The Family Shadow

SUZANNE WINTERLY

Alizester Books

ALIZESTER BOOKS

First published in 2021

www.suzannewinterly.com

A CIP catalogue record for this title is available from the British Library.

ISBN 978-1-9993168-1-5

Cover Design: Books Covered Ltd.

Alizester Books
Monasterevin
Co. Kildare
Ireland

"And the shadow flits and fleets
And will not let me be."

Maud - Alfred, Lord Tennyson (1855)

Novels by Suzanne Winterly:

The Neglected Garden
The Family Shadow

Chapter One

County Wexford, 3rd September, 1891

T he wheels of the trap rattled over stones as they passed the gates of Ardlackan House and the dark windows of the lodge stared back at the three figures huddled together for warmth. The pony in the shafts pricked her ears and shied at leaves whirling on the gravel sweep.

The girl pressed closer to her aunt and pulled the hood of her cloak over her head. It wasn't much of a carriage, a real boneshaker. Her uncle used it to ferry older locals to Mass on Sundays, or his wife on her visits as a midwife. She gripped her aunt's hand and leaned against the warmth of her ample bulk.

A crescent moon cast a cool light over nearby lanes and fields; on the right, a stand of evergreen oak trees stood dark against the inky sky. It was a cold night for the beginning of September and an autumnal chill hung in the air.

The pony trotted on and her driver helped himself to a few sips of whiskey from a battered hip flask. He gave a yank on the left rein and the carriage headed into the darkness of the wood, its lamps glowing like huge cat's eyes.

"Why are we going through the wood?" her aunt enquired. "Is that a good idea at this late hour?"

Her uncle snorted. "What, woman, are you afraid of ghosts

1

and ghouls? Look at the pony! She knows this is the shortest way home."

A shiver pricked the back of the girl's neck. She'd heard stories of these woods; tales about gangs of robbers jumping out from behind trees and demanding money at knifepoint.

Her eldest brother had been only too happy to tell her about the ghost that haunted Ardlackan woods. A phantom who rode a white horse and was headless. Locals claimed he was the dispossessed owner of the dwelling that once stood where Ardlackan House was now, thrown out by one of Oliver Cromwell's captains who forced it from him. He hadn't gone quietly and had been decapitated in the struggle.

The girl bit her lip and glanced at her aunt, who slid her arm round her waist, giving her a comforting squeeze.

They'd reached a clearing in the trees when the carriage jolted to a halt and the old man let out a long whistle. "Would ye look at that?" He pulled the reins and barked at the pony to stand still.

"What, you fool? What have your drunken eyes seen now?" Her aunt's voice cracked with fatigue after her strenuous night delivering a baby boy.

The pony pawed at the ground and tossed her head, impatient to move on and she received a quick reprimand. The man pointed to their right where a deep ditch ran along the side of the laneway, moss-covered banks where ferns wrestled with brambles. The tinkle of running water rose from below.

They craned their necks to peer down into the dyke. Something lay under the fronds and tangled briars, a dark shape with a glimmer of white.

"What is it?" The girl's breathing quickened. The headless phantom? Had they stumbled upon his resting place? Her heart thumped faster and she looked behind, as if expecting to see a white steed tethered to a branch.

"We'd better find out. Stay here, child," her aunt said, "and you, come with me." This last command she tossed at her husband.

The old couple made their way down into the stream, kicking the brambles and ferns aside, trampling them with their leather boots, while her uncle cursed under his breath. The girl shivered and cast another look over her shoulder. Were there shapes hiding behind the tree trunks? Was that the shadow of a robber falling across the dead leaves? She peered again into the bushes. Nobody there, only her imagination; her brother's stories unnerving her.

Her uncle and aunt reached the stream and bent to examine the creature, or whatever it was, their heads close together. They exchanged urgent but inaudible words. A series of mumbled sentences that the girl strained to hear. Several minutes passed before they climbed back up to the lane.

"Don't say anything to the child." Her aunt's face was pale, the hue of skimmed milk.

The girl gripped her arm. "What is it? Please tell me. Is it… is it the ghost?"

Her uncle tilted his head back and helped himself to a long gulp from his hip flask. "Ghost, is it? No ghost, indeed. It's a man and he's stone cold."

"Drunk?" The girl stared at his face, grey above his whiskers in the moonlight.

Ignoring a sharp look and reprimand from his wife, he hoisted himself back onto the driver's seat and shook his head. "Not drunk… dead. A man lying cold and dead in the stream, God rest his soul. There's nothing we can do for him now except drive on to the doctor's house. We'll let him take charge of the rest."

"Perhaps we should tell the constabulary?"

He frowned at his wife. "No, we want nothing to do with them. There'll be hell to pay when they see who it is."

Chapter Two

"I think you should consider this, Fiona. Remember the months we spent at Ardlackan?"

Jessica and I often reminisced about long summer holidays in County Wexford, swimming as fearless teenagers in the icy sea and running back through the woods to dinner in the former farmhouse where her uncle and aunt lived.

Ardlackan conjured up memories of light and shade; fingers of sun sliding up the stone house nestled into the hillside, with its cloak of Virginia creeper and protected on two sides by arms of evergreen trees that held the sea winds at bay.

Jessica and I stood by the wall running along Strand Road in Sandymount, gazing at mud flats where wading birds dug for lugworms under coiled castings.

"Aunt Daphne needs your help," she said. "She needs you to save her from a journalist and her far-fetched claims."

"Hmm."

"You'd be just the right person to do the research and find out the truth, I know you would."

I smiled.

"You're so…"

"Organized?" I asked. Jessica always insisted that was my

strength although far more successful than me with her modern, spotless apartment and career in the bank.

My eyes lingered on the Poolbeg chimneys, those faded red and white striped stacks that rose against a bank of dark clouds. Perched together since the late 1970s, they had become iconic landmarks of Dublin on the south bank of the port, visible from above the airport as we flew in; beacons that welcomed me home when I caught my first glimpse of the sprawling city and drew me to my father's house on the edge of Sandymount village.

My poor father's house, soon to be sold to another family and stripped of his possessions.

The dog. Where was the dog? I'd forgotten all about him, lost in my thoughts. I glanced around.

An oystercatcher hopped and tipped forward to probe with its orange-red bill. And there was the dog racing towards the black and white bird, his tongue lolling and his ears pricked. My father's dog. Mine now, at least for the present until I decided what to do with the little fellow.

"I know it's been difficult for you, Fiona." Jessica's dark brown eyes looked into mine. "You've had two very stressful events. Your father's death... and now a divorce looming. A change would do you good. Get you away from here for a while." Dear Jessica, always so forthright and certain.

The thought seeped into my mind that the incoming tide was like time passing; relentlessly sweeping everything away; an empty cola can, that crushed cigarette packet tossed by a careless person already sucked up and borne away on the last wave.

Further along Strand Road I watched a flicker of sunlight on the Martello tower, one of fifty built by the British in the early nineteenth century when they feared Napoleon would invade. There was something calming about history, events safely stored in the past and no longer able to hurt us. I found history reassuring.

It was the middle of June. A warm breeze tossed Jessica's

dark, shiny hair across her even features and her eyes, always kind and somehow earnest, gazed into mine as she placed a hand on my arm. "You have to move on now, Fi. No point dwelling on… you've got the whole summer ahead… your whole life ahead of you."

I spun round and my voice rose. "To do what? To forget and to forgive? Is that what you expect me to do? How can I forget about it? How can I forgive the man who has nearly ruined me?"

Her fingers squeezed my elbow. "I don't mean you should forgive him, not yet, but if you had something to do for the summer, something to take your mind off things." She tugged at my sleeve. "How did your Leaving Cert pupils cope this year?"

"Quite well, I think. I had the usual mix of genius and indifference in my history class, but they seem to have got through the exams without a crisis."

Always a poignant time when I had to say goodbye to my sixth-year students, even the troublesome ones pretending they would miss me.

Now two and a half months of holidays stretched ahead. Too much time. Too many hours to brood on what had happened so unexpectedly.

"Let's walk to the restaurant," Jessica suggested. "It's nearly time for lunch. We'll get coffee and lunch. I'll tell you more about what's happened to poor Aunt Daphne."

I whistled for Archie the terrier and slipped on his lead when he came bounding towards me, short tail wagging with excitement.

Jessica linked her arm in mine and we strolled along Strand Road, walking towards the centre of Sandymount village.

She was my dearest friend and the one who always listened.

The restaurant on the Green was filling up with customers, but we found a table on the pavement. Jessica sat down on a chair with an exaggerated sigh, tossing her long hair over her shoulder.

I attached Archie's lead to a wrought-iron leg and told him to lie down and be good. Perhaps all the running along the sand had exhausted him because he flopped beside my feet, resting his head across my shoe.

A tall, Italian-looking waiter brought us our coffees and we ordered lunch. He returned with two plates of salad piled high with goat's cheese, beetroot and mixed seeds. What my father would have called rabbit food.

I blinked away sudden tears.

I raised my mug. "To the future," I said. "Here's to the summer holidays."

Jessica tapped hers against mine. "That's the spirit. Onwards and upwards, my friend. Now, wait till you see this." She rummaged in her large leather handbag.

I watched with a feeling of unease.

My husband gone, my father's house placed in the hands of an estate agent that morning and an overdrawn bank account. Things could only get better.

Jessica shook out a folded newspaper and placed it on the table. She pushed it towards me. "See that headline? You can imagine what Daphne felt when she saw that. A bolt out of the blue. None of us knew what the woman was up to." The *woman* was obviously not Daphne because the word shot with contempt from my friend's lips.

I sipped my coffee and looked at the newspaper.

Murder haunts trainer's family.

"My father's brother," Jessica pointed out. "The racehorse trainer."

"*The* racehorse trainer," I emphasized, for he'd been a household name among the racing fraternity and one of my husband's idols. Dominic won over one thousand euro once at Leopardstown on a treble of winning horses trained by Charles Thornton and boasted about his victory for weeks afterwards. It paid for our Christmas holiday in Lisbon where my mother lived with her latest boyfriend.

People often thought my mother and I looked alike with our blue eyes and wavy dark blonde hair, but she assured them that was where any similarity ended. She claimed I was too serious and bossy, which came from being a teacher and from taking on too much responsibility when I was in my early twenties, marrying Dominic and settling down when I could have gone off to travel the world. My mother was always adept at shirking responsibility.

Jessica continued, "Poor Daphne has been besieged by the press since this headline. You'd think no one would be interested in a murder that happened more than a century ago… over one hundred and thirty years ago, but no, they love it… can't wait to read about it. The locals haven't been so excited for years and everyone is claiming to have known about it. Daphne knew nothing until the journalist phoned her a few days ago."

"I've never heard of this murder. Where did it take place?"

"In the woods between the house and the village. The victim was a Thornton man apparently, and also a racehorse trainer. Why didn't Uncle Charles say something about it before he died?"

"Perhaps he didn't want to." Charles had been a quiet man; a man who would have turned the key and kept family skeletons securely locked in the cupboard.

Jessica added, "If you go to stay with Daphne, I could come down at weekends. We could relive our youth."

"Summer holidays after my mother decamped for Portugal? I expect Dad was pleased to get a break from minding my brother and me."

"It was fun. Remember Daphne's cooking, though? I once suspected she mixed turpentine in the gravy instead of stock." She frowned at the newspaper. "Daphne still paints, more than ever when she's upset. So, this journalist is doing research for a British television producer. Daphne wants nothing to do with it. There's a ghoulish longing for details about true life murders these days. Why can't people leave the past alone?"

Why indeed? But if we all ignored the past and abandoned our history books, I would be out of a job.

Our days at Ardlackan had always seemed baked in sunshine. The only cloud in that blue sky was the bad-tempered glower on Uncle Charles's face. He wasn't a blood relation of mine, but I'd always called him that because Jessica did. Truth be told, I was afraid of him and felt sorry for Daphne. Later she confided that he suffered from depression and an uncharacteristic string of losing horses sent him into depths of despair. It wasn't his fault, she explained, he was a hero and a brilliant trainer. Under a lot of pressure. Most of the journalists agreed and were prepared to indulge him the occasional outburst in the parade ring after a race, when he let out a roar of exasperation and sent them scattering like sheep.

"What's the name of the writer?"

"Doesn't say."

"Poor Daphne," I murmured. "She had a lot to put up with, didn't she? The difficult owners and Uncle Charles's moods..."

"Hmm, I suppose so, but he secretly adored her."

Perhaps Jessica was right. Daphne had once tried to persuade me to eat a boiled egg for breakfast. I remembered shaking my head and refusing. Uncle Charles lowered his racing newspaper and glared at me, demanding to know what was wrong with the child.

But Daphne had just smiled and assured me that it was a special egg, laid by Rosie her most intelligent hen, and she added that Rosie told her I was the only special girl in the house who was allowed to eat it. Uncle Charles raised his eyebrows, snorted and laughed out loud before returning to his newspaper.

"And so..." Jessica paused and frowned slightly, lines wrinkling her brow.

"So?"

"I thought you might like to help her. Help Daphne deal with this persistent woman. I thought you'd be the ideal person to sort it all out." She put down her fork and opened her hands with the palms upwards, as if waiting for me to applaud her wonderful idea.

"Why?"

"She'd really appreciate it."

"What exactly am I expected to do?"

"Defend her. Find out what really happened. It couldn't possibly be a relation of ours who did that. A murder, for goodness sake. It has to be nonsense. Look, Fiona, wouldn't it be a distraction?"

"Sounds like it might take up a lot of time."

"Maybe, but I think that would be an advantage. Tell Dominic you can't possibly talk to him about the separation agreement until you get back. It would give you time to think."

I swallowed the last of my lettuce and glanced across the road at a girl in a red dress, who was leaning against the park railings and peering at her mobile phone. Young, innocent and her whole life ahead of her. She wouldn't be foolish enough to marry her first boyfriend at the age of twenty-two.

"Well?" Jessica interrupted my thoughts.

"It's… thanks for thinking of me and I was always fond of Daphne but… I'm not sure if I want to get involved in anything to do with horse racing. I'm sick of it, to be honest. I'm thirty years old and now I have to start all over again. It wasn't fun being married to a gambler."

"Uncle Charles wasn't a gambler. We could never accuse him of that. You used to like going to race meetings, didn't you?"

"It will remind me of Dominic. Have you forgotten why he left and what he left me with? A pile of debts and an unpaid mortgage while he ran off with a…"

"Trollop?"

We both laughed and somehow her use of that old-fashioned word pricked the balloon of my indignation, diminishing my anger.

"Yes," I said. "A trollop from an internet gambling forum. What sort of future will they have together? Tiffany the trollop. That's a good name for her."

"An impoverished future, no doubt. Come on, Fi, please consider it. Think about it for a few days and let me know. Daphne would be so grateful and I'm sure it would do you good. A change is as good as a rest, they say, and I know how much you love rooting around in the past. That old house is full of stuff – boxes piled high with papers and notebooks and photographs. If anyone can find out what really happened, it will be you. There might even be a few ghosts."

"Ghosts?"

"Metaphorically speaking, of course. Not real ones."

I got to my feet and bent to untie Archie from the leg of the table. "All right, I'll think about it. I only wish it would help me forget about Dominic. He was nothing but trouble."

"You were too kind to him. You treated him like one of your students, always making excuses for him."

"I have to go now."

"If he wanted to come back… if he tried to get you back, you wouldn't take him, would you?"

"I'd like to pay for lunch." I couldn't answer that question. Not yet.

"I'll pay for it," Jessica replied with a sigh. "You need to save what little money you have left. I hope Dominic doesn't come crawling back because I'm worried that you'll feel sorry for him."

I said nothing.

"I think living with Daphne for a couple of months will give you a chance to get things in perspective and to look around for somewhere else to live. You've still got your dad's home but for how long?" Jessica got to her feet.

We paid and left the restaurant together with Archie trotting at my heels. I gave Jessica a hug before we went our separate ways. As I strolled past the red brick houses along Sandymount Avenue, my thoughts flew to Ardlackan with its long sandy beach and wilderness of sand dunes. Jessica mentioned ghosts and Daphne was all alone with her phantoms of the past. In her late seventies and in need of my help. Selfish to refuse, really.

My friend, in her usual persuasive way, sowed seeds that promised change. An urge to return to Ardlackan swept through me. I would tackle those old dusty rooms, with piles of papers in cardboard boxes. I would leaf through photo albums of people long dead. Perhaps their past might provide a distraction and it couldn't be as painful as my own.

Chapter Three

The present - 23rd June, 2019

I drove up the avenue of Ardlackan with Archie panting in the back seat, secured in his harness. The oak trees crowded in on either side, so tall that they cast dancing shadows on the front of the car. I rounded the final bend and the house appeared in front of me and, as the shade gave way to sunshine on the gravel circle edged with lawn, I felt a flash of disappointment for it seemed diminished somehow, still wearing its cloak of Virginia creeper but smaller, as if it had lost its vitality. Paint on the sash windows peeled in the bright light and the small glass panes had gathered dust, like eyes glazed over with age or disappointment.

"You stay here, Archie, like a good boy. I'll be back for you in a few minutes." The terrier put his head on one side and his ears drooped.

As I rapped the brass door knocker in the shape of a horse's head, sympathy for Daphne Thornton swept over me. The place was too much for a widow of seventy-eight and Jessica was right to send me here. I would immerse myself in helping her aunt, drive away my resentment about Dominic and surely then, surely I would feel better?

I banged again on the door, louder this time and determined to banish all thoughts of my husband from my mind. He'd made his decision to be with his new girlfriend. I'd never met her or even spoken to her. I didn't even know her surname, but I could imagine what she looked like. Young and gullible. She would have to be gullible to be taken in by Dominic. I certainly was.

Footsteps clattered across a wooden floor and the door creaked open.

"Why, it's Fiona! How wonderful to see you, darling. Do come in." Daphne's lined face beamed as if my arrival was an unexpected treat and I wondered if she'd forgotten that I was coming.

Her hair was longer than before, white and pulled back from her face with an ornate silver slide. She wore pale blue cropped trousers and a pink blouse with tiny roses on the collar and cuffs.

"It's hot today, isn't it?" She fanned her face with a thin hand. "Come this way, please. I'll put on the kettle."

Daphne led me to the kitchen where photographs of racehorses covered the apricot walls.

A grey and black striped cat lounged on a cushion on the sofa and turned to stare at me with interest. Part of one ear was missing and he had only one eye.

"Oh, I didn't realize that you have a cat." I frowned. Daphne would hardly want Archie the cat chaser in her house.

"Yes, that's Balor. No, no, don't touch him! He likes to get to know people first."

The cat yawned and stretched, continuing to fix me with his single yellow eye.

"Charles called him that after the giant from Irish mythology. He's a bit of a fighter and hence the battle scars."

"Did Jessica mention that I have a dog… my father's dog? He's in the car, but I see now that…"

Daphne waved a dismissive hand. "Oh yes, don't worry. I know about the dog. The cat… my Balor is well able to look after himself. He's good at keeping dogs in order."

"That's just as well. Can I bring Archie in, if you don't mind? It's hot out there and he doesn't like staying in the car."

"Of course. You go and fetch him while I make tea. I'm sorry about the mess. I'm so confused these days... don't know whether I'm coming or going. This exhibition, I'm struggling to finish some of the paintings and I promised the art group that I'd have ten ready so..." Her voice trailed off and she moved over to the counter and switched on an electric kettle. "You do drink tea? I suppose you young people prefer coffee, but I haven't got any. It keeps me awake and gives me indigestion."

I assured her that tea was perfect and went back to the car to retrieve the terrier. Archie leaped out and shot off towards the house. When I caught up with him in the kitchen, he was barking at the cat which had climbed onto the dresser by the garden window and sat hissing at him with ears flattened back, a menacing growl rumbling from his throat.

"Archie, come here and be quiet!"

"Just ignore the two of them." Daphne poured tea into a blue and white striped mug. "They'll soon be good friends, don't worry. Sit down, my dear. Sit on that chair at the table and tell me all your news."

I sat and noticed that the large pine table was strewn with sketches and sheets of paper dabbed with oil paint. Daphne trying out new ideas, perhaps. I picked up one of the drawings and saw that it was of the bell tower in the yard, perched on top of a stone arch at the end of a row of stables. We'd loved being allowed to pull on the rope and send echoing peals out across the woodland and sand dunes. It was one of the treats Uncle Charles permitted when he was in a good mood.

"I was sorry to hear about Uncle Charles," I said, sipping the strong sweet tea that Daphne handed me. She'd deposited a spoon of sugar absent-mindedly into it and stirred vigorously, but I didn't want to make a fuss. "Sorry I couldn't make it to the funeral. I was so… so busy, I'm afraid. A year ago, wasn't it?" Leaving Certificate time and all the frenzy that the State exams created in school.

Archie let out a yelp and ran to me. I picked him up and put him on my knee. He cast a sorrowful glance at the cat, which turned away and curled up on the cushion. Balor, named after a terrifying giant, had soon shown the dog who was boss.

Daphne's vivid green eyes regarded me for a few seconds. Unusual eyes that suddenly seemed much more discerning. Did she think I was making feeble excuses about not attending the funeral? I swallowed a gulp of tea. I should have made an effort to go. Jessica had offered me a lift, but I'd been caught up in school problems. Students panicking before their exams or still not getting down to revision. And Dominic… that was the time he'd lost several months' salary on what turned out to be a remarkably slow colt in the Two Thousand Guineas.

"We're all so busy these days, aren't we?" Daphne grimaced. "And I was sorry to hear about your poor father. Such a nice man. I only met him once or twice when he came to collect you and Jessie, but I thought he was kind. Was it sudden?"

I cleared my throat. "Not really. He had a series of strokes."

"Poor man. Jessie said you looked after him for several months. You need a rest, my dear, I'm sure you do."

The tea calmed me; the strain I'd felt driving down shifted and ebbed away. It was good to be here after the two and a half hours journey from Sandymount. I held up the sketch of the bell tower. "I like this drawing. It brings back memories."

Daphne reached out her hand and stroked Archie's head. "Yes." She fixed her eyes on my face. "It's kind of you to come… I believe Jessie told you about the… this ridiculous murder story and the proposed television series."

I said that she had.

"He would hate it, of course. Charles would absolutely

hate this. He was such a private man." Her gaze flitted away
to a photograph of her late husband in the parade ring at
Leopardstown, Daphne beside him holding a large cup, her eyes
alight with pride. That was his first year as champion trainer.

"Jessica told me the woman claims your family is somehow
connected to this murder."

"Some long-distant relative maybe. Charles never mentioned
an Edward Thornton. He would have told me if he knew anything
about the murder, I'm sure he would."

Charles had been secretive though. There must have been
things he hadn't divulged to Daphne throughout their married
life and she'd always been reluctant to bother him; to interfere
in his business. Daphne spent a lot of time in her own world,
painting flowers and seascapes or tending to her beloved plants
in the garden.

"I'll talk to the journalist," I said. "I'll help you find out what
really happened. That's why I'm here."

I noticed the balls of cat hair on the black and white tiles
and suspected that the floor hadn't been brushed or mopped for
weeks. I would see to that. I would throw myself into housework
and research, rescuing poor Daphne and hopefully myself at the
same time.

Daphne's brow wrinkled and she pushed her glasses up on
the bridge of her nose. "Find out what really happened? Oh no, I
don't think you need to go that far, Fiona. I think you should just
try to stop the woman researching the murder."

"Don't you want to know what happened?" I hoped I didn't
sound disappointed.

Daphne stood up, brushing crumbs from her trousers onto
the floor. "We'll see. You remember where your old room is? I
haven't had time to paint the walls, but I've vacuumed the floor
and made up the bed."

She led the way up the staircase. Ardlackan was a Georgian

farmhouse that had been built at the end of the eighteenth century. It wasn't a large house back then but had been added onto over the years, with an extra wing for servants and rooms opening off long corridors. Photographs lined the walls up to the second floor, mostly black and white of racehorses from long ago and an occasional one of Charles with his early winners.

I heaved up my suitcase filled with neatly ironed clothes to last me several weeks. We passed the bedroom that Daphne had shared with Charles and walked on to the end of the corridor where she opened the door of the room where Jessica and I had slept all those years before.

I hesitated in the doorway. The primrose striped wallpaper peeled in one corner but it was a bright space where strips of sunlight ran across the floor from the two south-facing windows.

"I'll just let in some air." Daphne stepped over to open the window.

I stood beside her and gazed out at the view stretching above the treetops, a sweeping expanse of glittering sea. White sails of a yacht broke the line of the horizon and I knew that just beyond the wood and out of sight lay the tall spine of sand dunes that ran along the beach.

"Are you still keen on gardening?" I asked.

"I try my best. Only one herbaceous border now and the roses, of course. I've given up vegetables. My back isn't up to it."

A flower border lay below the window, pink peonies edged with lavender. Tall clumps of fluffy pampas grass sheltered plants at the back of the lawn. Hadn't there been a summer house there? Perhaps it was further away out of sight.

"I'll leave you to unpack. Come down when you've finished. I'll be in the kitchen."

After she'd gone, I emptied my suitcase and lay on the bed, yawning and closing my eyes. I would relax for a few minutes. I must have drifted off into a doze and I woke to hear footsteps on the stairs. The dog barked and ran out into the corridor.

A sense of unease surfaced. The footsteps had come from the main staircase, hadn't they? Not the wooden flight to the right descending from the side wing. Those were hidden behind a door, as far as I could remember.

Daphne came into the room. "Everything all right? Did you drop off to sleep? You must be tired after your journey."

I sat up and swung my legs over the side of the bed. "I was more tired than I realized."

"Let's go down to Charles's study. I'm hoping you might like to sort through some of the papers? I really ought to get rid of... but haven't been able to make myself."

"I understand. It must be sad to stir up the memories."

Her green eyes, magnified by the lenses, sought mine. "It's not that I don't want to, it's just I can't seem to make a start. So overwhelming. Such a lot of paper to wade through and you know I can't cope with that... and now there's this journalist... and the painting exhibition. If you feel like you can sift through it, I would be really grateful. I know you've had your own troubles recently, apart from your father's death. That can't be easy."

"Ah, Jessica mentioned that, did she?"

"She told me about your husband leaving."

What could I say? I didn't want to explain and, in the end, I said nothing and she didn't push me.

I followed Daphne to the study at the bottom of the stairs. The room faced the garden and appeared surprisingly tidy.

She reached out, her fingers resting for a moment on my arm. "I'm so glad you've come. I've been here on my own since Charles died... all alone except for Balor... and Ben, of course."

"Ben?"

"He's the young man who has been helping me with a few renovations this summer. I'll make you a mug of tea." She clicked her tongue and the terrier trotted out of the room after her.

Poor Daphne would find this distressing, of course she would. When sorting through my husband's belongings, I'd found birthday cards we'd sent each other during the first happier years. And photographs of our honeymoon in Tanzania, paid for by an unusually lucrative gamble on an outsider in the Aintree Grand National.

I would have to stop thinking like this. I would have to force myself to forget him because he'd forgotten me. Just a short note left on the kitchen table that shocking morning two months before.

A *Dear John* letter, people call them. *Dear Fiona*. It began with an apology. Sorry, sorry, sorry. Dominic was always sorry afterwards. Each time he lost money. Each time he failed to pay his share of the mortgage. When he forgot my birthday. He could produce a bunch of flowers from behind his back like a conjuror. I forgave him. Of course I did. Until this time. This time there'd been no flowers and no box of chocolates. Only one short note propped against the marmalade jar.

Dear Fiona, I'm sorry. I hate to do this to you but…

I pulled open the top drawer of Charles's desk. Inside lay a fountain pen with his initials on it, a pipe and a packet of tobacco on top of a dark brown notebook. I sat on his office chair and placed the book on the desk.

My eyes lingered on the silver-framed photograph to my right. Daphne and Charles on their wedding day. I had to admit that Charles looked handsome in his morning coat, with his short black hair and dark Thornton eyes. Eyes like Jessica's and the same fine cheekbones.

Lists of horses' names and their breeding ran down the pages of the book in Charles's neat handwriting. Sandy Bay, Clarissa's Hope, All the World. I remembered All the World, a small chestnut gelding with four white stockings up to his knees ploughing through the mud at Fairyhouse to win a steeplechase.

I closed the book and replaced it in the drawer. I stood up and wandered over to a glazed bookcase that contained Charles's collection of stud books.

All the World's breeding would be in one of those volumes. I turned the little brass key and took out one from 1988 and held the smooth, creamy hardback in my hands, admiring the gold lettering across the spine. I leafed through the lists of horses' names at the beginning. So many horses long dead by now but carefully recorded for all time. There was a Fiona's Fancy there and many names beginning with Rose. Charles had placed a dot beside a few of the names, perhaps ones he'd been interested in buying for an owner or ones he'd trained. A large tick beside one called Ardlackan Rosalind. I'd no memory of her.

I turned the page and a small black and white photograph fluttered to the floor. A sheet of writing paper with faded ink remained, foxed and creased as if folded to fit in a pocket. I bent to pick up the photograph and saw that it was of a young woman with hair piled high on her head, falling in curls on either side of her smiling eyes. I placed the book on Charles's desk and smoothed the writing paper with my fingertips. It was a verse, written out neatly in old-fashioned handwriting with elaborate loops. I scanned it quickly:

She is coming, my own, my sweet;
Were it ever so airy a tread,
My heart would hear her and beat,
Were it earth in an earthy bed;
My dust would hear her and beat,
Had I lain for a century dead,
Would start and tremble under her feet,
And blossom in purple and red.

A beautiful woman who looked no more than mid-twenties and a verse brimming with sentiment. Who was she? Had Charles written out the verse? Surely not, because the paper was old and the ink faded.

A man dead for a century would hear the light footsteps of his beloved and tremble in his grave. Very romantic but unfamiliar. I would have to ask Daphne about it.

I pushed the stud book back onto the shelf and went over to the window to take a better look at the photograph. The woman's dress was plain with satin-covered buttons up the front and a collar of delicate lace. Late-Victorian era by the look of it as the skirt was quite narrow with a small bustle at the back below her neat waist.

I turned it over and saw *Rosalind 1890* written in dark blue ink on the back. Who was Rosalind?

Charles would have known because he must have hidden this photo and verse in the book. The two objects might be connected.

I glanced again at the exquisite face and the finely shaped nose before folding the piece of paper and slipping both it and the photograph into the pocket of my jeans.

Ten minutes later Daphne returned with a mug of tea and Archie.

I handed her the photo and she considered it with a slight shake of her head. "No, I've never seen this before. In the stud book you say? Was it a relation, do you think?"

"There's a horse in the book called Ardlackan Rosalind. Do you remember her?"

"There were so many over the years but that sounds like one that was bred here. Maybe one of Charles's own mares." She handed back the photo. "I ought to be able to remember them but… I'm going to take your dog for a walk down to the beach." Archie's ears pricked and he let out a little yelp. Yes, he would like to go to the beach as he'd taken to Daphne in spite of her cat.

"I found this too." I held out the paper with the verse and she read it.

"No idea," she murmured. "I don't recognize it. Who's the poet?"

"It wasn't Charles, I suppose?"

She flashed a quick smile and turned away. "Charles was a dear sweet man but I would never have called him romantic."

"Daphne?"

"Yes."

"The name of the journalist who rang you, the one who's doing the research... can you remember her name?"

Her pale forehead wrinkled with concentration. "I wrote it down at the time. Didn't it say in the newspaper? Let me think. The surname was Ryan... I remember that because our postman's called Ryan and he's a lovely young man with golden curls. His mother is my hairdresser in the village. Ryan, Ryan... what was the first name? Oh, I've got it. Tiffany. Tiffany Ryan, that's it."

Chapter Four

The past - Ardlackan Lodge – July, 1890

Rosalind Thornton rested her palm against the windowpane and sighed. Did it ever stop raining? It was July and supposed to be summer. Surely even in Ireland there should be a summer? Clouds hung low over the house, shrouding the gravel path along the terrace in a damp mist and a sodden blackbird huddled under the box hedge.

She looked towards her writing desk in the corner of the room, on which lay an unfinished letter to her aunt. So little news to titillate her lively Aunt Catherine. She could tell her about progress in the garden and the plan for the new summer house, but her aunt disliked gardening. She could mention the racehorses and perhaps she would be interested. What had Edward told her early this morning before he departed for the gallops? Mighty Maiden was showing promise over fences and he would like to send her to a race meeting in a month's time. She was the big bay mare that always laid her ears back when Rosalind reached out a timid hand to stroke her glossy coat. She shrank back when the mare stamped a hind leg and Frank – she must remember to call him O'Rafferty – warned his mistress not to go too close.

Rosalind walked across the blue oriental rug and pulled the bell lever. Aunt Catherine had grown to approve of Rosalind's marriage and now believed it was an opportunity, a wonderful chance to make something of her life and get her away from books. Aunt Catherine wrinkled her nose when she thought about books. Novels and poetry were bad for a young lady, she'd assured her niece in last week's letter, which lay open on the desk demanding to be answered. No man enjoyed keeping company with bookish females.

But why not? Rosalind longed to protest. Why shouldn't she make an effort to expand her mind? She imagined her aunt's eyes glazing over as she read these impertinent questions.

Rosalind moved back to the desk and sat down. She picked up her aunt's letter and ran her eyes down the fourth page. So much going on in London. She hadn't mentioned Mama. She never did.

One book Aunt Catherine approved of was the latest edition of Mrs Beeton's *Book of Household Management* and she'd presented it to Rosalind on her marriage. Rosalind dutifully read the chapters on organizing the household and pointed out to her husband those concerning the groom and coachman. Edward interrupted and reminded her that Frank O'Rafferty was in charge of the stable yard and wouldn't take kindly to him interfering.

Rosalind recalled her attempts to win over the cook. Mrs O'Brien, queen of the kitchen at Ardlackan Lodge for over fifteen years, stared suspiciously at the culinary recipes and enquired whether Rosalind had ever prepared them.

No, of course she hadn't, but wouldn't it be interesting to try a few different dishes?

Mrs O'Brien sniffed and said that Mrs Gertrude Thornton had never seen fit to complain about her cooking. Rosalind apologized and left the kitchen with a consoling slice of coffee cake and Mrs Beeton's heavy tome under her arm. She'd placed it in the bookcase in the morning room and reached for Tennyson.

Rosalind glanced at the black marble clock on the mantelpiece and saw that it was almost midday. The door opened and she turned her head to face the tiny maid who flashed a smile and bobbed a curtsey. Her mother-in-law had trained Sadie well.

"You rang, ma'am."

"Yes, thank you, Sadie. Would you bring me a jug of water, please?"

"Yes, ma'am, I'll bring it straightaway." Sadie's golden curls bobbed under one of the new caps Edward's mother had ordered for the maids in an attempt to make them resemble those in Cousin Hugh's household. Gertrude liked to emulate Hugh and Beatrice Thornton.

Sadie turned to leave.

"By the way, have you seen Mrs Thornton?" Rosalind asked.

"She's in the garden." Sadie pronounced each word carefully and with individual emphasis. Gertrude had been trying to improve her diction and her own lady's maid had been given strict instructions to take Sadie under her wing. Rosalind would have to try to find more work for Sadie in order to rescue the poor young woman from Gertrude.

The maid left the room and Rosalind turned back to her letter. Perhaps she should tell Aunt Catherine about the garden and her plans for a rose pergola. Would the roses grow so close to the ocean? The salt-laden winds ruined so many of her beloved plants. Edward hadn't shown much interest in her idea, but he hadn't forbidden it. Rosalind picked up her pen. It was her money, after all, her father's money that had kept this place going since their marriage almost nine years before. The rest of the Thornton family conveniently forgot that. They never mentioned how indebted they were to Rosalind and her inheritance.

When darling Papa had been carried off by pneumonia and left his only child and sister everything, Rosalind and her aunt were reasonably well off. She would have loved to point this out to Gertrude but didn't have the courage because her mother-in-law would probably only turn up her nose and a chill would creep into her voice as she breathed that word *trade*. Rosalind was never allowed to forget that Papa had made his fortune in the manufacturing industry and had owned factories that produced cotton undergarments. Definitely not a subject of conversation at a polite county dinner party.

The door swung open and the handle crashed against the wall, dislodging a circle of plaster.

"Mama, Mama!" Harriet ran towards her and fell into her arms. "Papa says I can't go down to the stable yard today. Please, please speak to him."

Rosalind permitted her to scramble onto her knee, as no one else was watching, and noticed too late the mud on the bottom of the heels of her daughter's little leather boots that was now streaked across her own pink silk dress. "What is the matter, my angel?"

"It's not fair." The girl scowled, her freckled nose wrinkling. "Papa says I can't ride Bumblebee today. I want to. It's not fair."

Rosalind admired her chestnut curls. "Perhaps he's too busy to keep you company today, Harriet."

"Will you take me?"

"You know that Papa doesn't like us to go to the stable yard on our own. We could send word to Frank to saddle up Bumblebee and bring him to the front door for you to ride. How does that sound?"

The girl struggled out of her mother's arms and ran to the window, pressing her nose against the glass. "Oh, look at the rain. When will it stop?"

Rosalind had forgotten about the dismal weather. "We'll have to leave your riding for another day. Now would you like to help me write a letter to Aunt Catherine? She's looking forward to hearing how you're getting on and what new dresses we've had made for you. You know how much she loves to hear about you turning into a pretty young lady. What would you like to tell her?"

"Dresses!" Harriet snorted. "I couldn't give a fig about my dresses. Will you tell her about my new pony? How fast he is and how he spat grass all over Grandmama's fur coat? That was funny." Harriet chuckled and skipped back to her mother's side. "I'll draw a picture of Bumblebee for Aunt Catherine."

She settled down on the rug at Rosalind's feet with a pencil and a sheet of paper, sticking her tongue out of the side of her mouth. She always did that when concentrating and, so far, the child had resisted all attempts by her grandmother to discourage the habit.

Sadie arrived with the jug of water. Harriet drew a caricature of the pony with a long mane and tail flowing as he galloped along the beach and Rosalind sealed it in the envelope with her own news about her plans for the garden, the rose pergola and more details concerning the building of the new summer house. The clock struck the hour. Time for luncheon.

She helped Harriet brush the creases out of her navy pinafore and they walked hand in hand across the hallway to the dining-room.

"What are you going to do this afternoon, Rosalind?" Gertrude peered at her from the other end of the long mahogany table. "Your daughter needs exercise. I found her running along the top corridor early this morning annoying the maids. She is too boisterous."

Harriet made a face and flopped onto her seat beside her father.

"High-spirited, Mama," Edward replied with his broad smile. "She's like Hugh's new filly, a three-year-old who is very skittish. Just young, that's all. The maids don't care, I'm sure."

He was kind to defend his daughter. He could get away with contradicting Gertrude as she doted on her only son.

"Skittish is a nice word," Harriet replied.

Gertrude picked up her napkin and shook it onto her lap. "Not when you're supposed to be a young lady. Grown-ups won't tolerate a skittish girl for long. You'll be the talk of the county and no self-respecting parents will wish to invite you to play with their children as they will consider you to be a bad influence."

"Pray don't be so hard on Harriet." Edward opened up his newspaper and scanned the headlines. "She has plenty of time to grow into a young lady. I see here they are talking in England about holding steeplechases for lady riders in the future. Good heavens, what next?"

His mother cast a glance at her son and Rosalind wondered if she would complain about him reading the newspaper at the dining-room table. Gertrude's eyes lingered on him for a few seconds, her lips moved, but she pressed them together and said nothing.

"That sounds interesting, my love." Rosalind smiled at Edward.

Gertrude turned to her. "Now Rosalind, you didn't answer my question, dear. Where are you going this afternoon now that the rain has stopped?"

"I thought I might walk over to Ardlackan House to call on Beatrice and her girls. Harriet will enjoy the exercise and she loves playing with her three cousins."

Edward looked over the top of his newspaper. "Would you bring a note for Hugh?"

"Of course." Rosalind took a plate of beef stew from Sadie. "Thank you, that smells delicious."

Harriet peered at the food the maid placed in front of her and sniffed. "Is that turnip?"

"Yes, Miss Harriet, and very good for you," Sadie said. "Would you like another spoonful?"

The girl rubbed her nose with the palm of her hand. "No, it's disgusting."

"Harriet!" Rosalind frowned at her.

"The cook says it's very wholesome, indeed she does." Sadie allowed the spoon to hover over Harriet's plate.

"That will be all, Sadie," Gertrude said. "Eat it up, Harriet, and be grateful."

The girl put a forkful of turnip in her mouth and made a face as Sadie left the room.

Edward folded his newspaper and placed it on the floor beside his chair. "There's a special horse train going to the North of Ireland for the race meeting at Down Royal. I must remember to tell O'Rafferty."

"How many runners will you send?" his mother enquired, glancing at her reflection in the window pane to her left and patting a stray grey curl into place.

"One or two. It's a long way. Hugh won't allow me to send the horses he owns unless they have a good chance of winning. It's a two-day meeting."

Rosalind gestured at Harriet's stew. "Eat up, dear. Edward, which horses will you send?" If she made a point of asking their names, perhaps they would be easier to remember.

"Ardlackan Lass is entered in a steeplechase over three miles," he replied, his brown eyes searching her face. "Would you like to go?"

"Oh, I don't know… it's a long journey to the North of Ireland and the weather has been so dreadful."

"Better to wait for a closer meeting. A new grandstand has been built at Clonmel racecourse with a complete view of the start to the finish. How about that?" He added, "Leopardstown would be the best if you'd like a fashionable day out. That's three hours away on the train."

"Can I go, Papa?"

"You're too young for race meetings," Gertrude said. "Too much goes on that isn't suitable for your eyes."

"What goes on?"

Her father waved a hand. "Gambling, drinking and all manner of vices. Only last week a man was hit on the head with a broken bottle outside a racecourse and the constabulary had to intervene."

Harriet's eyes widened and she opened her mouth but closed it again when she saw her grandmother frowning at her.

"Of course she can't go. What a suggestion!" Gertrude turned to Edward. "Anything else of note in the newspaper?"

"Only more complaints about the racing authorities' new regulation fence. Some hate it because they think it's too unnatural. There's also a letter from a man complaining about the cost of the Royal Irish Constabulary. A report from the House of Commons mentions objections to the annual cost of over one and a half million pounds. Apparently the constables here in Ireland are paid more than their counterparts in London."

"They're not popular here," Rosalind said. "It must be difficult to work for the constabulary. All those evictions…"

"Who told you that?" Gertrude demanded.

Rosalind blushed, a heat rising from her neck and creeping up her cheeks. "Oh, I just heard Frank… I heard O'Rafferty mention something."

"O'Rafferty? What would a coachman know about such matters?"

Edward placed his knife and fork together on his plate. "O'Rafferty's a fountain of knowledge. His mother is the village schoolmistress, don't forget."

"And I wonder where he gets his opinions? His connections in the Land League, no doubt. Perhaps he too is keen to get rid of landlords and snatch land back for tenants?"

Her son shot her an impatient glance. "Frank has no connections in the…"

"His father was a keen Parnellite, I seem to remember,

31

before he drowned at sea. I can't help but feel the Royal Irish Constabulary deserves every shilling that is paid towards it, what with the trouble being stirred up nowadays." Gertrude's face flushed with anger.

The door clicked open and Sadie carried in a tray on which sat a steamed ginger pudding and a jug of custard.

Rosalind felt relieved at the interruption. Politics was one of the few subjects that could raise an argument between Edward and his mother. Now was the time to mention progress on the design for the summer house; Rosalind's ideas about the rose pergola and extending the herbaceous border. She knew from previous quarrels that a tactful interruption about the state of the garden would help to distract Gertrude from her concerns about the state of the nation.

She steered the conversation towards smoother waters and her mother-in-law relaxed and listened while Harriet spooned down two helpings of steamed pudding.

After luncheon was over, Edward picked up his newspaper and walked towards the door. "I'm going to write my note. Let me know when you are ready to leave, Ros."

"Of course. Please excuse me, Gertrude, I must go and change my dress." Rosalind rose and beckoned to her daughter. "Harriet, come along, you and I will go upstairs and make ourselves look respectable while Papa is writing his note to Cousin Hugh."

"Enjoy your walk," Gertrude replied.

She doted on Hugh and Beatrice, no doubt about that. Since they'd moved into the big house higher up the hill, she often mentioned the improvements they'd made and constantly reminded her own family about Beatrice's good taste in wallpaper and furniture.

Gertrude believed that Hugh's late uncle had carelessly allowed the house to fall into disrepair when he grew old and senile. How fortunate that Beatrice, like Rosalind, had brought money with her to the marriage. Rosalind wondered where these racing men would be without their wealthy wives.

Chapter Five

Harriet danced beside Rosalind, humming a tune she'd made up that morning. Unlike her mother, she was musical and could already pick out several pieces on the piano, her little fingers stretching to reach the keys, her brow furrowed into a frown of concentration and her tongue as usual peeping out of the side of her mouth.

They passed the main gate into the stable yard with its granite arch and carved motto across the top. *Gradatim vincimus*. Rosalind had looked it up in her dictionary. *We overcome step by step*. A competitive and bold statement to cut in stone over the entrance of a racing stable. Typical Thornton confidence.

"Mama!" Harriet shrieked, making her flinch. "There's a man hiding in the bushes."

Rosalind saw a man with a straggly grey beard and flat cap on his head. When he noticed their eyes on him, he strolled out from behind the laurels and away through the stable yard gates.

"How strange," Rosalind said. "I wonder what he's up to. He looks a bit unkempt, doesn't he?"

"Unkempt? What does that mean?"

"A scruffy appearance. His clothes look old and worn."

"Perhaps he's a friend of Frank's."

"I don't know. We'll ignore him and continue on our way but I'll mention him to Papa later. I know he doesn't like strangers around the stables."

"Why not?"

"He might not be trustworthy."

Harriet put her head on one side as she considered this. "Will he try to steal Bumblebee?"

Rosalind stroked her daughter's hair. "No, I don't think he's interested in Bumblebee. Perhaps one of the others like Mighty Maiden. She's worth a lot of money, Papa says, and Cousin Hugh would be most upset if she was stolen."

They continued their walk into the wood and Rosalind pulled the wrought-iron gate closed behind them. No sign of the mysterious man.

"I hope Grace and Irene and Nora are at home," Harriet said. "We can play croquet on the lawn. I am able to beat them all. I'm good at croquet."

"Don't say that to them, please. It's not polite to boast about one's talents."

"But I am the best at croquet. I always beat them. Nora can't even hold the mallet properly."

"Nora is only four years old and she's half your age, the youngest of your cousins so be kind and allow her to win sometimes."

They continued along the damp path through the trees, Harriet chattering about the games she played with the girls.

A twig snapped. What was that? Rosalind swung around and spotted the same man they'd seen in the shrubbery walking about two hundred yards behind them.

She caught hold of Harriet's hand and strode on at a faster pace. "Come on."

"I can't walk faster. I think there's a stone in my boot." The girl bent to unhook the buttons. Rosalind gripped her arm to support her as her daughter tipped the boot upside down and a piece of stick fell out. The man was getting closer. Perhaps she should wait until he caught up and ask him who he was. That might deter him from following so close behind.

He came to a halt a short distance away and grinned at them, lifting his cap with exaggerated courtesy. "Good afternoon, ma'am."

Harriet pulled on her boot and moved nearer her mother.

"Good afternoon." Rosalind attempted to keep her voice even. Couldn't let him see how her hands trembled. She clasped them in front of her.

"Out for a stroll this fine afternoon?" the man asked, moving a step nearer. He had a crooked nose and had lost a tooth at the front of his mouth.

Rosalind smelled whiskey. "I saw you at the stables. What is your name?"

"Maguire, Mick Maguire. And you are Mrs Thornton, I believe."

"Yes, I am. Well, Mr Maguire, I wonder what you are doing following us like this." Her voice sounded surprisingly confident.

"Am I following you? This is my way home, a short cut through the woods and I had no intention of causing you concern, I assure you." He chuckled and coughed several times, rubbing his chest with a grimy hand.

Rosalind reached out and gripped Harriet's arm. "We'll step aside and allow you to continue on your way. What was your business at the stables?"

Gertrude would be proud of her if she could hear her speaking out like this.

She would make a point of telling her mother-in-law later.

"I wanted a word with Frank O'Rafferty about a wagonload of hay," Maguire said.

Was he telling the truth? Edward could ask Frank later.

Rosalind pulled Harriet aside and beckoned at the man to walk past.

He grinned again. "I hope you don't meet the headless horseman in these woods."

"There's no such... no such thing," Harriet said loudly. "That's just a silly story."

He moved past her and raised his cap again.

Rosalind and Harriet waited until he'd disappeared around the next bend in the lane. The gates of Ardlackan House stood on the left and the old couple who lived in the lodge might come to their aid if necessary. She squeezed Harriet's hand and they walked on.

There was no sign of Maguire when they reached the lodge and they continued along the avenue. Harriet resumed skipping and humming while Rosalind wondered if she would dare tell Beatrice her good news. If it really was good news. Still too early to be certain but she had to tell someone.

The house rose out of the trees and towered over them. An early nineteenth century three-storey family home with a granite portico. Not as old as their house but much more elegant, or so Gertrude thought.

Rosalind and Harriet climbed the steps to the polished front door. Hugh and Beatrice had a much better view of the sea too. An uninterrupted expanse of vivid blue stretched above the woodland. She raised the knocker and banged loudly.

Within minutes it swung open and Gilton appeared. "Good afternoon, madam. Please step into the hall and I will tell Mrs Thornton you are here." The butler turned to Harriet. "Good afternoon, Miss Thornton."

"Are Grace and Irene and Nora in?"

"Yes. I'm sure they'll be delighted to see you."

He left them in the hall and went to inform Beatrice, who was in the drawing-room sketching. She welcomed them and Gilton went on his way. That was another of Gertrude's peeves. She resented the fact that Hugh and Beatrice could afford a butler. A butler would have seemed far too grand for their smaller house. How uncomfortable it would be to have Gilton hovering in the background and listening to everything. Rosalind wouldn't be able to relax. Mrs O'Brien in the kitchen was bad enough with her airs and graces and fiery temper.

"How lovely to see you both," Beatrice said. "Come in and sit down. Tell me all your news."

Grace, Irene and Nora arrived, so polite and calm compared to Harriet, who jumped up to fling her arms around their necks and kiss them with unbridled joy. The girls left to play upstairs as Irene wanted to show Harriet her new collection of dolls.

"Would you like tea?" Beatrice asked. She wore a beautiful yellow silk dress with embroidery on the bodice and her dark hair shone.

Rosalind smiled at her friend. "No, thank you. It's too soon after luncheon. Let's take a stroll in the garden."

They wandered between the flower borders that flanked the pathway down towards the tennis court.

"My plants are all a little bit behind this year," Beatrice said. "It's because it was so cold in the spring. They didn't dare come out before now and I'm concerned the rain will spoil them. This Bourbon rose goes into horrid brown balls if it gets wet. I'm so glad you like them because I know you're the one with gardening knowledge, not me."

"Oh, I rely on Troy to keep me informed."

Beatrice laughed. "Your head gardener is quite formidable, isn't he? He knows a lot about the countryside as well."

"I'm terrified of Troy. He's nearly as frightening as Mrs O'Brien." Rosalind took her friend's arm. She'd inherited servants who spoke their minds, that was the truth. She couldn't imagine Beatrice and Hugh's well-behaved cook contradicting them.

They moved on towards a paved area near the tennis court and she admired the view of the sea.

"Yes," Beatrice said. "It's wonderful, isn't it?"

Rosalind agreed and wondered again if she should tell Beatrice her news. She would be delighted of course but was it too early? How terrible if she said something and then... No, she mustn't think like that but was she risking bad luck like last time?

Beatrice led her to a wrought-iron table and chairs set out under the shade of a large oak. Overhead the swallows swooped and dived. One of the huge mastiffs appeared from the gate into the wood and trotted towards them. Prince or Duke, Rosalind wasn't sure which one.

The dog flopped on the ground at Beatrice's feet. "I think you've got something to tell me," she murmured, patting the enormous head.

"What do you mean?"

"A secret maybe? I love secrets."

Rosalind blushed.

"Come on, Ros, you can tell me. I'm the soul of discretion. I promise I won't breathe a word."

Rosalind hesitated. What harm could it do except... She gave her friend a smile. "I have a little secret, actually. How did you guess?"

"Something different about the way you look today."

"Well, I hope I'm not taking a risk mentioning this so soon but... I'm expecting another child."

Beatrice reached for her hand and held it in her cool fingers. "How wonderful! I knew there was something. Edward will be thrilled."

"Please don't mention it to him. I haven't said anything because... well, after last time, you know I don't want to go through that again. He so longs for a son."

Beatrice's grip on her hand tightened. She'd been a great

support when Rosalind lost the baby four months into her pregnancy. A baby boy too. She couldn't bear to think of the disappointment in Edward's eyes when the doctor told him what had happened. If she let him know she was pregnant too early, he would fuss over her; would stop her gardening and taking exercise. Gertrude would be unbearable with her sharp glances at her swelling stomach and voicing aspirations about an heir. Suppose it wasn't a boy? Rosalind closed her eyes for a couple of seconds and willed herself to be strong. She was young enough, only twenty-seven; she would have time for more children.

Beatrice kissed her on both cheeks with a sudden display of affection. "I'm so pleased for you and I promise I won't breathe a word. Our husbands are so obsessed about sons, aren't they? With three daughters, I'm under pressure to produce a boy. Well, my dearest one, I also have news. I'm expecting too and the baby is due in December. A little Christmas bundle, isn't that just wonderful? Hugh is longing for a son to inherit all this." She waved her hand towards the house. "We'll be able to commiserate together if we feel ill or tired. When is your baby due?"

It really was too early to have mentioned this. "Not until February. I might not even be… You mustn't tell Hugh, please Beatrice, don't tell him yet."

"Of course I won't. You may tell Edward about my news because Hugh already knows and word will spread. Please God it will be a boy this time and make him happy. I don't want to have to give birth to ten children." A flash of fear glimmered in her eyes.

Rosalind looked down at the sleeping dog and tried to blot out the memory of Beatrice's white terrified face the last time. She'd had a difficult birth with baby Nora and it had taken her several months to get back to her usual cheerful self. Gertrude whispered the dreaded word *melancholia* but Rosalind was certain her mother-in-law was wrong. Beatrice had been tired, that was all. She was four years older and not as robust as Rosalind.

They stood and strolled back towards the front steps while Rosalind told her friend about the man she and Harriet had encountered at the entrance to the stable yard and who followed them into the wood.

"Mick Maguire? He sounds like a tout," Beatrice said. "They're the curse of racing yards these days."

"A tout? What's that?"

Shrieks of laughter came from the front door and the four girls ran towards them as Harriet shouted something about beating them at croquet.

Rosalind shook her head at her daughter.

"Hush, girls," Beatrice called. "Don't fall down and hurt yourselves." She turned to face Rosalind, a frown drawing her fine eyebrows together. "I'd mention that man to Edward if I were you. A tout is not nice to find loitering in your shrubbery. He'll bribe the stable boys for tips. Hugh will be angry if he hears about this as he told me yesterday that Mighty Maiden is lined up for a nice win next time out at Leopardstown and, if the betting odds go down because of some wretched tout, he'll be furious. Tell Edward to get O'Rafferty to run Maguire out of the yard, if that really is the scoundrel's name. Touts supply other unscrupulous punters with information about the form of racehorses and Hugh won't tolerate that. Oh, hush, here he comes. Don't say a word."

Her husband walked out onto the steps and treated Rosalind to his wide smile. He was dressed for riding in a well-cut black coat, his dark curls under a tall hat.

"What a lovely surprise!" He kissed her on the cheek. "And looking as pretty as ever."

His dark brown eyes appraised her. Did his gaze rest longer than necessary on her stomach? Surely he couldn't have guessed? No, he was just appreciating her new green walking dress and the way it emphasized her waistline. That was all. She reached into her pocket and produced her husband's note.

Chapter Six

The present - 24th June, 2019

I climbed the sand dune and lay down on my towel in a sheltered hollow. Overhead a gull soared, white wings outstretched against the blue, borne on a breeze that brought the scent of seaweed and something sweeter.

Archie lay beside me, panting and wet. He rested his head on a clump of small yellow flowers and a cloud of red and black flies took flight. The plant turned out to be the source of the sweet scent and lured tiny pale blue butterflies that flitted from clump to clump.

No message in reply to my text to Jessica earlier. She was probably busy but I needed to talk to her about the latest development. I'd asked her to find out if Tiffany Ryan the journalist was the woman who lured away my husband. If so, Daphne's revelation had tossed my new project into complicated territory.

As the mobile phone signal was stronger at the beach, the first line of the poem accompanying the photograph of Rosalind came into my mind. *She is coming, my own, my sweet.* I typed the words into the search engine and saw a link to a poetry page on the screen. *Maud* by Alfred, Lord Tennyson. That was a surprise. Tennyson was a famous literary figure in his own lifetime, the longest serving Poet Laureate, but neglected by modern critics.

I clicked on a commentary on Maud and learned I'd been wrong to consider the poem romantic. Lyrical it certainly was but with a darker tone than I'd realized. The narrator's father died in the woods, taking his own life after being betrayed by a more affluent business partner whose daughter Maud, darling of the narrator, was considered socially above the poor man lingering by the gate and an unfortunate incident followed where he shot her brother in a duel. Did that really still happen in the nineteenth century? Overall it was a tale of death, hopeless love and insanity. Not the flowery love poem I'd expected and infinitely more intriguing.

Archie barked and leaped to his feet, disappearing over the top of the dune. I stood and shook sand off the towel. Where was he going? I hoped it wasn't to annoy someone else with a dog. The barking ceased but Archie didn't return. I would have to follow him.

With the damp towel round my neck, I moved back up the dune, the sand sliding under my bare feet. I would try calling Jessica again later. "Archie, Archie, come here!"

A figure moved in the distance at the foot of the dunes. Was that Archie bouncing up and down beside him? A man, I could see that much. I blinked and held my hand above my eyes to block out the sun. A black silhouette against the rough grass and sand, shimmering in the light, but difficult to see what he looked like apart from the fact he was tall. Walking in my direction.

My mobile rang and Jessica's name flashed up.

I tapped the screen. "Hi there."

"Hello you. What are you doing?" She sounded slightly breathless, perhaps because of the weak mobile signal.

"Waiting on the beach for Archie to bring me a random stranger with whom he's made friends."

"Oh, that's fun. Is he handsome?"

"Can't tell from this distance. Hope so." I laughed. "He looks like he might be too young for me though."

"Listen, Fi, Dominic called me five minutes ago. I have to be quick because I'm just trying to cross O'Connell Bridge and there's a crowd of Spanish students chattering away behind me… can hardly hear you."

"Dominic? What did he say?"

"It is her. Tiffany is a racing journalist. Isn't that freaky?"

A weight in my stomach shifted and turned over. "That's all I need."

"You have to stop her, Fiona. Just think of Daphne and my dad. She has to be stopped… for my family's sake. This could be your chance for… for revenge."

Revenge. I hadn't considered that and I wasn't sure if I wanted to.

A voice came from beside me and I turned. A young man with dark brown hair pointed at Archie. "This fellow yours? I wondered who was up so early but the dog gave me a clue."

The terrier scampered back to me wagging his tail, his tongue hanging out, proudly showing me who he'd found.

"Who's that?" Jessica asked. "The random stranger?"

"Yes, I'll ring you later." I ended the call.

"Lovely weather today," the man said. "Daphne told me you arrived yesterday. I'm Ben Davidson."

I held out my hand and shook his. "She told me you are helping her."

"I'm repairing the summer house."

His hair was wet and clung to his forehead so I decided that he must have been swimming too. He had a deep voice with a slight English accent that I couldn't quite place.

"Where are you from?" I asked.

"London."

"Nice to meet you. I have to get back soon because Daphne's

taking me to a café with Wi-Fi in an hour's time. She doesn't have a connection to the internet at home."

"I know. It's frustrating at times. She's not the tech type. You're doing research on her family?" He glanced at his feet and away across the beach.

"I don't really know what I'm supposed to be researching yet."

We moved back into the sand dunes as I led the way along a path into the pines with Archie trotting beside my ankles.

"Daphne said you're here because of the murder," Ben said.

I wondered what else Daphne had told him about me. "Do you know anything about it? There's a difficult journalist apparently. Have you met her?"

"No. Just heard about her. She sounds tough. Though I'm sure you'll be able to manage her. Daphne says you're a teacher."

"Yes. I'm used to dealing with awkward teenagers. I teach history."

A silence dangled between us. Ben pushed the pine needles around with the toe of his shoe, hanging his head as if wondering what to say.

"Have you finished college?" I decided to stick to education, an easy topic for me.

He cleared his throat. "Sort of. I dropped out this year. Law… not for me."

"Ah. I understand."

"If you're interested in the family history," Ben said in a louder tone as if keen to change the subject, "there's a house near here you might like to see. It was owned by an ancestor of the Thorntons in the 1890s. Did Daphne mention it?"

"No, she didn't."

"A ruin." He clicked his tongue at Archie, who had returned to us panting. "It's not far… just a slight detour on the way back to Daphne's. Would you like to see it?"

I considered this. There was something intense about this young man with his serious expression and dark eyes. When he asked a question, his gaze lingered on my face but his thoughts were difficult to read. He was making an effort to be friendly though and a ruined house sounded fascinating.

"Okay," I replied. "Thank you."

We walked on to where the Corsican pines parted to reveal a steep track that wound up a hill. I followed behind him until we reached a bend at the top that brought us onto a laneway, overgrown but still passable.

Briars stretched out thorny limbs that grabbed at my jeans and I had to stop several times to untangle them. Archie ran off into the undergrowth, yelping with excitement when a rabbit shot out and doubled back in panic.

"I hope we see him again," Ben murmured. "It's like a jungle up here. I don't suppose anyone comes this way now but I reckon the two houses were connected by this lane decades ago."

"I wonder why Charles never mentioned a house belonging to his relations. He was always keen to keep my friend Jessica and me away from the woods when we were children."

"I suppose he thought you'd come to harm or get lost." Ben broke a light branch from a tree overhead and used it to slash his way through the undergrowth. "This way. Follow me."

The track led us deeper into the trees, a mixture of pine and evergreen oak forming a canopy overhead. We reached a clearing and Ben waved his hand at the view of the ocean below us. "Beautiful, isn't it? I never get tired of looking at it."

I took in the sweep of sand dunes and the sea beyond them. A heat haze shimmered below and on my left Daphne's house sheltered in the hollow of the hill, the windows of the top floor shuttered. I could see the garden and the half-finished summer house on the lawn in front. Virginia creeper smothered the east side, reaching leafy fingers towards the roof.

It seemed secretive, furtive somehow. I thought of the corridor that ran past my bedroom and on towards the stairs leading to the top floor. That dark narrow staircase used to give me shivers after dark when I was a teenager, and I remembered the night Jessica and I had crept up them with only a small torch to light the way, along the gloomy corridor above until a creak of a door brought us to a standstill, clutching each other with fright in the darkness. We'd turned on our heels and thundered back down the stairs. Only the wind, Daphne told us afterwards, nothing to worry about.

"If we go over the top of this hill, the lane runs down to the next band of trees," Ben said. "We go through them and onto the road that takes us to the gates of Ardlackan House."

"Ardlackan House? You mean Daphne's place?"

"No, Daphne's is Ardlackan Lodge, or it used to be called that name before the big house became a ruin. This place was built at a later period, probably Regency or early Victorian. I noticed it when I was running past one day."

The oak woods felt cool and dark after the warmth on the hill. Patches of light filtered through the leaves as we pushed our way along a path swallowed by briars and bracken. Overhead a blackbird piped its fluid song. Archie reappeared out of the undergrowth, bounding over to me with burrs clinging to his coat.

Ben pointed to a building on the left. I stopped to peer into the shadows. It looked like an old gate lodge with windows that had long since fallen out, leaving only gaping rectangles. The door lay open, sagging on its hinges, with slates lying in broken heaps among the nettles. Tall pillars struggled out of ivy and an ornate wrought-iron gate leaned against the trunk of an oak.

"Ardlackan House." Ben pointed in front. "This was the main entrance once upon a time. The road used to come past this lodge and there was a carriage sweep over there." He waved a hand.

"You seem to know a lot about the place."

He blushed, suddenly looking younger. "Oh… I… I'm interested in history, I guess. I looked the house up on the Ordnance Survey map."

"Who owns the land now? Will they mind us trespassing?"

"No, it's okay. An old fellow in the pub told me it belongs to a farmer and he never goes near the house. His cattle graze the fields. As long as we don't actually go into the ruin where it might be unsafe, he won't object."

"All right then, lead on."

Ben stepped through the gateway. The dog shot out of the hedge, making both of us jump and we exchanged amused glances. Ben relaxed a little as we walked on.

The woodland thinned and the broken walls of the old house towered in front of us, its granite steps and pillared portico still intact. Ivy, that ruthless strangler, climbed up the ornate scrolls over the lintels. Sycamores self-seeded inside the roofless interior and thrust their clawlike branches through gaping holes. Part of the front wall had collapsed and stone blocks lay covered in moss.

"Wow!" I murmured, "Wow, that's some house, isn't it? A big house. Do you know what happened to it?"

"A fire. It was destroyed at the beginning of the twentieth century. I don't know why or how. Perhaps it was one of those political burnings; you know what I mean, around the time of the Civil War or earlier. So many big houses were destroyed then. Have a look behind you."

I spun round to see a stretch of grass sloping down towards the coast and a wide expanse of sea. No other houses were visible. "They certainly knew where to position their homes in those times. The view is amazing, isn't it? It must have been a beautiful place to live. Is that an archway over there on the left?"

"Yes, it leads to a yard and to what used to be the stables and coach house. None of those buildings have slates on them now and the timbers have rotted away."

I watched jackdaws flying in and out of the open windows. "It's so forlorn… but it must have been beautiful once." I gazed back towards the sea and screwed up my eyes against the sun. "Is that a building down there by the trees? Do you see it? It looks like an old summer house."

"We could walk down and take a look."

I glanced at my watch. "No, I haven't got time. I can always come back another day now I know this is here. Daphne will be tied up with her work for the art exhibition for another week and this would be a good walk for the dog."

"You're kind to her. She's lonely… I know she is. It's good that she has you to talk to."

"She has plenty of friends though, don't you think? The art group keeps her busy."

"Yes, it does. But before you came… when I dropped in to check up on her in the evenings, she was always glad to see me and wanted me to stay for a chat. Time hangs heavily for older people with only their past to keep them company."

"I suppose they have more memories and have lost more people than we have."

He nodded. "I was brought up by my grandmother."

"What happened to your parents… if you don't mind me asking?"

He turned away and I wished I could snatch back my words. "Sorry," I said.

"It's okay, don't worry. A long time ago." His mouth twisted to one side. "They died. A car crash when I was two."

"I'm sorry." I would have to change the subject. I stared at the house; at the elegant but ruined plasterwork on the inside of the hall door; the smothering cloak of ivy creeping up the façade. "I wonder who lived here and what happened to them? What stories could those old walls whisper?"

"If only the walls could tell us. Do you think it's difficult to escape from our memories?"

"I don't think we can," I replied. "I think our memories accompany us wherever we go and are often reluctant to release their grip."

Chapter Seven

"Are you ready to go to the village?" Daphne stood back from the canvas on her easel and tilted her head to one side. "Hmm, what do you think of this tree? It looks a little lopsided, doesn't it?"

I peered at it, conscious that I knew nothing about art. "Aren't trees often lopsided? Especially ones growing near the sea where they must get a constant buffeting from the wind."

She reached for a piece of cloth on a nearby table. Jars of brushes stood among bottles of white spirit and turpentine. She wiped the bristles on the cloth. "I'll be finished here in a few minutes."

"No problem. I met Ben, by the way. He took me to see an old ruined house."

Her hands stopped moving. "Oh… a big house?"

"Huge but the roof has come off and there's no glass in the windows. Looks like it has been a ruin for a long time. Ben thinks since the Civil War maybe."

She gave the brush a final wipe. "Ben would know. He's keen on history."

"You must have seen the house."

"Yes. I remember walking up there with Charles. I think it

belonged to the Thorntons… many decades ago."

I took out the photograph of Rosalind again and held it in front of her. "Do you think Charles would have known who this woman was?"

She squinted at it, pushing her glasses back on her nose. "He must have put that photo in the stud book. Who else would have? Not me anyway. I never went near his study if I could avoid it as he didn't like being disturbed… used to get quite irritated by interruptions."

"Perhaps she was a relation of his. The date on the back is 1890. What age do you think she looks?"

Daphne turned away and began to dab at her tree with a smaller brush. "Late twenties? They looked older in those days, didn't they? Mid-twenties, maybe."

"But the man who was murdered in the woods… he must have been related to your husband."

Lines furrowed her brow. "I suppose so but what has the murder got to do with Charles? It's all so long ago and I can't understand why people are getting excited about it. Why make a fuss about this murder, for goodness sake?"

"Was there a reason why the family never talked about it?"

"Families didn't talk about unpleasant events in those days. They brushed them under the carpet. Far too much is talked about now, if you ask me. Why don't they leave the dead alone?"

Her voice had risen as if agitated and I didn't want to distress her, but I needed to know more if she expected me to outwit an experienced journalist. "Is there a family tree of the Thorntons anywhere?" I asked. "Could Rosalind be Charles's grandmother?"

"Too old, I think. He never mentioned much about his family. I suppose I should have asked but you remember what he was like, Fiona. Never any use trying to force him to talk. Not that he got angry with me but he could go into a silence that would last for hours if he was in one of his moods. Poor Charles, he used to take everything so much to heart."

"What about the people who trained racehorses here before him? His uncle was quite successful, wasn't he? The man who left him Ardlackan when he died? What was his name?"

"John Thornton. I'll have to think about it because Charles wasn't really a family person… would have hated all these details dredged up." Daphne peered at her painting. "This tree is really giving me grief and I don't know how I'm going to get it right. Look at those leaves there… don't they look too large? Horse chestnut leaves are distinctive but these are deformed. They're definitely deformed. I think I'll give up for today and we'll drive down to the village and you can spend some time on the internet." Daphne tightened the cap on a tube of white oil paint and placed it back among the others. "I think I'll have to scrape this off and start again."

I waited while she did so.

She dipped a rag in white spirit and rubbed at what was left of the offending tree. "There, that looks better. I'll start again tomorrow morning. I don't know how I'm going to get five paintings finished in time for the exhibition." She went over to a sink in the corner near the window and cleaned the brushes with washing-up liquid and water.

We set off for the village in Daphne's car with Archie strapped into his harness on the back seat. She suggested taking him for a walk along the pier while I looked up the census records on the computer in her Dutch friend's café.

I thanked her and reached out to stroke Archie, pulling his soft ears through my fingers. The 1901 census would list the inhabitants of the house and I would find that on the National Archives website. A pity there wasn't an earlier one available but 1901 was only eleven years after the date on the back of the photograph of Rosalind.

Daphne's mobile rang in her handbag beside my feet.

"Shall I answer that?" I asked.

"Would you please? It's probably Andrea wondering where we are because I said we'd be there half an hour ago."

I fumbled for the mobile in a jumble of small notebooks, pencils of various sizes, two purses and a pair of glasses.

"Hello?"

A man's voice asked, "Is that Mrs Thornton? I've a few questions about the murder story…"

"The murder story?" I glanced at Daphne, who shook her head and changed gear to slow down at a crossroads.

"I don't know anything about that," I said. "I'm Mrs Thornton's friend and she's not available. Can I take a message?"

"Can you ask her to ring me? I'm writing a piece on Victorian murders and I'd like to talk to her urgently."

I wrote down his number in one of Daphne's notebooks and ended the call. "Do you get a lot of those?"

She sighed, swinging the steering wheel to the right and narrowly avoiding an old man on a bicycle who wobbled to a halt and turned to wave at her. She raised her hand in acknowledgement. "All the time since the woman… since Tiffany Ryan… I really don't know what to say to these people. Why don't they leave me alone?"

"Where is Tiffany Ryan?"

Daphne pressed her lips together and I thought she wasn't going to answer but she muttered, "She'll be back soon, I expect. Back to annoy me."

The first building in the village was a pub with the name O'Mahony painted in black over the door. Established in 1869. It had small, red-framed windows and a thatched roof like several of the other cottages.

Had Rosalind passed its doors in her carriage or had she been inside? This would have been unlikely. Ladies like Rosalind didn't frequent public houses in Victorian times. It would have been frowned upon by both her family and the locals. Besides, Rosalind may not have lived in this area. She could just as easily have been a family relative in England or Dublin and she could have lived anywhere.

A row of six thatched cottages ran along the side of the road in the centre of the village. Daphne told me they were rented out to tourists. Each one was painted white with small dark blue sash windows and a border of plants up to a half-door. Rosemary flanked the path and Eryngium with its silver foliage and prickly blue cone-like heads. Clumps of thrift with pink pom-pom flowers swayed in the breeze.

We stopped outside The Lobster Pot café and I said I would see Daphne and Archie in about two hours.

I walked in and ordered a cappuccino at the counter from a teenage girl. An array of homemade cakes beckoned from behind glass and I couldn't resist a large slice of coffee gateau with walnuts on the icing.

"Is it all right to use the internet?" I asked, nodding towards one of the desks in the corner where two computers sat, sleek and modern in this old fashioned interior of red wooden chairs and pine tables. Paintings covered the walls and I wondered if Daphne had hung any of hers here. Perhaps that one of sea pinks against rocks freckled with yellow lichen.

"Sure, you go ahead," the girl replied.

I thanked her, picking up my mug of coffee and the slice of cake and settled myself on the chair at the nearest computer.

Where would I start? I typed in the name Rosalind and added the surname Thornton but nothing connected to County Wexford appeared. A few names in the United States and an expert in child psychology in Australia. All far too recent.

Time to try the census but first I had to find out something else. I entered the words *Tiffany Ryan journalist* and there she was. A freelance reporter with her own website, working for numerous racing papers and magazines. A photo of her too, with short brown hair streaked with vivid blonde highlights. A confident expression on her angular face and bright red lipstick. A woman who looked used to getting her own way and demanding her questions were answered. A stab of pity for Dominic pricked me but I shook it off. He'd made his own bed, as my grandmother would have said, and now he would have to lie on it.

I keyed in the National Archives website address and found the Census of Ireland for 1901 and also for 1911. I knew how to check this because I'd used it before for other research. A shame that most of the census returns for the nineteenth century had been destroyed by fire after a massive explosion at the Public Records Office during the Civil War. I chose 1901 and typed the name Thornton and then Ardlackan into the search box and selected County Wexford. I waited. The internet connection was slow and I took a few sips of coffee. It tasted smooth and creamy. I nibbled a bit of icing on the cake, yawning and glancing at my mobile. No messages.

A form took shape in front of me with a list of names. There was Ardlackan Lodge but there was also an Ardlackan House, the ruin Ben and I visited.

I clicked on the Lodge and first on the list was a Gertrude Thornton. I selected the Household Return and the looped handwriting of the enumerator who'd filled out the form appeared. Gertrude was listed as Head of House and a widow, aged seventy-four. Then a list of domestic servants: Betty O'Brien aged fifty-six, who was the cook; Ellen Mangan, a lady's maid from Dublin; Mary O'Brien, twenty-six, kitchen maid and obviously related to the cook as they were both locals from the village. Two men at the bottom named Cornelius Troy, aged sixty-nine, the head gardener and thirty-nine-year-old Frank O'Rafferty, the coachman and head lad.

I took another sip of coffee and broke off a piece of cake.

Was Gertrude alone in the house with all those servants? Troy and O'Rafferty must have lived on the property to be included in this census. Perhaps there was a gardener's cottage and another in the stable yard.

I took out my notebook and jotted down the names and ages. No sign of Rosalind or a husband, if she'd been married. Perhaps if she was part of the family, she'd moved away by 1901. Was she a daughter of Gertrude? Who had trained the horses? And what of Edward Thornton? Where did he fit in?

Seeing these names from nearly one hundred and thirty years before brought them alive and I wondered if one of these people could have been a killer.

I clicked out of the webpage and selected Ardlackan House and its Household Return. Would Edward or Rosalind be in this long list of names? Hugh Thornton was Head of House, followed by his wife Beatrice and three daughters Grace, Irene and Nora. There were many servants, including a governess from England and a butler from Scotland. This branch of the Thornton family had more money, no doubt about that.

"Hello." A voice behind me with a clipped foreign accent.

I swung round and saw a tall woman with blonde hair tied back. She wore sapphire blue beads around her neck and a long red dress, loose-fitting and made of linen.

She held out a hand and gripped mine. "I'm glad to meet you. I'm Andrea, the owner of this café."

"Fiona Foley. I'm staying with Daphne Thornton."

"Daphne's a dear friend of mine. She painted that." She waved a hand towards an oil of two trawlers tied together at the pier. "Did you get everything you need? Is the cake good?"

"Delicious, thanks."

"Is this research for Daphne?"

"Yes, I'm trying to find out who lived in the house in the late Victorian era." I pointed at the census form.

"It's because of this murder, isn't it? The village is alive with gossip about it."

"Yes, so I've been told."

Andrea's smile was warm. "I've only lived here for five years. You could ask a few people here in the village and there's always the graveyard. The dead can tell us more than the living sometimes."

I stared at her. "The dead can tell us more. What do you mean?"

"Tombstones in the graveyard… names of the family who were buried there. Dates, relatives, all that sort of detail."

"Of course," I murmured with relief. "Good idea. Where is the church?"

She gave me directions that would take me up a side road from the main square. "Try the little church first. I'd guess the family was Church of Ireland in those days."

Yes, I knew that from the census forms.

The lane leading to the churchyard climbed uphill and beads of perspiration broke out on my forehead by the time I reached the top. Dry grass, baked brown by the heatwave, straggled along the edges of tarmac that oozed underfoot.

A long, low wall on the right side of the lane was broken by two ornate wrought-iron gates with a chain wrapped around the centre and a grey stone church stood inside, a tall steeple at the front against a backdrop of Irish yews. No padlock on the gate, fortunately. I unwound the chain.

I tried turning the heavy ringed handle on the oak door. Locked. The parishioners of St Andrew's obviously didn't mind strangers wandering into the churchyard but weren't so keen on us getting inside.

Patches of dead grass dotted the lawn that flanked the front and side of the church. No graves were visible but perhaps they were at the back. I walked along a gravel path towards the rear and a row of mischievous gargoyles peered down at me.

I climbed onto a boulder under one of the windows and pressed my nose against the metal grid that protected the glass. Inside a brass rail gleamed in front of the altar and I saw a stand in the shape of a huge eagle with an open bible on it. Perhaps the Thorntons had paid for this church to be built as it probably dated from the early nineteenth century. The Victorian era in Ireland spawned an abundance of local churches but many of them had closed nowadays, their parishioners long dead. At least this one was still used. Stone tablets on the opposite wall listed names but they were too far away to read.

I was correct about the graveyard and found it at the back where headstones dotted mown grass. All the local Church of Ireland families were probably buried here and I moved over to a corner on the right-hand side where the tombstones looked older and more weathered. Lichen crawled across many of them and I peered closer at some of the inscriptions, running my fingers along the letters in an attempt to decipher them.

Samuel Archer, beloved husband of Eileen
and father of Thomas and Isabel. Died 1863.

His widow's name five years later, sadly missed by her loving children in 1868.

I spent fifteen minutes wandering among the oldest graves and noted how many children had died that century.

Annabel Louise, in heaven with the angels, aged six.
Robert and Joshua, aged two months.

They must have been a daughter and twins. Tragic for the parents to lose all of them. Was it tuberculosis? Or typhoid fever? The slightest bacterial infection in those days without antibiotics could have proved fatal. TB had wiped out entire families.

Hot and tired, I sat on the corner stone of a particularly grand-looking grave surrounded by chains linked to small pillars.

A jackdaw landed on the grass nearby and hopped towards me, putting its head to one side and considering me, its eyes gleaming with curiosity. I held out my hand but it took fright and flapped away to land on another larger gravestone.

I followed to read who was lying there and my pulse quickened when I realized it was Gertrude Elizabeth Thornton, born in 1838 and who'd died in 1913 at the age of seventy-five. I scribbled down the dates of her birth and death in my notebook.

Was I getting somewhere at last? The dead were beginning to talk to me as Andrea suggested. Gertrude's husband was mentioned but he'd died in middle age and was ten years her senior, another Charles.

Charles Thornton, departed this life in 1877 aged forty-nine.
Sadly missed by his widow Gertrude and his son Edward.

And there he was on the same stone: *Edward Thornton, died 3rd September 1891 aged twenty-nine*. A sister too: *Clara aged six*. Poor Gertrude had lost her daughter as a child and then her son.

I wiped my brow with a sleeve. The humidity was overwhelming but at least I'd found Edward. Pulling ivy from a grave on the left, I tried to make out the name where roots of the plant gripped the stone. Hugh someone. Yes, another Thornton. I ran my fingers along the names, tracing the letters. Hugh and his loving wife Beatrice of Ardlackan House. So perhaps cousins, the wealthier side of the family with the butler and governess. Hugh died in 1930 at the age of seventy-one so had survived the First World War.

And what of Beatrice? I noticed that she predeceased him by twenty-five years. She left this world in 1905 after a short illness at the age of forty-six. What ailment had carried her off?

I sat on the grass and lay back, gazing up at the sky. So easy to let my imagination run away with me here in this silent place among the dead. Swallows darted about overhead, landing to perch in pairs on a telephone wire that stretched above the graves. A bank of dark cloud was advancing towards the village. Was the rain coming at last?

"Hey there!"

I sat upright.

A woman with streaked blonde hair marched towards me. "Hey."

She stopped and regarded me. "You from around here?" More a command than a question. My heart thumped when I recognized the angular face and thin lips from the website. Tiffany Ryan.

"Well?"

I scrambled to my feet. "No, no I'm not."

"Know how I can get into the church?" She pointed towards the building.

"No."

She frowned, probably suspecting that I didn't know much. She took a step towards me, turning to look over her shoulder as if to check if anybody was hiding behind the yew tree beside us, listening to our conversation.

I glanced at the tree but no one was there. Only the shadows of branches playing on the grass beneath.

"I'm working for a British TV producer, Sebastian Rotherill. You heard of him?"

I shook my head.

"I'm researching a local murder," she said. "Know anything about it?"

What could I say? I remembered Daphne's reaction in the car.

"A man called Edward Thornton was murdered near here.

Haven't you heard about it?"

"Near here?" I decided to pretend I knew nothing. She wasn't a tall woman and her pink T-shirt was short and tight above a pair of clinging black jeans. A knot tightened in my stomach as I thought of her and Dominic together. "Murdered? I'm sorry, I don't…"

"He was murdered by his wife. I've heard his wife was crazy… a lunatic."

"Murdered by his wife?"

She uttered a short laugh. "Definitely insane. What do you think of that, eh? A good story and it will make a great TV series."

I cleared my throat, as swallows twittered on the wire overhead against the backdrop of ominous cloud. Thunder rumbled in the distance.

Better to let Tiffany think I was an innocent and she might divulge more. "You're working on a murder series? That sounds interesting. This Edward Thornton… do you know the name of his wife?"

She'd turned away; deciding I wouldn't be any use to her but my question made her spin round and her sharp brown eyes fixed on mine. "Oh yeah, I know that. Her name was Rosalind."

Chapter Eight

The past - 30th August, 1890

Mighty Maiden towered over the other five horses in the parade ring at Leopardstown. Joseph, the most able of the stable boys in spite of his diminutive stature, was leading her and struggling to keep her under control. She laid back her ears and snapped at a chestnut gelding that stopped in front. Rosalind stood at a safe distance behind the parade ring railing, admiring her dark gleaming coat and bright eyes.

"Would you look at our lady!" Edward turned to Hugh, clapping his cousin on the back. "She's in fine fettle, isn't she? Have you ever seen her look so well?"

Beatrice murmured to Rosalind, "Is your dear husband talking about one of us, do you think, or is he praising the mare?"

Rosalind smiled. "I only ever hear him talking about the horses in such glowing terms."

"You envy Mighty Maiden?" Hugh looked down into her eyes. He was taller than Edward and considered more handsome by the local ladies with his darker hair and self-confidence. She often thought that he and Beatrice looked alike and indeed they were occasionally mistaken for brother and sister by those unacquainted with them. A good-looking couple.

A flush warmed her cheeks. "I would never presume to

compete with Mighty Maiden."

Hugh reached out his hand to touch her glove. "All the ladies pale into insignificance beside you, my dear." Then, as if losing interest, he turned to Edward. "Come along, cousin. It's time to hoist O'Rafferty into the saddle. Wish us luck, ladies."

"Good luck," Beatrice said as she took Rosalind's arm.

The men moved into the centre of the parade ring where some of the jockeys already stood among the horses.

"Edward thinks the mare might win today," Rosalind said as Frank O'Rafferty moved towards her husband. Frank wore Hugh's pale blue and wine hooped jersey and he lifted a hand to tip the peak of his cap as Rosalind walked past. "Good afternoon, ma'am."

She replied, "I wish you good luck."

He smiled.

Rosalind's maid Sadie had told her that morning that Mrs O'Brien was going to put a small wager on Frank to win. Sadie said the cook liked him best of all the outdoor men, as she called them, and often gave him extra scones and cake when he came to the kitchen.

The flash of interest in Sadie's eyes made Rosalind wonder if she also had a soft spot for the coachman and stable head lad whose exploits were often the talk of the servants. She'd heard Ellen giggling with him the week before, which surprised her because Gertrude's maid was a serious woman who viewed the world with cynical eyes through a pair of round spectacles.

Sadie admitted that Frank O'Rafferty was a handsome man with his soft brown curls and Rosalind had found herself agreeing. Sadie added that all the girls in the village set their caps at him. Rosalind liked the way his blue eyes danced when he was amused by one of the horses. He was good with the animals and they loved him, raising their heads and nickering when they saw him approach.

Edward informed her that the horses only liked Frank

because of the time he spent with them and he was the one who fed them. Horses weren't clever creatures, her husband pointed out, but they became attached to their handlers.

Edward had asked Frank to teach Rosalind to ride and he'd shown nothing but patience as he led her along on one of the older horses, a sturdy cob with the unlikely name of Romeo. That was soon after she'd come to Ardlackan as a bride nine years before. She was quite a capable rider now thanks to him. She'd made slow but steady progress and could even tackle a small fence without feeling terrified.

Her riding would have to cease now that she was pregnant. She couldn't risk a fall and knew she would soon have to break the news to her husband.

A tall, well-built man passed by and Frank's smile vanished. The red-haired stranger, who had a thick moustache and beard, was wearing a bowler hat and long brown coat. His piercing eyes lingered on Rosalind for a few seconds before he pushed his way into the throng of bystanders.

"We're going up on the grandstand now so that we can get a good view," Beatrice told Frank. "We'll be able to see Mighty Maiden jumping away from the others."

Frank touched his cap again as she walked away.

Rosalind followed her, lifting the hem of her pale pink silk skirt. The waistband felt tight and she would have to have it loosened. She dreaded having to abandon her outfits for maternity gowns and wasn't looking forward to the tedium of her inevitable confinement.

Beatrice stepped through the crowd, holding her parasol over her head. She'd had several larger dresses made already and was wearing cream silk with lace at the cuffs and collar.

This was Rosalind's second outing to Leopardstown. Edward had reminded her in the train that the racecourse had only been completed two years before and its design was inspired by

Sandown in England. On arrival, she'd been captivated by the carriage enclosure with its assortment of vehicles from four-in-hands to donkey carts. Edward told her Leopardstown attracted big crowds because it was close to the city of Dublin. People from all walks of life gathered to watch the races from wealthy families and clerks to hawkers and fortune tellers. Already the ballad singers were gathering around the carriages in the hope of earning a few coins.

Beatrice and Rosalind ascended the steps of the grandstand and found a space against the railings halfway up.

One of the horses trotted out onto the course, a dapple grey with a silver mane and tail that reminded Rosalind of the rocking horse in the nursery at Ardlackan Lodge. Harriet loved that rocking horse, named it Twilight and told her mother tales of how it could fly her off at night to foreign countries like France and Italy where they ate grapes and chocolate. Twilight always brought her home at dawn so nobody knew she'd been away. Her daughter had a vivid imagination.

Below them fashionable ladies sporting ostrich feathers in their hats mingled with the men to place their bets with bookmakers.

"There goes Mighty Maiden." Beatrice nudged her. "Doesn't she look wonderful? Pray hard, Ros, that she wins. There is a fortune riding on that mare today."

"A fortune? You mean the prize money? Edward told me it was sixty sovereigns."

"No, the wager."

"What wager?"

Beatrice turned to face her. "You don't know, do you? Hugh and Edward have had a private wager with the owner of the grey. If our mare wins, our husbands will collect a thousand pounds."

Rosalind's chest tightened. A thousand pounds! Of course Edward hadn't told her this; she'd been kept entirely in the dark as usual. "And if Mighty Maiden loses?"

Beatrice flashed her quick smile. "She won't."

"Don't you worry about… what if something goes wrong?" She tried to keep her voice steady. "I don't like Edward gambling."

"That's just your upbringing. You never get used to us, do you? Don't worry, Hugh never gambles money he can't afford to lose. He's always been astute."

Was Edward astute? Rosalind feared not. He disliked her mentioning his gambling and always changed the subject. It was her money, after all, her father's money left to her. Edward had a right to it, of course, but there was the future to think of. Harriet and now the baby who would arrive in February. She would like to employ a new nursemaid to look after him. Or her. Perhaps when she told Edward about the baby it would make him more responsible with money.

"It's started." Beatrice raised her race glasses to peer through them. "The grey's off in front."

Six horses galloped towards the first fence and Rosalind closed her eyes as they rose into the air in a bunch. If only Beatrice hadn't mentioned the gamble. Now she could hardly bear to watch in case something happened to the mare. How much had Edward risked? She opened her eyes and saw that the grey was still half a length in front. Mighty Maiden looked like she was pulling hard, her head lowered towards the ground and Frank leaning back in the saddle in an effort to prevent her galloping into the lead.

The horses jumped three more fences and swung round the bend towards the grandstand for the first time and a murmur of excitement rose from the crowd.

Beatrice laid a hand on Rosalind's shoulder and squeezed with her fingers as the mare took off too early at the fence, stumbling on landing and shooting Frank up onto her neck. The gentleman beside them groaned and a ball of worry tightened in Rosalind's stomach. If Edward and his cousin stood to win a fortune, that meant they also stood to lose one if their horse fell.

Mighty Maiden struggled to her feet again and set off to catch up with the rest of the horses, with Frank safely back in the saddle. He loosened the reins and allowed her to stride on until she challenged the grey in front and took the lead.

"Too early, too early," Beatrice muttered. "She's not supposed to go to the front until the last furlong. I heard Hugh discussing it with O'Rafferty. Why doesn't he listen?"

Why was it Frank's fault? Rosalind suspected that the head lad, who knew more about training horses than her husband or his cousin, had to accept the blame if their plans did not work out. Frank might be anxious today if he knew about this wager.

He pulled again on the reins and managed to get Mighty Maiden back behind the grey as they approached the first fence on the other side of the course. A chestnut horse with four white socks galloped beside her and they took off together.

Had the jockey on the chestnut pushed against the mare? Rosalind strained her eyes and wondered if she should ask Beatrice. The chestnut shot out a hind leg and kicked back at the fence, going down on his knees on landing and hurtling the jockey onto the grass where he lay still.

"Oh!" Rosalind put her hand to her mouth.

But no, he was uninjured because as soon as the hooves of the other horses flashed past, he sat up and rose to his feet. His mount galloped off with the rest.

The men surrounding Rosalind and Beatrice nudged against each other and began to mutter in expectation.

"The grey is expected to win," Beatrice explained. "He won last time out at Cork Park. Trained by the champion Henry Linde, with more experience than our mare but she's a better jumper. That's what Hugh says and he knows what he's talking about."

Mighty Maiden looked like she was enjoying herself as she galloped behind the grey with her ears pricked.

Rosalind felt perspiration on her forehead and wondered what Edward might do with his winnings. Enough to buy that carriage for which her husband had been hankering, perhaps. And a matching pair of horses to go in the traces. She'd been standing beside him when she heard him joke with Hugh about a new carriage only the week before. He'd seen a dark blue landau with silver trimmings and lamps advertised for £220 by the carriage builders in Baggot Street in Dublin. With its two folding hoods that fastened in the middle, Edward told her it was a status symbol that he would dearly love to own. Hugh had bought one a year before and he and his family had been driven to the County Show where it was much admired. Hugh, of course, could afford a team of four horses but Edward assured Rosalind that two would suffice until he could justify purchasing another pair.

"And now," Beatrice's voice rose, "they're coming round the last bend. Come on, Mighty Maiden, show them how good you are!"

As the remaining five horses turned the corner into the straight, a little cry burst from Rosalind and she clutched the handle of her parasol with both hands in an effort to remain calm. Beatrice's fingers clasped her arm and tightened as the mare took on the grey coming into the second last fence. Mighty Maiden rose into the air and jumped into the lead, galloping on towards the final obstacle.

"Come on, come on, you can do it," Rosalind whispered.

The crowd began to roar, waving hats in the air and shouting encouragement. The grey battled back and appeared to be gaining on the mare. Rosalind squeezed the handle of her parasol until her fingers ached. The dappled head of the challenger edged closer and closer. Frank crouched lower and drove Mighty Maiden on with his heels. The mare surged past the winning post.

Beatrice flung her arms around Rosalind's neck and screeched in an unladylike manner while they hugged and kissed each other.

"We've won!" She sounded breathless with excitement. "Oh, Ros, we've won!"

Chapter Nine

The past - 5th September, 1890

"My love, what wonderful news!" Edward gathered Rosalind in his arms and planted a kiss on the top of her head.

"I have a long way to go yet but yes, I'm so happy. Harriet will be thrilled to have a younger sibling to play with and order about."

"A little brother," Edward murmured in her ear, his breath warm on her skin. "All these years... what age is Harriet? Seven or eight years old... and after the last… I really thought that we would never have another and now I might have a son to help me train at Ardlackan. Mama will be ecstatic."

Rosalind felt a chill like the touch of an icy finger. If it wasn't a boy? If this baby turned out to be another daughter, what then? She would love her, of course she would. A son didn't matter to her the same way as it did to Edward. After all, her father had only one daughter… Rosalind closed her eyes and allowed herself to be embraced again by her husband. It was a joy to witness his enthusiasm and to be the focus of his attention. She stroked his cheek and kissed it. She had to stop worrying. All would be well.

Gertrude declared herself quite taken aback and said that Rosalind wasn't getting any younger and it was certainly time for another child. She pointed out that Beatrice was only four years older and was already expecting her fourth baby.

Sadie placed a plate of cold roast beef in front of Rosalind with a secret smile at luncheon and Rosalind felt a conspiratorial thrill pass between them. Sadie, brought up in an orphanage in Wexford town, had been sent to work for a large family at the age of thirteen. She had practical experience of childbirth and babies. Rosalind looked forward to having the maid to help her this time.

"I have a suggestion," Edward said as Sadie piled mashed potato on his plate. "Why don't we go for a drive this afternoon in the new landau and call upon Hugh and Beatrice to tell them the good news? Now they aren't the only ones adding to the Thornton family."

Gertrude toyed with a piece of roast beef, slicing it in half and reaching for the gravy boat. "Is that wise, my dear?"

"Mama, what can you mean?"

"Rosalind has only just told us about the baby. February is a long way off and anything could happen before then. You remember the last time."

Edward frowned. "Do you expect me to wait until the boy is born before I announce this? Honestly, I thought you would be happy for me... for us."

Rosalind kept her eyes on the white linen tablecloth. No point interfering in an argument between Edward and his mother. She knew already who would win.

After the meal was over, Rosalind changed into one of her new dresses and went downstairs to wait for the carriage to be brought round to the front door. There was still no sign of Edward or Gertrude when Frank O'Rafferty appeared with the new landau, driving a pair of shining bay horses and wearing a brown suit of whipcord. He only dressed in formal white breeches, single-breasted frock coat and top boots when he was required to drive the family to parties or town. Rosalind knew he disliked having to wear the ceremonious outfit because the stable boys whooped with amusement and made jokes about him. Harriet had overheard their gibes when she'd sneaked into her pony's stable.

He raised his cap to Rosalind. "Good afternoon, Mrs Thornton."

She walked down the steps and smiled up at him on the driver's seat. "Good afternoon, Frank. My husband and my mother-in-law will be here presently. How are the new carriage horses behaving?" She reached out to pat one of the bay geldings on his glossy neck.

The horse rolled his eyes and moved away with a flick of his tail.

"A bit flighty so far. That one's the hardest to control. I'm not convinced they've much experience in the traces."

Edward had returned home in an exuberant mood after he bought the new pair. He'd seen them advertised and hurried to County Tipperary to purchase them without consulting Frank because they were matching bays with identical markings. Very unusual to get such a fine pair, he'd said, and not too expensive considering they'd come from a large stable that specialized in breeding carriage horses.

"My husband couldn't resist them," Rosalind replied, turning her head towards the house to see if there was any sign of the others. "I'm sure they'll soon settle down in your capable hands."

Frank laughed. "I'm glad you have such a high opinion of me... of my equestrian skills."

His smile lit up his blue eyes and she felt grateful that he treated her like an ordinary person and didn't show any of the respectful silence he displayed in front of Gertrude. With Edward, whom he'd known since they were boys, he maintained a professional manner but could always be counted on to give his considered opinion if he disagreed with something his master said.

The pair of bays caused a minor argument. Frank hadn't shared her husband's excitement about them being such a bargain. Ask him again in six months, was his immediate response the day they'd arrived snorting and shying in the stable yard.

As for the landau, Frank admired the beautiful carriage but considered it unsuitable for their local country lanes. A city carriage, he told Edward who dismissed his coachman's criticism with a careless wave of his hand.

Rosalind wondered if playing with Edward as a boy, running through the woods, galloping on ponies together and racing bareback across fields had encouraged Frank to feel less of a servant and more of a friend to her husband. Certainly, Edward relied on him to run the stables and train the racehorses.

Edward boasted often about how other trainers envied him such a capable head lad. Some had even gone so far as to attempt to poach Frank away from Ardlackan and offered him more money and a house of his own, instead of his few rooms over the coach house.

When Frank had given her the first riding lesson on Romeo, he'd been careful about what he said, not knowing how much of their conversation would be repeated to Edward and Gertrude but, as the weeks passed and her ability improved, he'd relaxed more in her company and they'd had interesting conversations.

Rosalind had been impressed by the fact that his mother was the local schoolmistress and taught him to read at an early age. Unlike Edward, Frank tolerated poetry, including that penned by the great Lord Tennyson although Frank, being a man, preferred to recite *The Charge of the Light Brigade* aloud and Harriet often joined him, marching behind him across the yard much to the amusement of the stable boys, who cheered and clapped.

"What do you think of the beautiful bays?" Frank asked. "I

suppose we are fortunate they have good bone and the one on the right has only mild stringhalt."

Rosalind looked over her shoulder to check they were still alone. The pair of horses were fidgeting and making ugly faces at each other. The bay on the far side rolled his eyes at the coachman. "They don't look like happy companions to me and I wonder how they're going to pull together in harmony."

"Very astute of you, to be sure. I wonder myself if this magnificent pair will ever get along. Harmony is important with carriage horses or else we end up in the ditch or wrapped around the trunk of a tree when these handsome creatures have a falling out and decide to go their separate ways."

She laughed because he also did, her eyes on the more aggressive bay pawing the gravel and snapping again at his companion.

A voice rang out behind her. "Be careful, girl! Step away from those horses. O'Rafferty, you should keep a better eye on her. She knows nothing about the danger of highly-strung animals."

Rosalind blushed and moved back to stand beside Gertrude.

"I beg your pardon, Mrs Thornton," the coachman muttered. "It was my fault for not paying attention."

"What is Edward doing?" Gertrude walked towards him. "Come along, Rosalind. Help us open the door, O'Rafferty, don't just sit there like a stuffed parrot."

His feet landed with a crunch on the stones and he pulled open the door with a flourish. Rosalind perceived a glint of amusement in his eyes but his face was expressionless when he turned to Gertrude.

Rosalind took his gloved hand as he helped her into the carriage. He returned to his perch behind the horses without another word when Edward appeared on the front steps, hurrying to join them and waving an envelope in the air.

"My apologies, Mama, I had to write an urgent letter. Drive

on, Frank. We'll go through the village on our way to Ardlackan House as I wish to deliver this letter personally and besides I want to show off my new landau and fine pair."

Frank picked up the reins and the horses shot forward causing the carriage to lurch and Gertrude to shriek and grab at her hat. The wheels spun in the gravel.

"For goodness sake, man! Keep those creatures under control, will you?" She glared at the coachman's back.

Rosalind suppressed a smile and looked down at her hands in her lap but could imagine the expression on Frank's face.

They set off down the avenue under the oak trees in the early September sunshine and out the gate onto the narrow road that dropped down to the village.

Frank gripped the driving reins and his jaw clenched with concentration, obviously trying hard not to give Gertrude another fright but the bay horses weren't making things easy for him. The gelding on the left lowered his head and was pulling hard, leaning on the bit, while the other kept trying to move to the right to escape from his fractious partner.

Strands of Rosalind's hair blew across her face and she could have done with more pins to keep her hat on. A rather lovely blue one with dark pink flowers posted to her by Aunt Catherine. A shame if it ended up in the cornfield on their right.

"Well, what do you think, Mama?" Edward took Rosalind's hand in his and gave it an affectionate squeeze. "What do you think of the landau?"

"Too fast." His mother's brow creased into a frown. "I feel safer enclosed in the brougham where there's no breeze."

Edward tossed back his head and laughed. "Poor Mama, you have no sense of adventure."

Just how this description of Gertrude went down was impossible to discover because a commotion up front threw the occupants of the carriage into disarray. The difficult bay horse leaped to one side and the other followed. The carriage tilted to the left, throwing Rosalind on top of her mother-in-law. Gertrude exclaimed and pushed her off while Edward jumped out of the landau and ran to hold the heads of the horses. The coachman abandoned his seat and followed his master.

"We'll have to lead them past," Frank suggested.

"Tidy your hair, Rosalind, you look a fright." Gertrude sat upright and gripped the door with a gloved hand. Her face was pale and her eyes glittered. She was about to have one of her fits of temper. What her son called her volcanic eruption.

"All's well now, no need to be alarmed," Edward called out.

"Just the pigs," Frank added.

"Pigs? What pigs? What are you talking about, man?" Gertrude still clutched the door.

"There, ma'am, in the field." Frank waved his whip in the direction of the hedge as both horses shuddered. "It's the smell, Mrs Thornton, the horses dislike it. . . and the noise too."

"What noise? I can't hear anything."

"The oinks, ma'am." There was mischief in the coachman's clear eyes now. "They hate the oinks."

Rosalind raised her hands to her face and swallowed her laughter, afraid that Gertrude would turn her displeasure on her. Frank was used to her mother-in-law's ways; was probably ordered about by her since he was a barefoot boy playing games with Edward on the lawn. Gertrude's husband had been, by all accounts, a quiet, tolerant man.

He'd encouraged the friendship between the two boys because it kept Edward occupied and young Frank was a natural on a pony, who inspired courage and enthusiasm in his playmate.

If Rosalind had been Sadie and not a happily married woman and mother, she'd have been tempted to set her cap at him, too, like all those young women in the village. She hadn't set her cap at Edward, but he'd handed his to her and it'd been a fine top hat at

Ascot races on the day she'd accompanied friends of her father.

She could still recall the look of alarm on Aunt Catherine's face when Rosalind informed her of her betrothal. Her aunt objected that Ireland was far away and rather an unruly country. The young man didn't appear to have much money. Granted he was well-spoken, quite good-looking and knew how to be polite to ladies but Rosalind hardly knew him. It had taken all of Edward's charm to talk Aunt Catherine into accepting the marriage as inevitable. Papa, had he lived long enough, would have taken to Edward.

Frank climbed onto the coachman's seat and picked up the reins, clicking with his tongue to urge the pair of bays forward while her husband led the troublemaker on a few steps. The pigs were left behind and Rosalind watched them grazing in the field, rooting in the dust with their long snouts. A sudden squeal from one made the horses flinch but Frank maintained a stronger hold on the reins and averted trouble.

"Edward, you must tell that farmer to remove those creatures."

"Yes, Mama."

"We can't possibly have this happen every time we wish to go to the village. What a nonsense!"

"Yes, Mama."

By the time they reached the first few cabins at the top of the hill, the horses had settled down and were happy to trot on without Edward's assistance.

He climbed back into the landau. "I think I saved the day and perhaps our lives as well."

A disrespectful snort of amusement shook the shoulders of the coachman in front but Gertrude ignored this.

"Well done, my dear. We can rely on you." Edward's mother patted her son's arm, smiling at Rosalind.

"He's wonderful," Rosalind said and noticed Frank's head nodding, as if in mock agreement.

When they reached the centre of the village, Edward gave the order to halt outside one of the cabins. Frank pulled the reins, applied the brake and got down to hold the horses.

Edward walked up the path to a half-door and rapped loudly upon it. A boy opened it and a smirk lit up his freckled face. Rosalind couldn't hear what her husband said but watched him hand over a coin. The boy grinned, reaching out to take the envelope.

A crowd of small children gathered around the landau, some of them daring to run up to touch it before they skipped away again. A motley lot, some wearing clothes too big and others with trousers so short that their ankles showed. Brown limbs and faces burned by the summer sun and sea wind.

"What are they staring at?" Gertrude frowned at them. "Do they think we're the circus come to town? O'Rafferty, ask them to move off."

"It's the landau. I don't think they see one that often." He raised his cap in greeting to a group of young girls who giggled and put their hands over their mouths.

Gertrude addressed one of the taller ones. "You, child, what's your name?"

"Ruby."

"Ruby who?"

"Ruby O'Brien."

"Do you know who I am?"

"Yes, Mrs Thornton, my auntie is your cook."

"Mrs O'Brien is your aunt? Why, everyone must be related in this village. Well, Ruby, you look a sensible girl. Can you encourage the children to move away?"

Ruby did her best for the formidable lady in the carriage but without much success. The boys grew more brazen, rubbing the horses and tapping at the woodwork of the landau as if inspecting its quality, grinning at each other and bowing mockingly at Frank, who smiled back at them.

"O'Rafferty, don't just sit there, do something," Gertrude demanded.

Frank began to address the children just as Edward returned from delivering his letter and, standing up in the carriage, the coachman threw a handful of coins onto the road. With whoops of excitement, the children fell to their knees, pushing each other aside and scrabbling in the dust.

"Now do move on, O'Rafferty," Gertrude ordered.

The horses walked on through the village, snorting when anyone ventured too close, eyeing passing women and a group of men outside the public house with suspicion. As Edward gave the local constable a cheerful wave, Rosalind wondered how much experience the pair of bays had in the traces and whether her husband had been told the truth about them. Frank had once informed her that horse dealers could look a buyer in the eye while telling bare-faced lies. A shameless breed according to him.

What had been in Edward's letter? The envelope looked bulky, as if stuffed with pages of handwriting. He wasn't much of a letter writer. Hopefully it hadn't held bank notes.

Chapter Ten

The present - 24th June, 2019

Daphne listened to my encounter with the journalist, taking off her glasses to polish them with kitchen paper. "A murderer here in this house? But how does the woman know? It might not be true. I never heard Charles say..."

I decided not to mention Tiffany's connection with my husband. That could wait. I'd also decided not to mention it to the journalist. I would bide my time before that revelation.

Daphne reached out a hand to stroke the cat, which was sitting on the table and glaring at Archie. "You'll have to convince her it's not true, Fiona, you will be able to do that, won't you? To think that poor Charles had been in the process of commissioning a biography when he had the first heart attack... he would turn in his grave." She stood to pour boiling water into the teapot and tossed in two teabags.

"We'll have to find out what she knows. It might all be gossip and lies. Thank you, yes, just milk and no sugar. I think I should continue sorting through Charles's papers in the study and perhaps I might think of a few ideas... how we should manage this."

She walked over to the kitchen window and stared out on

the yard below. The room overlooked the stables on the right where a line of navy-blue doors stretched towards the hay barn. Rows of fine thoroughbred heads once looked out over those doors, watching for Charles with ears pricked. A circular stone mounting block stood in the middle of the yard.

"Why can't she leave us alone?" Daphne asked.

I hurried over and laid my hand on her shoulder. "I'm sorry, it must be hard, must be so difficult for you. She's dragging up the memories."

She forced a smile. "I know he has gone forever but sometimes, especially if I wake during the night, I believe he's still here… watching over me. Does that sound crazy to you?"

"No, I'm sure that's only natural. I remember when my father… just after my father died… I used to imagine I saw him in the street sometimes. It would look so like him and then the man would turn to face me and it would be someone else. My imagination, I suppose."

"I see his shadow in the bedroom." Her words sounded matter-of-fact, as if pointing out the dog in the garden.

"His shadow?" Jessica had reminded me that Daphne sometimes saw things that the rest of the family put down to her vivid imagination and artistic temperament.

She knocked on the glass pane and raised a hand to wave at Ben as he looked up at the window, before turning to me. "I'm worried that Tiffany Ryan will stir up what should be left in peace."

"You think Charles would come back and haunt her?" The question shot out of my mouth before I could stop it and sounded flippant. I hoped she wouldn't be offended.

"Not just him."

"Other inhabitants of this house? I don't think they will, Daphne, but then I haven't… I've never seen…"

"Oh, I'm well aware that the rest of the family thinks I'm

off my rocker. Say what you like, my dear, but don't denounce something you don't experience or understand."

"Of course I won't, I'm sorry." I decided to change the subject. "Some of the rooms in this house are empty. Did Charles clear out furniture before he died?"

"Yes, he moved some pieces into the coach house in the yard. I suppose he meant to sell them at auction but he never got around to that. He just took a notion one month and got the boy who mows the lawn to help him lift them out."

"Are they still there… in the coach house?"

"I expect so. I really must do something about them. Perhaps you could phone some of the auctioneers in Wexford town and see if there are any furniture sales coming up… add them in. What do you think?"

"It's a good idea. Would you like me to have a look through them first, just in case there's anything inside them that you'd like to keep?"

"I expect Charles would have done that already. He was always very thorough."

Would Charles have got rid of a lot of family papers? Perhaps there was something he knew that he didn't want his relations to find out. I decided I would have a look in the coach house. It would be better for Daphne if I found something before Tiffany got her hands on it. I had a hunch that Charles, if he was trying to hide some family information or history from his wife, would definitely have moved papers out of the house before he died. It was hard to bring oneself to burn letters, photos and diaries, wasn't it? People usually kept those things and hid them away.

Daphne smiled at the cat and turned her green eyes on me. "I do remember something… he told me years ago… he seemed upset… quite put out, in fact."

"What about?"

"I wish I'd paid attention but Balor was yowling to get out the window so I didn't really concentrate… he said something about a letter he'd received from a woman in England."

I waited for more. If only Daphne wasn't so absent-minded. "About the family?"

"Hmm, yes it might have been. He had a letter in his hand and he was telling me something about… someone who lived in England. Perhaps I'll remember later on. I'm going back to my painting now, dear. If you find anything in the coach house, do let me know, won't you?"

I assured her I would, standing up and calling Archie to come with me. He was glad to escape from the single malevolent eye of the cat and bounded ahead of me into the hall.

Fifteen years since I'd last been in the stable yard and it'd been full of racehorses, beautiful heads over the half doors with their dark eyes and sleek thoroughbred coats gleaming. I stood in the middle of the old stone yard and felt an aching sadness. All empty now, those stables, with only swallows flitting in and out to care for their young in nests on the rafters inside. The clock on the bell tower had stopped soon after Charles died and Daphne never bothered to get it going again. A place where time stood still. What had it looked like in 1890? The second and third yards behind this older one wouldn't have been built as they were added by Charles after his first major successes on the racetrack and new owners came flocking.

I walked over to the old coach house where a strong padlock secured the double doors. I rattled the metal clasp but nothing gave way.

As I looked up at the windows above, something moved. Someone watching me behind the panes draped with cobwebs? No, only the reflection in the glass of a bird flying behind me, a house martin landing on a telephone line.

I turned and saw a man standing in the shadow of the doorway into the garden. I strained my eyes. So hard to see with the dazzling sunshine. He walked towards me, stepping out from the shade and I saw it was Ben.

His serious dark eyes surveyed my face. "Hello, Fiona. What are you up to?"

"I'm helping Daphne... there's some furniture stored here and I offered to look at it before she sells it."

"Furniture?"

"She said it was stored in the coach house. Charles put it here before he died. I want to sort through the drawers in case there's anything left in them by mistake, anything that Daphne might want to keep... but this is locked."

"I know where she keeps sets of keys." He led the way to the back door. "See that tin box on the windowsill beside where the coats are hanging? That's where most of the keys to the sheds are kept."

I picked up the box, opened the lid and saw that each key had a label. Charles's handwriting. Coach house. There it was. "Thank you, Ben. How's your work going?"

"I've spent the last two hours pulling up the floor of the summer house. I'm going to remove all the rotten boards and replace them with new ones. You should come and have a look at it when you get a chance. It must have been wonderful once, with its revolving mechanism."

"It was." I remembered the time when Jessica and I pushed it around with my younger brother inside while he encouraged us to go faster. "I think it revolved so that people could avoid the sun in Victorian times. Now we'd do the opposite, I guess."

"Daphne just told me you met the journalist."

I looked up at him. "Yes, that's right."

"She's staying in a guest house in the village."

"Really?"

He hesitated, looking away. "I... I came across her in a local pub." He added, "She seems nice enough. We had a few drinks last night."

Had she told him about Rosalind the lunatic, the woman who murdered her husband? No, I wouldn't tell him what Tiffany told me about Edward Thornton. Not yet. It might not even be true.

"I'll go and have a look inside the coach house." I held up the key.

"I'll help you with the lock." He walked beside me across the yard.

The key was stiff in the padlock and refused to turn. I stepped aside and watched him twist it backwards and forwards several times before the catch clicked open. I blinked in the darkness inside. Dead leaves lay in heaps and cobwebs dangled from the ceiling. On the right at the back, a wooden staircase climbed up into the gloom.

"No one has been here for a while," Ben said.

"You live in the yard, I think you told me."

He pointed towards the bell tower. "Over there. Charles had an apartment made for his head lad. It's in reasonable condition and I'm not fussy."

Furniture draped with dust sheets stood against the back wall and I walked over to lift a couple of them to peer underneath. A large chest of drawers, heavy dark oak with brass handles and a matching wardrobe. I opened a drawer and peered inside. Empty. I closed it and pulled out another lower down.

"What exactly are you looking for?" Ben leaned against the door, his shadow lying across the flagstones where the sun threw a strip of light into the gloom.

"Just checking there's nothing personal inside these pieces of furniture before Daphne sells them."

Near the foot of the stairs, a pile of folded horse rugs sat on what looked like an old school trunk with heavy leather straps and wooden banding across the top. The initials *CHT* on the end.

I lifted the rugs onto the flagstones and knelt, pulling at the leather straps. They had stiffened with age and lack of use. One of my fingernails chipped as I fiddled with the rusty metal buckle. Ben came over and crouched down beside me to push the leather back and forth until the buckle released and he could raise the lid of the trunk.

Stacks of plastic-covered books lay inside with dates inscribed on the front.

He picked one up and flicked through the pages. "Charles Thornton's collection of racing results from his training days."

I moved a few aside to search underneath.

Ben sat on the floor and pushed away dry leaves with a hand. "Are you looking for photographs, diaries, that sort of stuff?"

I remembered that he'd made friends with Tiffany and that they'd shared a drink together. She might even have told him something about her research and asked him to keep an eye out for anything relevant. I would have to be careful. "Yes, anything that we don't want to send to an auction. Ben, did Tiffany… did she tell you about Sebastian Rotherill, the TV producer?"

For a moment his eyes rested on mine.

"Did she?" I repeated.

"Only a little bit. We talked about the house and I told her I knew Daphne. She told me she's been to the National Library and looked up newspapers from 1891. Why do you ask?"

I hoped I hadn't sounded accusatory and murmured, "Just wondering how she's getting on, that's all."

I removed some of the form books and piled them on the ground while I searched inside the trunk. Could I trust Ben?

There was a cloth section like a long pocket at the back and I could see a notebook sticking out. A notebook, when I glanced inside, similar to the one I'd found in Charles's desk with lists of horses' names and breeding.

Ben was still sitting on the floor, looking at his mobile. Perhaps he'd lost interest in what I was doing.

I picked up a thick brown envelope at the back of the cloth

pocket with Charles's neat handwriting on the outside. *Thornton family* written in faded black ink. That looked interesting. I opened the flap and pulled out the contents. More envelopes, smaller with stamps and postmarks.

I took the large envelope and its contents over to the door, where the light was better. The letters looked foxed and smelled musty. Had Charles found these when he was sorting through the furniture, perhaps when he was convalescing after his heart surgery? Had he stashed them here in an old trunk where nobody would think to look? My heart raced in spite of my attempt to pretend the letters were nothing out of the ordinary. I would take them back to the house and read them later.

Dark clouds were gathering over the treetops outside the yard. The storm getting nearer.

Ben got to his feet. "Anything interesting?"

I pushed them back into the envelope. "Just some old letters. I'll have a look through them and give them to Daphne who will probably burn them. She doesn't seem interested in family history."

His eyes remained on my face, as if trying to read my thoughts. "Yeah. Most people aren't."

Chapter Eleven

The present - 25th June, 2019

I sat up in bed, every nerve in my body tingling, my heart thudding against my ribs. Darkness surrounded me as I gulped a few breaths to calm myself.

A crash of thunder rolled outside but what was scratching at the door? I fumbled for my mobile but it slipped through my fingers onto the floor. Damn. Swinging my legs over the side of the mattress, I groped for the lamp and switched it on. Light flooded the bedroom and I found the phone under the table.

Another scratch at the door. I walked towards it, holding my breath. I reached for the handle and pulled the door open, peering out into the dark corridor. Nobody there. I turned back and something brushed my leg, something warm and furry. Balor stared up at me with his one yellow eye, uttering a soft *burr* as he trotted past, as if to thank me. He jumped onto the bed and settled down.

My head ached, a throbbing at my temples. Of course it must have been the wine after dinner. I should never have drunk four glasses of it. That acidic red Daphne produced for us and Ben had brought a triangle of blue cheese. No wonder I was having nightmares.

I couldn't remember the dream but it'd been one of those

terrifying ones where something, a nameless unrecognizable presence, drew so near to my face that I could feel its breath brush my skin.

I swallowed the water in the glass on the bedside table and walked to the window, pulling back one of the curtains. A sliver of silver moon bobbed in and out of the hastening clouds, dangling as if on a thread over the black treetops like a toy above a baby's crib.

Above the roar of the wind and waves there was an intermittent clanging; the bell tolling in the stable yard tower when gusts of wind hit the heavy iron. Jessica and I had heard it long ago on stormy nights and used to imagine ghostly hands pulling the rope below.

I remained standing at the window until my pulse returned to normal.

The cat sat up and kept his eye on the window as another roll of thunder echoed. He landed softly on the floorboards and climbed onto the windowsill to stare out.

It was then that I saw the figure in the garden. One of my hands clutched at my throat while the other gripped the top of the sash. The dark form moved across the lawn, stopping to bend as if looking for something, a hood pulled over its head and hiding its face.

Was it my imagination? Having woken from a nightmare, was my mind conjuring up this apparition?

Or the wine was still at work, giving me hallucinations as well as a headache.

The figure stood still, turning to look back at the house.

I stepped aside, hiding behind the folds of curtain and peeping round it after several seconds passed. Still the shape remained staring in the direction of my bedroom window. Daphne's words came into my mind. I'd suggested foolishly that Charles might come back to haunt Tiffany and she'd said, "Not just him." I'd smiled afterwards but not now, not when alone in the middle of the night.

I walked back to the cupboard and opened the door. My fingers closed around the thick envelope inside, the letters still where I'd concealed them. I'd meant to read through some earlier but the wine had sent me straight to sleep.

Could Daphne be out there in the garden? I would have to check.

The corridor was lit only by the skylight halfway along and sudden flashes of lightning. Daphne's bedroom was on the left and I tiptoed towards it as the thunder crashed and the storm marched closer. No light showed under her door so she was either lying in the darkness or walking about in the garden. Unlikely to be out on a night like this but Daphne was unpredictable. I clasped the door handle and twisted it.

I groped my way over to the bed between the two windows, both with their shutters bolted so the room was even darker than mine. My hand touched the silky bedspread and I could hear breathing, a steady rhythm punctuated with an occasional soft snore.

The light flashed on, dazzling me, and Daphne sat upright in the bed, hair dishevelled, fumbling for her glasses on the bedside table.

She pushed them on. "Fiona! What on earth… what are you doing?"

I stepped backwards. "Oh, sorry. I'm really sorry. I thought… I just wanted to check…"

"For goodness sake, you gave me such a fright! Were you checking I was still alive? You nearly gave me a heart attack." She sounded angry as well as frightened.

I apologized again. "I didn't mean to terrify you. I was checking you were here in bed."

"Where else would I be at this time of night?"

"In the garden," I muttered lamely.

"If you think I'd be in the garden in the middle of the night… Is that thunder? What time is it?"

"Nearly half past three. I saw something in the garden, a figure dressed in black with a hood… I… I thought it might be you."

Daphne's eyes rounded. "A figure in the garden?" Intrigued, she climbed out of bed and flung open the shutters of the window on the right. Her voice rose. "Where? Where is it?"

I pointed towards the lawn but there was nothing there except shrubs blowing against the darkness of the wood.

"Are you sure you didn't imagine the whole thing? Perhaps it was a dream."

"Perhaps it was. I woke up suddenly as if from a nightmare… Balor was scratching at my door… I opened the curtain to let the light in and there it was."

"Was it a shadowy female? Did she have long light brown hair? Long… down her back."

I hadn't expected her to be so specific. "No, this was a real person. It had to be. She or he seemed so… solid, yes, definitely solid. Nothing transparent at all. No, not a ghostly figure."

"I wish I'd seen it. And out on a night like this. How strange." She frowned and climbed into bed, lying back on her pillows. "You mustn't worry when you see something like that here. You'll get used to us all eventually."

"Goodnight." I walked away, wondering who she included in the word *all.*

"The dead can't harm us." Her voice sounded calm. "It's the living we have to be careful of. They're the dangerous ones."

My hand gripped the door handle. "I suppose you're right. The dead are safely in their graves."

"That Tiffany, she'll try to make a big deal out of nothing… this old story she's heard. Charles was a famous man. I know there are many who've never heard of him, people who don't

93

follow horse racing, but they too might be attracted by a scandal."

"Was there a scandal?" The old-fashioned word hung in the air.

Her face looked pale and lined. "I would have heard, I'm sure… I'd have heard if there was anything."

On impulse, I walked over to her and planted a light kiss on her brow.

I returned to my bedroom, more wide awake than ever. I couldn't go back to bed now. I would creep into the garden and find the person, for that must have been what it was; not a ghostly figure like Daphne hinted but a real human.

I pulled on a cotton sweatshirt and a pair of jeans. Using the flashlight app on my mobile phone to find my way across the kitchen, I kept the main light off as I didn't want to alert the intruder outside.

I told Archie to stay in his bed and pulled open the door into the garden, stepping out. The gravel crunched under my feet and I held my breath, glancing towards the lawn as another flash of lightning lit up the dark outline of the summer house near the gate into the wood. Was that where the figure had gone?

I made my way along the path running beside the herbaceous border. The back of the summer house was hidden by clumps of pampas grass. I would sneak up behind one and peer in the window. A faint light flickered inside and I switched off my flashlight.

Yes, definitely a movement of light. A shadow dancing on the inside wall.

I steeled myself to creep closer. Who could be in there at this hour? And why? It couldn't be Ben. He wouldn't need to behave in such a clandestine manner.

I stole nearer, reaching out to push the stems of pampas grass aside and cried out in pain when I touched the sharp foliage.

The light inside went out.

I wiped the blood spurting from my finger on my jeans and put my head through the open window, my heart pounding against my ribs.

Someone sat upright on the floor. "What are you doing here?" I called, trying to keep my voice steady.

The person stood up and swung round to face me.

Tiffany.

For a few seconds she stared at me, the hood of her long coat pushed back and the bleached highlights in her hair almost white in the torchlight.

"You gave me a bloody fright!" she shouted. "What the hell were you doing sneaking up on me like that?"

"What the hell are you doing sneaking around Daphne's summer house in the middle of the night? I saw you from my bedroom window. What are you doing?"

She pulled out a packet of cigarettes from her coat pocket. "You're the woman I met in the graveyard. Who are you?"

I didn't answer.

Her lighter flamed and she drew on the cigarette, blowing smoke up into the air, her eyes on my face. "I don't know who you are but I was just having a nose around, that's all. I knew Daphne Thornton wouldn't like it so I decided to come after dark. You won't tell her, will you?"

"She already knows. I woke her up when I saw you."

"Oh… why did you do that?"

"Because you're an intruder, that's why."

Tiffany took another drag from her cigarette. "I found nothing so there's no need to make a fuss." A deep voice and a slight Dublin accent more noticeable than before.

I glanced at the broken floor boards ripped up by Ben and yawning gaps between the joists. "But you obviously expected to find something here, didn't you? And you must have wanted to find it urgently if you came out in a storm."

Her eyes narrowed. "Look, if you're a relation of Daphne's…
I know you don't trust me… whatever you've heard. I only want
to find out the truth about Charles Thornton and his family,
that's all. I'm being paid to discover the truth."

"You don't need to go back into the distant past. Why not
just stick to his racing days? Why upset Daphne and her family?"

Tiffany laughed, pulling again on the cigarette. "But that
wouldn't be much of a story, would it? I don't think the television
producer would be happy with that."

Irritation flared inside me. "But who told him about this?
How do you even know it's true? That Edward Thornton was
murdered… how do you know it's not just local gossip?"

"The TV producer has a good source."

"He or she must be pretty old by now. You're talking about
the late nineteenth century."

"A descendant of someone."

"Who?"

She drew her shoulders up to her ears and smirked. It gave
her power, withholding this information. "Besides, some people
know about it here… down in the village. I met an old man in a
pub with Ben."

"Ben? He introduced you to the old man?"

"Ben's good-looking, isn't he? And helpful. He's a bit young
for me but seemed happy to help."

I'd been right not to trust Ben. "I bet that old man is a drinker
who doesn't know what he's talking about."

"Maybe… but his story matched the one I heard. You can't
stop Sebastian Rotherill making this series, whoever you are. It's
quite a tale, the best I've heard in a long time. Far too exciting to
abandon… an insane wife of a racehorse trainer kills her husband
and then disappears, never to be seen again."

I shivered in the rain, cold seeping through my clothes. "I'm
going back into the house and I won't tell Daphne I found you

here if you keep away in future."

Tiffany smirked at me, triumphant in the gloom. No point arguing with her. I left her without another word, walking back across the lawn. I could have mentioned Dominic. The nearer I got to the house, towering above me in the shadows, the more determination burned like a fire inside me. Tiffany could think what she wanted but I would prove her wrong. It wasn't Rosalind who'd done this. I was good at research, at ferreting out historical facts and I would prove Tiffany wrong. The woman in the photograph with that sweet expression was not a murderer.

Back in bed, I tried to sleep. After half an hour tossing from one side of my mattress to the other, I gave up and switched on the lamp, retrieving the envelope from the cupboard and emptying out the letters onto the bedspread. The more I found out about Rosalind, the sooner I could stop Tiffany.

I flicked through the names on the outside of the envelopes, noting the dates of the postmarks. Some were addressed to Charles from his mother, reassuring letters written to a lonely young boy in boarding school. Others to his parents from a variety of relations around the world. An uncle in Australia seemed to have been a prolific letter writer. I wondered, as I often did, what would happen to family records in the modern era of texts and emails. Would researchers have anything to look back on in decades to come?

Two envelopes caught my eye. Both were addressed to Mrs Edward Thornton at Ardlackan Lodge. Rosalind. The postmark was London and the first one I opened was dated 26th November 1890.

> *"My dearest Rosalind,*
>   *It was wonderful to receive your letter last week. I had so longed to hear news of you, Harriet and Edward.*
>   *I was delighted to hear that Hugh's horse, Mighty Maiden (what*

a wonderful name for a racehorse) won again at Leopardstown and that sounds a worthy reward for Edward's training skills. How proud you must all have been!

Most of all, my dearest love, I was overjoyed to learn that you are expecting another child. What wonderful news! Your papa would have been so happy for you if he was still alive. I hope that you will take good care of yourself and not become overtired like last time.

What does Harriet think of the prospect of a younger sibling? You will have to make certain she does not feel left out. I think you should talk to Edward about hiring a nursemaid. Two children will be too much for Sadie as well as all her other duties.

Please tell Harriet I enjoyed her drawings very much.

My dearest, I was alarmed to hear about the trouble you are having with that horrid man called Maguire. It can't be nice having someone like him following you. You really must insist that Edward keeps him away…"

The rest of the letter sent news of London and what this woman, who signed herself Aunt Catherine, had been doing. Parties and occasional expeditions to the country with friends. Her friend's husband had been ill with influenza and had alarmed the family for a few weeks but had recovered. There were no antibiotics in those days and complications from influenza could prove fatal. Catherine referred to an outbreak at the beginning of 1890 and hoped it wasn't going to return. She pointed out that it had been the worst since 1840.

What had I learned from this letter apart from the fact that Rosalind had an aunt in London? I now knew that she had a young daughter named Harriet.

There had been no Harriet in the graveyard in Ardlackan village but I would have to go back there and check. Rosalind was pregnant and had a servant called Sadie to help her.

My eyes returned to the paragraph Aunt Catherine had written about the strange man. Why was he following Rosalind and her daughter?

I pulled out the contents of the other envelope and read the letter dated 12th February 1891, also in Aunt Catherine's flamboyant handwriting.

> *"My dearest Rosalind,*
>
> *Such wonderful news reached me yesterday about your baby boy. A boy! Edward must be thrilled and I'm sure Gertrude had a few words, or several hundred, to say about him. I hope you are not too exhausted and that my letter finds you in good health. I look forward to hearing all about the son and heir whenever you are rested and able to write to your anxious aunt. Please remind Edward about employing a nanny. I am sure you can afford one.*
>
> *I was so sorry to hear of Beatrice's loss in your last letter. What a tragedy to lose the baby! It will be difficult for her now that your own son has arrived safely.*
>
> *I will write again soon as the carriage has just arrived to take me to stay with Cousin Albert who has become so doddery and forgetful that I am certain one day I will arrive at his house in Hampshire and he will no longer know who I am!*
>
> *My love to you always, my darling girl."*

I placed the sheet of notepaper back in the envelope, feeling gratitude to the effusive Catherine for her letters. A baby boy would have been important in those days. No mention of a name for him but at least he'd arrived safely. But Beatrice, wife of Hugh, had lost her baby. A tragedy, Aunt Catherine called it. What had happened?

I placed the letters on the table and switched off the lamp, lying back on my pillow in the darkness while the thunder grumbled in the distance, the storm moving inland. Tiffany was wrong, I was certain. Rosalind was the wife of a trainer, a respectable mother of two children and a beloved niece of an aunt who lived in London. She was an ordinary Victorian woman, living a normal nineteenth century life. She would never have committed murder.

Chapter Twelve

The past - 20th February, 1891

Frank O'Rafferty pushed the liver chestnut gelding forward and Sailor trotted to the top of the hill and stood as his rider held up a hand to shield his eyes from the sun. The strip of training gallop snaked round the copse of sycamores and straightened out up the hill.

They were cantering towards him now with the two horses' heads close together, Ardlackan Lass's flaxen mane upright in the breeze and Mighty Maiden's ears flat back as she leaned on the reins. The Lass wouldn't stand a chance of keeping up with the Maiden if the boys allowed their mounts to gallop. Frank waited as their hooves thundered past him and Sailor flicked his ears but didn't move.

Frank gave the gelding a pat. "Good boy, you're a fine old man, aren't you? You might not be the fastest point-to-pointer in the county... not speedy enough for your owner, the grand Hugh Thornton, but you're a reliable old fellow and you never fret when the others leave you, eh?"

Further down the other side of the hill, Joseph and Peter pulled up the two mares and turned to jog back towards Frank. A white foam of sweat clung to Mighty Maiden's neck as she threw her head in the air and almost snatched the reins out of Joseph's hands. He was an experienced rider for his twenty-two years. The master was lucky to get him from a big stable on the Curragh.

"Did you see her go, Frank?" Joseph called out. "She's like a hurricane when she's given her head."

Peter grinned at his companion. "A shame you're like a sack of potatoes on the poor mare's back." A tussle between them almost dislodged Joseph when the big bay mare objected to this rough play and reared.

"Hey, hey, you boys!" Frank shouted. "Come over here and stop that tomfoolery. The master will be giving us all our marching orders if you lame that mare before Leopardstown next week. A handicap steeplechase with one hundred sovereigns to the winner and her owner has his eyes on them."

The stable boys grinned at each other and asked their horses to trot towards Frank. Together the three men rode down the hill in the direction of the lane leading to the stable yard. The slate roof of the house reared above the top of the trees in the wood. A fine house, no doubt about it, a curl of smoke furling from the kitchen chimney into the cold February air.

Frank's eyes lingered on the second-storey windows above the front door. The mistress would be there with her baby boy. He hadn't seen her for several weeks; not since the day she knocked on the glass from above and raised a hand in recognition as he drove the pair of bays onto the gravel. He'd smiled and returned the greeting.

Edward hadn't taken the landau out since the dreadful day. Fortunate nothing terrible had happened to the mistress but Beatrice Thornton was still confined to her house. Mrs O'Brien whispered this as she buttered his morning scone and added that Dr Richards was concerned about the poor lady. The cook had a reliable network of informants in big houses throughout the county.

Joseph interrupted his thoughts. "I hear Mr Hugh wants to aim her at the Grand National." He pulled a cigarette out of his jacket pocket and looped the reins over his arm as he attempted to strike a match.

"And where did you hear that?" Frank frowned at him. He didn't like the stable boys gossiping about the horses. Too many touts around who might make use of such information and tip off the bookmakers. He warned the boys regularly about talking to men who made money by passing on the form of horses in training.

"Didn't you say something to the master last week loud enough for us all to hear?" Peter winked at Joseph. "Our head lad thinks he's the most discreet man in the county but he doesn't realize he forgets what he's saying when he lays eyes on the master's lovely wife, isn't that the truth, Frank?"

Joseph, who never dared to initiate a joke about Frank, concealed his mouth behind a hand.

Frank narrowed his eyes at his young cousin. "You be careful what you say or I'll tell Mrs O'Brien you're on half rations this week because of your weight." He couldn't help smiling. "Mrs Rosalind Thornton is nothing to me, I'll have you know."

Peter and Joseph looked at each other and smirked. Frank didn't mind the stable boys making jokes as long as they carried out their work; as long as they cared for the horses and listened to his instructions when they were on the gallops or in the stable yard. They were good-natured lads and didn't mean any harm.

"The English horses didn't get a run during January because of the snow, we all know that, with all the race meetings abandoned, but I reckon The Maiden will have her work cut out, all the same," Joseph muttered and sucked on his cigarette until the tip glowed. "I hear that Royal Meath will be in the field for the National." He imitated a French accent. "Ze winner of ze Grand Steeplechase in Paris no less."

Frank had read about the big liver chestnut's victory in France. Royal Meath was an Irish equine hero, a powerful horse with quality and stamina. Frank rejoiced in the grandstand with the rest of the jostling crowd the year the horse had cantered home the winner of the Conyngham Cup at Punchestown. He would certainly be a force to be reckoned with if he ran in the National.

"And there's Ilex, last year's winner and he'll be back again to retain his title, I reckon," Peter said. "Two thousand sovereigns, that's what the National is worth and I heard Arthur Nightingale went home with a thousand extra for riding the winner. That's a fine sum of money for a jockey, isn't it, Frank?"

"It could be Frank's next year if the Maiden's on form," Joseph replied. "I'd have a wager on our mare, to be sure. Didn't the mare Frigate win last year and she's from our home county of Wexford? She was unlucky this year but she'd a lot of weight to carry over those big fences."

"The mares and the women have to be taken into the reckoning, don't they, Frank?" Peter sniggered again and winked at his cousin. "And Frank has an eye for the women all right."

Joseph and Peter let out whoops of amusement and took off at a canter, heading for the gate that led into the lane; their laughter lingering on the air behind them with the smell of cigarette smoke.

Frank reached out to stroke Sailor's neck, his hand sliding on the glossy coat. He didn't begrudge them their fun because the boys had a tough life. Getting up at five o'clock in the morning and working hard all day, mucking out stables, grooming the horses, riding out the racehorses before all the farm work began and then scraping the mud off the cart horses afterwards.

Sailor suddenly shied at a rustle in the hedge on the right. Frank regained his balance and gripped the reins, speaking softly to calm him. Unlike the gelding to react like that. He glanced into the undergrowth and saw the cap of a man duck out of sight.

"I see you! Come out here this instant!" Frank called out. "Don't think you can run away from me because I'll be after you on this horse and…"

"Hold your tongue!" The bloodshot eyes of Mick Maguire peered out from behind a clump of young sycamores entangled with briars. "Is it me you're addressing in that insolent manner, Frank O'Rafferty?" He pushed aside the branches and ambled over to the horse, a long-haired dog trotting at his heels. Maguire's lurcher with his sandy hair and intelligent brown eyes. "And that old gelding couldn't keep up with me… don't make me laugh. I saw him galloping today and he's past his best. The point-to-pointers have nothing to fear from that old nag." A harsh snigger burst from his purple lips and he spat on the grass.

"Why are you trespassing on the master's land?"

Maguire scowled. "I'm biding my time, that's all." He turned to the dog and ordered him to sit.

"I've warned you before about spying on the horses out on the gallops. The master won't be pleased to hear this. You've no right to be loitering here."

The other man fixed him with cold grey eyes. "I'm not afraid of Edward Thornton. I know a lot more about your employer than you do. I'd keep a sharp eye on your position in the stables here, my lad. Make the most of it while the money lasts."

"I've a mind to tell the owner of the bay mare. I've read the newspaper reports about you thieving his salmon from the river and rabbits from Ardlackan woods. You and your dog."

Maguire coughed and spat again, a glob of spittle that landed near one of Sailor's front hooves. "Hugh Thornton is it? The grand Hugh Thornton of Ardlackan House. I don't care much for the likes of him."

Frank didn't care much for Hugh either but he wasn't going to say that to a notorious tout who crept into the bushes beside the gallops and reported back to the gambling men on the form of the horses. The less he mentioned to the rogue the better.

Frank had heard Mick Maguire's name associated with that

of a prominent bookmaker who was feared throughout the county. Many a gentleman who owed Martin Chance money lived to regret the day he'd engaged his services. Frank had seen the giant bear of a man at various racecourses, strutting around in his fancy fur-collared coat, his pockets stuffed with rolls of five pound notes and weighed down with sovereigns, and a fat cigar clamped between his yellow teeth.

His type was to blame for the penury and misery of the gamblers. He was the one who encouraged the weak-minded to part with their money before they drank their losses away afterwards, staggering back to their unfortunate wives without a penny in their pockets.

That was the sort of bookmaker Maguire fed with information without a flicker of remorse in his shallow, unscrupulous heart.

"You'd best be gone," Frank said, turning Sailor's head towards the lane. "Go on with you now. I'll tell the master about this."

Maguire's face turned pale in the sunshine but Frank knew there wasn't much the tout could do to him while he was on a horse. He could hardly drag him off and beat him senseless with the boys only fifty yards away. With another shrug and ejection of green spittle, Maguire called his lurcher and slouched off in the opposite direction.

Chapter Thirteen

The past - 27th February, 1891

"Your little boy is two weeks old today, Mrs Thornton." Sadie beamed down at the bundle in the baby carriage and reached out a finger to stroke his cheek. "A bonny lad, isn't he? And very like his father."

Rosalind looked up from the letter she was writing to Aunt Catherine. "He's the image of his papa, or so his grandmother says, but I think he will have my light brown hair." Her eyes slid over the sheet of paper on her writing desk. "Will you take Ivor out into the garden? Harriet and I are driving over to Ardlackan House this afternoon. It's a mild day and I think it will be good for him to get some fresh air as long as he is well wrapped up."

"Yes, of course I will. I would love to do that, wouldn't I, darling baby? You and I will have a lovely walk together while your mama goes visiting."

Rosalind sat with her pen poised, watching the maid. Sadie was so good with children and Harriet adored her. Aunt Catherine might like to hear that, although she was the one who suggested a German or French governess for Harriet, one who could teach her another language, to sew and to play the piano. Aunt Catherine had developed some grand ideas when her brother set her up in the house in Hampstead and provided funds to employ a cook and housemaid. She and Papa had always been close.

Harriet was getting on well with the governess at the big house, sharing lessons with Grace and Irene. Hugh had suggested this arrangement and Rosalind was grateful to him.

She'd mentioned to Edward about hiring a nursemaid for Ivor but he'd been surprisingly uninterested. He said that Sadie could manage and Mrs O'Brien's niece Mary, who was fifteen and a strong girl according to her proud aunt, could take over some of the maid's duties.

Rosalind was happy to agree as the thought of having to recruit a nursemaid unnerved her and no doubt Gertrude would interfere and make her feel inadequate, although her mother-in-law had been kinder since the birth of Ivor and considerably less critical. Rosalind and her father had lived a harmonious and simple life in London with only a handful of servants to look after them. It was a challenge to keep control of the Ardlackan staff, much more outspoken than those employed by Hugh and Beatrice.

There was also Cornelius Troy in the garden but, although grumpy at times, he treated her with respect because he appreciated her love of plants and interest in his work. Troy had been in charge of the gardens at Ardlackan for many years and even the stable boys were afraid of him. When Frank's eighteen-year-old nephew Patrick was sent out to the walled garden by Mrs O'Brien to help Troy dig up vegetables, he rolled his eyes at the maids and made out that the head gardener was a tyrant.

Frank would probably be outside now, sitting patiently on the carriage with old Romeo in the traces, waiting for her and Harriet.

She tucked the letter into a drawer. She could finish it later and add in some news of Beatrice. Poor Beatrice hadn't come to visit since the accident, claiming she felt too tired. She needed company and perhaps Rosalind and Harriet would be able to coax her out into the garden to take tea in the summer house.

The door swung open and Harriet rushed in, eyes sparkling and cheeks glowing. "Are we going now, Mama? I can't wait to see Grace and Irene and Nora!"

Rosalind stood and crossed the rug, catching her daughter in her arms and impulsively giving her a hug. "Yes, let's go. Say goodbye to Sadie and little Ivor."

"Goodbye." Harriet blew a kiss to the baby.

Outside they found Frank stroking the cob. Rosalind knew Romeo wasn't the best looking of horses and he had feet like a plough horse according to Hugh but she liked him for his steadfast nature. He would never shy or rear the way those two bays… But no, she wouldn't think about them today, not when she was going to see Beatrice.

"Good afternoon, Mrs Thornton," Frank said and bowed in a mock formal manner to Harriet before adding, "and how are you today, young lady?"

"I am well, thank you, Frank." Harriet spread out the skirt of her navy dress on the seat of the carriage.

"You are growing tall," he said, with a glance at Rosalind. "What age are you now, seven isn't it?"

"Nearly eight. My birthday is on the tenth of March and Papa is going to buy me a new saddle for Bumblebee and then I will be able to go jumping with him."

Frank laughed and gave Romeo a gentle tap with the whip. "Walk on, old fellow. Well, I'm sure you'll look the picture, Miss Harriet, out jumping across the country on your fine pony."

Rosalind tapped her daughter's arm. "No jumping yet. Not until you're ten years old. Beatrice says she…"

"Bumblebee will be perfectly safe, you needn't worry about me. I'm not going to end up in bed like Cousin Beatrice."

Frank pretended not to hear and sat facing forward, humming a tune. Rosalind frowned at her daughter.

"Cousin Beatrice thinks all horses are dangerous just because she was knocked over by one." Harriet shook her head. "That's just silly."

Rosalind noticed Frank's shoulders stiffen and she leaned closer to her daughter to whisper, "Hush, Harriet."

They hadn't told the girl the truth but Frank knew. She was certain he knew because even though he'd been up on the hill gallops with several of the racehorses and stable boys, they must have seen the carriage as it hurtled down the road and would certainly have heard Edward's cries of alarm as the pair of bays raced towards the ford in the river, the landau bouncing and jerking behind them like a fish on a line.

Rosalind closed her eyes but the memory pushed to the surface. Beatrice had thrown herself towards Edward, as if to grab the reins before the horses met the water. Rosalind sat rigid beside her, too terrified to speak, gripping the seat with her frozen fingers. She heard her husband shout and saw her friend's face turn white.

The difficult bay swung away to the left, snorting at the water, and the other pulled to the right. Both horses stumbled onto their knees and Beatrice, already too far forward, hurtled from the carriage into the river.

Rosalind's eyes stung with tears as she remembered Edward clambering down and splashing in after Beatrice, reaching to pull her to her feet. Rosalind followed, desperate to help her friend, who was sobbing with shock. Miraculously there were no bones broken and Edward left Rosalind to comfort Beatrice while he checked the horses who were both unharmed apart from one cut knee.

If only she had managed to persuade him to wait for Frank to get home from the gallops before taking out the landau but her husband had been in an impatient mood after he'd received a letter. He'd insisted on driving Beatrice home and wanted

Rosalind to accompany them. He pointed out that Frank O'Rafferty wasn't the only man in Wexford who could handle the bay pair. He would show the ladies how capable he was. Wasn't he the one who had chosen the carriage horses in the first place and not O'Rafferty?

They'd explained to Harriet that Beatrice had been knocked over when walking beside Hugh's horse in the stable yard after one of the dogs gave the gelding a fright. The tumble had brought on the baby and that was why he died. Too early to arrive in this world, poor little mite. Harriet had listened, her big brown eyes filling with tears. They'd had to tell her the same story they told Beatrice's daughters, the same lies because they didn't want the girls to blame Edward. Hugh had helped them concoct this deceit and Beatrice, in bed for several weeks afterwards, didn't care what they said. She wanted to be left alone and turned away all visitors, even Rosalind. She needed time to come to terms with losing her son. Hugh told them a month later that the doctor didn't think she'd ever be able to have another child. There must have been internal injuries because she'd lost so much blood.

The pain of these memories constricted Rosalind's throat and she dabbed at her eyes with a handkerchief.

"Mama? What's wrong? Why are you crying?"

"It's only the wind," she said. "It's the salt on the wind off the sea. It's stinging my eyes and making them water."

Frank glanced over his shoulder, concern on his open features as Rosalind hid her face in Harriet's chestnut curls.

When they arrived at Ardlackan House and were admitted by Gilton, they found that Beatrice was up and dressed, waiting for them in the drawing room.

"How lovely to see you both." She smiled down at the girl.

"We've been looking forward to seeing you, haven't we, Harriet?" Rosalind noticed the dark circles under her friend's eyes, the skin stretched tight across her cheeks and pale from lack of fresh air and exercise. She was dressed in black and had lost weight; her dark brown hair, usually so glossy, looked dull and lifeless.

Beatrice motioned towards the door. "You know where to find the girls, Harriet. Off you go, my love."

The girl lingered, gripping the skirt of Rosalind's dress with her fingers. "Mama, where will I find you? You're not going to leave me here, are you?"

"Of course not," Rosalind replied. "Why would you think that?"

She twisted her mouth, looking down at the rug. "Irene said…"

Beatrice put out her hand, lifted Harriet's chin and looked into her face. "Tell me what Irene said."

Harriet glanced at her mother. "She said… she said that I might have to come and live here now because Papa can't afford a nanny."

"Well really!" Beatrice said. "Where does Irene get this nonsense from? What silly things you girls talk about. That's nonsense, Harriet, so don't take any notice of her. Now run along and don't worry."

The door closed behind the girl and Rosalind looked at Beatrice, who waved a hand towards the sofa by the fire. "Sit down and tell me all your news." Her voice sounded tired and weak.

"You are taking care of yourself, aren't you?" Rosalind plumped a cushion behind her back. "You're not overdoing things?"

Beatrice sighed. "Ah, how can I overdo things when I have Hugh watching me like a hawk? I'm not allowed to ride… not allowed to walk on my own. I feel I'm suffocating here, Ros… feel I'm going slowly but surely out of my mind."

Rosalind laid her hand on Beatrice's arm and gave it a

comforting squeeze. "Hugh is concerned, that's all. I'm certain he's only trying to take care of you. He doesn't want you to fall into a… to become ill again."

A wary look crept into Beatrice's dark eyes. Thornton eyes, like her husband's and Edward's. She was a distant cousin, Rosalind remembered. Her great-grandfather had also been a Thornton, one of the wealthier branches of the family that owned linen mills in Northern Ireland. Fine damask cloth and napkins graced the tables in Ardlackan House, products of the looms from factories dating from the previous century.

The drawing room was a light-filled space, with long windows and shining glass panes. Portraits of Thorntons hung on the pale blue walls with the most recent beside the Regency glazed bookcase. Hugh, Beatrice and the three girls seated on the lawn, a tumble of flowering roses behind them. There would have been another commissioned to include the son, no doubt, if he'd lived.

Beatrice's eyes rested on the painting. "What will happen to this place now, Ros? What will become of it when the girls marry and leave home?"

"The girls might decide to live here. Don't distress yourself with thoughts about the future. Who knows what will happen?"

"Hugh longed for a boy and now… You heard what Dr Richards said, didn't you? Hugh said he told you. I won't be able…"

"Don't talk about it. It's too upsetting. You have the three girls…"

"You don't understand how it works, do you? What would you know? You weren't brought up in our tradition."

Rosalind flinched. "I'm learning. Don't forget I have Gertrude to instruct me and tell me what I should be doing."

"Ah yes, the perfect Gertrude. Always eager to be the authority on everything. Her grandmother was a governess, did you know? I don't suppose she told you that."

"No, Gertrude never... Are you sure? She never mentioned anything of the sort."

Beatrice uttered a mirthless laugh. "No, she wouldn't, would she? She wouldn't want you, of all people, to know that her grandmama was as poor as a church mouse and only married into the family because she was expecting the master's child."

A cold chill hung on the air and Rosalind moved closer to the fire. She'd never seen her friend in this mood before; never heard such bitterness in her voice; words weighed down with sadness but tinged with anger.

"Well?"

"No, she never told me that," Rosalind replied. "I'm surprised at what you say, of course I am. Gertrude wouldn't want me to know that. How do you know?"

"Hugh found out. He's good at finding out secrets in families. It came through his horse racing connections. A friend of a friend knew a family in County Mayo, where Gertrude's grandmother came from. Everyone knows each other's secrets in Ireland. People may pretend that they don't but all it takes is a few drinks and..."

"Does it really matter though? Does it matter where we come from?"

"It does to men like Hugh and Edward."

"I don't believe Edward cares. Gertrude does but not Edward."

Beatrice shrugged and stood to walk towards the window. She pulled at the silk curtain as she looked out at the lawn, a frown creasing her brow while her hand brushed the fabric over and over, as if trying to remove an imaginary stain.

"Beatrice, please... let's have some tea and forget all about this conversation," Rosalind said, desperate to distract her friend. Beatrice had been so cheerful before the accident, looking forward to the future.

"Hugh knows everyone's secrets... even yours."

"But I don't have secrets."

Beatrice pulled the curtain towards her and rearranged the way it fell, standing back as if to check it was straight before turning to face Rosalind. "Don't you?"

"No, I don't."

"Of course, it's all right for Edward, isn't it? He has what he wanted. He has a *son*." She spat the word out. "You've done well, haven't you? You've provided him with money and an heir."

Rosalind picked at the lace on the end of her sleeve. "You don't mean to say that, I know you don't. You're upset, tired..."

She spun round, fury flashing in her eyes. "These racing men! We're like brood mares to them. That's what they think of us."

"Beatrice!"

"And you've done well, my dear. You've produced a colt foal while I..." She broke into loud sobs and covered her face with her hands.

Rosalind moved over to the window and placed her arm round her friend's shoulder. "Don't, don't... please stop talking like this. Can I get you anything? Would you like me to fetch Aileen to help you?"

Beatrice jerked her head away. "I don't want Aileen. I'm tired of her obsequiousness. I nearly told her to pack and leave this morning. Do you know what she did? She put out my red dress instead of my black one. How stupid of her!"

"Perhaps you would like to come for a walk with me down to the summer house? We could look at the daffodils in the grove. Would you like to see them?" When Beatrice declined to reply, Rosalind continued, "I saw some when we drove up. I do love those *poeticus* types. Such delicate scent and lovely as cut flowers. I'm interested to see how your 'White Lady' is growing." Perhaps mentioning the garden would take Beatrice's mind off her troubles.

She looked at Rosalind and her expression softened.

"Will you come out for a walk with me?" Rosalind smiled.

"I think perhaps I will. I'll have to get my coat. I feel the cold dreadfully these days."

They walked down the path along the side of the grove, stopping now and then to admire single white narcissi while Rosalind pointed out clumps of snowdrops spreading like a blanket under the trees. "Aren't they beautiful? I can't resist the little darlings. *Galanthus nivalis*, the Fair Maids of February, such pretty, pretty things."

"You and your plants." Beatrice gripped her arm. "Do you know what the girls have been doing?"

"What have they been doing? Do tell."

Beatrice peeped over her shoulder, as if to check that they were alone. "They've been writing puzzles, or perhaps I should call them riddles, and leaving them under the loose floorboard in the summer house. I read some the other day. Rather sweet little rhymes about ponies with drawings of the dogs. Your Harriet is really quite an artist. I found several of hers written last summer. Her drawing of one of the mastiffs is very lifelike and she captured his sleepy look perfectly."

How good to hear her praise Harriet, who always seemed so boyish compared to her more graceful cousins. She was the best rider, of course, and quite fearless when it came to cantering along the track in the wood that Hugh marked out for them. Frank's instruction had improved Harriet and he seemed proud of her progress. If only Edward could find the time to take her out riding with him and praise her equestrian skills. Harriet longed to be noticed by her father.

Beatrice pushed open the door of the summer house. It was made of wood with a slate roof, painted white with grey panels and an oak floor. Rosalind always admired it and had asked Troy to build one for her. Its construction had already begun on the lower lawn near the wood and she looked forward to reclining on a sofa like Beatrice's and reading her books. The men had just finished laying the base. Her summer house was going to rotate on a pivot, a room outdoors that could be turned to follow or avoid the sun depending on the time of year. Aunt Catherine, in spite of her reservations about her niece's thirst for poetry, had sent over a lovely little edition of Lord Tennyson's *Lyrical Poems* for Rosalind's birthday. She longed for a haven to read where she wouldn't be interrupted by Gertrude or Mrs O'Brien with some culinary request.

"Here they are." Beatrice stooped to pull up the section of floorboard. "You mustn't say anything to the girls or they'll stop using this secret hideaway." She held up a sheet of paper. "This is Harriet's, I recognize her writing. It's really quite good for a girl of seven."

Rosalind took the child's note and read out loud:

> *My first is in Peter but never in Grace,*
> *My second is in oats and I love to race,*
> *My third is in Nora and also Irene,*
> *My whole ends with Y and is Harriet's dream.*

She considered. "Well, the first line tells us the word starts with a *P* or a *T* and the second and last lines make it obvious, don't they? I suspect your governess has had a hand in this although Harriet loves writing and drawing but Miss Temple's tuition is certainly helping. Did you guess the answer?"

"A pony," Beatrice said. "How talented your daughter is! My girls have composed lines about their dolls and the dogs but they don't scan as well. There's a rather uncomplimentary one about poor Duke slobbering on Hugh's best coat. I think Harriet was very clever to include all their names. Who is Peter?"

"Peter is one of the stable boys. A young cousin of Frank O'Rafferty's and he often assists Harriet with her pony."

"Well, she must be keen on him to include him in her rhyme," Beatrice said. "Imagine what we'll read about when they are a little older. I suspect they will all fall in love with your handsome coachman. How is O'Rafferty, by the way?"

Heat glowed on Rosalind's cheeks. Beatrice liked to tease her about her camaraderie with Edward's head lad and make sly remarks about his good looks. She would brush this off with a careless shrug. "Oh, Frank is well. He's always in good form. I suspect my maid Sadie is in love with him."

"Poor Sadie, she will have to stand at the back of the queue, won't she? My friend Maria... you know who I mean, the one with the fat husband and three pugs, thinks that Frank O'Rafferty is divine... quite divine."

"Beatrice, don't be ridiculous!" Rosalind frowned. "I don't think Maria would appeal to Frank."

"No, he likes English beauties like you."

"You shouldn't say such things... even in jest. What if the girls hear you?"

"That would certainly give them material for their riddles, wouldn't it? Don't be alarmed, Ros, I'm only teasing so there's no need to look prudish. It doesn't suit you. If the wind changes, you will be left with that disapproving expression."

"Would you like me to go up to the house and ask Aileen to send down tea?"

"Now you're changing the subject. No, here come the girls. Quick, hand me back the riddle. I don't want them to see me with them. I'll never find out their secrets if they know their hiding place has been discovered. You go and distract them while I put back the floorboard." Beatrice added as Rosalind moved away, "Ask them to order tea and persuade them to wash their hands. I bet they'll have been in the stables, knowing your daughter as I do."

Rosalind moved over to the doorway and waved at the three

girls running down the lawn towards her.

"Of course," Beatrice muttered behind her back, "we all know that O'Rafferty would do anything for you, sweet Rosalind. He makes no secret of that."

Chapter Fourteen

Beatrice's words still stung Rosalind as Frank drove them home. Had she hinted that Edward only married her for her money and it was her duty to produce a son? Edward was a loving husband. Granted he didn't show Harriet enough attention, not as much as a father should, but perhaps Rosalind had been spoilt with her papa who had been so eager to spend time with her.

"Mama."

"Yes, Harriet."

The girl's brown eyes glowed. "Cousin Hugh said I was a talented rider."

"That was kind of him. Did you meet him in the stable yard? I'm not sure he likes you all going there without permission. I know Papa prefers you not to pester the stable boys…"

Harriet sniffed. "Cousin Hugh doesn't mind. He showed me his new horse. He's called Lancelot."

"Lancelot?"

"Yes, like in *The Lady of Shalott*."

Rosalind gazed into the shade of the trees where shadows flittered across the pine needles. Beatrice had been in a strange mood. Her sorrow was understandable but she'd switched so suddenly to that mocking manner. It wasn't Edward's fault that she'd lost the baby. No, it was nobody's fault. It was an accident. A terrible accident. Edward couldn't help it if the horses took fright and bolted but Beatrice had looked at her almost accusingly.

Harriet tugged at her sleeve. "Look, there's that man."

Rosalind's heart thumped painfully against her ribs. Mick Maguire was standing in the trees about two hundred yards away. She didn't want to have to talk to him today.

"Frank, please drive past that man. Don't stop."

"Yes, ma'am, I'll do my best."

Harriet continued in a loud voice, "He's the one who followed us last year. Do you remember? I don't like him. He frightens me."

"Hush, I don't like him either, my love, but we don't want him to hear you say that. Don't look in his direction as we pass by… try not to catch his eye."

Frank flicked the reins on Romeo's back and the cob plodded on.

Mick Maguire waited for the carriage to approach, leaning against the trunk of an old oak and filling a pipe he'd taken out of his jacket.

Rosalind turned her head away, determined to ignore him.

Frank urged the cob to trot on but Maguire stepped out in front of the horse and Romeo came to a halt.

"Out of the way, please." Frank's voice rose.

"And who do you think you are, Frank O'Rafferty, to order me out of your way in that cold manner?"

Rosalind turned her head away. She would let Frank deal with this man. What did he want with her?

"A word with the lady, if you please, O'Rafferty," Maguire said with a laugh. Not a kind laugh but jeering, mocking.

"The lady doesn't wish to speak to you, Maguire. Now step aside or I will be obliged to run you over."

"Run me over, is it? I don't think that would be a good idea, young Frank. And I don't think you would like the consequences. A quick word with the lady is all I ask."

Frank opened his mouth to object but Rosalind spun round to face the man on the ground, who was looking up at them with a smirk.

He struck a match and sucked hard on his pipe, blowing smoke in Frank's direction.

"What is it? What do you wish to say to me?" Her words sounded high-pitched and she made an effort to speak slowly. "Say what you want to say and kindly allow us to go on our way."

"I don't think that's a good idea," Frank muttered but Rosalind silenced him with a glance.

Mick Maguire stepped nearer and put a hand on the side of the carriage. He raised his eyes to Rosalind's. How cold and grey they were, like the sea in winter.

"I would like you to give a message to your husband, Mrs Thornton."

"Very well. What is it?"

"I'm warning you, Maguire," Frank said. "You leave her alone."

"Hush, Frank. I'll deal with this. What is the message, Mr Maguire?" Perhaps if she showed him some courtesy, he might be brief.

Harriet's eyes grew large as he said, "I would like you to tell your husband that Mick Maguire is waiting for his money. You tell him that."

"I don't know what you mean."

"Your husband will know what I mean and I imagine young O'Rafferty also knows but he's too mannerly… too considerate to say. Aren't you, my lad?"

Frank stiffened as Maguire blew yet another cloud of smoke towards his face. Rosalind worried he might leap off the seat and tackle the man who stood below them. That would only make this situation worse.

"I'll give Mr Thornton that message," she said. "Now please allow us to drive on."

Maguire raised his cap to her. He moved aside. "Most grateful, ma'am. I'm indeed grateful to you." His tone sounded more insolent than thankful.

Rosalind's fingers trembled as Frank tapped Romeo's broad flank.

"And good day to you, O'Rafferty," Maguire called after them. "You might regret the day yet that you decided to stay at Ardlackan Lodge."

"I don't understand. What did he mean?" Rosalind asked when they reached the turn for the woods, the shortcut home. "Could what he said be true? Does Edward owe him money?" She knew she shouldn't be saying this, especially in front of Harriet, but she desperately needed reassurance.

Frank looked at her and didn't reply.

What was in his eyes? Pity. It seemed like pity. Her heart raced. "Frank?"

He flashed a smile at Harriet. "Cheer up, Miss Harriet. He's gone now. If I catch him hanging around these parts again, he'll be sorry, I can assure you."

"Will you hit him, Frank? I was hoping you'd jump down and grab him by the neck and… I'd like you to hit him," Harriet said.

"Please!" Rosalind cried out. "Both of you, stop talking!" A pain in her temple throbbed and she put her hand to her forehead.

They pulled up at the front door and Frank leaped down to help them out. He held Rosalind's hand a little longer than usual and gave it a gentle squeeze, barely perceptible but like a signal of some sort. Of sympathy, of friendship; surely nothing more.

She thanked him and he replied in a low voice, "If I were you, Mrs Thornton, I'd mention Maguire to the master straight away."

"Yes, yes, I think I will. Has that man been in the stable yard recently?"

"No, but I spotted him watching the horses galloping last week. He makes a habit of concealing himself behind a hedge or a stand of trees and I know he's taking note of the horses in form."

"Why would he do that?"

"So he can sell his tips for winners to desperate men, I reckon, or to other more unscrupulous trainers. He's a tout. That's what they do. They act like spies for the gambling men."

"I understand. I don't like him… and he's frightening Harriet."

He placed his hand on Romeo's broad forehead and stroked the horse. "Tell the master."

Rosalind found Edward in his study writing lists of horses' names into his book of race entries. He glanced up when she entered the room. "Hello, my dear, did you have a pleasant afternoon?"

"That Mick Maguire. He stopped us again."

Edward muttered a few words under his breath and ticked off a name on the list. "Frank said Pirate has gone off his feed. I'll have to get the veterinary surgeon to look him over."

Impatience swept through her and she stepped towards him and snatched up the notebook.

He stared at her, surprise in his eyes. "Rosalind! Whatever is the matter with you? This is most unlike you, my love."

"Please listen to me! I'm sorry, but please listen to me. Please pay attention. Maguire says you owe him money and he was… well, he was threatening… threatening in his manner towards me. Do you owe him money?"

He waved a hand carelessly. "What of it? A few pounds here and there. He knows he gets it back and, besides, he gets information."

"Information?"

"Yes, you wouldn't understand, my love. It's information about the horses."

She digested these words, turning them around in her mind. Surely a tout wasn't a good person to have on the premises? Especially if he was feeding information to gamblers or bookmakers. Would Hugh approve of that?

Edward held out his hand. "Now please return my notebook. I have important things to consider. Pirate doesn't seem himself and he has been entered for a steeplechase at Punchestown in two weeks' time. I'll have to see what the vet says. I may have to take him out. Mighty Maiden has lost a shoe and I told McNally not to ride her back from the training ground without a front shoe but what did he do? He rode her down the road, if you please. He could at least have gone through the wood. Now it looks like she has a stone bruise and we've been aiming her at the big Aintree race in April. This might set her back a week or two… Frank gave McNally an earful, I can tell you."

"Does Hugh know that you give information to Maguire? Information about his horses?"

He took back the book and opened it on the desk, leaning forward and sucking his pen. "If the Maiden misses the Aintree meeting, Hugh will be… he'll… well, he won't be happy, put it that way."

"Why do you owe Maguire money, Edward? Why would you want him to hand out information about horses trained here… horses owned by Hugh to others? I don't understand what this is about."

Edward held out his hand, catching hers and pulling her to him. She sat on his knee and put her hand on his shoulder. He was incorrigible. Why couldn't he treat her like a woman with intelligence instead of some silly little doll? He sometimes called her his darling doll and she disliked it. She would have to put a stop to that. "Edward…"

He interrupted. "All right, my darling, all right. I'll have a word with Maguire… tell him to stop pestering you and Harriet. He'll be paid his money tomorrow morning. I'll ride down to the village first thing and get the Darcy boy to deliver it." He stroked her hair and planted a light kiss on her lips. "You mustn't worry your pretty little head about such things. You know I would never do anything to upset you – or Harriet. Did she tell you about the saddle?"

She tried not to smile. "Thank you. Yes, she told me about the saddle. And that's another thing; I don't want you to take her out jumping until she's at least ten years old… at least ten."

Edward snuggled his face into her hair and breathed in. "How lovely you smell. I could eat you all up. No, no, Rosalind, don't struggle and look so cross. I'm listening. I promise you, promise on my… on my life, I won't take Harriet out jumping until she's well and truly capable of managing that pony."

Rosalind put her arms around his neck and looked into his eyes, his dark Thornton eyes. "Edward, you know how much I love you."

"Of course I do, my sweet. I love you too, more than anything."

"You wouldn't tell me lies, would you?"

"Of course not, my dearest."

"We've been married nine years now – it will be nine years this May."

He kissed her ear and she wriggled away. "Nine wonderful years. The best years of my life."

"Do you really mean that?"

"Of course. Why would I say it if I didn't? You mean the world to me, my darling doll… the world."

She pushed him away and got to her feet. "I do wish you wouldn't call me that."

He raised his eyebrows. "You don't enjoy it? But you are a

doll, so like a doll, with your beautiful clear skin and shining hair. Your rosebud lips." He stood and planted a firmer kiss on her mouth. "I'm envied by many men."

"By whom?"

"Aha, as if I'd tell you that! Men admire you and you're too good and sweet to even notice. How lucky I am."

That was how he'd won her heart with his disarming flattery. Only four weeks after they'd met at Ascot races, he'd knelt at her feet on the grass in The Regent's Park and begged her to marry him. He couldn't live without her.

Her husband stroked her hair. "How was Beatrice today?"

Rosalind frowned. "I found her in a strange mood at first. She seemed almost angry but she relaxed when we…"

"She's not herself, Hugh says. It's like the last time, only worse… much worse. I hope it passes because it puts a strain on him."

"A strain on Hugh? But what about Beatrice? She's lost her baby, her son. We have to make allowances. Hugh has to make allowances for that. Besides, she may not be able to help it… how she behaves."

"Her mother was always a bit hysterical."

Rosalind stiffened. "I don't think Beatrice is hysterical. She's sad and she's tired. She needs rest and plenty of sympathy."

"If you say so, my love. You always know best. Now I have to tell you something and promise me you won't be upset."

"What is it?" Her pulse quickened. How easily alarmed she was these days. She put her hand to her chest, feeling her heart flutter. Perhaps it was because of the baby. She hadn't regained her strength yet and her emotions hadn't settled down. Alarm rose and swept through her at the slightest worry.

"Hugh has invited me to go to England with him."

"Oh."

"Not for long – only a week or two."

She was embarrassed to feel tears prick at the back of her eyes and turned her head away. No, she wasn't yet fully recovered after the baby. She wasn't usually so sentimental.

"A week or two," he repeated. "We're going to look at horses. Hugh knows a man, the best judge of a racehorse he has ever met, who lives near Lambourn and we're going to stay with him. He has a fine stud, Hugh says, and plenty of young horses from which to choose. We need to find another younger steeplechaser. Pirate is ten years old; we can't rely on him forever. We won't be gone long, I promise."

"Two weeks you say."

"Yes, no more than that. You have my word. Mama wouldn't let me stay away for longer. She relies on me so much, you know. Hugh and I have a plan. We've got this wonderful plan and, if it comes off, we will all be… we'll be one of the best racing yards in the country."

She forced a smile. "Of course, you must go, my love. I'd like to come…"

A wary light crept into his eyes. "You… well, I'm sure we'd love you to come but what about the baby? And you can't leave Harriet. We will be visiting other parts of England, not just the Lambourn area, and Hugh is depending on you to keep an eye on poor Beatrice. He said your visits make such a difference to her mood. You must watch over her, Rosalind, you must try to cheer her up and take her out of herself. It's worrying to see her so despondent. Hugh has had to talk to Dr Richards again and he's concerned about her. If she doesn't improve, if she can't seem to…" He cleared his throat. "She might have to go away for a little while."

"No, not that! Beatrice would hate that. You can't mean to a sanatorium? She will be better when the good weather comes. She cheered up when I took her into the garden and we had tea with the children in the summer house."

He raised his hands. "You see the influence you have over her? You'll help her to recover, I know you will. You're such a kind-hearted soul and you see only the good in others. Beatrice and the children need you here at home with them."

"Yes, you're right. I can't leave them or Beatrice. Not at the moment but perhaps when she has fully recovered and the children are older, we could go away together, just you and me. I would so love to do that. Perhaps France or Italy. Somewhere warm where there are no racehorses."

He squeezed her hand. "Of course, I'd love that too. Of course, I would. Now, if you don't mind, I really have to get back to my work and try to decide whether Darling Doll and…"

"Darling Doll?"

"Yes, the new three-year-old filly that Frank is driving in long reins. He's so good with young horses… I called her after you, my pet. I'll have to change her name perhaps if you object. Though that might be unlucky – or does that only apply to ships?" He laughed again and caught her in his arms, holding her so close that she could feel his heart beating.

Chapter Fifteen

The present - 29th June, 2019

I kept my word and didn't mention Tiffany's nocturnal visit to Daphne. Had Ben talked about the summer house to the journalist and planted an idea in her mind? Why would she think there was something hidden under the floorboards? I would have to ask him. My chance came the following Friday when he offered to drive me to the village market.

He looked pleased to see me and politely opened the passenger door of the jeep. I waited for several minutes, until we'd turned out of the gate and were heading towards the steep hill down to the village. "Ben…"

He glanced at me and then back at the twisting road in front, pushing his foot on the brake to negotiate a sudden turn.

"I met Tiffany last night. She was in the summer house."

He kept his gaze on the road, slowing down the jeep to pass a herd of black and white Friesian cows that ambled along the verge with tails flicking away the flies. The farmer waved a hand as we drove by.

"Tiffany Ryan? I told you I had a drink with her."

"I found her in the summer house after dark… during the storm last night."

He remained silent.

"She was searching for something under the floorboards... where you'd pulled them up."

He didn't answer as we reached the village, driving past the row of thatched cottages and the old red pump outside O'Mahony's pub.

I tried again. "What was she searching for?"

"You think I told her there was something there? Is that what you mean?"

"She implied you were keen to help her." I kept my eyes on his face.

He didn't meet my gaze. "I've only met her once when we had a drink together. I bumped into her in the street outside O'Mahony's and the old fisherman was there so she began asking him questions. He loves telling stories."

"True stories?"

"Possibly not. He said the local story is the family always insisted Edward Thornton died from striking his head on a rock when he was thrown from his horse but the villagers back then knew better. His grandmother was good friends with the cook's family. He believed the man was murdered by his wife."

"I bet Tiffany enjoyed hearing that."

He accelerated the jeep towards the café. What was he thinking?

"In the summer house," I repeated. "Did you tell her there was something there?"

He looked at me, a sharp glance. "No, why would I?"

"She was definitely looking for something under the floorboards."

Was there something he wasn't telling me? Something he didn't want to say?

His forehead creased with concentration as he gazed ahead.

"Where's this food market?" I asked.

He pulled in to the side of the road opposite Andrea's café

and switched off the engine. "We have to walk from here. We go down that lane to the pier." He pointed to the left.

"If Edward had toppled off his horse, struck his head on a rock and died, people might not have been interested."

"Maybe not in those days. Something jumped out of the undergrowth... spooked the horse and perhaps that's all it was. An unfortunate accident." Ben pushed open the door of the jeep.

"Perhaps you're right." I kept my eyes on his face. "But Tiffany believes it was a murder."

He rubbed the back of his neck and looked away. "I never met Tiffany... never saw her until the other night."

We crossed the road together and headed down a narrow lane. A herring gull perching on the low stone wall beside us rose into the air with a harsh cry, spreading its broad wings and flying towards the pier far below where vans were parked among a crowd of people.

Ben stopped and leaned on the wall, running one hand along the rough stone. "Tiffany's a tough one, isn't she?"

"Yes, I don't like her much." The words slid out of my mouth. Too late to pull them back.

"You're fond of Daphne, of course. You want to protect her and her family."

I took a deep breath, exhaled and muttered, "Tiffany also lured my husband away."

His eyebrows shot into his hair.

"They met on the internet," I said. "I didn't mean to tell you about him. He left me a couple of months ago. I drove him away, my mother said, with all my nagging."

"Your mother said that? Sympathetic, isn't she?"

I gazed down at the brightly painted trawlers moored along the pier. "She lives in Lisbon with her boyfriend. She told me that men are easy to find and that another one will come along. No need for me to worry about all those debts he's left me with..."

"I'm sorry to hear this. It can't be easy for you."

"That's why I'm here, I suppose. It's a distraction arranged by my friend Jessica, Charles's niece, who suggested I came to help Daphne... a change of scene."

"Daphne told me your father had died but didn't tell me this..." He tilted his head to one side, sympathy in his eyes. "I'm sorry."

The words kept tumbling out, a feeling of relief warming inside me. "Daphne doesn't know about my husband and Tiffany. Dominic told me he'd met a woman on a gambling forum on the internet. I'd no idea she was a journalist until Jessica found out who she was. I haven't said anything to Tiffany yet so please... say nothing."

The smell of fish mixed with freshly baked bread wafted up on the breeze, mingling with the sound of merriment and raised voices.

Ben didn't move. "Well, I've no experience of... but it must be difficult for you."

I decided I'd burdened the young man with enough and changed the subject. "I'm planning to go to the National Library tomorrow morning and look up old newspapers to see if I can find anything about Edward Thornton's death. There were a lot of provincial papers in those days so a local one might have more details."

"That's a good idea."

We continued our walk down to the pier where stalls lined the quayside; bright umbrellas and canopies under which local food producers sold everything from tomatoes to toffees. Ben stopped to chat to a woman and bought a slab of home-produced cheese, dark yellow with blue veins running through and a pungent smell. He broke off a piece and handed it to me. "Taste it. I like this little market and come here on Fridays to buy home-made food. You should try the brown bread over there."

I nibbled at the cheese. "Delicious. Are you interested in cooking?"

He said he was and slipped a chunk into his mouth.

A warm smell of yeast lured me to the baked bread and I bought a dark brown loaf with sesame seeds sprinkled on top. I asked the woman at the stall if she could slice it for me. While I was waiting for this, Ben paid for two cups of takeaway coffee.

We stood looking down on the trawlers moored alongside each other with thick ropes attached to huge iron rings on the pier, painted in strong reds and blues emblazoned with appropriate names: Sea Gull, Misty Morn and even one called Fantasea, obviously owned by someone with imagination.

"It looks quiet here," I said. "Let's sit down in the sun and eat some of this bread with your cheese. I bet they'll go well together."

We perched on a low wall, looking over the boats as they shifted and nudged each other on the oily water and we shared the rest of the cheese and half of the bread.

Why couldn't Dominic be more like Ben? So easy to get on with and at least he was interested in what I had to say. I felt I'd known him longer than the time I'd spent in Wexford. Had Dominic ever been like that? Or was it always all about him?

I suppose in the beginning we had shared interests but I struggled to remember what those might have been. I'd been so keen to be the perfect housewife, to make his life run smoothly and keep him organized.

Too young to marry, Jessica pointed out. She said I'd been looking for stability to compensate for my missing mother and was always trying to fix problems, everyone else's problems while my own were desperately jumping up and down, pulling at my sleeve and demanding attention. Jessica had studied an evening course in psychology and liked to practise on her friends.

"Where are they then? What happened to Edward Thornton's

family?" Ben's voice sounded low, more a whisper to himself than a question to me.

I glanced at him, surprised. "You're interested in them too, aren't you?"

"I am. It's because of you, Fiona. You've brought them alive for me. I'm sure you're a good history teacher."

"Not really. I'm considering giving it up, actually. I don't feel I'm making much progress with the students. Now we have a new principal and I don't think she's taken to me." I was beginning to sound quite depressed. I would have to stop this outpouring of self-pity.

He murmured, "So hard to know what our lives have in store for us... I have something to show you. It's in the jeep."

I followed him back through the throng of customers at the market stalls and stopped to buy another loaf of bread for Daphne and a few jars of homemade raspberry jam. We made our way back up the steep hill towards the café.

What was he going to show me? Something he'd made? He was an accomplished woodworker and Daphne had pointed out a teak handle he'd made for her old French chopping knife, smoothly turned and stained dark brown.

We got into the jeep and he reached across to open the glove compartment, taking out a small leather-bound book. He handed it to me and I flipped open the first page. Large childish handwriting in old-fashioned loops and dark blue ink stretched across the flyleaf:

Harriet Thornton.
My journal of riddles and secrets - March 1891

The leather felt old and cracked between my fingers but growing warmer where I gripped it. "Harriet Thornton! Rosalind's daughter?" A thrill of excitement fluttered inside me. "Where did you find this?"

"Underneath the floorboards in the summer house about a week ago. This might have been what Tiffany was looking for."

Chapter Sixteen

I'd always loved the National Library and my spirits lifted when the curved exterior with its familiar domed roof came into view. I stepped off the bus in Nassau Street and walked the short distance up Kildare Street to the wrought-iron railings the building shared with Leinster House next door. I followed the path to the colonnade and stone steps.

The impressive late Victorian building was designed by Thomas Deane and had first opened its doors in August in 1890. Had Rosalind Thornton hurried to visit along with others from Dublin society? Perhaps she'd strolled across the mosaic floor in the entrance hall and admired the different hues of light filtering through the windows. She might have climbed the main staircase and trailed her hand along the marble.

I'd put in a request the previous week for one of the local Wexford newspapers published in the nineteenth century that was now no longer in existence. The librarian handed me a box of film and I walked into the adjacent microfilm room, originally the Ladies' Reading Room, again wondering if Rosalind had come here.

I had the whole morning to devote to my research and the reading room beside me was quiet; only a handful of people with their laptops on desks early in the morning. I opened my shoulder bag, taking out my small notebook and the slim volume handed to me by Ben the day before containing Harriet Thornton's secrets and riddles. I hadn't had time to study it but the contents were mostly drawings and lines of verse.

Her pencil sketches looked competent, a pony named Bumblebee featuring often, small and rotund with a bushy mane and with eyes full of mischief.

I flicked to the last page where her handwriting looked less tidy, as if hurriedly scrawled, with a riddle at least twenty lines long in four sections; the ink slightly blotched where a hand might have smudged it or water dripped on it. The title 'Farewell' sat above the verses and there were a number of references to Tennyson's famous poem, *The Lady of Shalott*, including a drawing of a tower with ivy smothering the stonework and the face of a woman with a sad expression at the top window, long hair falling around her shoulders.

My first is in people but not in river,
My second in rye and also in shiver,
My third is in lily but not in towers,
My fourth glows sweetly in space and in flowers,
My fifth is in royal, but not in island,
My sixth is in casement and also in hand,
My seventh is in weave and also in verse,
My final in reaper and wicked in curse.
My whole cruelly locked up behind iron bars,
No company but the galaxy of stars.

The more I perused the first verse, the more I recognized words from Tennyson's poem. Perhaps Harriet had composed the riddle with it open beside her. There'd been an island and a river with a woman locked in a tower who could only look at the world through the mirror in her room or she would be cursed. Wasn't that it? The first letter was obviously *P, O* or *L,* the second letter *R* or *E.* The clue at the end hinted at a prisoner looking out at the stars. That was it! Yes, the last letter of the word had an *R* in reaper and curse. *Prisoner* was the answer to this puzzle and matched the drawing of the tower. Not as difficult as I'd first imagined. But who was the prisoner? Had Harriet been locked up in her bedroom for a misconduct? The pages were blank after this last entry except for a brief sketch of a boat. That was familiar. The Lady of Shalott floated down the river towards Camelot in a boat, the curse had come upon her and the poor woman died before Lancelot laid eyes on her.

Deciding to check another time, I pushed the leather-bound book back into my bag and turned to the screen of the reading machine in front of me.

I turned the dial and advanced the microfilm, skimming through a few pages from the late Victorian era, soaking up the vivid journalism; the local news, the dramas and accidents, the births and deaths, the reports of cholera and influenza outbreaks.

There was a report of a race meeting. I ran my eyes down the list of horses' names and found Mighty Maiden owned by Mr Hugh Thornton and ridden by Frank O'Rafferty. An easy winner of a steeplechase. The mare was trained by Mr E Thornton. Edward.

What had Rosalind thought of horse racing? Was her husband a gambler like mine?

Chewing the end of my biro, I wondered why I'd never thought of that before. Had splurging money on horse racing destroyed him? Had someone fallen out with him because of this and knocked him off his horse one dark night as he rode home through the Ardlackan woods? Had this person bashed him on the head with a rock and rolled his lifeless body into a ditch?

I scanned the columns of births, marriages and deaths in the

Wexford paper for the year 1891 and found the death notice of Edward Thornton. Described as a sudden death, much missed by his grieving relatives, his mother Gertrude and cousins Hugh and Beatrice, his nieces. How weird there was no mention of Rosalind! What had happened to his widow? No mention of his daughter either. I scrolled down the column. Had Gertrude refused to allow the wife's name to go into this death notice?

My mobile phone sat on the desk beside me, on silent so that it wouldn't suddenly go off and startle the other few people reading along the desks that ran to my left. I thought of Ben and wished he was there so that I could share the anomaly with him. He might be interested. Since the day he'd taken me for a walk to the ruined mansion, he'd seemed curious about the Thornton murder. I glanced again at my mute mobile. I could send Ben a text. No, I would wait until I next saw him.

A thought surfaced in my mind. Had he known that Harriet's book of riddles was hidden under the floor of the summer house? Or had he found it by coincidence? I scribbled a line in my jotter to remind me to ask Ben about this.

Returning to the newspaper, I discovered a report on the death of Edward Thornton in September 1891. I read it carefully with my biro poised to make notes:

The body of Mr Edward Thornton of Ardlackan Lodge was discovered lying in a ditch in Ardlackan Woods on Thursday, 3rd September by Mr Jeremiah Murphy, a labourer, and his wife Molly, a midwife. They were accompanied by Mrs Murphy's twelve-year-old niece, Bridget.

Mrs Murphy stated that she had attended the birth of a baby boy at a cabin situated two miles from where the body was found. Her husband had decided to take a short cut through the woods as it was late, approximately four in the morning, and he wanted to get to his bed.

Mr Frank O'Rafferty, head lad and coachman to Mr Edward Thornton, stated that his master's horse had returned to the stable yard unaccompanied at approximately half past four. Mr O'Rafferty had heard the clatter of the horse's hooves on the cobblestones in the yard and added that the horse was covered in sweat as if it had been galloping hard.

The report continued with further evidence from a stable lad (called a stable boy in those days) who assisted Frank O'Rafferty and cleaned down the mare, putting her in her stall for the rest of the night.

Mr O'Rafferty alerted the household and the Royal Irish Constabulary. Subsequent details mentioned the bloody injury to Edward's head. Rosalind was referred to as the grieving widow.

I moved on through the next few editions of the newspaper.

The next reference jumped out at me and my heart began to thump. A headline screamed: *Wife of deceased trainer missing.* I scanned the words.

The Royal Irish Constabulary has appealed for information concerning the whereabouts of Mrs Edward Thornton of Ardlackan Lodge. Mrs Thornton has not been seen since the day of the death of her husband and police officers have appealed for witnesses to come forward. Mrs Thornton's two children, Miss Harriet Thornton, aged eight years, and Master Ivor Thornton, an infant, are also missing. Any person with knowledge or information should come forward immediately.

I read the names again. Miss Harriet Thornton. My eyes rested on my bag, thinking of the book. I would have to study those riddles with more precision when I got back to Ardlackan.

Rosalind was missing. Both her children also missing. What could have happened? Had some crazy lunatic come upon the family late on that September night? He might have murdered Edward, thrown him in a ditch and abducted the wife and children. No, that couldn't have taken place as Rosalind and her children would not have been walking through Ardlackan Woods at that hour. They would have been in a carriage. Perhaps the carriage had been taken and Edward left behind. But there was no mention of a missing carriage in the report.

I checked the date of the newspaper article. Four days after the fatal accident. The police must have kept it quiet for a few days, hoping she would reappear. They would have been working on it behind the scenes. A shock for the rest of the family and for Edward's mother, Gertrude.

My mobile screen showed me it was almost half past twelve. If I went for lunch now ahead of the crowds at one o'clock, I would have more time in the library before I caught an afternoon train back to Wexford. There was one leaving Connolly Station just after half past four that would get me back there in about three hours.

I tossed my biro and notebook into my bag. It was time to begin putting pieces of the puzzle together and I could make a start over lunch. A quick sandwich or a salad in a pub near the back gate of Trinity College would suffice and this was only about five minutes' walk from the library.

Heavy clouds hung above the rooftops outside and drops of rain already spotted the pavement. I stood by the gate of the National Library, wondering whether to wait under the shelter of its colonnade or risk making a run for Lincoln Place. Drizzle ran down the back of my neck and I retreated to the main door.

A woman with short hair and wearing a bright pink raincoat caught my eye. She walked across the mosaic floor and turned to face me.

My heart skipped a beat. Tiffany.

"Hey," she said. "Hey, it's you!"

For a split second I considered running down the steps into the rain but it would have looked foolish.

She stepped towards me, holding a large green golf umbrella in one hand, which she raised in a mocking salute. "What are you doing here?"

"I could ask you the same question."

She peered out at the rain. "Bad day, isn't it? I'm going to do some research, that's what I'm doing here. Strange I didn't see you come in."

"I'm going out."

"Yeah? Where are you going?"

"I'm going to get lunch, if you must know."

She looked amused, her thin red lips curling at the corners. "Well… maybe I'll keep you company. If you don't object, that is?"

"I do object actually."

Tiffany raised her carefully shaped eyebrows. "Huh, I don't know why you don't like me. Maybe we just got off to a bad start. Listen, I'll buy you lunch and we'll kiss and make up. How about that?"

I watched her sharp face, the neat eyebrows and her confident expression. Should I tell her? Was now the time to mention Dominic? She would have to find out at some stage.

"What do you say to lunch?" Tiffany's smile vanished. "That's a fair offer, you have to admit."

"My husband left me for you." The words sounded oddly flat on the damp air. But at least I'd startled her.

Her mouth fell open in surprise. "What?"

"I said, you stole my husband."

"Stole him? But I don't even know your name. Who are you talking about?"

Really, this was ridiculous. I swung away from her.

She reached out and gripped my elbow. "No, don't go. Who

143

are you talking about? Who is this man? You can't just accuse me of stealing your husband and walk off."

"You know who I mean. Dominic Foley, of course."

No trace of recognition or guilt on her features. Just bewilderment. "I'm Fiona Foley, married to Dominic," I said loudly, as if she was deaf and struggling to hear me.

Her mobile phone rang, a piercing interruption to this farcical scene. She pulled it out of her handbag and peered at the screen. "Sebastian, my boss," she said. "Wait a minute… wait please, Fiona. Don't go." She barked a few words into the phone and told him that she would call back.

I felt calmer now that I'd confronted her. At least I'd cracked her overconfident smirk.

She raised wary brown eyes to mine. "Yes, I have a boyfriend called Dominic Foley. I'd no idea he was married. Well… well, that's news. That's definitely news." She pressed her scarlet lips together and frowned. "Dominic's got a few secrets it seems."

I wasn't sure whether to believe her. Was she putting on an act? Pretending to be an innocent?

"Let's have that lunch I mentioned." She sprang out onto the steps and opened the umbrella. "Here, come under this so you don't get wet. Where are you heading?"

I hesitated.

"Come on," she said. "I'm trying to be friendly and it sounds like we have a lot to talk about. Where are you going for lunch?"

I told her and we walked out into the rain together, out through the elaborate wrought-iron gate and on past the entrance to Leinster House where a group of sodden and miserable-looking protesters huddled together under a placard that demanded *More Top Jobs for Women*. They'd be lucky if members of the government ventured out to eat in weather like this. Tiffany was silent for a few minutes, thinking about my bombshell perhaps.

"Where did you meet him?" I asked.

"Horse racing group on the internet."

"And he never mentioned being married?"

"Never. I swear it."

Anger tinged with exasperation gripped me but I said nothing more.

"A shock when I turned up in Wexford, eh? No wonder you hate me." Tiffany's voice rose. "Wait till I see him… I'll give him a piece of my mind. How dare he… how dare he not tell me he's married!"

Because he always tried to avoid confrontation, I thought. He lied to keep me happy. About his gambling. About his debts. About Tiffany until he plucked up the courage to leave me that cowardly note. And now he was lying to her.

She reached out and touched the sleeve of my jacket, her voice a degree warmer. "You and I have a lot to talk about."

Chapter Seventeen

Tiffany poured herself a glass of white wine. "Want some? No? Oh well, all the more for me then."

The pub buzzed with voices, the clatter of plates and clink of glasses. A smell of damp clothes mingled with coffee. While we ate our salads, Tiffany persisted in protesting her innocence. She never knew that Dominic was married; wouldn't have gone near him if she had and wasn't it too late now anyway? He'd made his choice.

"Surely you don't want him back?" Although a question, she made it sound more like a statement.

She held down a difficult job, no doubt about that. I would never have made a good journalist because I hadn't the tenacity and the determination to pursue people who declined to answer questions. To keep phoning those who ignored me and cut me off. I wondered for the first time why Ben had decided to give Harriet's book of riddles to me and not to this woman. Perhaps he was being loyal to Daphne.

When I asked Daphne how she'd ended up with him as a tenant in the stable yard apartment, she'd told me she'd advertised for a carpenter in the local newspaper.

I wouldn't tell Tiffany about Harriet's book but it was obvious she knew about its existence if she was searching in the summer house after dark.

I considered her question. Did I want Dominic back? I didn't know. A few months before I would have but my father's death and my husband's lack of support had proved how little he cared. He'd turned up at the funeral of course, muttering sympathy and offering a half-hearted and embarrassed hug but had made no attempt to contact me since, apart from referring the bank to me when they rang him about our joint account. And Ardlackan had taken me further away from him, distancing me emotionally. Perhaps I no longer wanted him back. Perhaps Tiffany was welcome to him.

"Well?" She was unwilling to allow her question go unanswered.

I shook my head. "I don't know… maybe not."

"Why would you? If I were you I wouldn't, not when he behaved like that. Left you without warning for another woman. I'm almost tempted to dump him myself." She directed her peculiar mirthless smile at me and sipped her wine, wrapping her fingers around the glass and tapping it with red fingernails. "He's a gambler, you know."

As if I didn't. "Yes."

"It doesn't bother me," Tiffany said. "As long as he doesn't gamble with my money, it's all totally cool."

I reached for the wine bottle and poured myself a half glass. I didn't have to drive and it might help me relax. "So, what are you going to research in the library today?"

"What were you researching?"

"Reports in the local newspapers of Edward Thornton's death and the inquest," I replied.

"Oh yeah, I read through those a few weeks ago. The inquest ended with an open verdict, disappointingly inconclusive and no use to us. Shall we compare notes?"

"You know I can't encourage you for Daphne's sake... for her family's sake, I can't."

She rolled her eyes. "Daphne's too eccentric to care for long."

"She does care. She feels she's letting down her late husband."

"Charles Thornton won't be bothered now, will he?" Tiffany muttered. "The man's dead, Fiona. Charles Thornton is dead. It doesn't matter to him now."

I breathed out. "His brother is... bothered as you put it. It's not fair on his family. His daughter is one of my dearest friends and she doesn't want her ancestors on television. It matters to her family. Her uncle's good name... his position in Irish horse racing history. His biography was supposed to highlight his successful training career. He wouldn't want to be remembered for a sensational family murder that had nothing to do with him."

She shrugged and popped a prawn into her mouth.

"How would you like your relations exposed in an unsolved murder?" I asked.

She considered this for a moment before she put her head to one side and said, "I don't think I'd care." She obviously didn't have a conscience. I wondered if Jessica's father had considered consulting a lawyer. Was there a legal way to stop Sebastian Rotherill?

"I've changed my mind about the murder suspect, by the way. You want to know what I think now?"

The chicken on my plate tasted dry and I added a dollop of mayonnaise. "Go on."

"I think it was the head lad who did it. That guy O'Rafferty was besotted with Rosalind Thornton so he bashed Edward on the head and rolled his body into a ditch. Or perhaps both he and Rosalind killed him together. Then he ran off with her and the kids."

The waiter approached with the dessert menu before I could respond to this dramatic pronouncement. I shook my head but

148

Tiffany ordered ice cream with salted caramel sauce.

"Why do you think that?" I asked. "I don't know much about O'Rafferty. I saw his name on the 1901 census for Ardlackan Lodge so he must have stayed there with Gertrude Thornton until then."

"I noticed that too. Perhaps he killed Edward in a fit of jealousy and Rosalind fell out with him and left on her own." Her eyes gleamed as she added, "A crime of passion!"

I took out my black notebook. "What do you know about Frank O'Rafferty?"

Tiffany topped up her wineglass. "His family still lives around the Ardlackan area. I tracked down one of his descendants who is a nurse in Wexford hospital and she sent me to her aunt, who has a box of family letters and photo albums and is keen on tracing her ancestors. She signed up to that ancestry website on the internet so she's a bit of an enthusiast."

This sounded promising but I tried to keep my voice casual. "Really? I doubt the letters go back to the 1890s."

"They do. There are some earlier than that because O'Rafferty's mother was a schoolteacher in the village and an educated woman. She wrote and received hundreds of letters. This aunt is planning to deposit them in the local library or the National Archives, whichever will take them. The letters are fascinating, full of gossip and social history... details of births, deaths and marriages. It was a turbulent time in Irish politics and one of her father's uncles was a friend of Parnell. The schoolteacher had a big family, at least eight children, and some of them emigrated to America and Australia."

"Where is Frank buried? Did you look in the local graveyard? I've only been to the Church of Ireland one, not the Roman Catholic cemetery."

"I looked through the register of deaths but he's not listed. That's why I wondered if he went away. I checked the website where we can get death certificates from 1864 onwards. I know he was in love with Rosalind because his mother received a letter from her sister in America that hints at this."

"You're reading too much into this."

"You think so? Who do you think murdered Edward?"

"I don't know."

She slurped a spoonful of ice cream. "Perhaps we'll never know for sure but I'm compiling a list of suspects and Frank O'Rafferty is now at the top."

"So you've gone off Rosalind as the main suspect?"

Tiffany sucked her spoon. "Not strong enough to bash her husband's head in by all accounts. She wouldn't have been able to do it. One of the letters from an O'Rafferty sister mentions her as a sweet lady who loved flowers and poetry. She doesn't sound like a killer after all."

I smiled with relief. "I've never thought she did it. She looks innocent in the photograph I found."

"But she might have put Frank up to it, all the same. She might have caused the row that ended Edward Thornton's life in those dark woods that night. Maybe she wasn't as innocent as she looked."

I found it hard to think of Rosalind committing a murder. That lovely face, guileless with a hint of shyness. Perhaps she had been driven to it. Or perhaps it was an accident. In those days what would happen to a woman who committed murder? She would have been hanged or put in an asylum, wouldn't she? Locked up for life in some horrendous Victorian madhouse and experimented on by psychiatrists who used restraints, cold baths and leeches amongst other horrors.

"No, she couldn't have been involved," I said. "I'm sure she couldn't. Perhaps she wanted to get away... to run away from her marriage. We don't know what her husband was like. Perhaps he drove her away."

"Rosalind disappeared. I know that much but I don't know if she was caught. I need to find out what became of her. That's what I'm gonna search for this afternoon… gonna trawl through more newspapers… check the local asylums just in case she ended up in one of those."

"I hope she didn't. They were grim places." I glanced at my watch. Time to get back to the library if I was to get more research done before the train left in the afternoon.

"I'll pay for lunch. I said I would." Tiffany got to her feet and slung her large handbag over her shoulder. "It's the least I can do now that I know who you are… wait till I see Dominic this evening. There'll be a murder in Milltown." She looked pleased with her joke.

I followed her to the door. "Would I be able to see those letters written to Frank's mother?"

Tiffany handed her credit card to the man behind the cash register. "Maybe. I'll mention you to the aunt and let you know. She talks for ever so make sure you allow plenty of time. She won't let you take them out of her house though. She's very protective of them. I reckon she was afraid I might steal them." She grinned and tapped the side of her head. "A bit crazy, she is."

"Thanks, I'd like to have a look at the letters."

Tiffany leaned towards me and lowered her voice. "Sebastian was given diaries written by Grace Thornton."

"Grace?"

Tiffany nodded. "Yes. Hugh and Beatrice's daughter. Grace married a man from London. Her son was quite a well-known MP in the 1950s in Winston Churchill's government. Her grandson passed on her diaries to Sebastian. In the 1890s she mentioned that her cousin Harriet wrote…" Tiffany stopped.

"Wrote what?" I attempted to make my question sound innocent.

"Harriet wrote a book about her time at Ardlackan. A book

of riddles apparently and her cousin noted in her diary that she often hid these riddles under the summer house floor where her parents wouldn't find them. Both houses have summer houses so..."

"So that's what you were looking for that night. But you found nothing?"

"I found nothing. Nothing in the summer house of the bigger house either because I checked there."

"Perhaps Grace was mistaken."

Tiffany frowned. "Perhaps. It's disappointing."

Chapter Eighteen

The past - 15th March, 1891

Sadie opened the door and announced, "Mrs Hugh Thornton has arrived."

Rosalind stroked the baby's cheek. "Oh good, please show her in. Isn't that a lovely surprise? I wasn't expecting her today. Harriet and I called to see her yesterday but she wasn't feeling well. Do come and look at this little angel."

"She must be feeling better now." Sadie walked over and tickled Ivor's tummy. "He's getting big."

"Yes, he is."

Sadie left the drawing room to fetch Beatrice.

Edward was missing this, missing his son changing week by week. He'd also missed his daughter's eighth birthday five days before.

Harriet had been disappointed when he sent word to say that he and Hugh would be away for at least another week. The longed-for saddle for her pony would have to wait until his return and Rosalind saw the hurt in Harriet's eyes. Gertrude, of course, had offered excuses. The two cousins were making excellent contacts in England.

Beatrice swept into the room. "Good afternoon, Ros, I was out walking in the woods and I thought I would call to see if you were in. And is this Baby Ivor? My goodness, he is so like his papa."

Rosalind kissed her cool cheek. Beatrice had not yet regained weight but at least she didn't look as pale. The dark smudges under her eyes had faded.

Beatrice turned to Sadie. "Fetch us some tea, would you?" She leaned over the baby carriage. "I haven't seen him for so long."

"Thank you, tea would be lovely," Rosalind said, "and perhaps Mrs O'Brien has some of her fruit cake?"

When the maid had left the room and closed the door behind her, Rosalind took Beatrice's hands in hers and squeezed them. "I'm so glad you called in. It's lovely to see you looking more your old self."

Beatrice returned the affectionate grasp. "I am, indeed. I certainly feel better today and I think the walk has done me good. Tell me, have you heard from Edward recently?"

Rosalind asked her to take a seat on the sofa beside her. "Just this morning, actually. He said that he will be away for another week."

"I received a letter from my dear husband too. I dread to think what they are up to over there... buying too many horses, I expect. Has Edward told you of their plans?" She regarded Rosalind with a glint of sympathy in her eyes.

"No, no, he hasn't. What plans are these?"

"Oh, I understand, he hasn't mentioned... well, I won't say anything. I'll let Edward tell you himself. I just thought he might have mentioned something by now."

A stab of anxiety pricked Rosalind. "I hope it's nothing too extravagant. Edward often has ambitious ideas."

Beatrice changed the subject and asked questions about Harriet. Her eighth birthday party was a wonderful success and the girls enjoyed it. Grace and Irene couldn't wait until their own birthdays now. Such a good idea of Frank O'Rafferty's to hold that little riding competition in the meadow to keep them all occupied.

Rosalind agreed. "Yes, it was fun for them. I hope Irene recovered from her fall."

Beatrice waved a dismissive hand. "Oh, it was nothing, nothing. A minor tumble over the pony's head. Your girl is by far the best rider of the three of them. If she was a boy…"

"She's not a boy."

Beatrice hesitated. "I know, but… oh, well, never mind, she's perfect the way she is, of course she is."

Sadie returned with the tea tray and the blue floral china; the best tea set. She'd obviously informed Mrs O'Brien about the importance of the visitor. The cook had also baked queen cakes, little sponge buns glistening with plump raisins with a dusting of icing sugar. Heart-shaped shortbread piled high on another plate and moist dark slices of fruit cake with chopped walnuts. Beatrice lifted her hands in the air and exclaimed with delight.

She seemed in much better spirits but almost too cheerful, as if she was making a great effort to appear normal, hoping that Rosalind would think her fully recovered or perhaps trying to convince herself that she was well again before her husband's return home. There'd been no further mention of Dr Richard's suggestion that she be admitted to a sanatorium for a short rest. That was a relief.

Rosalind had heard tales of those places and Aunt Catherine once let slip how upset she'd felt when she'd visited a friend's daughter in Surrey in the new sanatorium for members of the middle classes, who were considered temporarily deranged and could afford to pay for treatment. Deranged, such a horrible word, and not at all apt for that silent, withdrawn girl.

No, she wouldn't dwell on such distressing thoughts. Rosalind turned to thank Sadie, who picked up the baby and left the room.

"She's very good with Ivor, isn't she?" Beatrice passed the plate of fruit cake to Rosalind. "My nanny is hopeless with the girls. She lets them run wild all over the house. It gives me a headache some days. They're always shrieking and chasing each other." Her voice rose but she pressed the tips of her fingers together as if trying to regain her composure. "But I don't wish to complain, they're just being children, aren't they? The rain recently kept them indoors when they need to get outside and run off their energy."

"I'm very happy with Sadie," Rosalind said, taking a slice of cake.

"Would you consider letting Sadie come to me?"

The sudden question made Rosalind sit up. "I'm sorry, I couldn't part with Sadie. I'm sure you'll find someone else just as capable."

Her friend added quickly, "Don't worry. Please forget I said anything. I will put an advertisement in the newspaper or I'll ask other ladies around here if they know of anyone."

They took a queen cake each and Beatrice began a conversation about the men in England; how Hugh's letter had described days at the races and visits to stable yards.

"Our husbands might return home with a train full of young horses," Beatrice said, amusement in her voice. "Your Edward is so adept at spending money."

"My Edward? What about your Hugh?" This sounded impolite and Rosalind added, "Both of our men have a weakness for thoroughbreds."

Beatrice picked a currant out of her bun and laid it on the side of her plate. "That's the truth but my Hugh isn't a gambler."

"Edward only gambles small sums of money. I have his word on that."

Why did Beatrice glance at her like that? The glitter in her eyes alarmed Rosalind. Was she deliberately trying to provoke a reaction? Everyone knew Edward liked a wager on horses occasionally but this was normal for a man who loved racing.

"Not just money, Ros. Still, you know him best."

Rosalind kept her voice light and steady. "What can you mean?"

Beatrice crumbled the remaining piece of queen cake between her fingers and reached for a linen napkin. "I don't feel hungry. It's warm in this room, isn't it? I think I'll walk home now." She rose to her feet, brushing the front of her skirt with the napkin. "Thank you for tea. Please come and see me soon. Our huge house is so lonely and quiet with Hugh away."

Hadn't Beatrice previously complained about the noise her daughters made? Really, she was all contradictions. Rosalind stood to kiss her. "I'll come with you to the door. Don't overexert yourself. Will I ask Frank to drive you home?"

"Oh, that would be kind. I feel tired now – all the talking, I suppose, and the heat from your fire."

Rosalind walked over to the wall and pulled the bell lever. She would send Patrick out to the yard to tell his uncle to bring Romeo and the brougham to the front door. She would have to ensure Patrick understood her message about the correct carriage because sometimes he got things wrong; she didn't want to terrify Beatrice with the arrival of the pair of bays and the landau.

Sadie appeared and was dispatched to find Patrick and issue the instructions. Rosalind and Beatrice walked to the hall and Beatrice put on her coat, a navy blue wool one with a fur collar and cuffs. Her cheeks certainly looked flushed. She'd seemed much improved when she arrived but now Rosalind wasn't so certain.

Rosalind touched her arm. "Tell me what you meant when you said that Edward doesn't only gamble with money?"

"Don't pay any heed to me today. I don't know what I'm saying. My mind feels quite confused sometimes."

That was all Beatrice would say and they waited in silence until the brougham arrived. Rosalind kissed her friend goodbye, promising to visit her the following day. She stood on the steps with a sense of growing unease, waving until the carriage disappeared behind the laurels.

Chapter Nineteen

The past - 20th March, 1891

"Whoa there, my lovely. I'm only here to help you, girl," Frank murmured as he ran a hand down the inside of the brown filly's foreleg. "Let's see what ails you. A splint, I fear. Yes indeed, a splint and quite a large one."

Frank pulled the lid off the tin of ointment and began to rub it over the bony swelling. He hummed a tune and the horse's ears flicked forward as she began to relax.

The shadows of two men fell on the wall inside the stable, the master and his cousin speaking in lowered voices about five yards away. Frank continued to stroke the filly but ceased humming.

"You're not to mention a word about this to Chance," Hugh muttered.

No reply from Edward.

Were they discussing Martin Chance, that blackguard of a bookmaker? Frank stepped out of sight behind the door, his hand still on the filly's shoulder.

"We'll get the weight down and put the money on at the Fairyhouse meeting. I reckon two poor runs will get us better odds." Hugh added.

"And if the stewards notice?"

"They won't. Not if we hire a cunning jockey." Hugh must have lit a cigar because a rich smell of smoke wafted over the door. "Have some faith, cousin. I know what I'm talking about. We keep the mare running down the field and then aim her at a bigger handicap chase with a nice low weight and make a fortune on the day. There's nothing to it."

"Frank won't like this."

Hugh snorted. "You won't tell him, Edward, my lad. You won't breathe a word of this to anyone."

Frank leaned against the stone wall and closed his eyes. A heavy weight churned in his stomach. Ardlackan Lass was entered for a big race at the Fairyhouse meeting in April. That must be what they were discussing. She had two engagements before, one at Clonmel and one at Cork. The mare was hitting form and her coat beginning to shine and he'd hoped to ride her on her next three outings if he could make the weight.

"We need to attract attention for this plan of ours to work," Hugh said. "No one will want to send us their horses to train if we don't show success in the big races. There are plenty of wealthy fools with money to spend these days. Those industrial men who know nothing about racing and want to look superior in front of their companions. Pheasants ready to be plucked, my lad, and as stupid as pheasants too."

Edward grimaced, displaying some resistance to his credit. Frank willed him to disagree, to turn Hugh Thornton down and walk away. Hadn't Edward's own father-in-law been one of the new breed of business men and, by all accounts, certainly no fool? Frank had met men like these at Irish race meetings and they'd impressed him with their enthusiasm and knowledge about racing.

But his master's silence masked another fear because Edward muttered, "I don't know. I'm nearly out of funds at the moment. That damn Maguire has been plaguing me… plaguing Rosalind too. I wish he would leave her out of this. I've had a string of losers recently. Nags I shouldn't have gone near and not much luck at the card tables either this past month. She knows nothing, she's an innocent and I don't want to alarm her because I need her to write to her legal advisors for more funds within the month."

Frank reached out and entwined his fingers in the filly's mane. She certainly was an innocent, the poor mistress.

Hugh lowered his voice. "Then listen to me and pay attention... I'll lend you some money to pay off Maguire for the time being, get him off your back... then we hire the jockey and you will tell O'Rafferty that he's not required to ride the mare until Fairyhouse... make up some excuse, man, if you need to. Remember that O'Rafferty works for you and not the other way around. We can do without him if we must."

"I can't... I can't risk that. You know yourself how good he is with the horses... and the stable boys. They worship the ground he walks on."

"There are plenty more men like O'Rafferty. Better men who will listen to their master's orders."

There were plenty more men better than Hugh Thornton. Frank had suspected something like this since he'd noticed him that day at Leopardstown races when Mighty Maiden won; seen him shaking hands with Martin Chance and sharing a packet of cigars before heading to his carriage in the enclosure for a few glasses of champagne. Leaving the mare in the care of Joseph and Peter, Frank had followed the two men, ducking behind a brougham to avoid being spotted.

Chance was a good name for the bookmaker because people who trusted him and handed over their money to him had more than a fair chance of never seeing it again. Trusting to chance took on a whole new meaning but deliberately scheming to outwit a powerful bookmaker was tempting fate.

"That owner we met in Lambourn, the man with the coal

mines… you must recall his vanity, his lofty ambitions," Hugh continued. "Nearly eighty horses in training at two pounds each a week. Imagine that, eh? We're talking about over eight thousand pounds a year from men who have more money than sense. If we could attract ten of them…. All it will take is a few big wins for these rich plump pheasants to notice us and we'll be able to start plucking."

"And this jockey that your friend recommended… will he mention us to Chance? How much will he want us to pay him to stop the mare winning and keep quiet about it? If he really knows what he's doing, if he knows how to do what you say, he won't come cheap."

Frank frowned. Indeed, this jockey wouldn't come cheap. He would fleece the master and his cousin for as much as he could get and might decide to blackmail them afterwards; threaten to tell the authorities and Martin Chance unless they handed over more funds. The road to hell was strewn with fools who got involved with crooked jockeys.

Frank waited in the stable, stroking the mare's soft velvet-like nose and praying that the two men wouldn't look in over the door. They talked some more about the jockey, whose name wasn't mentioned, and Edward agreed to speak to Rosalind about writing for funds. He pointed out that she'd seemed less willing to spend money over the last few months.

Hugh's laugh was without mirth. "For God's sake, Edward, what are you made of? The head lad runs your yard and your wife keeps your purse. Tell her you require the funds. You're entitled to the money. Tell her and if she makes a fuss…"

Frank clenched his fists.

What exactly was this man implying the master should do?

Their footsteps moved away from the stable as Hugh continued, "If she doesn't obey, then you make life a little difficult for her, you understand what I mean? A little less attention, a sharp word here and there. I could go on but I'm sure you can think of other ways to keep a wife in order."

After waiting another five minutes, Frank gave the filly a final pat and opened the stable door. No sign of Hugh but Edward was standing near the bell tower, looking in the opposite direction as he pushed a stone around with the toe of his boot.

Frank walked over to him and his master looked up.

"There you are," Edward said. "I was wondering what had become of you. There's no sign of Peter and Joseph."

"Fetching in the horses from the paddocks. They won't be long."

Edward threw him a glance before looking back at the ground. "I need to talk to you about Ardlackan Lass."

"Yes?"

His master shifted his weight from one foot to another. "I've decided... I'd like to... to try another jockey on her at Clonmel next week."

Frank remained silent.

"I didn't think her jumping was as fluent as usual..."

"There was nothing wrong with her jumping last time out. I should know as I rode her."

"That is perhaps the way it felt to you but from the grandstand... even Hugh noticed... my cousin pointed out that the Lass's blunder at the last fence nearly cost her the race."

"Is that so?"

Edward frowned. "I'm hiring another jockey for Clonmel, O'Rafferty, and that's my final word on the matter. I will expect you to prepare her for the race as usual."

Frank did not reply as his master spun on his heel and strode off towards the door into the garden.

Chapter Twenty

"The trouble with you, Rosalind, is that you worry too much," Edward slapped the reins against the flanks of the bay horses and they shot forward.

"Careful! You know how excitable these two creatures are. Frank told me they didn't have much exercise while you were away. Don't tip the carriage upside down in the ditch."

He turned to face her with a mocking grin. "Like I said, you worry too much, my love."

Was that a faint smell of brandy on his breath? He'd had a visitor an hour before they were due to leave for Martin Chance's dinner party. This unexpected guest was a small swarthy man whom Edward had hurried into his study as Rosalind watched from the landing, as if he didn't want to introduce him. She'd lingered in the hall for about ten minutes, pretending to be looking for a handkerchief she'd mislaid earlier but the men remained closeted in the room so she went upstairs to kiss the children goodnight.

Edward had been in a strange mood since he'd returned from England two weeks before. He'd talked enthusiastically about the places he'd travelled with Hugh; the racing stables they visited and the trainers they met at various race meetings. He'd found it exciting, a breath of fresh air after the Irish winter and had returned full of ideas for Ardlackan Lodge. What sort of ideas? He just smiled and stroked her cheek with a finger, adding that she would find out soon enough but he still had to finalize plans with Hugh and was sworn to secrecy until then.

The thought of secrets was unnerving. Who was going to pay for these grand plans, whatever they were? Perhaps Hugh would be the main investor if they involved his racehorses? A worried letter from Aunt Catherine had arrived the previous week. Her aunt informed her that the family lawyer had called upon her in Hampstead, voicing concerns that Rosalind was spending her inheritance more quickly than recommended and suggesting that her aunt dispatch one of her tactful letters.

"Have you known Mr Chance for long?" Rosalind asked as her husband raised the whip and one of the bays shuddered in the traces. She clutched at her hat.

The carriage jolted and moved forward.

"Hugh and I met him at Aintree last year and also at Leopardstown. You remember the meeting where the Maiden won? He's well known in Wexford society."

"A gentleman bookmaker, you say?"

Edward fixed his eyes on the two horses in front and gripped the reins. "A recent gentleman might be a better description. He's one of a new breed in Ireland... a man who's made his own money. Very clever... Hugh says he's a mathematical genius."

"It's kind of him to invite us to dinner. Will we know many people?"

"Major Langstown, Hugh and Beatrice, Ralph Murray and his wife... he trains a few horses... some other ladies you've met. The Major's sister, poor frail thing."

"Who was that man who called before we left?"

"What man is that?"

"Edward, you know very well. You took him into your

study… a small man who looked like a jockey."

He frowned. "No one you would know, my dear. Don't worry your pretty head about him. He wanted to talk to me about a horse, that's all."

"Have you been drinking? You nearly hit that tree trunk with the wheel on this side of the carriage. Please be careful."

"For God's sake, Rosalind, do stop nagging me. I saw that tree trunk and we missed it by several yards."

Martin Chance's pale pink late-eighteenth century house stood on the side of a hill looking over the River Slaney. An impressive pair of granite pillars with wrought-iron entrance gates led to a gravel avenue edged with lawn and tall Wellingtonia conifers, standing like a line of soldiers on the way towards the front of the building.

"An impressive dwelling," Rosalind said.

Her husband agreed. "The best that money can buy. Chance has spent a fortune doing this place up. You should have seen it before he bought it. Hugh said it was a ruin. The last owner lost all his money in the stock market crash, poor fellow, but Martin Chance was waiting to scoop up a bargain. An astute man, mark my words."

Edward hauled on the reins and brought the bay pair to a halt beside the steps with an abruptness that shot Rosalind forward and she grabbed at the woodwork in front. A boy waiting near the front door ran to hold the heads of the horses as Edward climbed down to help her out onto the gravel.

"Take them to the stable yard," he ordered the boy.

"I'm glad you asked Frank to ride over later to drive us home," Rosalind muttered.

Edward took her arm and hurried her up the steps. "It means I can enjoy myself tonight. Do try to relax. You've been on edge since I returned home. Don't mention money tonight in front of Hugh and Beatrice. You're embarrassingly bourgeois at times."

A flush sprang to her cheeks and she opened her mouth to reply but closed it again as the front door opened. No point trying to argue with him now that they were surrounded by people and while Beatrice was rustling across the hall floor towards them in a purple silk gown that shimmered in the lamplight. But it was unkind of Edward to reprimand her like that. She was always so patient with him.

He'd come home restless and fidgety, barely spending any time with Harriet who was desperate to go out riding with him and try out her new saddle. His long-awaited birthday gift had brought joy to their daughter's face. At least he'd remembered that.

Rosalind swallowed her indignation. "I won't mention money, don't worry." She reached out her hand to Beatrice. "How beautiful you look tonight! Your hair looks different. What have you changed?"

Martin Chance's guests came from nearby counties and all had an interest in racing. When they were seated at the mahogany dining room table, Major Langstown, an ardent admirer of Beatrice's, kept murmuring to Rosalind how beautiful Hugh's wife looked and how fortunate Hugh was to have married her. Her father was an old friend of the major with several thousand acres.

"And I suppose he has a big stable of horses too," Rosalind murmured.

The major raised an eyebrow. "Does he? I don't think so, my dear. I don't think Beatrice comes from a family with horses. Positively terrified of the creatures when she first arrived. It took Hugh months to train her in."

He made her sound like a horse, the way he put it, and an image of Beatrice trotting around in circles on the end of a rope popped into Rosalind's mind.

She looked away while he slurped his mushroom soup and

dabbed at his moustache with a linen napkin, his eyes back on Beatrice, who was whispering to a bald man on her left.

The major jerked his head towards this man and murmured in an exaggerated stage whisper, his hand cupping one side of his mouth, "Ralph Murray over there. Now there's a man that likes attention, to be sure, especially the attention of beautiful women. You heard his first wife ran off and caused quite a stir, didn't you? Much too fond of the wine, of course, but she was entertaining. We had some exciting evenings in their house over the years. Card games that lasted until the next morning and not just money at stake. No, I can't tell you what, my dear, you're too young and innocent. Yes, ran off with their groom, if I remember rightly."

Hugh raised his eyes from his soup and fixed them on the major. What expression was in them? Amusement yes, but something else. Exasperation, perhaps. "Now, now, Major, I hope you aren't spreading scandal and gossip."

Ralph continued his conversation with Beatrice, appearing not to have heard.

Beatrice tapped her husband's arm with her ringed hand, a sapphire sparkling and dancing. "Hugh, how impolite you are! Accusing Mr Chance's guests of scandal-mongering. What was that about the groom? Are you talking about O'Rafferty?"

The major murmured, "A good man, O'Rafferty. Knows his horses. They'll do anything for him." He added with a chortle, "And the ladies too. His father used to work for my cousin. Far too good-looking for his own good."

Ralph shifted in his chair and put a hand up to his throat as if to loosen his necktie. Perhaps the conversation had become too personal for him. Rosalind noted the mischief in Beatrice's dark eyes. It was unkind of her. Couldn't she see how uneasy the man seemed?

Martin Chance came to Ralph's rescue and began to tell a story about a recent gambling coup in a loud voice, glancing around the table in his commanding way as if to ensure his guests were listening. He filled the room with his presence, his brown eyes gleaming as he spoke. He reminded Rosalind of a large bear with his bushy beard and whiskers but his gaze also seemed calculating, as if he was measuring up his guests and knew exactly what they were thinking.

She watched as he raised a crystal glass of wine in a toast. His eyes alighted on her for a few seconds. She'd felt that appraising look before, she was certain she had. Chance was now watching Beatrice and Rosalind remembered where she'd seen him. Leopardstown races. He'd been among the crowd as she wished Frank luck before she and Beatrice walked towards the grandstand. He'd fixed her with that penetrating look that day and now she knew why. Martin Chance had recognized her. Rosalind shot a quick glance at her husband. He'd already drunk quite a lot of wine and was avoiding her eyes.

"Ladies and gentlemen, let us celebrate the wonderful sport of horse racing. The sport of kings. But we need to do more, we need to remember those less well off than kings and get more farmers involved in racing if the sport is to be kept going." Chance's eyes swept over their faces. "All this emphasis on flat racing, it's not good for the country… the public don't want too much of that."

"You're right," Hugh said, leaning back so that one of the servants could refill his glass. All Chance's servants were in livery for the occasion and Beatrice had whispered to Rosalind when she arrived that it was a deliberate attempt to impress.

"If the standards are too high at race meetings, we'll only see more unaffiliated fixtures taking place, that's the truth," Chance said. "Just think of all the top-class steeplechasers we know of that started off at smaller racecourses. Stringent rules will only encourage race committees to ignore the authorities."

"Indeed, indeed." Ralph drained his wineglass. "The modern

thoroughbred is sacrificing stamina for speed. Why, I read recently that over half the races run in Britain and Ireland last year were six furlongs or less. Gentlemen… and ladies, we need longer races. It's what the spectators enjoy."

Chance drank, his head tipping back. All eyes looked towards him as he continued, "We need longer races, yes indeed… much more challenging to bet on."

"What bookmakers prefer, eh?" Hugh's dark eyes glittered in the candlelight. "Longer races over fences help fill your coffers, Chance, don't they?"

Their host chuckled. "Ha, yes indeed. I must admit I have a particular love of four-mile steeplechases. Not nearly enough of them these days."

Major Langstown replied, "Indeed you are right, my friend, but you'll be considered too radical. Too radical by half. Next you'll be promoting the cause of professional trainers and all of us landowners will be drummed out of town." He looked at Rosalind and smiled.

"As a matter of fact," Hugh said, rising to his feet a little unsteadily, "we have an announcement for you all. You, our dearest friends, will be the first to hear of our ambitious plan. Cousin Edward and I wish to take on the professional trainers in this country."

Rosalind watched Hugh with unease. Was this what Beatrice had hinted at? She squeezed her fingertips together and slipped her gaze to the hair on the top of the major's hands, light and surprisingly fine in the flickering light.

"Expansion," Hugh said, "that's the grand plan. In spite of what the major says, you all know that professional racehorse trainers are the future. We only have to look at the illustrious career of Henry Linde of Eyrefield Lodge to see that. He sends his owners' horses to win at Aintree and Paris as well as here at home. Well, we intend to keep up with the times. Edward and

I will build a training establishment of excellence at Ardlackan Lodge where owners will line up to send us their horses." A gasp went around the table and several guests clapped their hands as Hugh continued, "We've visited over a dozen public stable yards across England in the last month and we've returned with some enterprising ideas to suggest to the architect in Dublin."

Rosalind watched her husband but his eyes were fixed on his cousin's face, a gleam of excitement in them.

She sighed and the major turned his head to murmur, "You sound distressed, dear lady."

She shook her head and took a sip of wine. Perhaps it would be all right; perhaps Hugh would pay for this lofty scheme. One thing was certain, she couldn't allow Aunt Catherine to learn about this until she'd ascertained exactly what sums of money would be involved and who, exactly who, was going to have to produce the funds.

Murmurs of appreciation rose and fell while the log fire sent shadows capering across the dark green walls. Servants cleared away and reappeared with pudding plates on trays.

Beatrice told Rosalind that Martin Chance's cook had been lured away from a friend in Dublin. He'd offered higher wages and even a job in the stable yard for her wayward son. Her dinners were delicious and beautifully presented but her baking could never compare with Mrs O'Brien's.

Chance laughed and clapped Hugh on the back.

A sherry trifle landed in front of Rosalind and the major passed a silver jug of thick yellow custard. Ralph's wife, new wife as the major called her, was staring at her with an expression of pity mixed with satisfaction on her sallow features. Rosalind poured custard over the mound of trifle on her plate and looked away. She would have to question Edward the next morning about these ambitious plans.

A crash and a thud startled them and Mrs Murray screamed.

Beatrice leaped to her feet, her hands over her mouth and the major brushed at the table with his napkin.

"What the… are you all right, my dear?" He turned to Rosalind as he swept small fragments of glass into his broad hand. A large stone lay by her chair and she reached down to pick it up.

Hugh hurried from the other side of the table and snatched it away from her, holding it aloft. "Look at this! What scoundrel has thrown a rock through the window? Out into the dark, men, and we'll catch the blackguard and sling him in the cellar until the constabulary arrive! We'll make him regret this." He led the way as the other men rose to join him. The clatter of their footsteps echoed across the hall towards the front door.

Rosalind was first to recover her equilibrium, ushering the ladies into the drawing room where she closed the door behind them and entreated them to sit down and remain calm. The major's sister sank onto a sofa and moaned to herself.

Rosalind sat next to her and spoke reassuringly, "I'm sure we'll discover that it was just a prank, a silly boy who has been dared to do this. Quite harmless, I'm certain."

"Harmless!" The major's sister held a hand to her breast. "How can you say such a thing, Rosalind? You have no idea what it's like around here these days. The… what do they call them? Those wretched Home Rule supporters and Nationalists, they're to blame… they have it in for people like us…"

"Oh really!" Beatrice objected. "I agree with Rosalind. We mustn't make too much of this. We've never had trouble with Parnellites or anyone else, for that matter. There will be a simple explanation, I'm certain of it."

The major's sister waved her hand. "The rock nearly hit Rosalind on the back of the head, didn't you see? She could have been badly injured. Oh, oh, how lucky you were to escape death, my dear!" She sank against the cushions with a shudder. "The stories I've heard about those sorts of people. And that scoundrel Parnell stirring up trouble for years."

"But Parnell is a member of parliament," Mrs Murray pointed out. "He believes in peaceful politics… not violence."

The door swung open, sending a sudden flame licking up the chimney. Beatrice rose to her feet as the men crowded in.

"No use," Hugh said, "he got away. Please don't distress yourselves, ladies. I'm sure it was just a boy."

"Or a disgruntled punter, perhaps," Edward said. "Some unfortunate who has lost his shirt to Chance on one of your old nags, Hugh." He meant it as a joke, Rosalind was certain, but the words slid out of his mouth edged with more sarcasm than he intended.

His cousin poured himself a brandy, offering one to the major and to Ralph. "Who trains the nags, I wonder? Perhaps the blame should lie with him."

Beatrice passed a glass of whiskey to Edward. "Now, Hugh, your cousin wasn't being serious."

"Yes, it was spoken in jest." Rosalind frowned at her husband whose eyes glittered with irritation.

"Is that what you think, Hugh?" Edward gripped the crystal glass until his knuckles whitened. "Is that what you believe? Do you think your horses are badly trained? What about our grand plan, eh? Am I expected to pay for more than half of the new racing establishment only to have you push me aside and install another trainer in my place?"

Rosalind reached up to touch his arm. "More than half the cost? Oh Edward, what have you agreed to?"

Hugh knocked back the brandy and poured another glass. "You mind your words, cousin."

"How can I when you insult me?" Edward pushed Rosalind's hand away.

She turned to Hugh. "Edward didn't mean anything of the sort. He's tired. He's been up since five o'clock this morning."

Edward glared at her and strode over to the fireplace, leaning his shoulders against the high marble mantelpiece and frowning at his cousin.

Hugh sipped his brandy. "You're the one who took offence."

"But that's what you meant, isn't it, to push me aside?"

"You're becoming paranoid, man," Hugh said, with a short laugh.

"My Ardlackan Lass could beat your best horse any day." Edward's voice grew louder. "Any day, I say. If you want a match race, I'll give you one… and I'll put money on it."

The major cheered and clapped his hands. "Now, Edward, you'll give us all a day out, will you? And Chance can make up the odds. What sort of odds are we talking about here?"

Rosalind turned to Beatrice. "Talk sense into the men, please. They can't start challenging each other to matches when they're planning to work closer together. Stop them, please!"

The major's sister opened her eyes and sat up, as if from a brief nap. "Matches? What are you all talking about?"

"A race between two horses, dear," Major Langstown explained. "Young Edward has challenged his cousin to a match. What say you, Hugh? What have you got to match Ardlackan Lass?"

"Major, please." Rosalind heard her voice rise. "Don't encourage them. This is just because of the fright we got with the broken window… the fact they didn't catch the culprit. It means nothing. In the morning Edward will have forgotten all about it."

She took a risk saying that, making him sound like a child in public and he wouldn't like it but she was upset he hadn't warned her about his extravagant idea. Aunt Catherine's letter still stung. She wasn't the one spending her inheritance; she knew perfectly well how to be frugal.

Hadn't she agreed to have only one maid to look after the children? Even Edward had resisted hiring a governess for

Harriet because he was concerned about the expense.

No, he was slightly drunk and full of bravado because he was overtired; excited about the new racing stables and fired up by the chase out into the darkness to find someone who would certainly turn out to be no more than a boy, dared by others to throw a stone through the window of the wealthy Martin Chance.

Edward swallowed his brandy in one gulp. "Please ignore my condescending wife. All right, Hugh, I will accept your challenge. I'll even ride the mare myself if you ride your horse. I think it would be more exciting if we ride across the country. Ditches, banks, some timber fly fences. I'll ask O'Rafferty to lay out a course for us. Why not? We'll see what you're made of, cousin!"

"Not for money, Edward," Rosalind pleaded. "Please, not for money. Why not make it a gentleman's bet?"

"Where's the fun in that?" her husband asked.

"Indeed, no fun whatsoever," Chance agreed. "I'll work out the odds and we'll all have a decent wager."

"Perhaps Ros has a point." Hugh caught Beatrice's eye for a few seconds before he smiled at Edward. "We shouldn't be gambling for money, not when we'll need every penny for our new training establishment. No, we'll think of something else to wager."

Did Beatrice's gaze rest momentarily on Rosalind with something akin to triumph on her face? What was she thinking when she turned to Edward and offered him another brandy? She looked suddenly happy, as if this was the outcome she'd been hoping for.

"Very well." Edward held out his empty glass. "We'll discuss this another time but I will win, Hugh. Mark my words."

Chapter Twenty-One

The present - 3rd July, 2019

Daphne climbed the stairs in front of me, calling over her shoulder, "It's kind of you to help me sort through Charles's old clothes." It was difficult to see her in the gloom because the door to the top floor was shut. She pushed it open and a long corridor with bare floorboards stretched ahead of us, lit only by one skylight; a row of doors on the right-hand side.

Like stepping back in time, I thought. It would have looked like this in the nineteenth-century as no luxury would have been wasted on the servants.

A memory niggled: a door slamming, the shuffling of what sounded like footsteps and two girls turning on their heels to thunder down the wooden staircase.

"You and Jessie were terrified of this wing," Daphne said, switching on the light. "Do you remember? You got a fright here and would never come up again."

"We sneaked up in the dark with a torch and thought we heard someone here."

"Yes, that was it." She walked ahead of me down the corridor and stopped outside a door, reaching for a key on the top of the frame. "This is where Charles locked possessions he no longer used but couldn't bear to throw out. Mostly old clothes and books."

I blinked as sunlight flooded the corridor.

The room was small with a jumble of boxes and an oak bookcase; two small windows with bars looking out over the trees on the seaward side. An old marble-topped washstand and a chipped jug decorated with pink roses.

She moved over to the windows and pushed them open. "Let's let in some fresh air. It smells musty."

"It's helpful for you… and for the family that Tiffany has decided the coachman was to blame," I said. Daphne seemed relieved earlier when I informed her of the journalist's latest brainwave.

A house martin swooped towards one of the open windows, shot into the room and landed on the top of the bookcase.

Daphne pointed at the bird. "That's for a message to be revealed, did you know that? A bird flying into the house. Some would say it's a warning of a death but I don't believe that. A beautiful bird like this could only bring good luck. A message to be revealed."

The house martin shook its blue-black feathers and tilted its head as if listening to her voice before taking off and flying out of the window. A chattering in the oval nest under the eaves broke out.

"The babies," Daphne said. "I always think the nests are like works of art, made from mud gathered from streams and puddles with a round entrance at the front. Charles would never allow the decorators to knock them down. He always said it was bad luck. He was surprisingly superstitious but perhaps people who work with horses often are. So much can go wrong."

I walked to the window and looked up at three nests running like a terrace under the gutter. Another house martin arrived with an insect in its beak and a chorus of frantic chirping rang out.

She picked up a tweed jacket from the top of a cardboard box and stroked it, holding it to her face as if to breathe in her late husband's presence. "This was one of his best jackets." She handed it to me.

Used to searching Dominic's clothes before putting them in the washing machine, I pushed my fingers into the pocket of the jacket and found a small sheet of notepaper.

I glanced down the names written on it. Harriet Thornton. Jenny Gilbert. Kitty O'Rafferty.

I knew about Harriet but how strange that Kitty was there. Tiffany had sent me her name in a text when I returned from Dublin, for she was the descendant of Frank O'Rafferty with shoeboxes full of old family letters. Charles must have known about Kitty O'Rafferty. He must have been doing some research into his family history after he retired as a trainer and before his heart attack. And for some reason he'd kept this secret from his wife. Or had he? I was growing suspicious of Daphne and her habit of pretending to be vague.

"Daphne, have you heard of these names?" I read them aloud.

Daphne's brow wrinkled. "Hmm, Jenny Gilbert... she was the woman who called here a few years ago. A woman from England claiming to be related in some way... Charles wouldn't speak to her about his family."

"Why did she call here?"

"Oh, the usual. Just turned up to try and trace her roots."

"Tell me more about her."

Daphne waved a hand. "She only stayed a few hours. Charles... you see he hated people asking about the family. I wouldn't have been allowed to say anything. That's why I can't bear this Tiffany Ryan woman digging up old stories. Charles would have been so upset."

Was she fobbing me off? I sighed. "Is it possible that you

haven't told me the whole truth? Is there something you know about Charles's family that would have made him so reticent? So keen to discourage others finding out?"

She closed her eyes as if to block out my words.

"I'm sure Charles would have helped me," I said. "He wouldn't have liked a TV murder series about his ancestors, would he?"

She murmured, "The house martin... a revelation. Perhaps the superstition is true but I'm afraid..."

"What are you afraid of? It was all so long ago... so long ago, Daphne. There's no reason to be afraid."

She shook her head. "Old sins cast long shadows. There are shadows here... shadows in this house, restless and uneasy."

"Only shadows. That's all. Shadows cast by the sunlight. Look, there on the floor, those dancing shapes. They're nothing. Only the afternoon sun flickering behind the trees in the garden. Nothing to be afraid of."

She looked at me accusingly. "You were afraid. You and Jessica were terrified up here. I found you both sobbing hysterically."

"You think something happened here long ago?" I asked. Perhaps it would be better to appease Daphne rather than rely on logic.

Silence hung in the room as she pulled a thread from the faded yellow curtains.

I tried again. "Do you know if something happened up here in 1891? What could have happened?"

She shivered. "I don't know. I just have a feeling, that's all. A bad feeling when I'm here."

I needed facts though, not feelings. "What's in that?" I pointed at a large trunk on the right of the bookcase.

"Just clothes... old clothes and linens."

Against the wall on the left of the fireplace stood a collection of large pictures, glass facing the wall. I moved over to them and lifted one to look at it.

I shot a glance at Daphne but she was staring out at the lawn below.

The first was of a fair-haired man of about thirty with dark eyes with his arm round a young woman. I reached out to touch the glass over the woman's face.

Rosalind. It had to be her. Those beautiful features.

A girl with long curly hair rested her head against her mother's hip and a baby, a bundle of linen and lace, lay in the woman's arms. The date *February 1891* was scrawled on the back.

"Look at this, Daphne! This must be Edward and his wife Rosalind with the children in 1891. Taken before the tragedy… before Edward died."

Her eyes swept over the photograph.

"Did you know this was here?"

Daphne didn't reply.

"Did you know who these were? It must be them… Rosalind looks just like she does in the photo I found in Charles's study."

She avoided my eyes. "Charles said they must be kept here, locked in this room. He didn't want them hanging downstairs."

"So he knew who they were. What's this one?"

I lifted the other framed photograph and turned it to face me. A dark-eyed young man stared back at me from the depths of a sepia portrait, a white necktie round his throat. I examined the back of the frame. The words *Hugh Thornton 1881* written in faded ink. Hugh Thornton of Ardlackan House… Edward's cousin.

He looked familiar in some way. Was it the nose or the dark eyes? Perhaps I was thinking of Jessica's father.

"Hugh Thornton… the cousin who owned the big house."

"Yes," Daphne replied. "He owned this house too. Charles's uncle John Thornton inherited it from him when Hugh died. Hugh moved here after… after the bigger house was burned down."

"But Jessica says you lived near here as a child. You grew up near here, didn't you? You must have known John Thornton."

She kept her eyes on the floor. "I remember him. He looked quite like Charles but not as handsome. His wife died young and he became quite reclusive in his old age when he stopped training. Lived here alone with his dogs. Charles used to visit him so it was only fair that he left Charles the property."

"Did John have any children?"

"One daughter. She wasn't interested in horses. She moved to England when she was in her early twenties."

I put down the photograph and stepped over to the bookcase, placing my hand on the nearest dusty cover, a faded green. *A Tale of Two Cities* by Charles Dickens. A foxed flyleaf displayed the title of the book and, in looped handwriting, *John Thornton 1883, aged ten.* Ten would make him about a decade younger than Rosalind.

My voice rose. "Look… look at this. John Thornton was only about ten years younger than Rosalind. He'd have known her, wouldn't he?"

"I suppose he might."

"Would he have known what happened to her?"

"I don't know. Charles never said."

"Did Charles tell you what happened in September 1891? Did he, Daphne?" I had to know the truth. I had to force it out of her.

She threw her hands in the air. "Oh, for goodness sake, Fiona! I don't know. I told you, he disliked talking about his family." She hung her head and moved it slowly from side to side. "None of this would ever have come to light if it hadn't been for the journalist. Why did she have to come here poking her nose into other people's business? Raising long-forgotten…"

I hoped she wasn't going to say ghosts.

Daphne walked towards the door. "I have to go out to the

181

garden now. I need to prune the herbaceous border."

I followed her but stopped by the photographs and held up the one of Hugh Thornton. "He reminds me of someone. Who is it? Do you see a resemblance to anyone?"

Daphne reached for the door handle, as if desperate to escape from my questions.

I looked again at the rather noble-looking nose, the dark eyes with their serious and intense expression. That stare, sharp and scrutinizing; yet somehow also secretive. And then it came to me.

As Daphne pulled the door open and scurried out into the corridor, the confusion in my mind cleared. The man in the photograph, taken when he was probably in his early twenties, was the image of another young man. No doubt about it. Hugh Thornton looked like Ben.

Chapter Twenty-Two

I took a photo of Hugh Thornton's image with my mobile, replacing the frame against the wall and hastening after Daphne. She'd already disappeared, the corridor empty and the door banging at the bottom of the stairs on the lower landing. I was aware of the gloom around me, the lurking silence of long-abandoned rooms.

The solitary light bulb dangling from the ceiling flickered and went out. A coincidence, but my pulse quickened and the lines of Tennyson's poem sprang into my mind:

She is coming, my own, my sweet;
Were it ever so airy a tread,
My heart would hear her and beat,
Were it earth in an earthy bed...

I took a deep breath and stepped forward, willing myself not to look over my shoulder but all the time anticipating the soft pad of footsteps behind me.

I reached the top of the wooden stairs, shot one look back down the dark corridor and hurried to the second floor. As soon as the door swung shut behind me, my heart rate steadied. Such overwhelming emotions! Really, I was worse than a child and should have stood my ground up there, waiting until I'd calmed down.

If I were brave enough now, I would head back up the stairs and confront my fears.

I didn't, of course. I needed to talk to Daphne and pin her down. I needed answers more than I needed to assuage my teenage memories.

The dog was curled on the rug outside my bedroom door. He jumped up and wagged his tail when he saw me coming towards him, as if he'd been waiting for me. I bent to stroke his soft ears, reassuringly warm and definitely belonging in the present. "Hello, Archie, have you seen Daphne? Did she come scurrying past you just now?" For her age, she could move with agility.

He tipped his head to one side, his bright eyes staring at me.

"Let's go find her," I said and he ran on ahead of me.

The sunlight outside the garden door was dazzling. Where would Daphne have gone? She'd mentioned the herbaceous border; always a place of solace for her, a retreat away from distasteful conversations. Her sanctuary when Charles was still training and difficult owners dropped in unannounced.

Archie spun in circles of joy in front of me, convinced a long run on the sand lay ahead.

"We'll track her down," I assured him. "We'll track down Daphne and we'll make her answer our questions, won't we?"

As for Ben, why did he look like Hugh Thornton?

I'd been kept in the dark and not told the truth. Not by Ben and certainly not by Daphne. She knew a lot more than she was saying, of that I was certain.

Her pink cotton hat with the wide brim bobbed over fluffy yellow flower heads and purple delphiniums. A gloved hand reached out for a spiky blue globe of Echinops but froze in mid-air when she spotted me.

"Daphne, I would like to finish our conversation, if you don't mind."

She shrank into the flowers. "Oh, I'm busy here. I've got a lot of pruning to do. This meadow rue will fall over if I don't snip off some of the side flowers… get too heavy to…"

Archie looked up at me, his brow wrinkling at the delay, disappointment evident in his eyes.

"I'm sorry, Daphne, I really am, but I'm concerned that you… and Ben… that you both have been concealing the truth from me."

The red-handled secateurs snapped at a delphinium with faded flowers. "I… I don't know what you mean."

"Ben looks like Hugh Thornton in that photo. Surely you've noticed?"

A bright pink phlox was beheaded and dropped into the foliage as Daphne snipped and chopped, ignoring me.

"Perhaps Ben doesn't know he looks the image of the cousin of a man mysteriously murdered in the woods near this house. Why do you want me to stop Tiffany's research? Is it because you actually know what happened here? Is it because you don't want that to become common knowledge?"

She reached for the Echinops again, her head on one side, her lips pressed together.

"I'm going to stand here until you tell me the truth." I folded my arms. "I won't move until you answer me."

A sigh rose from the herbaceous border and Daphne peered at me from behind a clump of bright yellow Verbascum, her glasses glinting in the sunlight.

"I'm waiting, Daphne."

"I wanted you to stop Tiffany because she's going to make up lies. I'm afraid. That's the truth. I'm afraid that she's going to sensationalize everything and then Charles's name will be remembered for all the wrong reasons. All the wrong reasons when he was a champion trainer for ten years… ten years in a row."

"The woman who came here… you said she was from England. Who is she?"

"Jenny Gilbert is Ben's grandmother."

"His grandmother! How do you know she's his grandmother?"

"I know because he asked me questions sometimes… questions that only her grandson would know to ask. He thought he was being discreet and that he could fool me but…"

"So you knew all along who he was."

"Yes." Her voice was barely audible. "Yes, I knew when I first laid eyes on him. I can sense these things."

"And you kept those photos of Hugh, Edward and Rosalind locked away from me until now because you realized I would recognize him too."

"I… I forgot they were up there this morning. I suppose I wanted to protect Ben. I've grown fond of him. I can understand if he wants to discover… if his grandmother wants to discover what happened to Harriet."

I frowned, trying to follow her logic, not always easy with Daphne. "But what if he encouraged the journalist? Weren't you worried about that?"

"I didn't think he would. They are his relations too."

Archie flopped on the grass near my feet with a whimper, abandoning hope of a walk. I bent to scratch his ear. A peacock butterfly fluttered on a golden flower at the edge of the lawn, the false eyes on its outstretched wings staring up at me. I'd been duped by Daphne. She'd been happy to let me blunder along, discovering names and dates that she'd known all the time, while I foolishly imagined I was making progress.

I sat on the grass beside the dog and ran my hand along his back. "Tiffany has been to see Kitty O'Rafferty, the third name on the list. Tiffany thinks that Frank and Rosalind had an affair and that Edward was killed because of that."

"For goodness sake, what will she come up with next? First Rosalind was a crazy murdering lunatic and now she was involved in a scandal. How can we stop this journalist?"

"We can stop her by finding out the truth."

Her eyes widened behind the round glasses. "How will that help?"

"The truth might not be as lurid as Tiffany's imagination. But I'll need your help. I can't do this if I'm being fed misleading information all the time."

Daphne pulled off her gardening gloves and emerged from the foliage. Archie woke up and threw himself at her legs, hopeful again. She bent to stroke him. "All right, I'll admit that I knew Charles had been working on a family history before he became ill. He showed me the photograph of Rosalind with Edward and the children."

"Do you think John Thornton told him anything about the family?"

She considered, twisting her mouth to one side. "I'm not sure. They used to spend hours together talking about horses."

"And his daughter who went to England?"

"Died long ago…in her forties from some horrible disease. I forget what. She never married."

This was better. At last I was getting somewhere. "Did Charles tell you… did he show you what he was working on? Did he share any of his ideas with you?"

"He said the Thorntons were a secretive family and had to adapt to survive. Not easy back then. 1916 and all that happened in the years afterwards… the fight for Irish independence. So many other families left… went to live in England. I think the racing helped. It's a great leveller, horse racing, in spite of what people say… certainly National Hunt racing is. In National Hunt racing people talk to each other with few airs and graces."

I nodded encouragingly to show that I agreed with her.

She continued, "The Thorntons employed local people and mixed with the farming community. Hugh Thornton lost his house and came to live here so he had to make an effort to get on with others after Ireland became independent. You either got on or you got out in those days."

"It must have been difficult."

"Yes, it was." She bent to pick up the dog. "I'll take Archie for a walk on the beach, if you like."

"Thank you… and thank you for telling me this. I'm going to have a word with Ben now."

I found Ben fitting slates to the summer house roof. I stood at the bottom of the ladder and called his name.

He looked down. "Hey there, Fiona. What's up?"

"Can you come down here, please? I'd like to ask you something."

He climbed down the rungs and stood on the grass beside me. He was wearing a red T-shirt and blue cotton shorts. A modern double of Hugh.

How would I begin? Perhaps best to launch straight in. "Ben, I've seen a photograph and… and it looked the image of you."

His dark eyebrows rose. "Me?"

"Yes you." I kept my voice level. "Hugh Thornton, who owned the ruined house that you took me to see… you look just like him."

"Like Hugh Thornton?"

"Yes, but I expect you know that. Daphne knows who you are. She told me your grandmother came here."

He took a step back and dropped his eyes to the lawn at our feet, the tiny heads of daisies bobbing in the breeze, but didn't reply.

"You've been telling me lies, haven't you?"

"I've told you… half-truths." His mouth twitched at one

corner. "I apologize for misleading you. I thought it best at the time."

"Please explain your connection to Harriet Thornton."

He pushed his hands into the pockets of his shorts. "How did Daphne know? My great-great-grandmother was Harriet Thornton. I didn't find Harriet's book here in the summerhouse… not here under the floor boards. That wasn't true. I wanted to make sure I could trust you before I told you. I thought you might hand it over to Tiffany."

"Who gave you the book of riddles?"

He looked at me. "Harriet gave the book to my grandmother the year before she died. My gran used to visit her in London."

"So your grandmother was Harriet's granddaughter? And you didn't tell Daphne who you were?"

He shook his head. "I'm sorry to admit that I misled her too. I didn't come just to mend her property… her summer house and stable yard. I came here to find out what happened on that September night in 1891."

"Harriet must have lived a long time if your grandmother remembers her well."

"Yeah, she did. She died in her nineties in 1977. I'm close to my gran… she brought me up… and she asked me to come over here to find out what happened to Edward Thornton… her great-grandfather." Ben's dark eyes were fixed on mine, no longer shy or secretive but with a gleam of… of what? Excitement, perhaps. "The truth is my gran says Harriet had a terrible secret. Gran said that Harriet… well, that Harriet always believed she might have killed her father."

Chapter Twenty-Three

The past - 25th April, 1891

"Has it started yet, Frank?" Rosalind peered out of the carriage window.

The woods of Ardlackan reared against a black bank of cloud sweeping in from the sea. A shower was coming, one of those sudden spring squalls that hit with fury and ended in a burst of sunshine.

A crowd had gathered to watch the race, pushing past the carriage and a few children even climbing up onto the sides and standing on the wheels for a better view, until Frank waved his arm and ordered them to move away.

He'd positioned the carriage on the top of the hill beside the gallop where they could see the fields roll down towards the church, its grey granite bell tower rising above the rooftops of Ardlackan village.

Harriet rested her forehead against the glass. "I think some of them are Papa's stable boys. I recognize Peter over there. Do you think they're gambling on Papa to win?"

Rosalind reached out a gloved hand and touched her shoulder. "Don't stare at them like that."

"Can I get out and watch from the other side of the hill?"

"Certainly not. You'll be trampled underfoot."

"I won't."

"When people get overexcited and take too much drink, they might not see you in the crush."

Harriet frowned. "Please let me get out. Frank will keep an eye on me."

The rain shower soaked the grass and forced the crowd to huddle under trees. When the sun slipped out again, Rosalind fastened the buttons of her coat. She would have to accompany Harriet because she couldn't risk letting her young daughter run loose among the churning mass of people and horses.

Many had come on horseback in order to follow the race and get the best view possible and they would gallop with abandon after the two racehorses, cheering with delight, and might not see the girl on the ground.

Rosalind prayed that Edward wouldn't be thrown off Ardlackan Lass. She'd tried to persuade him to let Frank ride the chestnut mare and, for once, even Gertrude supported her and added her concerns to the argument.

At luncheon earlier, his mother refused to watch the spectacle and expressed fears about her son lying in a ditch with a broken neck. She pointed out that this had happened to a young man in Kilkenny only the previous year. His horse hit a solid fence; the rider shot off and landed on his head on a stony track. That was the end of him, Gertrude said, dead as soon as he hit the ground and leaving behind a grieving widow and six children. Was that the way Edward wanted to go? Was that what he wished to bring upon his beloved mother and family? She'd sniffed loudly and reached for the sherry decanter.

Her son waved his hand dismissively and said Ardlackan Lass knew the course well as both he and Frank O'Rafferty had ridden her over several of the obstacles on countless occasions.

Harriet pulled her cloak around her and put up the hood. Her eyes sparkled with excitement as she stepped down from the carriage and clutched her mother's hand. She would love to be part of this; riding in this senseless match. If only Harriet would show more interest in ladylike pursuits. If only she was less like her reckless father and more like her cautious Mama.

"Be careful, ma'am," Frank called after them. "I'll wait here with Romeo until you return. I'd advise you to take the young lady over to the stone wall where she'll get a good view of the start and stay away from the horses' hooves."

Harriet dragged Rosalind towards the wall, pushing her way through the crowd. They scrambled up large stones that shifted under their leather boots, clutching each other for support.

At the back of the crowd Rosalind saw two horses and riders approach the wooden box on top of which Major Langstown balanced precariously, bouncing with self-importance as the official starter. He clutched a stout stick with a white handkerchief tied to it, his moustache twitching in anticipation, while his sister looked on from their carriage beside him.

A cheer went up from the crowd as Edward and Hugh lined their horses up beside the major's wooden box. Arms raised and caps waved.

Frank had mentioned the great rivalry between the two stables. Many of the stable boys had gambled on their own master. Rosalind had been informed by Sadie that Hugh was tipped to win because his gelding Pirate was judged to be a better jumper than Ardlackan Lass with more experience in point-to-points, winning several with his owner in the saddle.

Rosalind shifted her weight on the wall. What if Edward lost? What was really at stake here apart from his pride, his foolish pride? He promised her that he wouldn't put money on the outcome of this match. He wouldn't lose a penny.

When she asked him what he might possibly lose, he strode away and shouted over his shoulder that she fussed too much and was even more irritating than his mother.

The major raised the makeshift flag in the air and, as if obeying the conductor of an orchestra, the people around him fell silent. Hugh and Edward reached out; their mounts shivering with anticipation, and the men shook hands. Rosalind heard Hugh's voice call out, "May the best man win."

A flock of mute swans flew overhead, a humming throb from their wings as they stretched their necks towards the shore, heading for the salt marshes. A flutter of foreboding ran down Rosalind's spine and she put one hand to her throat.

Where was Beatrice? She screwed up her eyes, placing a hand above them to shield them from the breeze.

There was Hugh's black carriage further down the hill, with its gold-painted monogram on the door. The coachman stood at the heads of two well-behaved grey geldings, wearing his formal uniform of white breeches, top hat and black coat.

Rosalind glanced over the heads below her towards the brougham and Frank flashed a grin in her direction and tipped his whip against his cap. She smiled back at him. What was he thinking about this match?

She knew he hadn't been happy about it because she'd overheard him muttering to Edward when he brought Romeo and the carriage round to the front. She'd seen the stubborn flash in her husband's eyes and the flush on his cheeks as he moved away.

Not even Frank could get away with reprimanding her husband without an angry reaction these days.

"Are you ready?" the major called. "Edward! Get your horse back in line."

Edward turned the mare and walked her in a circle. She came to a halt beside Hugh's big black gelding, swishing her tail and kicking out with a hind leg. The gelding swung his head and snapped at her, huge teeth bared. The mare squealed and stamped a foreleg.

"Let us go, for God's sake," Hugh yelled, "before these creatures devour each other!"

"On your way!" The major shouted and dropped the flag.

Hugh's gelding was first away with Edward and his mare a couple of lengths behind. The crowd gasped as the horses galloped with their ears pinned back towards the stone wall near Rosalind and Harriet.

"Good luck, Papa!" Harriet screeched as the horses rose together and landed on the other side. A few divots thrown up by the galloping hooves struck Rosalind's coat. While she was wiping off the mud, her daughter climbed down and ran after the horses.

The crowd surged forward and enveloped her. Rosalind's eyes scanned the melee, beckoning to Frank to bring over the carriage. Thank goodness, there was Harriet sitting on the grass laughing. A boy, who looked like Patrick, stopped to hold out his hand to help her to her feet and she ran back, waving at Frank.

"That was an exciting start," Frank said as he reined in Romeo a few yards away. "The stable boys are obsessed about this match. They've been in a fever of excitement for days. Why, Peter said this morning even his grandmother has money on the master."

Harriet brushed leaves from her dress. "Mama believes gambling is a sin."

Frank's amused blue eyes rested on hers. "Your mama is probably right. Look at the ruin and misfortune it brings to many."

Harriet, her hair streaming behind in the wind, pulled open the door of the brougham before he could get to it. "I heard her tell Papa he was stubborn and irresponsible to take part in this match."

"Harriet!" Heat burned Rosalind's cheeks.

"Is that so?" Frank scrutinized her face. "It's strange your mama married a horse trainer. She could have been a fine lady in

London, driving out in Regent's Park in the mornings to visit her friends instead of mixing with our mob of Irish ruffians."

Harriet grimaced. "I'm glad I wasn't born in London. What a dull life!"

"That's enough, both of you," Rosalind said.

She took Frank's hand and he helped her into the carriage.

He gave her fingers a light squeeze. "I didn't mean to offend you, Mrs Thornton. It was a compliment, even if it didn't sound like one. You're far too good for the likes of us."

Was he joking? He was smiling into her eyes but was that a mocking glance from under his thick dark lashes?

"Let's go, Frank, or we'll miss the race."

He touched the peak of his cap and offered a little bow. "Of course. I can't allow you to miss the action." He turned and climbed onto the driver's seat and muttered to Romeo, "Move on there, old man, the lady is keen to see her husband break his bloody neck."

Rosalind cast her eyes down so that she didn't have to look at Harriet or see her amused expression. Harriet adored Frank and the girl would presume that he was joking. He often played the fool with her, pushing against her like an older brother and teasing her in a genial manner.

The brougham lurched forward and bumped across the field towards the stony track leading to the village. Spectators pressed on ahead, leaving the occupants of the carriage alone in silence as the sun slipped from behind the clouds and bathed the hill in sudden light. The swans circled again overhead, wings beating out their rhythmic hum.

When they reached the track, Frank drew Romeo to a standstill. Rosalind opened the door and looked up at him.

Frank pointed with his whip. "See there, can you see the river? Halfway to the church now… see the horses over there, and it looks like the master is in the lead."

She could see the crowd swarming after them, the men on foot at least two fields behind while those on horseback cantered in a group. Major Langstown on his solid grey mare rode in front, a portly but capable rider who occasionally turned his head to roar over his shoulder in order to keep the others behind him.

"Look at the major go!" Frank cried out. "He's a fine rider for his age. When he occasionally hits the ground in a point-to-point, he bounces back on his horse in a flash. A tough old geezer. The major will die with his boots on, to be sure."

Hopefully that wouldn't be today.

Hugh's gelding was gaining on Edward and the mare as they reached the river at the bottom of the hill, only five yards or so behind them. Ardlackan Lass slowed down when she saw the shallow crossing at the ford and, objecting to the sunlight glittering on the water, tossed her head in the air. Edward gave her a few kicks and drove her in, spraying Hugh behind.

Pirate regarded the ford with suspicion, deeper than usual for April, the rain earlier in the month causing flooding in the fields and swelling the streams that flowed into this stretch of river so that it rushed and roared by the mill in the village. Hugh pushed his horse past Edward in the strong river current and clambered out onto the muddy bank several yards ahead. Ardlackan Lass stood still for a moment, lifting a front leg to paw nervously at the water but decided she didn't want to be left on her own and leaped high in the air before sliding down on her knees on the top of the bank. Edward shot off over her head and sprawled in the mud near a gorse bush.

Rosalind clutched at her throat and shrieked. Harriet screamed and even Frank looked worried. Edward climbed to his feet within minutes and remounted.

Hugh was ahead by about fifty yards and was nearing the gate out onto the lane that led to the churchyard. Surely they weren't going to ride across the graves? The rector, obviously fearful of that outcome, ran towards the gate with his black cassock flapping in the wind, waving his arms above his head like a demented crow.

A roar ascended from the crowd as Hugh turned Pirate to the right to canter down the main street, children and dogs scattering out of his way.

"A mercy no one was killed," Frank murmured. "The master better get a move on or he'll be left with too much to do at the finish."

"It's not over yet." Rosalind replied. "He has time to catch up. Don't they have to ride back up that hill and finish where they started?"

"Yes, indeed. The quarry is next. They have to go through the quarry over there and then into the woods and back to the gallops that way."

A group of men walked past the brougham, casting glances at Rosalind and Harriet as they passed and nodding at the coachman. Another gathering stood on the far side of the church beside the gap in the wall that led the riders back towards the granite quarry. She could see women among the men, shawls pulled over their heads to protect them from the wind and children in trousers that looked too short, their skin blue with the chill.

She'd recently sent a box of boots to the school and would give Harriet's pair that she'd just grown out of to Mrs O'Rafferty and ask her to hand them on to a deserving child. Frank's mother would know best; would give them to one of the poorer children.

But so many of them were poor. So many lived in crowded, smoky cabins coughing and wheezing their way to death. The graveyards of both the Church of Ireland and the Roman Catholic churches were strewn with headstones of departed children.

Tuberculosis was the silent killer that crept into the damp, thatched cabins and claimed these unfortunate families with its deadly breath. Even though Mr Koch in Germany nine years before had identified the bacterium that caused it, doctors were no further on with keeping the disease under control. Even wealthier people died of consumption as their bodies wasted away.

A shiver ran down Rosalind's spine. She would have to try to shake off this feeling of dread that gripped her today.

Onlookers lined the sides of the quarry as the riders approached, cheering and waving their caps. Hugh was still in the lead and asked Pirate to jump over a paling. The gelding landed safely and slid down the bank to the bottom. Edward, urging Ardlackan Lass into a gallop, failed to slow sufficiently to take the fence and ran into the crowd. Yells and screams rose from frightened people as Edward emerged the other side and swung the mare back to face the obstacle again. This time she popped over it without hesitation and followed the gelding across the bottom of the quarry.

"Well, ma'am, your husband is a goer, I'll say that for the man." The bloodshot eyes of Mick Maguire peered at Rosalind. He was sitting on a heavy black cob. "He doesn't give up easily, not even when he knows he's beaten."

Frank frowned at him and jumped onto the grass. "What do you want, Maguire? You leave Mrs Thorton alone, do you hear me?"

Maguire ignored him and pressed his horse closer to the door of the brougham, taking out a bent cigarette from his jacket pocket and placing it between his purple lips.

Rosalind felt tempted to close the carriage door and lock him out. He struck a match and lit the cigarette, pulling on it and coughing loudly before spitting on the grass. She shrank back.

"On your way." Frank walked towards him.

Maguire shrugged and coughed again. "All right, man. No need to be like that. I'm not going to harm her or the child. I'm passing the time of day, that's all… trying to be civil. Where's the harm in that?"

"Go and be civil somewhere else." Frank narrowed his eyes.

Maguire raised his bowler hat to Rosalind. "Good day to you. I'll be on my way so, but I hope you're keeping well and Miss Harriet too."

Frank leaned against the carriage and tilted his head in the direction of the quarry. "You'll miss the finish if you don't get a move on. I hear you've got a tidy sum riding on Mr Hugh."

Maguire uttered a hoarse bark. "Who told you that? As if I'd share that sort of information with you. If my man wins, you'd be down to the public house to claim a free drink off me. You'd be my friend then, all right. Turn up your nose at me and drive me off the property one day and rub shoulders with me the next."

Rosalind shot a quick look at Frank, who shook his head.

Maguire kicked the cob into a trot, calling over his shoulder, "I'll be going, so. I need to keep an eye on my wager." The horse broke into a canter as his rider steered him towards the stone wall and, jumping neatly over it, went on up the hill towards the wood.

"Thank you," Rosalind said to Frank. "I don't know why that man likes to harass me."

"I had to chase him off the gallops too. I don't trust him. He's a slippery snake at best. I think we should head back so that we're there at the finish. The riders will be in the woods now and it won't take them long to reach the other side near Ardlackan House. Then it's only half a mile down the lane towards the Lodge. We'll go back there now and be waiting for the master and the Lass when they arrive in front." He called to Romeo, who was munching contentedly on fresh spring grass at the side of the road.

"Frank knows that Papa will win. He knows Ardlackan Lass is the fastest horse," Harriet said, chewing one of her nails and peering at it.

"I hope so. Don't do that, please. It's so unladylike."

Harriet's wide mouth stretched into a grin. "If I'd been born a boy, I would inherit the stables and Papa's horses if he breaks his neck."

"Harriet! How can you say such a thing!"

"I'm joking. Why do you take me so seriously? Papa will win. He's a good rider. The best in Wexford county. And besides, I've got my penny on him and, if he wins, Sadie is going to give me another one."

Rosalind decided not to continue this line of conversation. Harriet could be argumentative and enjoyed teasing.

Frank urged Romeo on up the hill, the horse slowly moving forward, reluctant to leave the rich grass. Harriet settled down and rested her head against Rosalind's shoulder in her affectionate way. Rosalind yawned as the motion of the carriage soothed her, glancing out of the window.

It was then that she saw Major Langstown on his grey mare galloping towards them with a look of alarm on his florid features.

Chapter Twenty-Four

"A bad fall," the major panted. "A rush of men came swarming at him. Supporters of Hugh, I've no doubt."

"Where is he?" Rosalind reached for Harriet as her daughter's face turned pale.

"Someone had a pony carriage nearby and they lifted him into it. I've sent a man to fetch Dr Richards."

His words spun in Rosalind's head. A bad fall. Rush of men. Dr. Richards.

Frank appeared at her elbow and he walked Harriet away, his arm round her shoulders.

"But how… how did it happen?" Rosalind stammered.

The major frowned. "I saw a man deliberately run in front of the mare. A scoundrel who disappeared back into the crowd as quickly as he came out of it. The horse reared in fright and Edward fell off backwards over her tail. I think one of her hind hooves caught him on the side of the head as he went down." He lowered his voice, his pale blue eyes full of sympathy. "I'm sorry, my dear. I hate to be the bearer of bad tidings."

Rosalind reached out to hold onto the wheel of the brougham, her chest tight and painful. "Is he… is he…"

The major shook his head. "He's unconscious but Hugh said he was still breathing before I left to find you."

"I'll have to go to him immediately. Where… did you say?"

"The house… home. That's where they're taking him. Try not to worry. Edward's a strong young man."

Frank persuaded Harriet to get back into the carriage and he climbed up on the driver's seat and picked up the reins.

"Thank you, Major, for coming so quickly," Rosalind said. "We'll go back to the house now."

The older man helped her into the brougham. "I'll ride with you." He clambered back onto his mare and pushed her into a trot to keep up as Romeo was urged forward by Frank.

Harriet stared out of the window, avoiding Rosalind's eyes; her fingers clasped together in her lap and her lips pressed into a tight, thin line.

Sadie waited on the steps at the front door as the brougham approached the house and Rosalind searched the maid's face. She looked composed. Had she good news? Was he still alive?

Frank stepped over to open the door and helped Rosalind out, his hand reassuringly warm through her glove. He turned to Harriet and caught her round the waist and lifted her down.

"Oh, Frank!" Rosalind said. "What if…? What if he's…?"

"Please God he won't be. Go on inside and find him. I'll put the horse back in the stable and go to the kitchen. If you need me, that's where I'll be. I'll wait in the kitchen for news. If you need anything…"

"Yes, yes, thank you."

Sadie said, "Don't worry, ma'am, he's in bed upstairs now and Dr Richards is on his way."

Major Langstown handed his mare to Peter, who'd appeared from behind the laurels and was muttering something about coming back in the pony carriage with the master. "As white as a sheet, he was, and blood streaming from his head." He made the sign of the cross. "Sure, we thought he was done for."

"Yes, that's enough," the major muttered. "Now hold your tongue and take my mare round to the stable yard and rub her down." He turned away, took Rosalind's arm and led her to the steps. "We don't want that young rascal making up stories that might not be true."

Harriet trailed behind them into the hall, her head lowered as she wiped away tears with the back of her hand. Rosalind put her arm round her and gave her a hug.

Major Langstown said he would wait downstairs and keep an eye out for the doctor.

Rosalind's heart pounded again and nausea rose from her stomach, a bitter taste in her mouth. She summoned a smile for her daughter. "Perhaps you'd better go to your bedroom and change, my love."

"No, I want to see Papa. I want to see if he's alive."

"Of course he'll be alive."

"How do you know?" She burst into loud sobs and Sadie, who'd followed at a discreet distance behind them, hurried to her and took her in her arms. Harriet cried against her shoulder while Rosalind stroked the girl's hair.

As they climbed the staircase, a portrait on the wall regarded them. Edward's sister, Clara. An enigmatic expression on her young face, her eyes seeming to follow Rosalind. Only six years old when she was taken from this world.

Rosalind led Harriet into the bedroom.

Edward lay back against the pillows, his face ashen and a red gash on the left side of his head, snaking over his brow and crusted with blood. His eyes turned towards them as they approached but flicked away again as if he didn't recognize them.

Rosalind held Harriet back as she strained to throw herself onto the bed. "No, darling, wait here. Don't confuse him." She turned to Edward and said softly, "How do you feel?"

He blinked at her. "My head hurts... such pain. Where have you been? What took you so long?"

"We came as fast as we could."

"Where have you been? Where's Mama? I've been lying here in agony. What happened to me?"

"The major said you had a fall... thrown off the mare when she reared up."

"Reared up? I... I don't remember."

"He said... he said someone... he said someone ran out in front of you and frightened the mare."

"No, I don't think that..." Edward winced with pain. "I can't remember. My head is so sore. It's throbbing."

Rosalind sat on the edge of the bed and held his hand. "Don't think about that now, dearest. Try to rest. The major has sent for Dr Richards and he'll be here shortly. Sadie, could you fetch a basin of warm water and a flannel, please. I'll bathe his head."

The maid moved across the rug and out of the door.

Harriet shouted, "We'll find out who did it, Papa! We'll find out and we'll... we'll throw him in jail."

"Horsewhip him," the major barked from the doorway. "We'll make him regret this, you mark my words. The doctor is here now."

Rosalind heard the sound of wheels and she went to the open sash window that looked out over the gravel sweep. Hugh and Beatrice had arrived with Dr Richards, his bald head gleaming in the sunlight as he stepped down and reached for his bag.

"The doctor has arrived." She turned to Edward. "He'll soon have you well again."

Edward closed his eyes and shrank back into the pillows. "My head. My head hurts... can't you understand me? Can't you hear me? How can I be well if I can't even sit up? Where is Mama? For heaven's sake, woman, go and get me a brandy before I pass out!" He let out a groan.

"I'll go," Major Langstown said.

"No, thank you, I'll get him a small glass. What harm can it do? You stay here until the doctor arrives. Harriet, come with me."

"But Mama…"

"Come with me."

The girl followed her to the door, stopping to glance back at the moaning invalid on the bed. Rosalind gestured towards the corridor.

"Will he die?" Harriet whispered, when the door shut behind them. "He looks so pale and sick. And all the blood on his head, did you see all the blood?"

"Yes, but I will wipe that away. Where is your grandmother?"

Gertrude appeared from her bedroom on the left. She frowned when she saw Rosalind and Harriet.

"Gertrude, Edward's been injured. Haven't you been told?"

"Of course I was told. I've been searching for my smelling salts. I thought they might bring the poor boy back to consciousness. Have you seen him?"

"Yes. He's awake now and looking for brandy. Dr Richards has just arrived with Hugh and Beatrice."

"Go and get the brandy. I'll keep the child here."

Harriet opened her mouth to object but Rosalind squeezed her arm and whispered, "You help Grandmama, my dear. You can fetch anything she needs."

At least Gertrude would prevent her climbing on the bed and aggravating her father who, still dazed from the fall, was in a difficult mood. His mother would know how to handle him and keep Harriet quiet.

Rosalind hurried down the stairs as Sadie opened the front door and curtsied at Hugh and Beatrice.

"Oh Ros," Beatrice cried. "How is poor Edward? Hugh told me what happened. So unfortunate. The mare took fright at the crowd by the timber fence out of the wood." She pulled off her gloves. "A horrible accident."

Hugh stood looking down at Rosalind, a guarded expression in his eyes. "One of the men by the fence had a large dog on a lead and perhaps that frightened the mare," he murmured.

"Oh, but Major Langstown said... he said that a man deliberately ran at the mare."

"Did he indeed? Well, I was riding just behind Edward at the time and I didn't see a man do that. I saw a dog barking and straining on a leash. It was an accident. An unfortunate accident but that was all it was. The major's eyesight isn't the best, is it, Beatrice?"

"It's not, to be sure. He sees more than we do, that's for certain, and he's well able to embellish the truth." She added, "Hugh would have seen a man running out. If he says there was no such man, I believe him."

Rosalind blushed. "Oh, I didn't mean... I didn't doubt you... not for one moment. It's just not what I heard from Major Langstown but perhaps he was mistaken."

"He was mistaken," Hugh said. "Now where are you hurrying off to and how is the unlucky patient? Poor fellow, when he was riding so well."

"He's asking for brandy and I was on my way to fetch him a glass when you arrived."

Hugh's eyes flicked towards his wife. "Calling for brandy, is he? He can't be too bad. We'll come with you to the drawing room and help fill the glasses. We're all in need of a drink after what happened."

Rosalind led the way and held open the door. It was strange that Hugh's version of events differed from the major's but perhaps he and Beatrice were right. Perhaps Major Langstown had imagined the man running out. He'd said it happened in a flash but maybe it hadn't taken place at all. She opened the cabinet and took out a cut glass decanter.

"I'll have a brandy," Hugh said, standing behind her. "And my beautiful wife will have a sherry, won't you, my love?"

Beatrice took the decanter from Rosalind. "You're very pale. I think you're still suffering from shock. You sit here and Hugh will pour us both a brandy. We need more than sherry today."

Rosalind did as she was told and sank down on the sofa. The strength ebbed from her legs and her hands trembled. She closed her eyes and prayed that she wasn't going to faint. Dr Richards had climbed the stairs to greet Gertrude on the landing. He would be examining Edward now. She would have to take the doctor aside when he came down and ask his opinion. What if Edward's injuries were more serious? What if there was internal bleeding? A haemorrhage?

Beatrice pushed a glass into Rosalind's frozen fingers. "Take a sip, take a sip. This will give you strength and courage."

Rosalind felt the liquid burn the back of her throat. She pulled a face. "I don't like brandy."

"Drink it," Hugh urged. "Swallow it down and you'll feel better."

"Perhaps I should go upstairs to Edward. He seems confused... needs me..."

"Edward will be up and about again before you know it," he said. "Only a little tumble over the mare's tail. His pride is more injured than anything else."

Rosalind lifted the glass and swallowed another mouthful.

Hugh leaned on the mantelpiece. "His pride took a tumble. He won't be pleased when he hears that I rode on and finished the race. That will hurt him more than a kick on the head, I can tell you."

"Hugh, please don't gloat. Now is not the time." Beatrice shook her head at him. "We can sort everything out later. Plenty of time for that."

"Plenty of time for what?" Rosalind asked. "What are you talking about?"

"Why, the wager, of course," Hugh said. "Edward lost the bet... but Beatrice is correct. This isn't the time or the place to discuss such a thing. It can wait until Edward has recovered."

The brandy warmed Rosalind, slowing her pulse rate and she permitted Beatrice to pour a little more into her glass. "I hope it wasn't too much money. Edward promised me..."

Beatrice dropped her voice. "It wasn't money, dear Ros. Not money. Don't worry. It was just a little agreement... the tiniest agreement but we'll discuss it later when Edward has recovered."

The door swung open and Harriet ran in. "Mama, Mama, can you come with the brandy? Papa is shouting for it and Dr Richards is arguing with Grandmama. He's asking for blankets and hot water bottles... and something called camp fire. She's getting very cross with him."

"Camphor." Rosalind rose to her feet. "Very well, my love, I'll come now."

Beatrice handed her a heavy crystal glass filled with the amber liquid. "For your husband. Poor lamb, it sounds like he needs it."

Chapter Twenty-Five

Dust rose like a cloak behind Ben's jeep, shrouding the overgrown hedgerows where stalks of cow parsley and grass withered in the heat.

"You said you'd tell me about your grandmother," I reminded him, winding up the window. "Kitty O'Rafferty's cottage is down this hill and the first entrance on the right... on the edge of the sea. Please tell me about your grandmother... why did she persuade you to come here?"

Ben kept his eyes on the narrow lane ahead as the ocean swept into view, a vivid blue against jagged rocks. "Are you sure this is the correct laneway? I hope we don't end up underwater." He winked at me. "Just kidding."

"Hey, watch out! This bend ahead..." Briars in low grass grabbed at the side of the vehicle.

Ben laughed, his dark eyes dancing, and swung the steering wheel to the right. A different young man to the one I'd met at the end of June; no longer reticent and withdrawn. Was it because I now knew who he was? It must have been a relief to drop the pretence.

"Gran knew I was at a loose end... that I'd dropped out of college, so she suggested I might like to do a bit of research

209

for her. She said there was a mystery about her grandmother Harriet because she never talked about her past, but once Harriet mentioned that she might have killed her father. Just like that, just the once, as if she didn't really know."

"Where did Harriet live?"

"She lived in London most of her life and Gran said she was an interesting woman, tall and full of energy. She loved animals, especially horses. My grandmother likes horses, was brought up in the country and used to ride when she was young."

Instinctively, I reached for my notebook and took a pencil out of my handbag. "And Harriet never mentioned her mother? She never mentioned Rosalind?"

Ben slowed the jeep at a bend in the lane. "Never. It was like Rosalind didn't exist. Is that the house?" He pointed ahead.

"High gate pillars with a red letter box... yes, look there's the letter box. So when was your grandmother born?"

"In 1943 during the Second World War. She was a war baby and her father was a pilot in the RAF. He survived but was captured by the Germans after his plane went down near Frankfurt."

"And your gran knew Harriet well?"

"Yeah, I think so. She said Harriet was good fun and used to write imaginative short stories for her grandchildren but she never talked about her youth. She was a suffragette and she married a member of parliament."

"A campaigner for women to have the right to vote? That's interesting. Did she get arrested?"

"Several times. She chained herself to railings and... do you remember reading about several hundred women who marched on Buckingham Palace in 1914? Yes? Well, Harriet was one of those. Emmeline Pankhurst led a delegation to talk to the King. Quite a number of them were arrested by police before they got as far as the palace." His eyes lit up. "They were brave women in those days. Would you do that now?"

"I don't know. If I felt strongly enough about social change, I'd like to think I would but life is easier for us… though not for all women, of course. There are countries where women still remain downtrodden. What made Harriet think she'd killed her father? Did she ever say?"

"Gran told me that Harriet left her the book of riddles when she died. She left it in an envelope with Gran's name on it and a note asking her to find out what happened. Harriet explained that she'd always meant to return to Ireland… to Wexford, but never got around to it."

"So that's why your grandmother asked you to do this. Turn right, this must be the house."

"If only Harriet had talked about it to Gran before she died, but she didn't say a word. Gran came here but she couldn't find out anything. She met Daphne and Charles but they didn't know what happened and were reluctant to discuss family history."

The jeep rattled over a cattle grid and came to a halt in front of a two-storey house with a bright red front door.

Two black and tan dachshunds shot across the gravel, barking as they leaped up and down. I was glad that I'd decided to leave Archie with Daphne.

Ben pushed the door of the jeep open, turning to look at me. "She wasn't called Harriet, though. She had a nickname, I suppose common in those days… everyone always called her Maud."

Maud.

Harriet was called Maud. Interesting and perhaps significant. Could she have been named after the Maud in Tennyson's poem? Maud the love of the poor protagonist's life. I'd read the lyrical verses many times since first finding the lines hidden in the stud book:

Come into the garden, Maud,
For the black bat, night, has flown,
Come into the garden, Maud,
I am here at the gate alone...

Lines of poetry that resonated in people's minds in the late-nineteenth century because they'd been set to music and sung in drawing rooms around the country. *Maud and Other Poems* was Lord Tennyson's first collection published after he became Poet Laureate in 1850.

A small woman with white fluffy hair appeared round the side of the stone cottage and raised a hand in salute.

"That's her," I said. "She's eighty-four but looks much younger."

Kitty O'Rafferty advanced and held out a soft white hand decorated with turquoise nail varnish and a large silver ring set with a turquoise stone. "Hello, hello! So glad you managed to find me. Many don't, you know, and as for the couriers, well they haven't got a clue, spend hours driving around in circles. But you had no bother..."

"None at all." Ben stepped out and shook her hand. "What a wonderful view of the sea from your garden! A beautiful place to live."

She moved round the front of the jeep and grasped my hand. "Welcome to Seal Rock. The view is beautiful, of course, but you should see this place in winter. Oh my goodness, the waves almost reach my lawn. See that damage to the stone wall down there?"

We turned to look.

"That was caused by last year's storms. I thought my little cottage was going to be washed away." She shushed the little dogs that continued to hurl themselves at her legs, stooping to pick both up and tucking each one under an arm. "Excuse the boys.

They rarely see anyone so they get over-excited."

I reached out to stroke the nearest dachshund, which wriggled and licked my hand. "We don't want to take up too much of your time. Perhaps we should go inside." I remembered Tiffany telling me that the retired librarian was a keen talker and, once she got going, was difficult to stop.

She led us to her study, a room with a plate glass window looking out on the lawn that sloped away to the stone boundary above the cliff. Books lined all four walls and sat on shelves over the door and window. Rows and rows of hardbacks displayed Kitty's diverse interests from architecture and history to cooking and knitting. A basket with balls of bright pink wool lay on the wooden floor beside her desk.

She sat in an armchair and pointed towards the sofa. "Take a seat. Would you like tea?"

"No, thank you. We've just had lunch," I said. "We're interested in anything you have to tell us about Frank O'Rafferty and the Thornton family of Ardlackan. It's a village about an hour away from here. Have you been there?"

She got to her feet and hurried to a pile of shoeboxes in the corner, selecting a bright green one and returning to her chair with the agility of a younger person. "Oh yes, indeed I have. Ardlackan was the school where my ancestor taught but you know that, of course. Her name was Johanna O'Rafferty and the primary school was in the village… still open now and thriving. They had an exhibition there to celebrate its one hundred and fiftieth year. I was asked to contribute letters and deliver a speech about its history. I still have the details here… looked them up for you. I divided this shoebox into decades so it's the 1890s you're interested in, isn't it?" She flicked through the letters stacked inside. "Here we are… 1890. These are letters from the schoolmistress's many siblings and children. Her children lived all over the world in the end… eight of them. Two daughters stayed at home but most of the sons left. I suppose because there wasn't anything for them to do in those days and they were poor and in need of work… couldn't have been easy for them all."

I reached out my hand. "May I have a look?"

She clutched the shoebox to her chest. "I'll read out anything interesting. I know some of them almost off by heart after my talk to the schoolchildren and parents."

Ben was staring out of the window at the glittering water. I could imagine how cold and windswept the cottage would be in winter; how isolated. Kitty lived a lonely life with her books and her two little dogs, which had now curled up together on a large cushion under the window and were snoring softly.

Tiffany was right about this woman being reluctant to part with her letters.

"Perhaps I could have a photocopy or you could scan the letters for me?" I asked.

She shook her head. "I don't have a photocopier or a computer. I write everything down in an old-fashioned notebook. My relations think I'm crazy. They don't share my enthusiasm for the past."

"Tiffany told me you were a librarian in London."

"Years ago. I retired over twenty years ago. Books have always been my first love."

I shifted my weight on the sofa and looked at Ben.

He cleared his throat. "We're interested in … in anything to do with Rosalind and Harriet Thornton."

"Ah, yes, and the death of Edward."

I opened my notebook and clicked the end of my biro.

"Yes, the murder of Edward Thornton but also anything about the two women. Where did they go? Any details about them?" Ben asked encouragingly.

"Murder, you think? I don't know if it was a killing. The Thorntons claimed it was an accident." She placed the shoebox

214

on her lap. "A journalist came here. I didn't take to her at all, I'm sorry to say. She asked me all sorts of silly questions about Frank O'Rafferty... thought he might've had something to do with it and insisted it was a murder. So ridiculous. I know he didn't. He would never do such a thing." She spoke as if he was still alive and this made me feel uneasy. Perhaps it was because she was used to reading about these family ancestors in the present tense in intimate correspondence, bringing them to life. I'd felt that way in the National Library when reading through the old newspapers about people long dead. The journalism seemed vivid and immediate.

I thought of Tiffany with her stubborn chin and determination. No, she wouldn't hit it off with Kitty O'Rafferty. They were opposites. I would need to be patient in order to extract information from this eccentric woman and patience was not Tiffany's strongest characteristic.

A surge of triumph swelled inside me but I tried to repress it. Kitty might not take to me either; she might not appreciate my bossy teacher's tone, as my mother called it. I would do well to curb any self-satisfaction I might feel and let Ben ask the questions. Kitty appeared to have taken to him and was keeping her eyes fixed on his face, ignoring me.

"I'm sure he wouldn't have killed anyone," Ben replied. "He was the coachman at Ardlackan Lodge, wasn't he?"

"Coachman and head lad in the racing stables. He was wonderful with the horses, so gentle and kind to them. His mother wrote that the horses loved him."

"Did he ever fall out with Edward? Any evidence of that?"

"Oh, perhaps the occasional argument," Kitty ran her finger along the top of an envelope. "They had disputes about the horses of course, but that's only natural."

"Any rows about Rosalind?" The question sprang out of my mouth before I could stop it.

Kitty's pale blue eyes flicked to me. "Why do you ask that?"

"Tiffany said… well, perhaps it's just hearsay."

She rolled her eyes. "Just nonsense. The two men knew each other well… played together as boys but Frank knew his place. That's why he stayed on afterwards."

"Afterwards… after what?" I asked.

"After the master died, of course." Her voice prickled with irritation. "Frank went on working for Edward's mother, Gertrude Thornton, and he continued to train the horses for Hugh. Hugh owned most of them anyway. He was the one with a bit of money in that family." She looked at Ben.

"And where did Frank go after that?" he asked.

"America. Frank wasn't much of a letter writer but he had an aunt in Richmond and she took him in. Horse racing was popular back then in Virginia so that would have suited Frank. He found work training thoroughbreds over there. I know that because his cousin Alfie… I think he was a cousin… Alfie wrote letters to Johanna from England and also kept in touch with the aunt in Richmond. That's how I know she was a teacher too and her letters were most interesting about the education system in the States compared to Ireland in the late nineteenth century…"

I interrupted her to head off a looming and possibly lengthy diversion. "That's fascinating about Frank and the horses. Did he know Rosalind Thornton?"

Suspicion in her clear eyes. "Of course he did. He taught her to ride on the master's orders… but nothing more than that. Not at all what that journalist with her bad mind implied… and little Miss Harriet too, Frank taught her to ride as well. I call her Miss Harriet because that's how she was described in the letters, you understand. That's how I see her… Harriet, I should say, but… isn't she the one you're interested in?"

"Yes." Ben frowned at me, a warning to remain silent and not alienate our host. "We're interested in both Harriet and her mother. Did Johanna O'Rafferty keep a diary of her teaching days?"

"She did. She was a keen writer, as I may have mentioned. I learnt a lot about the teaching methods… quite basic in those days, of course. Reading, writing and arithmetic but she only taught boys. The girls' school was at the other end of the village and it's gone now. Demolished, I believe, in the early 1950s after a bad outbreak of tuberculosis. They built a modern school further down the road with better ventilation and heating. Listen to this from 1880." She turned a few pages and read aloud,

> *"My boys are a mixed bunch, God help them, some so poor that they don't even have boots and their feet are blue with the cold in winter when the frost is sparkling on the grass outside."*

"Poor children," I murmured.

"Yes, but Rosalind Thornton was kind enough to donate footwear. When she married Edward in 1882, she made a present of boots to all of the village children and continued to do so every year after that. Wasn't that nice of her?"

Ben and I murmured agreement.

"She was a wealthy lady when she first arrived from London," Kitty continued, "and I suppose she felt sorry for the poor children. Boots for every boy in the school. Johanna O'Rafferty was grateful and wrote to thank her. That's mentioned in her diary."

Kitty leaned back in her chair and lapsed into a silence, perhaps carried away by the generosity of the rich English lady.

I didn't dare disturb her thoughts.

Ben pushed his fingertips together and waited until she looked up at him. He asked, "Did Mrs O'Rafferty mention Edward in her diary or letters? You have some of her letters, I presume?"

"Yes, I do. They were collected together by one of her daughters after her mother died. It's thanks to her that I know so much about my family. She would have made a good librarian, that's evident from the way she collected and managed the boxes of letters and diaries for the whole family. I'm hoping that the National Archives will take the originals as my nephews and nieces show no interest. No one shows interest, I suppose, in family history until they reach middle age. And even then..." She spread her hands and grimaced. "Even then some never do. Some burn the lot. Imagine!"

"Terrible," I agreed. "All that history going up in smoke."

"Fiona is a history teacher," Ben added.

Kitty turned to me with more warmth in her eyes. "Oh, why didn't you say? I presumed you were another journalist like that other one. Tiffany Ryan. What a charlatan! She thought Frank was a murderer and expected me to hand over letters about him. As if I would! As if I'd encourage that TV series maligning him... maligning my family. A liar and a charlatan."

I tried not to smile. How would Kitty react if I informed her that Tiffany Ryan, liar and charlatan, had also made off with my husband? Would she throw her arms in the air in disgust? I decided not to give her the opportunity and raised my eyebrows at Ben to encourage him.

He cleared his throat again, obviously a habit when he was apprehensive. "I've met Tiffany and she's a forceful woman, that's for sure. She's a little hasty at jumping to conclusions and upset Daphne Thornton."

"Poor Daphne, I can sympathize. I know her. I met her at an art exhibition last year. Bought one of her paintings actually because it resonated with me. Would you like to see it?"

Before we could answer, Kitty trotted from the room and returned with an unframed oil on canvas and held it up with a flourish. "Here you are. What do you think?"

We examined the painting in silence. And astonishment. I'd expected a sea view with pinks and tufts of spiky grass on a cliff edge or bright trawlers bobbing against each other along the pier but this was different. So different that I could feel the hair rising on the back of my neck and a sudden chill in the sunlit room.

Dark trees lined a path in a wood and a figure, a woman wearing a long white dress with light brown hair pinned up, hurried between the pines towards a light in the distance.

"What do you think? I love it. Such atmosphere, such mystery. Where do you think she's going? Who is she going to meet?" Kitty leaned the painting against the armchair and chuckled. "You both look surprised."

"It's unusual... for Daphne," Ben said. "When did you buy this painting? Last year, did you say?"

"Last year at the exhibition, yes. As soon as I saw it, I thought of Rosalind Thornton, poor lady. Her husband dying like that. It must have driven her crazy. Poor tragic young woman. I expect that was why she had to go away... to be sent away."

I couldn't restrain myself and blurted out, "Sent away? What do you mean?"

A guarded look crept across Kitty's soft features. "You don't know what happened, do you?"

"No." Ben narrowed his dark eyes at me, urging me to keep quiet. "Where was she sent?"

Kitty hesitated and turned more pages of letters, smoothing the paper with the tips of her fingers, a glitter of excitement in her eyes. She was a good actor, I decided. She could be scolding and uncooperative one minute and consumed with the enthusiasm of a gossip the next. Perhaps she liked to entertain her visitors, playing them along, capturing their attention.

"I expect it was an asylum in Dublin. No one really knows."

I gasped. "An asylum. Are you telling us that she was... insane?"

"Johanna O'Rafferty wrote about it in her diary but not in her letters. That would have been unsuitable for a letter, I imagine, in those days. Just a quick paragraph in her journal. Frank told his mother that the mistress was so devastated that she took to her bed and wouldn't leave it for weeks on end. She must have slipped into a depression and never come out of it. Johanna sounded so sorry for her. She'd always liked her because of the boots."

"What happened to Harriet and the baby boy?" Ben asked while I was trying to absorb this bombshell.

"They might have gone to live with a relation, I suppose. Perhaps in Dublin or London, who knows? There was no mention of them, no mention at all. I would imagine that the whole episode was hushed up for the sake of decency. A death in the family in suspicious circumstances and then the poor widow losing her mind. It's not something that would have been talked about in those days. Quite a large skeleton rattling in the cupboard, I would say. I didn't tell Tiffany Ryan this so if you don't mind…"

"We won't say a word to her," I assured her and scribbled in my notebook. Aunt Catherine in London. Would Harriet and Ivor have gone to her? I underlined Catherine's name and put a question mark in the margin. I would follow that up.

Harriet's drawing in her book surfaced in my mind. The woman in the tower. A prisoner like The Lady of Shalott. Was that poor Rosalind locked away somewhere?

"Gertrude would probably have sent the children away," Kitty said. "I don't think she was fond of them, as far as I can make out. She doted on her son and on her daughter who died young. She lost them both… both her children dead, it doesn't bear thinking about."

"Don't you think that should have made her appreciate her grandchilden though?" I remembered the headstone in the church graveyard. "Why would she want to send them away?"

Kitty shrugged. "A difficult woman, apparently. So, Frank O'Rafferty, kind man that he was... I say that even though he is an ancestor of mine... he stayed with her at Ardlackan Lodge for another ten years and trained the horses there for Hugh Thornton the cousin. Frank was there to tend to her needs, drive the old lady around in the carriage and take her to visit her friends. He remained with her until the early 1900s when he departed for America, as so many did in those days. He was a kind soul, was Frank." She closed the shoebox on her knees with an air of satisfaction, waving her hand towards the pile in the corner. "I have plenty more work ahead of me; months of it... there are letters and cards in those boxes that haven't been read for more than a century. I've only got to the 1920s."

It appeared that our interview with Kitty was over but I would have to mention the intimidating man Aunt Catherine wrote about; the one Rosalind and Harriet had come across on the way to Ardlackan House.

"Ms O'Rafferty..."

"Call me Kitty. Everyone does."

"Kitty, have you ever heard of a man called Maguire who used to hang around racing stables? He's mentioned in another letter I saw."

"No, I can't say I have."

"I wondered if he had a connection with gamblers... men who might influence Edward Thornton... bribe him perhaps, if he had debts."

She moved towards the door. "No, I know nothing about him. There wasn't much about racing in these letters and diaries. Mostly family matters, personal information, that's all."

"All right, thank you." I got to my feet. "If you discover anything else relevant, anything about Frank or Rosalind or the... Edward's unfortunate death in the woods, would you let us know? You have my phone number."

Kitty reached for the doorknob. "Of course, dear. If I find anything useful, I'll give you a call."

Chapter Twenty-Six

"What do you think?" I asked Ben as he reversed the jeep away from the house. "Was she telling the whole truth?"

"Why wouldn't she tell the truth?"

"If Frank wasn't as wonderful as she made out... she might try to cover that up. If he'd been involved with Edward's death or had an affair with Rosalind. She would hardly tell us that."

He drove out of the gate and turned left. "Wouldn't she? It was a long time ago and nobody would care nowadays."

"I think someone like her would. She spoke as if Frank was still alive, still part of her family and I think she'd try to protect him if there was something in the letters that implicated..." My mobile rang, vibrating on my knee. "She might have let something slip to Tiffany by accident and that would make her more careful about what she said to us. I don't like to think that Rosalind ended up in a lunatic asylum. Could that really have been the case?"

I glimpsed the name of the caller on the screen of my phone. My heart lurched painfully against my ribs. Dominic.

The jeep bumped over stones on the lane as the shrill ringing persisted.

"Aren't you going to answer that?" Ben asked.

I tapped the button. "Hello."

"Fiona… you've got to help me!" I hadn't heard Dominic's voice for so long that I almost didn't recognize it, sounding more high-pitched than usual.

"Hello, Dominic. What's wrong?"

Ben shot me a look and his eyebrows rose.

"Fi, something terrible… Tiffany and me, we've had a row… a terrible row and she's…" Were those really sobs breaking his voice?

"Stop, stop please," I said to Ben. "I'll get out and walk for a bit."

He slowed the jeep to a halt. I pushed open the door and climbed out, shutting it behind me and moving back down the lane towards Kitty O'Rafferty's house.

"Fi, are you still there? You've got to help me."

"Yes, yes, I am. What's happened?"

His tone was accusing. "This is your fault. You told her. You told Tiffany you're my wife."

"What? But I am or have you forgotten? You should have told her."

"I would have, if only you'd given me a chance. I would have eventually. Now she says it's all over… she's thrown me out. I'm homeless, so you're going to have to help me. Your father's house… I can go there."

My voice rose. "No, you can't. The house is for sale. I gave the keys to the estate agent."

"But you have other keys. You must have. I've nowhere else to go."

"No, Dominic, no! Not my father's house."

"I've a right. You know I have. I used to live there with you for months before he died. I must have a legal right."

"A buyer has put in an offer for it. You can't move back in."

The sobs burst out and I held the phone away. What could

I do? Dominic was always prone to dramatics, especially if he thought I wasn't going to help him. After a few seconds, he grew silent. I put the mobile back to my ear. "Dominic?"

"You need to do something." He sounded calmer. "I can't live on the streets. How would you like that? Can't I come down to Ardlackan? Daphne must have plenty of rooms. She could put me up till I find somewhere else. Just for a few days? Will you ask her? You shouldn't have told Tiffany about me. This is your fault."

I took a deep breath and let the air out through clenched teeth. "All right, all right. I'll talk to Daphne and I'll call you back."

Without even thanking me, he muttered something about ringing me again the next day and was gone. I stood in the dusty lane, staring at the sea, feeling an emotional shift inside me.

Did I want Dominic back? Did I want him moaning and following me round at Ardlackan? No, I did not. Jessica had been right to send me here. I'd been so engrossed with Rosalind and my research that I hadn't thought about my husband, my ex-husband, for at least two weeks.

Ben raised his eyebrows when I returned to the jeep.

"My ex-husband. Tiffany has kicked him out." I wouldn't go into details until I'd thought this through.

"Okay," Ben said. "Shall we go to O'Mahony's pub in Ardlackan village for a quick drink and compare notes?"

I agreed and he drove on.

He parked outside the front door of the pub and we found an empty table beside the window. The room was quiet and dark, only a handful of people and a family with children sipping cola with straws.

I watched the light fading outside, the shadows deepening on the thatched roofs of the houses opposite; a pale pink glow seeping across the evening sky.

Ben placed a gin and tonic in front of me and grinned, a glint in his eyes. "Tell me, Tiffany kicked your husband out, did she? I can see why he's upset about that."

"It's not very funny because now he wants to come down here. I'm going to ask Daphne if she has a spare room. You might like to have him to stay in your apartment in the stable yard."

"No thanks. Have you seen my apartment? He'd need to be keen on wildlife to live with me. There are swallows nesting next door and house martins flying to the window where they have young under the eaves and as for the spiders and mice..."

I remembered the house martin flying into the room packed with boxes. A revelation, Daphne said. "Dominic has never lived in the country so I expect that might be a bit much for him. Perhaps I'll suggest the haunted floor above where I am."

"Why do you call it haunted?"

I sipped the gin and tonic, ice clinking in the bottom of the glass. "Jessica and I used to go up there as teenagers when it was dark. One night we heard noises like a door slamming and footsteps on the bare boards. That floor hasn't been used for generations but Charles stored boxes of stuff up there. It was built as a wing for servants and the kitchen was underneath in those days."

"Daphne never mentioned it to me," Ben replied, "but I believe she is often in another world."

"I sometimes wonder if she's as scatter-brained and vague as she likes us to think. It's a good way to avoid answering questions, isn't it? To pretend that she doesn't hear and then come out with something completely unrelated. Everyone puts it down to Daphne being absent-minded and she ends up never having to answer the question."

"I told you my grandmother got no information from her or from Charles about Harriet when she visited. Daphne gave her tea and biscuits while Charles watched the racing on television.

When he did actually speak to her, Charles claimed he knew nothing about his ancestors and had no interest in the past. I haven't mentioned Harriet's book to Daphne. Have you?"

"No, not yet. I was afraid she would take fright. I've got it here in my handbag." I put the book on the table and placed my finger on a drawing dated April 1891. "It's difficult to know how much is in the girl's imagination and how much actually took place. An eight-year-old might dream up a lot more than the facts happening in front of her. See this drawing called *The Match between Papa and Cousin Hugh*. Her horses are good... I mean they really look like horses. There's one of a man falling off with *Poor Papa* written underneath. It looks like a competition of some kind."

Ben glanced where I pointed. "Her father fell off? I think a match was a race between two horses, more common in those days than it is now. The owners put up the money and two or three horses took part for a simple wager."

"If I claimed my horse was faster than yours... that sort of thing? You'd challenge me to a match?"

"Yes, that's what it was like. They'd gallop across country in the early days and then on racecourses later on. I've seen a modern-day match between two top steeplechasers but it's quite rare nowadays."

"I expect Edward challenged or was challenged by Cousin Hugh to a match and he fell off. I wonder if he was injured." I looked again at Harriet's drawing. "This is like a jigsaw puzzle, isn't it? The riddles, the drawings, the letters... nothing really makes sense."

Ben frowned, vertical lines between his eyebrows. "The answer is somewhere. Someone had it in for Edward Thornton that night. But who?"

I flicked over a page of Harriet's book. "There's a riddle here called *The Tout*. Listen to this." I read it out to him.

My first is in greedy but not in race,
My second is in harm and also in face,
My third is in man but not in hate,
My fourth is in bet but not in fate,
My fifth is in luck but never in dread,
My last is in debt and writ in red,
My whole takes a risk I might end up dead.

Ben asked me to read it again line by line as he picked up my pen and a beer mat, writing down letters after each one. He crossed out a few and studied them again. "Not sure about the first line, but it's a *G*, *D* or *Y*. The second line is definitely *A*, the third is *M* or *N* and the fourth one is *B*. Then we have *L*, *U*, *C* or *K* followed by a *D* or an *E*. Why might he end up dead? Takes a risk?"

"Gamble," I said smiling. "Takes a risk… a gamble. That's the answer. Would it have been a deadly gamble? The race and her father falling off? Maybe she thought he could have died. Is that what she meant? But who is the tout… or what was the tout?"

"Nowadays it's someone who sells tickets for more than face value. Maybe the word meant something different back then. It doesn't sound like a nice person, judging by the words she used like greedy, harm, debt, dread, hate."

I peered at the page again. "She drew a stickman here in the corner with tiny writing underneath. It says *Maguire the tout.* He's standing by the carriage." I looked up. "Aunt Catherine's letter mentioned a man called Maguire. I think she wrote in November 1890 that Rosalind had told her that he had followed her. He must have been someone significant for Harriet to write a riddle about him."

Ben drained his beer. "A tout called Maguire and a gamble that could have proved fatal. What if this fellow Maguire, whoever he was, turned nasty and attacked Edward? Suppose Edward hadn't paid him the money he was owed."

"All so long ago," I said. "I'll have to look back through Aunt Catherine's letters. She lived in Hampstead in London."

"Would it be worth asking Daphne if she knows anything about Aunt Catherine?"

"I could try. If Rosalind disappeared after her husband's death, she would have fled to her aunt but now Kitty O'Rafferty says she was sent to an asylum. I wasn't expecting that. Suppose what she told us was true. If Rosalind had suffered some kind of breakdown after her husband's murder… if it really was a murder, the family might hush that up and tell their friends that she'd gone away. Perhaps she and the children vanished after her husband died and were found a few days later."

"That's possible. Rosalind goes away somewhere, possibly to Aunt Catherine in London, but suffers from mental health problems and ends up in an asylum." Ben looked out of the window at the setting sun slipping down the sky behind the lighthouse. "Victorian lunatic asylums had a terrible reputation."

"They didn't have our modern medication or psychology to help people in those days. Not all hospitals were bad but many people were locked away until they either recovered or died, and there were reports of various scandals in newspapers about women being certified falsely so that their husbands could snatch their possessions or inheritance. I remember researching it once and there was a new legal Act in Great Britain to make admission to asylums more difficult. The Lunacy Act of 1890, if I remember right."

"What a memory for dates and details. I envy you. I can hardly remember one day from the next."

I laughed. "I teach history, don't forget."

"It's like looking for a needle in a haystack… so long ago."

"She could also have been kept in a private house. Sometimes people with mental illness were locked upstairs in the family home where no one ever saw them except for the servants who looked after them."

I thought of the dark corridor in Ardlackan Lodge and the small bedrooms where light crept in through barred windows and dust gathered.

Was that why Jessica and I had found that floor so frightening? Had something terrible happened there decades before? While I didn't believe in ghosts, some historic houses I'd visited over the years had what my mother would call atmosphere.

"Aunt Catherine would have known what became of Rosalind, wouldn't she? Perhaps I should try to track down what happened to the aunt."

Ben picked up the beer mat and flipped it between his fingers. "If Frank O'Rafferty was involved with Rosalind... if he was responsible for Edward's death, would he have continued working at Ardlackan and training horses for Hugh Thornton?"

A good point. "He wouldn't. He'd have tried to get as far away as possible."

Ben dropped the beer mat and drummed his fingers on the table. "But even if it was Frank who was responsible or possibly Maguire, why did Harriet tell my grandmother that she might have killed her father?"

Chapter Twenty-Seven

A tang of salt hung on the warm April air and primroses peeped at the riders from the banks of the lane as the horses ambled past. Rosalind couldn't resist climbing down from Romeo and asking Frank to hold the reins while she stepped over to breathe in their sweet scent.

"Mama, what are you doing?" Harriet demanded, obviously restless to reach the beach. "Please let's ride on. They're only flowers."

"Only flowers! Listen to the girl!" Frank exclaimed. "Don't you realize, young lady, how much your mama loves plants? She loves them as much as you love that fat little pony."

"He's not fat," Harriet replied with a glower. "I wish you wouldn't insult him like that. And how can flowers compare with a pony? Bumblebee is a real live creature, not like those silly things." She clicked with her tongue. "I'm going to the beach and you can follow. I'm longing to gallop."

Frank's eyes danced with amusement when he jumped down from Sally, Edward's mare, to help Rosalind back onto the sidesaddle. Romeo stood patiently, nibbling at young hawthorn leaves at the side of the lane.

"She's a wild one, your daughter," Frank said.

Harriet turned to scowl at him, in a petulant mood because she didn't want her parents to go away. Rosalind was well aware of that and had tried to reason with her daughter earlier and explain how a visit to Auteuil Racecourse, in the Bois de Boulogne area on the west side of Paris, would be just what her father needed. It would give him something to look forward to after his convalescence and help restore his spirits. He'd raised his voice in front of Harriet several times during the week, and Rosalind felt obliged to keep her away from him as much as possible because he complained that he couldn't bear her loud laughter and exuberance. The girl gave him a headache.

It was Hugh who'd suggested a trip to France's famous racecourse for the prestigious Grand Steeplechase de Paris on the thirty-first of May. He would accompany them and he pointed out that it would be a unique event for Rosalind to witness as the fixture attracted an enthusiastic and fashionable attendance.

Hugh told them how Royal Meath, an Irish-trained gelding, won the race in fine style the year before and galloped home to a greeting of loud cheers from both the English and Irish among the crowd. Owners longed to have a runner there and he explained how Lord Dudley had bought the horse for the princely sum of £5,000 plus half the winning stake before the race and he hadn't been disappointed. Hugh's dark eyes glowed as he recounted this and said Edward would enjoy the outing and Rosalind would appreciate the French fashion, even if she wasn't interested in the horses. She felt a stab of irritation that he should think this but she thanked him graciously and encouraged him to organize their voyage.

Frank vaulted back onto the mare's back as Rosalind gave Romeo's solid neck a quick pat with her gloved hand, pulling on the reins to force his head out of the hawthorn bush. How the old cob loved eating and was always ready to stand with his head down, munching on whatever grew nearby.

"I hear you're heading for Auteuil and the Grand Steeplechase of Paris?"

"Yes. The whole family is in agreement that it will be a welcome change for my husband."

Harriet frowned. "We have to stay with Cousin Beatrice while Mama and Papa are away."

"You and the baby, Miss Harriet?" Frank glanced at Rosalind for a second before fixing his eyes on the girl. "Are you looking forward to that?"

"No, I'm not. Cousin Beatrice doesn't allow me to talk unless she speaks to me first."

Frank failed to suppress a smile. "Indeed, that must be a strain for you. Will Baby Ivor be going with you?"

"Yes, he will."

Again he flicked his gaze in Rosalind's direction, this time keeping his eyes on her face. What was he thinking?

"My parents are going on a long train journey," Harriet told Frank. "Mama showed me on a map. They're taking the steamship to Wales and then all the way to London to Victoria Station… then to Dover on another train. Then they go on a steamship to Calais and another special train to Paris. Cousin Hugh is paying for the special train because it's very, very expensive."

"Harriet!" Rosalind exclaimed, "How on earth do you know about the expense?"

"I listened at the door when Papa and Grandmama were discussing it. That's how I know so many things."

"Don't be too hard on her," Frank said before Rosalind could open her mouth to object. "She's an intelligent child and I'll admit that her methods of finding out information are somewhat unorthodox but she certainly shows initiative."

Harriet giggled and challenged him to a race. She trotted on ahead and down the lane towards the sand hills that ran like a towering spine along the top of the beach.

The pony's shiny flanks and the dark dapples over his sturdy rump gleamed in the sunshine. She'd spent an hour that morning grooming him and untangling the coarse black hair in his mane and tail. She'd even asked Frank to put oil on his hooves. If only she showed such an interest in her own clothes and hair. Gertrude had wrinkled her nose with distaste and complained about a lingering smell of the stables when her granddaughter appeared for luncheon.

Edward had looked up from his plate of roast beef but glanced away again, a faraway look in his eyes. Something was bothering him, Rosalind was certain of it, yet he would say nothing. She tried asking him if anything was wrong when he came to the front door to watch Frank help her climb onto Romeo, but her husband just shook his head and turned away.

"*Queen rose of the rosebud garden of girls,*" Frank quoted, interrupting her thoughts. "Miss Harriet could be a good jockey if she were a boy."

Rosalind waved a hand at him. "Don't encourage her, please. Have you been reading the poetry book your mother gave you? That's from *Maud.* I recognize it." He'd claimed he was forced to read Tennyson aloud at home but sometimes Rosalind wondered if this was true. She knew the stable boys made fun of the head lad when he quoted their mistress's beloved poet.

"Yes, my mother is fond of *Maud.* She asked me to thank you for your generous donation… for the children's boots. It was most thoughtful."

"It's the least I could do. I cannot endure the thought of them going barefoot in the cold. We have so much… it hardly seems fair." She hadn't mentioned the boots to Edward or Gertrude.

"Mother asked me to give you this." He reached into his coat pocket and produced a small package wrapped in brown paper, tied with a scarlet ribbon.

"Oh, how kind of her." Rosalind flung the reins on Romeo's

neck and removed the wrapping. "A little brooch, how beautiful! A little blue enamel butterfly."

"Just a trinket but she thought you might like it."

"Oh, I do. I love it. Please thank her for me. I must walk down to the school and thank her myself before we leave for France. Did she choose it for me?"

Frank hesitated, reaching out a hand to stroke the mare's mane into place. "I found it when I was last in Wexford town. She told me what to look for so I don't deserve any credit."

Rosalind's fingers lingered on the brooch for a moment as her eyes met his.

"I'll tell Mother that you liked it."

"Yes, please do." She slipped the brooch into the pocket in her riding habit. "My husband tells me you are riding Ardlackan Lass in a valuable handicap steeplechase at Fairyhouse next week with £600 to the winner, no less."

Did concern crease his forehead for a moment before he looked down at the mare's silver mane? "Yes, that's correct. She hasn't been running well of late."

"I heard she finished down the field at both Clonmel and Cork but Edward didn't seem perturbed. The other jockey wasn't good, he said. Perhaps the Lass was missing you, Frank. I'm sure she'll be back to winning form at Fairyhouse."

He bowed his head to acknowledge the compliment but his voice remained unusually cool. "I hope so. I like to see her run to the best of her ability." He pushed Sally forward and rode away.

Ahead of them, Bumblebee floundered through the soft sand of the dunes while Harriet urged him on. "Go on, go on, good boy. We'll soon be on the beach and then we can gallop. Yes, we'll leave Mama and Frank miles behind us."

"Harriet, no! Please be careful. Frank, can't you try to dissuade her? You know what she's like when she sees an open space."

But her daughter was gone before he could say a word. The

pony reached the firmer sand on the beach and away they went, Harriet's chestnut curls streaming behind as she galloped into the wind and whooped with delight.

Frank pushed his mare into a canter and took off after her while Rosalind asked Romeo to stand. He raised his big head and pricked his ears, listening to the drumming of hooves on the sand but was content to wait for his equine companions' return. He wasn't fond of galloping and it took all her strength to force him out of a trot.

Her daughter looked like she was leaving Frank behind. That little pony could go like a racehorse when he felt like it. He might suddenly swerve and Harriet would be off over his ears. He'd unseated her once already that week and she accepted the tumble without complaint, getting to her feet, brushing off the dead leaves and clambering back onto Bumblebee's broad back.

Golden sand stretched away on both sides of Rosalind, seven miles of deserted beach, studded here and there with pieces of shell: scallops, periwinkles and inky blue halves of mussels.

Rosalind stroked Romeo's shoulder and murmured encouraging words to him. Such a good creature, he made hacking a pleasure.

It was a joy to get out of the house and ride with Frank through the woods and over the hills towards the church or down here to the sea. She felt safe on the cob and Frank always kept an eye on her. He never expected her to overstretch herself. It was only when Harriet insisted on coming that the trouble began.

Would the trip to France drag Edward out of his gloomy mood? Hugh and Beatrice had come for dinner during the week and not even several glasses of wine helped restore Edward to his usual cheerful self. He'd seemed particularly reluctant to take part in the conversation and only brightened up when Hugh mentioned Auteuil and the Grand Steeplechase.

Beatrice had been in a lively mood and appeared quite

recovered from her unhappiness earlier in the year. She chatted with Gertrude and Rosalind in the drawing room before the gentlemen came in, asking after the children and Ivor in particular. She'd seemed enthralled by him when she came over for afternoon tea the previous Saturday, when Edward and Hugh were away racing, and she'd taken him from Rosalind's arms and carried him around the room, showing him the paintings and chattering to him in an endearing way. It was wonderful to see her feeling so much better. Beatrice assured Rosalind that she was looking forward to having both children to stay at Ardlackan House.

Unfortunately, it seemed that as soon as Beatrice felt better, Edward was next to slip into despondency. Dr Richards wasn't concerned; certain this would pass. The blow to Edward's head and subsequent concussion of the brain were bound to leave him feeling tired and depressed but summer was coming; he would soon regain his former spirits. Rosalind hoped the doctor was correct as she found her husband's irritable moods difficult, especially when he snapped at her and the children.

Rosalind held up her hand to shield her eyes from the sun, squinting into the distance to see what had become of Harriet and Frank. The mare and pony were at the far end of the beach with two figures on foot. Had Harriet been thrown off while Rosalind worried about Edward? How could she have missed that? Her daughter seemed unharmed and was walking beside Frank, holding his arm and bending over as if in a fit of giggles.

All was well. Harriet had not fallen off and broken a limb. She and Frank would be back presently and Rosalind would slip down from Romeo's back and examine that pretty butterfly over there on the little yellow flowers. It was a beautiful powder-blue and, if she took a closer look, perhaps she would be able to remember the details and paint it later.

Romeo pricked his ears and, before she had a chance to

dismount, turned his head to look behind him, shifting his large hooves in the sand. A big dark horse clambered over the top of the dune, one leg sliding to the side and nearly dislodging the rider.

"Hello," Hugh called, raising an arm to salute but lowering it to snatch up the reins when his horse dived forwards. "Whoa there, steady! How are you, Rosalind? I'm on this wild creature so I don't have much control. His first time to see the beach."

She returned his greeting. "I'm well, thank you. I'm fortunate that Romeo thinks it's all quite normal. Indeed, he's a rock of sense."

"Certainly you are blessed. Perhaps you would be kind enough to give me a lead down to the edge of the water? Lancelot will not like the sea. The noise and movement of the waves frighten horses until they grow used to them."

"Of course I'll help you. What would you like me to do?"

Hugh noticed the others. "Ah, I see you are not alone. Harriet and..."

"Frank O'Rafferty."

"The gallant coachman. Does he ride out with you often?"

"You must remember that he taught me to ride. I would never have learned to manage Romeo without his help. Shall I walk on ahead of you towards the sea?"

His dark eyes fixed on her face and she felt her cheeks glow with embarrassment and resolved to turn her horse away. Hugh cast another glance in the direction of the others before following.

Lancelot seemed relieved to have a solid and fearless equine companion and he pranced alongside, sweat on his fine thoroughbred coat and white foam in his mouth as he chewed the bit.

"How is Edward?" Hugh pressed his right leg into his horse's flank to move him further away from the cob. "Feeling better? The trip to France will bring him out of himself, I hope."

"He's looking forward to it."

"Beatrice is looking forward to having your children to stay. She's taken to the baby."

"It's kind of her to have them," Rosalind murmured. "Her health appears to have improved. I'm delighted she is so much better."

"As indeed am I. I was worried about her for months but all seems well again now. Melancholia is an unpleasant malady, I'm afraid. It changes people beyond recognition."

Romeo plodded on towards the water's edge with Hugh's mount snorting and shying beside him. The young horse stopped and spun around several times, his eyes bulging and his nostrils flaring.

When Lancelot was walking calmly again, Hugh said, "Of course, you have experience of melancholia in your family, so you understand what it was like for me and for the girls."

What did he mean? Who could he be talking about? Surely not her? Edward had recently accused her of lack of sympathy for him but her husband hadn't mentioned this to his cousin, had he?

A secretive smile lingered on Hugh's lips.

"I'm sorry I don't know what you mean." Rosalind turned to look towards Frank and Harriet who were slowly making their way back, now both up on their mounts. Her pulse gathered speed. Hugh had a way of making her feel uncomfortable. If only the others would hurry up.

He inclined his head in a small bow of apology. "I beg your pardon. Perhaps it's not talked about in your family, my dear. I can understand that, indeed I can."

Beatrice came into her mind at that moment. Beatrice smiling mockingly when she told her that he knew other people's secrets. He had contacts, informants who passed on information. What did he do with this information and why would he need it?

She pushed Romeo forward, switching direction away from the waves and towards Frank and her daughter. She urged him to trot but the cob ignored her and continued his ambling walk with Lancelot more relaxed beside him.

"Your mother," Hugh murmured.

Her heart leaped. "My mother is dead."

That same strange smile flickered on his face, a glimmer of satisfaction in his eyes. He said nothing.

"My mother died from a haemorrhage after I was born."

"I understand, Rosalind. It is natural that your family would prefer to protect you."

"Protect me from what?" Her hands were shaking as she gripped the reins. "Trot on, Romeo, for goodness sake! You are the slowest creature." She raised an arm and beckoned to Frank and Harriet. "We must go home now. Come along, you two!"

"It's a painful subject, to be sure," Hugh said. "None of us like admitting that a family member. . ."

Exasperated, she muttered, "I don't understand what you're talking about. Let's ride on and join the others."

He bowed his head in agreement.

They were less than one hundred yards away from Harriet and Frank. Hugh fell silent for a few moments before adding, "At least she was in a private asylum and near to your father and aunt. Those institutional asylums are horrific places… to incarcerate a loved one. That must have been comforting for your papa."

A knot twisted in Rosalind's stomach. Surely he was mistaken?

"I'm sorry, my dear. I will drop the subject as I can see it pains you too much. Rest assured that I will mention this to no one. I will be as silent as the grave. You can rely on me and now I'll take my misbehaving horse home. Thank you for assisting me with him." He raised his hat to Frank and Harriet, turning Lancelot to face the dunes.

Harriet called out as she approached. "Frank nearly beat me but I won. I won! Isn't Bumblebee the best pony ever? Best pony in the world! I shall have fun racing Grace when you and Papa are away. I've decided that I don't mind going to stay with Cousin Beatrice after all. I will be able to write more riddles in my book and you may solve them when you come home."

Rosalind's eyes followed Hugh's retreating back. Of course he was mistaken. Papa and Aunt Catherine would not have lied to her, would never have deceived her. She would send a letter to Hampstead the following morning and ask about her mother. Tightening her grip on the reins, she forced a smile for her daughter. "I look forward to solving them, my sweet. You have such a talent for puzzles. Now, let's go home before your grandmother sends out a search party for us."

Chapter Twenty-Eight

The past - 4th May, 1891

Betty O'Brien carried a fruit cake to the pine table and deposited it in front of Frank, as a cheer from the four stable boys rose to the rafters of the kitchen. They clapped their hands and stamped with their boots on the paving stones.

"That's a fine cake, to be sure. You're spoiling me." Frank hushed their enthusiasm. "Now, boys, please settle down, you'll have Mrs Thornton coming to see what riot has broken out below stairs."

"And you wouldn't mind that, would you Frank? Young Mrs Thornton, that is, not the old lady." Peter spluttered with amusement.

Mrs O'Brien clapped one hand on Frank's shoulder and slipped her arm around him, giving him a hug and planting a quick kiss on his cheek. "You're the hero here, my lad. You took Fairyhouse by storm, you and Ardlackan Lass. You're the best jockey in Ireland."

Another jubilant outcry echoed to the ceiling and Peter winked at his cousin. "All the women in Wexford are in love with you. Who else would have a special cake baked for him with congratulations written in pink icing on the top? Only our Frank, that's the truth."

Even shy Joseph turned eyes that danced with amusement

towards his more boisterous companion. The cook gave Frank's shoulders a final hefty squeeze before picking up a knife and pointing it at Peter.

"Less of your cheek, boy, or you'll get no cake."

Peter let out a wail of dismay but his grin told all there that he didn't believe she would carry out the threat.

"A glass of porter for all the men," Mrs O'Brien said, reaching for the nearest bottle, "and one for the lady present too." She looked around, beaming at the eager young faces, "I see I'm the only lady here today so I can't leave myself out."

They laughed politely at her joke, holding out their glasses to be filled with the thick black liquid.

"There'll be no work done for the rest of the day, I can see," Frank said. "Ah well, it's not often we have a fine celebration cake like this one. Enjoy it, lads, while you may."

The cook cut the cake and handed out a thick slice to each man, reserving the largest for Frank.

He muttered as he reached for the plate, "I'll not make the weight for the next race if I eat all of this."

"You're like a greyhound, you never put on weight." Peter nudged Joseph and went into a fit of giggles that made him choke. Another man thumped him none too gently on the back and pushed a bottle of porter towards him.

Mrs O'Brien took her seat at the head of the table and held up her glass. "A toast, boys, to Ardlackan Lass, the best steeplechasing mare, and Mr O'Rafferty, finest trainer and jockey in the county of Wexford."

"In the whole of Ireland!" Peter shouted.

Frank shot him a sharp look. Peter found it difficult to keep his exuberance in check and it wouldn't take much to irritate the cook, who was known for her sudden outbursts of temper but, for the moment, Mrs O'Brien beamed benignly back at the men, as if enjoying the sense of occasion.

Frank stretched his legs out under the table and swallowed a gulp of porter. It was nice for the lads to be able to celebrate and fruit cake was a luxury for them. He could see Joseph's pale blue eyes glow with appreciation as the cook pushed another slice towards him. Poor young fellow, with his father a drunkard and his mother not much better. Where would Joseph be without the horses?

The cake disappeared and more bottles of porter were opened with Mrs O'Brien playing the affable hostess. Half an hour passed and the huge kitchen clock chimed on the wall. The cook had a soft spot for the stable boys, no doubt about that. She loved to play mother to them and Frank knew they appreciated both her cooking and her kindness. The young man sitting beside Joseph had never had a mother. She'd died of consumption one month after he came into the world.

Peter's cheeks glowed as the effects of the alcohol loosened his tongue. "I heard there's one man who wasn't so pleased when the Lass came galloping in at Fairyhouse."

Joseph turned his head to stare at him. "And who might that be?"

Frank watched Peter's wide mouth twitch into a grin.

"Why Mr Martin Chance, of course. They say he was furious. White in the face with fury, like the phantom who rides through our woods at night."

Mrs O'Brien fixed him with her gimlet-eyed gaze. "Well don't stop now, Peter my lad, continue your story because I for one have no idea what you're talking about."

"I believe Peter may be exaggerating," Frank said softly.

His cousin sniggered. "Mrs O'Brien was kind enough to bake you this cake and she wants to hear me out."

"Indeed I do," the cook replied. "Don't you go interrupting him, Frank, let the boy finish what he started. I've had little excitement this past week so I could do with a good story."

Peter cast a mocking glance at Frank before continuing. "Mr Chance is a bookmaker of renown, one of the wealthiest in the land… in the whole country, it's said. He's not a man to be deceived by anyone but at Fairyhouse he was certainly taken for a fool." His eyes flitted around the table before he continued, "I have it on good authority how he raged and roared."

"Unlikely," Frank murmured, "because Mr Chance is one of the calmest men I've ever come across. There are not many that can pull the wool over his eyes."

"Ah, but that's exactly what happened. Our bold master and his cousin managed to do just that… and they did it in style. Didn't the Lass win in a canter? You only had to sit there and steer her to the winning post. And the look on Mr Chance's face in the winner's enclosure was more like thunder than pleasure… or so I was told."

"By whom were you told, may I ask?" Frank said almost under his breath.

Joseph's eyes dropped to the table, as if sensing trouble.

"One of Mr Hugh's stable boys… so it was straight from the horse's mouth, if you please."

The other men expressed amusement at such wit and Peter nodded knowingly, delighted with his own performance. Even Mrs O'Brien watched him with a hint of admiration on her rosy features.

"That's enough now." Frank raised his voice. "I won't have you gossiping about the horses."

"Hush, Frank," Mrs O'Brien said. "Let the boy continue. This is shaping up to be a fine tale."

Peter smirked. "I heard it on good authority, mind you, that Mr Chance almost exploded in front of Mr Hugh and our master… he swore that they'd treated him badly and that the mare had been pulled by the previous jockey."

Frank got to his feet. "Back to work now, all of you."

Mrs O'Brien's sharp glance fell on him. "Is there any truth in this story? Would Mr Chance be telling the truth about the horse not running true to form? We were all wondering why you didn't ride her at Clonmel and Cork, weren't we, boys? We thought maybe you'd eaten too much and couldn't make the weight but we know that's not like you. No, there was a reason for it, wasn't there? You were taken off the mare and that useless… that good-for-nothing rascal put up in your place and my pennies lost down the drain not once but twice."

Frank shook his head, trying not to smile. "More fool you for gambling on her. You should have asked my advice before investing such a grand sum of money on the mare."

Peter elbowed Joseph in the ribs. "Yes, Mrs O'Brien, Frank would have told you that the mare wasn't going to win that day, nor the week after. The master was looking for a low weight for Fairyhouse, you see, and that's exactly what he got and then he put Frank back on…"

"Peter, be silent! You shouldn't speak like that about the master." Frank frowned at him.

Of course the boy was right. Frank had seen Martin Chance's face darken when he reckoned how much money he'd have to pay out on the mare's win. One of Hugh Thornton's stable boys must have overheard the altercation beside Edward's carriage afterwards and Chance's threat that nobody got away with treating him like that. They were mistaken if they thought they could make a fool of him, he threw over his shoulder as he walked away. They would rue the day. Rue the day. The master had turned a shade paler but Mr Hugh remained expressionless.

Frank thanked Mrs O'Brien for the cake and the porter, declined another slice and hurried the stable boys out of the kitchen. He pulled Peter aside, grasping his arm none too gently, and ordered Joseph and the others to go on about their business.

"Ow, that hurts!" Peter moaned. "Let go of my arm."

"You watch what you say in front of the others, do you hear me? You don't want to get on the wrong side of Martin Chance and his men. If you weren't my blood relation, I'd threaten to report you to the master."

"Ah, Frank, go easy, will you? I didn't mean any harm. I was only entertaining the…"

"You were spreading dangerous words… sowing seeds of suspicion in the minds of the others and, like I said, you'd need to be careful of the likes of Martin Chance and his man Mick Maguire. They eat boys like you for their breakfast."

The smirk slipped from his cousin's face. "Do you think so?"

"Certainly, I do. If you're found dead in a ditch tomorrow night, I'll know what's happened to you."

Peter had the grace to blush and look nervously over his shoulder, as if expecting to see Maguire standing behind him. Frank gave him a pat on the back, winked at him and walked off through the door into the stable yard.

Chapter Twenty-Nine

The past - 8th May, 1891

"Goodbye, my dear. Have a wonderful time and give my fondest regards to your aunt." Gertrude bent forward to kiss Rosalind's cheek. "Look after my darling boy and ensure that he rests."

"Of course, I will do my utmost to bring him back to you in good health." Rosalind bent to hug her daughter, who clasped her arms around her waist and wouldn't let go until her mama had kissed her six times, three on each cheek. Sadie had to prise open her fingers and take her hand firmly in hers before Rosalind was allowed to straighten her hat and step away to plant a quick kiss on the baby's forehead.

Beatrice moved forward to grip her hand. "And don't worry about the baby for one moment. Sadie and I will take good care of him, won't we, Sadie?" The maid opened her mouth to agree but Beatrice added, "We will… and Harriet will have fun with her cousins. We'll be such a cheerful household while you and the men are away. A whole month of fun and games."

A pang pricked Rosalind when she saw Beatrice take Ivor into her arms and smile down into his chubby face. She mustn't become sentimental in front of Gertrude, who would only chide her for upsetting the children. Harriet had been quite tearful at breakfast and Rosalind didn't wish to encourage another bout of emotion. A whole month away from the children seemed difficult to bear but she was looking forward to seeing Aunt Catherine. Edward had consented to a week with her in Hampstead and that would be a treat. Hugh would join them in Paris at the end of the month.

Frank brought Romeo and the brougham round from the yard. Edward and Rosalind climbed into the carriage and turned together to wave at the assembled party one final time, before Frank clicked his tongue and the cob stepped forwards.

"Thank goodness that's over," Edward said, sliding back on the seat with a sigh. "I thought we'd never get away." He took out his pocket watch and fiddled with the chain. "I hope we make the Wexford train. All those farewells delayed us." There were dark smudges under his eyes and his face looked drawn and pale.

"But we won't see them for a month. A month is a long time for Harriet and a baby."

"The baby won't know. All he cares about is his next meal. They're quite unresponsive at that age."

Rosalind peeled off her gloves and tapped his knee with them. "How can you say that? He gurgles happily at you when you visit him in the nursery, doesn't he? I shall miss him dreadfully. I shall miss them both dreadfully. I do hope Beatrice looks after them."

Edward groaned. "Pray don't start fussing. Beatrice has Sadie to help her. My headache is back and it's because of this palaver."

"Well, you can relax now, my love. Close your eyes and have a sleep. We'll be at the railway station in no time at all and then you can rest all the way to Dublin."

He shut his eyes and leaned his head on the side of the window. He sighed again and stared out into the laurels as the brougham passed them by. He sat upright and asked, "Who was that? Did you see who it was?" His mouth twitched at the corner and he raised his voice. "It looked like Mick Maguire and his damn dog. He was skulking around in the shrubbery waiting for me to leave. I'll stop the carriage and give him a piece of my mind." He raised his cane to tap on the roof.

Rosalind reached out to him. "No, please, no. Leave him be. He'll only be back again tomorrow, in any case. Frank will keep him out of the stable yard while you're away. He listens to Frank."

"Meaning he doesn't listen to me?" A bitter note in his voice.

"No, of course I didn't intend to imply that. Please don't upset yourself. Frank knows to keep Maguire away from the stable boys... knows that he tries to bribe them for tips."

"Maguire is a drunken unpleasant scoundrel."

"He is that. I don't like him any more than you do."

Edward frowned and scraped at the wood around the corner of the window with a fingernail.

"Won't you close your eyes, my love? Forget about Maguire."

He put his head in his hands and groaned.

"What is it? What is troubling you? You don't usually worry about Maguire."

He shook his head, ignoring her question.

"Has he... has he done anything else?"

No answer, only another deep sigh.

"Edward?"

"For heaven's sake, woman, leave me alone."

Rosalind lapsed into an offended silence. She tried looking out of the other window but needed something to distract her. She opened her bag, reaching inside to take out a letter.

"What's that?" Edward asked.

"A letter from Aunt Catherine. She's looking forward to seeing us."

"Seeing you, you mean."

"And you, of course. Don't be so difficult. I thought you were in better spirits this morning at breakfast." She would read through her aunt's letter again. She'd received a brief reply to her query about her mother. A guarded answer and one that Rosalind suspected didn't divulge the whole truth but Aunt Catherine had been honest enough to confirm that her mother hadn't died from a haemorrhage after childbirth. She had indeed been sent for treatment in a private sanatorium outside London before she died six months later of a fever. She had always been treated with kindness there and was visited regularly by Rosalind's father and aunt.

Why hadn't Rosalind been told of this? Why had they kept it secret? Her aunt merely stated it was to protect her. Her mother was dead and there was no need for her daughter to be told of the upset and distress. Rosalind tucked the letter away in her embroidered reticule. Did her husband know? Perhaps one of the reasons for their deception had been a deliberate effort to keep him in the dark in case it would blight Rosalind's marriage prospects. No man would be keen to marry into a family carrying the stigma of insanity. Rosalind would demand to know more when she saw her aunt. Why couldn't her mother have been cared for at home?

Edward was still complaining about the tout. "Yes, I was in better spirits but now my head is throbbing. I'm sorry, my dear, but it's that man. That blackguard Maguire!"

Somehow Hugh had found out about her mother. Did he intend to tell Edward? Perhaps it would be better if she mentioned her mother's illness to her husband before his cousin decided to. Suppose Edward thought she'd deliberately hidden it from him?

"If I find out…" he muttered.

Not today though. She wouldn't mention her mother today. He wasn't in a receptive mood. "Frank will…"

"Ros, do stop going on about Frank. He doesn't know what Maguire is capable of. Frank doesn't know what that man said to me last week." His eyes widened as if alarmed by what he'd let slip and he turned his head away.

"What did he say to you last week?" Rosalind felt a cold prickle at the back of her neck. Maguire had been unpleasant enough when he met her at the match race when Frank had asked him to leave. She repeated, "What did he say?"

"Don't you think it's odd that Major Langstown saw a man come out of the crowd and frighten the horse? Who would do that? The man was determined to cause an accident. I could have been killed."

"Yes, but Hugh said…"

"Suppose Hugh didn't see him? Hugh says the mare shied at a dog, I realize that, but suppose the major is correct. Suppose someone wishes me harm."

A silence fell in the carriage as they swayed with the movement. They were passing the front gates of Ardlackan House and the old woman came out of the lodge to wave as the brougham passed by. Edward ignored her but Rosalind bent forward and raised a hand to return the greeting. She sat back and noticed his creased brow and the worry in his dark eyes.

"It could have been a gambler, perhaps," she said. "Someone who'd put money on Hugh to win the match and didn't want your mare to…"

"And who do you think would be likely to do that?"

"It could have been anyone. Anyone desperate enough for the money."

"Maguire? He'd been drinking that day. I saw him earlier in the village and he was already staggering."

"He seemed sober when he rode over to talk to me."

Edward's voice rose. "He spoke to you? What did he want?"

"Nothing. He was just his usual unpleasant self. Frank said that Maguire had placed a wager on Hugh to win and he told him to be on his way."

As slippery as a snake. Those were Frank's words.

"When was this?"

252

"When you'd ridden through the quarry, I think. I don't remember exactly."

"And then we reached the jump into the wood. Do you think Maguire would have had time to catch up with us?"

"Perhaps. He was on a black cob. You don't think… surely you don't think that he would have… have got off his horse and run out from the crowd to frighten your mare?"

He brought his head close to hers, looking into her eyes, his breath warm on her face. "What do you think? You said yourself that he had a wager on Hugh."

"Frank said that."

"Frank would know. If Maguire left you and galloped over to the wood as we came out of the quarry…"

"Why? Why would he do such a thing? I'm not sure that he would have had time to get there."

"Why would he do such a thing? Because, my lovely innocent wife, that man threatened me only last month."

Rosalind's heart thumped against her ribs.

"Yes, he threatened me when he was drunk and I was throwing him out of the stable yard. I grabbed him by the collar and he spat on the ground and then whispered something in my ear."

Her pulse was racing at the thought of Edward fighting with Maguire. Better to let Frank persuade him to leave than tackle him himself. Suppose he'd hit him. Or suppose he had a knife? What then?

"I wish you wouldn't…" she began.

He reached out and caught her hands in his, giving them a painful squeeze. "He threatened to kill me. That's what he said. He said he would kill me if I… he said my sort were better off dead."

"Oh, Edward!"

"I didn't tell you because I didn't want to alarm you but now you see how having that man sneaking around my property is…

And the man that threw the stone through the window at Martin Chance's dinner party. Who do you think did that, eh? I bet it was Maguire out to cause trouble. He knew I was there and he wanted to frighten me. I bet it was that devil."

"But why? You don't want him corrupting your stable boys, that's fair enough. I'm sure all the trainers in the county run him out of their yards. Frank says gamblers pay them to nobble horses. They slip something into their food or deliberately lame them when no one is looking. If Maguire…"

"He's worse than that. He keeps company with villains, Ros. I've heard about the fellows he spends time with. Cock fights, dog fights, you name it. Anything a man can gamble on, Maguire will be there in the thick of it and when he has drink taken, he's the very devil. He threatened to kill me and I'm afraid that he means to."

She gripped his fingers in hers, an attempt to reassure him. "He was drunk, that's all it was. Pay no heed to him. Frank will keep him away from you. He knows how to handle him."

That was the wrong thing to say. He snatched away his hands and jerked his head to glare out of the window, his lips pressed together as if biting back angry words.

"I'm sorry. I didn't mean to make you sound like…" Rosalind spoke more softly.

"Like I am useless compared to Frank? Frank the paragon of virtue who has every woman in the county wrapped around his little finger. And you, Rosalind, are you one of those ladies, pray tell me?"

She blushed in spite of the stupidity of his question. "Don't be ridiculous. How can you say such a thing? You're tired, you're upset. Maguire has unnerved you and you're just lashing out at me because you can't hit out at him." She willed herself to stay quiet before she said something she would regret. She'd never spoken to him like this but he was behaving in such an irrational, childish manner and wouldn't listen to her reassurances. Of course Mick Maguire was unpleasant, of course he was untrustworthy and probably attempting to corrupt the stable boys in order to procure information but that was all. He was just a drunken troublemaker. That bang on the head had made her husband obsessively anxious.

Edward looked down at his hands. "I apologize. I know you would never… that you and Frank would never…"

"It was a foolish and unkind thing to say."

"Yes, you're right. It was foolish and I've said I'm sorry. But you mark my words, Maguire threatened me that day." He spoke more quietly now, more to himself than to her.

She reached forward to touch his face. "You must try to forget about him now. We're going away for a month. Try to enjoy yourself. You will have plenty of time to consider how best to deal with him when we return."

Chapter Thirty

Hugh was correct about Parisian fashion at Auteuil. Rosalind stood beside her husband and two of his friends from Ireland on the grandstand and surveyed the crowd. Ladies sported the latest in *haute couture* and a profusion of lace and beads abounded. Lace gloves held parasols of different hues to shield pale skin from early summer sunshine.

Rosalind switched her gaze to the thirteen runners lining up for the start of the Grand Steeplechase de Paris.

Madame Coubert, wife of a French trainer, stood on her left, her auburn curls topped with a brimmed hat adorned with silk roses, clusters of diamanté dancing and sparkling in their centres. Her dress was palest green silk with a lace edging to the collar and sleeves. A row of embroidered buttons ran down the front, with silver beading in a leaf motif. Rosalind felt positively dowdy in her plain suit of navy blue silk.

Madame whispered in Rosalind's ear, "What do you think of our Auteuil? It is a wonderful place, you think? *Trés belle, n'est-ce pas?*" She waved her tiny hand. "Such elegance, such tradition. *Là-bas...* over there... *oui*, there was a fire in 1879, the burning stand, yes? Did you hear? But everything was made right again. All beautiful again."

The horses surged forward and galloped towards the first fence, a cheer rising from the crowd around them. Several gentlemen waved top hats in the air.

A bay mare called Saida, owned by Baron Finot, was in front and Rosalind peeped at her husband. His face looked stiff with concentration, just a slight glimmer of anxiety in his eyes, his eyebrows meeting in the middle. Her heart sank. Had he put money on the Baron's five-year-old? Steeplechases were unpredictable as anything could happen. The Grand Steeplechase de Paris was run over four miles, too, so the mare would probably tire if she kept up that pace in front. Perhaps that was why Edward frowned, because he hadn't expected her to lead from the start.

Saida looked like she was jumping well and galloped into the final straight still in front. Cheers and encouraging shouts from onlookers rang out in several different languages. Madame Coubert seized Rosalind's arm and gripped it. She had obviously invested many francs on the outcome.

Edward let out a cry of joy and turned to his friends, an expression of triumph on his face. A tumult of sound erupted as the mare flew past the winning post in front of the grandstand and hats were tossed into the air, falling to the ground and trampled on in the excitement.

They hurried to the winner's enclosure, the sea of people moving as a wave across the neatly mown lawn. Baron Finot, one of France's most popular owners of steeplechasers, greeted the mare with enthusiasm. Friends and well-wishers gathered around to congratulate him. Edward turned to Rosalind and lifted her up, swinging her in a half-circle and planting a kiss on the end of her nose. She laughed and grabbed at her hat.

"Did you see that, my darling?" he cried. "The way she led all the way, jumped those steeplechase fences like they were nothing to her. What a mare! What a victory!"

She felt a mild nausea contemplating how much he might

have wagered but perhaps she was misjudging him. Perhaps he was just genuinely pleased to see the Baron win.

She smiled up into his face. "Wasn't she wonderful? Not an Irish win but everyone seems happy with the result. A popular victory."

A tall man put his arm round Edward's shoulders. "A good win for you, my friend. I heard about your bet. Not quite as exciting as Royal Meath's victory last year for Ireland but the Baron is well-liked and there'll be a celebration tonight. Bottles of champagne for all of us."

Rosalind stared at Edward. "How much did you put on the mare?"

He lowered his voice. "Not too much. Just think of the profit I've made. Why, this will pay for our trip, my love."

She decided to be happy for him, reluctant to create an argument in front of all these people. Let him have his fun for he'd been in such low spirits and he deserved some excitement.

Later, after several glasses of champagne and more stories about the famous French racehorse owner and his champion horses, Edward entertained his increasingly inebriated friends with tales of Ardlackan Lass and Mighty Maiden. Mares were the best, he claimed. When they were in good form, it was hard to beat a good mare. Mighty Maiden might even be here in the winner's enclosure at Auteuil next year if everything went according to plan. He and Hugh elaborated on their ideas for the stable yard at Ardlackan Lodge, the new buildings increasing in size and grandeur with every glass of champagne they drank.

When the celebrations were over, the carriages called for and the crowd beginning to disperse, Rosalind could hold back no longer. Now was her chance while her husband was in this cheerful mood, when he might actually tell her the truth about the match with Hugh.

She'd overheard Hugh telling Madame Coubert about the

race between the two cousins; how he'd finished the race and was the victor. What had he won? Madame congratulated him and bestowed many kisses on his cheeks until her husband came to claim her and escort her away on his arm, inviting Hugh to accompany them.

Hugh turned to his cousin. "You and Ros go on to the hotel. Coubert and I will join you later for a bottle of cognac."

"Edward…" Rosalind waited until they were alone beside the rails.

"What is it, my love?"

A pity to risk irritating him when he was so happy but it had to be done. She could contain her anxiety no longer. "Hugh told Madame Coubert how he won your match race. Please tell me, what exactly did he win?"

Did he look suddenly wary, a brief hesitation? "Not money, Ros."

"I know, you told me that before and I believe you but he definitely won something. What was it?"

A chestnut horse pulling a cabriolet came towards them.

"Here's our man, I think. He'll drive us back to the hotel."

"You can tell me, my dear, I promise not to be angry."

He frowned, creases running across his brow. "No need to think like that. It was just a little gesture really, a gesture of goodwill towards poor Beatrice."

She waited, a feeling of relief beginning to seep through her. She'd been wrong to be so suspicious of him.

"You know the way Beatrice has been so downcast, downhearted since she lost the baby. And it was my fault. I feel it was my fault because of those two damn bays that got out of control."

"An accident, Edward."

"I felt guilty… such a heavy weight on my conscience… and so, when Hugh suggested this idea, I thought it would be harmless really… make things better between us."

Rosalind still smiled. "You mustn't feel guilty. It was an accident."

"Yes, but my fault all the same. I was reckless and stupid. I should have waited for Frank and… anyway, I know you won't mind. I agreed to Hugh's suggestion that they take Ivor for a few months."

Her stomach jolted. "What? You agreed to what?"

"A few months, that's all. Just until Beatrice feels better, more normal."

"You gave our son to them? You gambled on something like that? But this is madness! What were you thinking?"

Edward's face flushed as he reached for her arm to guide her to the carriage door. "Hush, people will hear you. You're overreacting and becoming emotional." He helped her in. "We'll be away for another month on our extended trip to the south of France. Mama thought it was a wonderful idea. In fact, she agreed as soon as Hugh mentioned it."

"Mama? You mean Gertrude knew about this? Your mother knew about your wager to give away our baby son and not even she thought to tell me. I am his mother, Edward. You can't do this without my permission. How could you think such a thing? We'll have to go home tomorrow and sort this out. I'll have a word with Hugh. You can't use Ivor as a… a substitute son for Beatrice; a salve for your conscience. What if she becomes attached to him and doesn't want to give him up?"

"All will be well, don't worry. She will soon tire of the boy. When Sadie and Harriet come home, she won't want to look after him for long. He will fill the gap left by the death of the baby, you see, and I will have done something to make things right… to make amends. I blame myself for what happened, no matter what you say. I think they blame me too, Hugh and Beatrice. They lost their only son. Imagine how that must feel? Their heir to the big house and all that land and they may never have another chance. The least I… the least we can do is share ours with them for a little while."

He could be so convincing and confident he was speaking logically when what he was saying seemed all wrong. Why hadn't he told her of this plan? Why had he agreed to Hugh's suggestion with his mother's blessing and not hers? Surely he knew she would object? He knew she wouldn't go along with it and perhaps that was why it had been arranged behind her back and there was nothing she could do so far from home.

"The south of France," Edward murmured, sleepy now from the combination of alcohol and swaying of the cabriolet on its way back into Paris. "Just imagine Provence in early summer. Think how beautiful it will be. The children will be well cared for and, when we get home, we only have a few weeks before we get Ivor back. I said no later than the end of June. It will all work out perfectly, you'll see."

Chapter Thirty-One

The present - 12th July, 2019

A bat flitted overhead, darting behind the summer house. Daphne placed a citronella candle in a terracotta pot in the centre of the wooden table to keep away the midges as dusk fell. Its lemon scent curled into the warm evening air.

"I suppose it's good your husband has come back," Daphne murmured. "I thought he might like to have dinner with us to celebrate Ben finishing the summer house renovations but he wanted to go to the café."

"He took his laptop with him," I explained. "I think he had to finish something for work. I really don't believe he wants to come back to me... just wants a roof over his head."

She raised her eyebrows and glanced at Ben who was strumming his guitar and humming. "I suppose any man who could forsake you for Tiffany..."

"And you're very kind to take him in," I added.

She sipped her wine, a red Shiraz I'd found in the local supermarket. "I felt guilty putting him in the room on the old servants' corridor when there's a perfectly good spare room beside you."

Ben looked amused but went on humming.

"That bedroom will be fine for Dominic, don't worry."

I couldn't resist laughing. "I don't want to make him too comfortable or you might never get rid of him."

She looked down at the dog lying asleep by my feet. "Well in that case…"

No, Dominic hadn't been keen on the bedroom with barred windows, faded curtains and no carpet, but I'd told him it was all that was available as Daphne needed to keep her spare room for visitors.

The lack of Wi-Fi bothered him because he spent most of his day on his mobile or laptop. He was obsessed about the internet, watching racing and gambling. I explained about Andrea's café and gave him directions and hoped he would spend hours in the village.

Any feelings that I would be pleased to see him evaporated when he arrived without a present for Daphne or thanks for me. Dominic was selfish and childish and I wondered why I'd never admitted that before.

"Ben has written a new song for us," I said, changing the subject.

Daphne murmured, "Will you sing it for us, please?"

"Ben is a tenor. He used to sing in the church choir in London."

He rubbed the back of his neck, flushing slightly. "Yeah, my gran made me. Okay, I'll give it a go."

Daphne and I listened in silence, admiring his strong voice as it soared over the lawn towards the darkness of the woods. I realized I felt content; relaxed in their company and relieved that Dominic wasn't there. He would be jealous of Ben, of course, even though he was only a young man. Dominic always liked to be the focus of attention in a crowd.

Ben sang several verses. A surprisingly moving song about a man with a sweetheart who had died, quite Victorian in its sentiment. Ben had borrowed a book of poetry that Daphne found among Charles's old clothes, with John Thornton's name scrawled in the front.

We clapped and congratulated him when he'd finished as he stood to bow with a flourish.

"Excellent," I said. "You have many talents. Perhaps you should have sung that to charm Kitty O'Rafferty and she might have handed over her box of letters from the 1890s."

Daphne smiled. "I'm not surprised she didn't take a liking to that journalist. Who could blame her? Does anyone actually like the woman? Tiffany seems to aggravate everyone, going around asking impertinent questions and stirring up trouble... poking her nose into other people's business."

"Tiffany irritates people but that's probably because of her persistence. Maybe she's not even aware of how much she upsets you. She was nicer to me when I met her in Dublin."

Ben gently laid his guitar on the lawn. "It's a shame Kitty knew nothing about Harriet. Perhaps she and her little brother were sent away by Gertrude when her mother had to go to an asylum. I wonder if Rosalind ever came out again."

Daphne gazed at me, the candlelight reflecting in her glasses. "Poor Rosalind. We don't know for certain about that, just a line in the schoolmistress's diary. Her husband murdered... no wonder she could have needed help but perhaps she only went there for a short while."

"And then where?"

"I've no idea. John Thornton was a distant cousin of Hugh's and he didn't show interest in the family even after inheriting this place."

Ben cleared his throat. "Daphne, the painting Kitty bought from you... what inspired that? It's so different to what you usually paint."

She pushed the wine glass around on the table top with a forefinger and took several seconds to answer, avoiding our eyes.

"I woke up one morning with that image in my head. So vivid that I couldn't ignore it so I went to the easel and painted it. I've never done anything like it before... or since."

"She came from somewhere," Ben replied softly. "And Kitty was drawn to the painting. Kitty has boxes and boxes of O'Rafferty letters... a lot more still to read."

"Do you know what Hugh was like?" I poured myself more wine and topped up Daphne's glass. In front of me, the summer house doors stood open to the night. I knew a lot of the garden dated from the late nineteenth century. Had the summer house been Rosalind's place of refuge? Somewhere to sit and read her Tennyson in peace, perhaps.

Daphne frowned. "I'm trying to remember if Charles ever said anything about him. We know what he looks like, of course." She waved a hand at Ben. "We have his double sitting over there. He died the year before Charles was born, I think, so he never met him. John was surprised to inherit the place but he was the only one interested in racing so he sold his other premises and moved in."

"Did John mention him?" I asked.

"Occasionally. John was a typical Thornton, a silent man who didn't give much away. I think I heard that Hugh was difficult when he was old. He lived here with his dogs... Charles wondered why he never married again after his wife died."

Ben bent to pick up his guitar. "I wonder how well he got on with Edward and Rosalind. They'd have been close cousins, I suppose. I met the old man again in O'Mahony's pub last night... the one who claimed to be related to the cook here in the 1890s... told me Ardlackan House wasn't burned down during the Civil War. It was earlier than that... about the turn of the century, he thinks, so it might have been a broken lamp or a candle that started the fire. That often happened, I guess."

I considered this. "According to the 1901 Census, the house

was still standing and occupied… so it was later than that when Hugh and Beatrice and their girls moved in with Gertrude. Harriet mentions their names in a riddle about a pony: Grace, Irene and Nora. I wonder what happened to Beatrice. She was only forty-six when she died in 1905."

"Child-birth, influenza, TB… could have been anything in those days," Daphne replied.

Daphne had seemed interested in Harriet's book of riddles when Ben and I finally laid it in front of her the day before, particularly in the child's drawings as she thought she showed talent.

"I don't know where we go next," I said. "Perhaps we need to find out more about Hugh and Beatrice Thornton. They'd have known what happened to Rosalind. If only they'd written something down. Charles never found any old letters from Hugh or Beatrice, did he?"

She pushed her glasses up on the bridge of her nose. "No. I don't think Hugh sounded much of a letter writer. Probably only interested in horses and dogs, like many of those men. I was lucky Charles also liked opera and art and he'd come with me to galleries on the rare occasions I managed to get him to leave Ardlackan."

"The asylum is important," Ben said. "If Rosalind was admitted to one, we need to find out where it was. Who would know?"

Daphne slowly shook her head.

"Jessica's dad." I suggested. "He was Charles's younger brother. He might be able to find out something as he lives in Dublin. I'll ask him." I swallowed more wine. "I'm also going to write to Aunt Catherine's address in Church Row, Hampstead… see if anyone living there knows anything about her."

I looked towards the house in the semi-darkness of the warm July evening. A window on the top floor glowed above the

Virginia creeper. Dominic must have left his light on before he went out. He'd complained about mice scratching at night; the sound waking him. Perhaps he would like to take Balor, the one-eyed rodent killer, to bed.

Chapter Thirty-Two

The past - 2nd July, 1891

"Is Ivor coming home today?"

Harriet's question upset Rosalind, yet it was a perfectly normal enquiry. The girl missed her little brother and asked about him every night. Edward had promised Rosalind that he would talk to Hugh again; would explain how she felt about them keeping the baby two weeks longer than agreed. She wondered what they really had agreed. Well, if Edward failed to get the message across, she would definitely broach the subject with Beatrice that afternoon and make it clear that she wanted Ivor back before the end of the week.

Rosalind followed her daughter into the stable yard. Frank was standing on the cobblestones by the mounting block, his hand on the reins of Bumblebee's bridle as he chatted to one of the stable boys. He looked up when he heard their footsteps.

The boy grinned at Harriet. "Come to fetch the little racehorse?"

Harriet threw her arms around the pony's neck and planted a kiss on his broad forehead. "He's the fastest creature on four legs in all of Ardlackan."

Frank glanced at Rosalind with amusement in his eyes. "Romeo is in the stable. Peter, go fetch the old boy."

Peter helped Harriet into the saddle, the skirt of her habit trailing across the pony's hindquarters and already covered in bay hair. He walked away to lead out the cob.

A horsefly hovered in front of Rosalind's face and settled on her sleeve. She swept it away with her glove. She would confront Beatrice today and make it clear that Ivor was coming home. It wasn't fair to keep him away from his sister and family. She would point out how much she missed him. The nursery seemed empty and forlorn without his gurgling smile and dimples. He was her son and she'd been kind to allow Beatrice to have him for longer than they'd planned.

Gertrude had seemed strangely ambivalent regarding her grandson's departure. She'd thought it a practical solution when Edward and Rosalind were going away to France; hadn't wanted the responsibility of looking after the little boy and maintained it was a blessing that Harriet spent time with her cousins instead of skulking in the corridors; bored and sighing for her parents. As for Ivor, Gertrude pointed out that he was getting the best of care with Hugh and Beatrice and wasn't it wonderful that they were showing an interest in the boy? Perhaps if they never managed to produce another son and heir, they would look kindly on Ivor when the time came. Perhaps he would be master of Ardlackan House one day.

Rosalind's heart fluttered in her chest when she heard this and unuttered words of protest swelled in her throat.

Was this Gertrude's idea of a beneficial outcome? That Ivor should inherit the big house? Her mother-in-law often sounded envious of Hugh and sometimes downright critical of Beatrice only producing daughters. As if Beatrice had control over what gender her children were! Edward's mother could be hard-hearted and unsympathetic at times.

Although Edward agreed after breakfast to talk to Hugh and make her feelings clear, she wondered if he'd given her pleas his full attention. Something else was on his mind. The architect had visited the day before with the plans for the new stable yard and he wanted to discuss those with Hugh. He assured Rosalind he would ask Beatrice about the baby. Perhaps she would be glad to give him back. Perhaps she was growing tired of playing mother to him by now.

"Is everything all right, Mrs Thornton?"

She became aware of Frank standing beside her with the cob. "Oh, yes, I'm sorry, I was in another world." She reached for the reins and pommel of the saddle, lifting a boot for him to hoist her up. She landed lightly and sat upright, smiling down at him. "I'm well, thank you. I'm looking forward to seeing my son today."

"I'm sure you are. It must be strange without the little lad. A fine baby boy, he is too. One day he will be able to race along the beach with Miss Harriet. One day he might beat you, miss."

Harriet snorted. "Not a chance. Not a chance. No one can beat my Bumblebee. Let's go." She pushed the pony forward and headed towards the arched gate out of the yard.

"Have a good ride," Frank said.

"Frank?" Rosalind pulled at Romeo's mane.

"Yes?"

"You didn't… you haven't heard anything about… about the baby, have you?" Sometimes she believed he knew more about what happened in the household than she did.

She often saw her husband leaning confidentially towards him, whispering in his ear and the two of them laughing.

It made her feel excluded; an outsider. But they'd been friends since boyhood after all and perhaps he told him things that he might not want to tell his wife.

"Have you, Frank?" She asked again.

"I… don't know what you mean." A slight hesitation in his voice.

"Has Edward said anything to you about Ivor?" She was being foolish. Why would Frank know more than her about the baby? It was none of his business.

"No, not one word." His blue eyes filled with concern. "He is coming home, isn't he? They are not going to adopt him?"

She twisted her fingers in the cob's mane to stop her hands shaking. "Adopt him? Why do you say that? Of course not... of course not. That will never happen." Gertrude's words echoed in her mind. *Perhaps they would look kindly on Ivor when the time came.*

"The accident with the carriage and the pair of bays, that was a terrible blow for Mrs Hugh," Frank said. "To lose her baby like that and a son..."

She knew she shouldn't be discussing this with him but the soft, concerned note in his voice drew her to him and he loved children. He came from a family of eight siblings so he was well used to babies.

The pony's iron-shod hooves clattered back under the arch and Harriet shrieked, "Do come!"

Rosalind raised her arm to wave at her daughter in acknowledgement and forced a smile at Frank. "All will be well. He will be home by the weekend."

"I hope so, ma'am. If you need any help..."

"Help? With what?"

"With anything. If you ever need my assistance, you know all you have to do is ask."

"Yes, of course. I know that and I appreciate it, thank you." She turned Romeo's head towards the gate and rode away to join her daughter.

Chapter Thirty-Three

Beatrice suggested tea on the lawn, reaching for the bell pull in the hall. "Now Harriet, my love, the three girls are upstairs waiting for you. I've heard nothing but giggles and excited whispers all morning. I really don't know what you are all up to. Please ask them to come outside for milk and cake."

Rosalind watched her daughter scamper up the staircase. "She's going to read them one of her riddles. I don't know what it's about because she keeps them secret until they're finished. Only after she's tried them out on your girls, does she allow me to see them."

Beatrice reached out her hand. "Harriet is clever. Our governess thinks she's a genius. Ros, you must be longing to see Ivor. I'll ask Magdalene to bring him out and place the baby carriage under the lime tree, in the shade of course. We don't want our baby in the full sun, do we?"

Rosalind's cheeks flushed with indignation. *Our* baby. Not *our* baby, Beatrice. *Her* baby. Her special son and she wanted him back, but she would wait and bide her time.

She wouldn't object yet, not in front of the housemaid who appeared and took her mistress's order for afternoon tea. Coffee cake and scones, jam and cream.

"Yes, ma'am," the maid said as she bobbed a curtsey. Beatrice asked her to tell Magdalene to wrap up the baby and bring him out into the garden. The maid bowed her head obediently and was gone.

Beatrice took Rosalind's arm and they walked out onto the front steps. The lawns below shimmered in a haze and the sea lay like a strip of dull grey over the tops of the pine trees. Salt from perspiration stung Rosalind's lips and the suffocating heat clung to her dress.

They moved over to the white wrought-iron chairs and table under the branches of two lime trees standing like sentries at the beginning of the avenue. Navy blue damask covered plump cushions on the seats. Bees droned in the leaves above them, drunk on lime flowers; a constant buzz, both calming and soporific.

Beatrice sat beside her and spread out her skirt, smoothing out the creases with a hand.

"So," Rosalind said slowly and carefully, "Magdalene? I don't recognize the name. Is she a new housemaid?"

Beatrice's fingers touched a curl at the side of her forehead, twisting it into shape. Her dark brown eyes lingered on the view, the manicured lawns and the swallows swooping and diving for flies.

Rosalind followed her gaze. Was that a bank of heavy cloud on the horizon? An approaching storm?

"Is she new?" Rosalind asked.

Still Beatrice did not look at her but murmured, "Yes, she came last week. Excellent references as a nursemaid. A nice village girl from southern Germany who has worked in England and so good with young children."

Rosalind's heart lurched and she put her hand to her chest. "A nursemaid? But why? Your girls are too old, surely?"

Did her friend hesitate before answering? Did her eyes sweep across Rosalind's face, gauging her reaction, calculating her feelings? Could she sense Rosalind's barely suppressed outrage? Beatrice's gaze was back on the distant view when Rosalind opened her mouth, her fingers twisted together in a painful grip, her knuckles growing white.

"Why did you take on a nursemaid?"

"To look after Ivor while you were away." Beatrice enunciated each word, refusing to make contact with her eyes.

"But... two weeks ago, you said. She came two weeks ago. You knew we would soon be back from the south of France when you took her on."

Silence.

Except for the monotonous drone of the bees that now seemed more menacing in the branches above her. Louder and reverberating through the pale green leaves.

One of the mastiffs, probably Duke because he drooled more than his brother, appeared from the archway at the side of the house that led towards the stable yard. He trotted over and sat protectively beside his mistress's chair, laying his huge square head on his paws, great globs of saliva seeping from his jaws. He fixed his brown eyes on Rosalind and she wondered if Hugh and Beatrice kept him away from her baby. Not that Duke or Prince would mean to hurt Ivor but they were enormous dogs and weighed over fourteen stone. She remembered Hugh proudly giving Harriet that nugget of information.

"Beatrice." She tried again to attract her attention.

The four girls followed the dog, running across the gravel and flopping down on the picnic rug beside the chairs and Rosalind's chance to question Beatrice had gone. Harriet clutched her leather-bound book.

"We're making a spell," Grace said. She had her mother's shiny brown hair, tied back with a red ribbon, but her eyes were blue, a startling blue in her sallow face.

"That's nice," Beatrice said, obviously not listening.

"A spell?" Rosalind summoned interest. "How intriguing! What is it for?"

"Aha, that would be telling." Harriet poked her cousin with a forefinger. "We can't tell you that or it might not work. Besides, it's only an experiment."

Four heads gathered together on the rug, bent over the squiggles and neat handwriting in Harriet's book while two housemaids walked across the grass carrying silver trays with a teapot, cups and saucers; the second tray bore a coffee cake with fat halves of walnuts perched on gleaming icing and a gold-rimmed plate piled high with scones.

No one said a word as the food and teacups were placed on a white lace cloth on the iron table. Beatrice thanked the women and they returned to the house, walking round the path to the right where the kitchen lay in the shade of two tall sycamore trees beside the laurel shrubbery.

Beatrice poured out milk for the girls and handed them the china cups and saucers, instructing them to sit up and pay attention and to put the book away while they ate.

Still no sign of the nursemaid and Ivor in the baby carriage.

Grace nudged against Harriet and they both giggled. Such innocent faces, Rosalind thought. Clear skin and gleaming hair with a whole lifetime before them and no idea of what would be thrown their way. No conception of what could possibly thwart the dreams and fantasies of youth.

The girls drank their milk and ate slices of cake, brushing crumbs from the front of their dresses. They were excused by Beatrice and jumped to their feet, hurrying away to the summer house. Rosalind watched their departing backs with a feeling of relief. Now she could try tackling Beatrice again.

She turned to speak and spotted the baby carriage being wheeled across the gravel, a vast construction with ornate iron sides shaped like swirling stems of plants. The young woman pushing it was wearing a navy-blue dress with a long white apron, linen stiff with starch. A cap with a neat trim of lace perched on fair hair, coiled into a bun and pinned up.

"Ah, Magdalene." Beatrice stood, her cheeks flushed from the oppressive heat. "There you are, at last, and here is the most handsome boy in Ireland." She bent to look in at the swaddled bundle in the carriage, reaching out a hand that shook slightly to stroke his cheek. "Do look, Rosalind, he's asleep. The little angel!"

A mix of emotions wrestled within Rosalind. A wave of tenderness mingled with anger. Part of her wished to smooth the infant's soft hair, but this instinct battled with a wild longing to snatch him up and run with him towards the avenue.

She managed to smile at the young woman. "It's nice to meet you, Magdalene. I'm Ivor's mother."

The nursemaid bobbed a curtsey. "He's just gone off to sleep, madam. Been a bit restless this morning. I think he might be cutting his first tooth." Her English was perfect, with hardly a trace of a German accent.

"Poor baby," Beatrice cooed. "My poor precious darling. That will do for now, Magdalene. Mrs Thornton and I will keep an eye on him for the next half an hour and if we need you, we'll send for you."

Magdalene nodded obediently before walking back towards the house.

"A lovely young woman." Beatrice stroked Ivor's cheek again. "You need have no fear while she's looking after him."

Rosalind sighed. "I'm sorry she'll have to leave so soon because she's only been here for a fortnight."

"What did you say? Oh, that's not true at all. Why do you think that?"

Rosalind put a hand to her throat and touched the lace at

the front of her collar in an effort to remain calm. It was now or never. She had to seize this opportunity before they were interrupted again. "Beatrice, please listen to me. You must hear me out. It's time Ivor came back to his parents."

"Oh no, not yet. Not yet. I thought Edward told you?"

"Told me what? He said he was going to talk to Hugh this morning. I need my son back, surely you understand that. I *am* his mother."

She had got Beatrice's full attention now. Brown eyes filled with tears and hurt as they gazed at her. "Oh, but Ros, don't you understand? I can't let him go. I can't... not now. Not yet."

The girls ran out of the summer house and began setting up bamboos as jumps on the croquet lawn on the bottom terrace. Pretending to be ponies was one of their frequent games.

Rosalind wondered if her anxiety had caused her to sound too blunt and decided on a kinder approach. "I understand that you've become attached to him and it was really very kind of you to look after him so well... and his sister, of course, while we were away. However, I miss him, I miss him dreadfully and he needs to come home now. It's time he came home and Sadie..."

Beatrice's voice rang out, sharp and irritated. "Oh that Sadie, for goodness sake don't mention her! The girl was so careless with him. She hasn't an idea how to look after a baby. What he needs is a professional, a fully trained nursemaid and I can assure you that Magdalene comes with the best references. Why, she recently worked for a marchioness in England, no less. A marchioness with six children. She's a natural."

"I know you're only trying to be kind but... didn't Edward talk to Hugh this morning?" Rosalind's voice trembled and she closed her eyes. Really, Edward was hopeless. When did he ever stick to his word? He'd probably been distracted by a discussion about the new stables and the architect's plans. She would have to speak to Hugh herself.

Beatrice picked up the cups and saucers, placing them back on the tray. She swept crumbs from the gold-rimmed plate onto the grass below and piled the side plates on top. "I'm sorry, I should have asked if you would like more tea. I can ask for more if you're thirsty."

"No, thank you. I don't need more tea. I'm not thirsty. I'm upset that you, my dearest friend, can't seem to understand my dilemma. Ivor is my baby. He's mine. Do you hear me?"

Beatrice seemed to resent Rosalind's tone and stared coolly at her. "You should talk to your husband. He came here this morning, yes, of course he did and he had a little discussion with Hugh about Ivor. Don't forget that they came to an agreement, the pair of them a while ago so... before you become angry with me, please speak to Edward."

"What agreement are you talking about? I had nothing to do with any agreement. He is my son and I'm taking him back." Rosalind reached out to grip the table. She could scream at Beatrice for being so obstinate, so lacking in sympathy. This misunderstanding was Edward's fault for not making things clear.

Beatrice breathed in. "The agreement was the result of the match race. Have you forgotten? Or perhaps your husband didn't tell you?"

"He told me that you were only going to keep Ivor while we were away."

"No, that's not true. It simply isn't true. The agreement was if Hugh lost the race he would give Mighty Maiden to Edward, but if Edward lost we could have Ivor... forever. We could keep him forever."

A bolt of shock hit Rosalind and she gasped. For a moment the ground seemed to spin up to hit her in the face and she sank onto a chair. Long seconds passed before she opened her eyes and fixed them on Beatrice, horrified to notice a mocking smile playing round her friend's mouth.

"No, no…" Rosalind had to force the words out as blood drummed in her ears. "No, that's not true. It's nonsense, just nonsense. Edward would never risk such a gamble."

Beatrice finished tidying the tea tray and glanced at her gold pocket watch with the pale ivory enamel. "It's time to take the baby indoors for a feed."

"No. My baby boy is coming home with me now. I'm sending Harriet back on the pony to fetch Frank and the carriage. You and I will go inside and instruct Magdalene to pack up his clothes."

"So you intend to disobey Edward's wishes and go against the gentlemen's agreement?"

"No gentleman agrees to give away his son, for goodness sake. You're all out of your minds. I can't believe that my husband agreed to this folly. I won't believe it."

"Ask him, dear Rosalind, go home and ask him," Beatrice said curtly. "Don't forget that you have a husband and his opinion differs to yours. Ivor is his son, too, and this is what he has agreed for his boy's future. He knows it's the best idea in the long run. He and Gertrude understand what's right for the child."

Tears sprang into Rosalind's eyes, hot and stinging, and began to roll down her cheeks. She raised a hand to wipe them away.

Beatrice stood there, regarding her with that icy smile. Like a different person, not the woman she knew but a stranger who appeared cold and indifferent to her shock and incomprehension. Who could agree to take someone else's baby as a prize in a race? Who would even suggest such an idea? Had it been Hugh, anxious to placate his wife and give her a child to focus on to relieve her depression after losing her own? Or perhaps Beatrice had dreamed up this insane plan to keep Hugh on her side and prevent him and Dr Richards sending her to the sanatorium for treatment.

Sadie's words that morning sprang into Rosalind's mind. The maid had stood with her head bowed and murmured that she'd been reluctant to speak at first but her mistress's distress prompted her. Sadie heard something strange mentioned while she and Harriet were staying at the big house. A young girl called Ruby worked there as a kitchen maid, a niece of Mrs O'Brien the cook, and she told Sadie that before Ivor's arrival her mistress had a cot with a large doll in it. A baby doll in the nursery that she used to visit before bedtime and, Ruby whispered to Sadie, someone had even heard her talking to the doll and singing a lullaby. Wasn't that an unusual way for a grown woman to behave?

Sadie's comments worried Rosalind. Surely someone else should be told about the doll in the nursery? Someone who might agree to help.

If Beatrice was so determined to keep Ivor, Rosalind might have to resort to desperate measures. She might have to enlist Dr Richards's aid. She would tell him Sadie's story and ask him if a woman who suffered from melancholia and talked to a doll as if it was a real baby was a fit person to take away her child. He would help her get Ivor back. He would know what to do and how to convince Hugh and Beatrice that what they were doing was wrong.

Rosalind got to her feet, attempting to keep her voice calm and steady. "Very well, then. I'll come another day to bring Ivor home when you've prepared him to leave and packed up his things. I'll talk to Edward and we'll let you know several days in advance. Thank you for the tea. I'll take Harriet home now."

"You're welcome to the tea. It was good of you to come over. The girls love having Harriet to visit because she has such imagination and she keeps them all entertained with her games."

As if nothing had happened, as if no disagreement had come between them, Beatrice strolled off down the lawn towards the lower terrace to summon her daughters.

Chapter Thirty-Four

Rosalind and Harriet walked their horses into the stable yard as two of the boys lingered outside the tack room, one with a cigarette dangling in his thin fingers.

Rosalind looked around. "Peter, have you seen the master?"

He stood upright and extinguished the cigarette with the toe of his boot. "No, ma'am, not since he left in the carriage with Mr Hugh before noon. Gone for four hours now or thereabouts."

Another stable boy appeared with Frank close behind him.

"Joseph, take the pony and Romeo," Frank told him. "Wisp them over and give them fresh water and hay. Well now, Mrs Thornton, did you have a good ride?" He helped her down from the saddle and passed Romeo's reins to the small freckled boy with bright blue eyes. "Are you all right, ma'am?"

"Yes, yes, of course."

He raised his eyebrows. "If you say so."

"I do say so." She realized that sounded impolite and added, "I beg your pardon, I have a headache. Have you seen Edward?"

"He's due back shortly." He took out his pocket watch, a battered brass one with a cracked face, and squinted at it. "He went with Master Hugh to see a new gallop near Wexford. They have plans for extending the one here, I believe. New steeplechase fences, too. Nothing but the very best for Ardlackan Lodge." He flashed one of his quick smiles at her but it faded when she didn't respond. "I apologize, I was only… a little jest."

It took all her strength to suppress the tears that sprang into her eyes; to force them back, biting her lip with agitation. If only he didn't always sound so kind and sympathetic. She felt an urge to reach out and lay her hand on the sleeve of his jacket; to ask him for advice but she swung away and swallowed her words. She'd probably given too much away already as Frank was intuitive and she often suspected he could read her thoughts.

"Would you like me to tell the master you wish to speak to him when he arrives?"

She removed her riding hat. "Please do. I will be in the house. Ask him to come and find me." She knew she should walk away but she didn't move. She remained standing beside him, her fingers gripping her hat.

She would have to be determined this time; force Edward to listen to her and make him understand that the situation was getting out of hand. Beatrice taking on the nursemaid was the last straw and something had to be done immediately to convince her that Ivor was coming home. She was becoming too possessive, too fond of him and as for all that nonsense about Edward and Hugh having a wager and the winner taking the baby, that was all it was. Nonsense. As were many of the thoughts in Beatrice's mind these days. She obviously hadn't recovered her equilibrium since losing her own baby. It was all very well to indulge her for a few months but now it was time to reintroduce her to reality.

"Are you worried about Master Ivor?" Frank glanced at the cobblestones. "He's coming home soon, isn't he?"

Rosalind drew in a breath. If Edward drove into the yard now it would be all she could do not to scream at him in front of the staff and suave Cousin Hugh. Edward was easily led and she suspected that his older cousin was the perpetrator of this ridiculous scheme. She had been duped into complying with it.

She swiped a hand at the flies buzzing around her face. July was a bad month for the insects and they drove the horses demented. Romeo had tossed his head all the way home in an effort to stop the horrible things landing on his nose and clustering around the corners of his eyes.

"I hope so, Frank. Yes, I'm worried about Ivor and I know I shouldn't be saying this to you but I fear Beatrice doesn't understand how much I long to have him home again."

Lines of concern ran across Frank's brow and she was certain that he understood exactly what she was talking about. Had he also known about the result of the match race? About Hugh taking the baby? How humiliating and embarrassing!

Rosalind's voice trembled. "You know what happened, don't you?"

He dropped his gaze to the toes of his boots.

"Don't you, Frank? Tell me the truth, for heaven's sake. I don't wish to be lied to."

At her words, he stepped closer. "I never would lie to you. I never would."

She clasped the brim of her riding hat in her fingers. "Then what have you heard? Tell me. Tell me about the race. Did you hear what the prize was?"

He still didn't look at her but said in a low voice, barely louder than a whisper, "I heard something all right. I heard something that I could hardly believe. I didn't wish to believe it, to be honest."

She sighed. He obviously knew all about the nonsensical bet, the ridiculous wager between the two cousins. Between an arrogant man with a strong desire for a son to inherit his house and lands because his wife had so far failed, through no fault of her own, to provide him with an heir. The other weaker cousin always in Hugh's debt both financially and emotionally. If Frank knew about it, it must be true. The thought made her stomach lurch. A mist blurred her vision and she swayed.

Frank stepped forward and put his arm round her shoulders. "Do you feel ill? You look very pale."

She couldn't reply.

"Will I help you to the house? Perhaps you need to lie down."

This time she did nothing to stem the flow of tears that coursed down her cheeks. She dropped her hat to the ground and sobbed against his shoulder. "Oh, oh... I'm sorry... I'm so sorry... but I... I don't know what to do. I don't know how to get Edward to listen to me."

Harriet ran over to them. "Mama? Are you unwell? Why, you are crying! What is the matter?"

"Your mama is feeling poorly," Frank replied and waved a hand at Peter to keep him at a distance. "Run into the house, there's a good girl. Go, quickly! Bring back a glass of water."

"I'll be well soon," Rosalind muttered. "Pray don't distress yourself, Harriet... my darling."

Her daughter's worried eyes peered into her face. "I'll go straight away. Oh oh, perhaps you should sit down."

"I'll assist her over to the mounting block," Frank said. "You go now."

Harriet's boots pounded across the cobblestones as she headed towards the door into the garden.

Frank supported Rosalind by her elbow and they walked to the granite block by the dark pink rose. She sank onto the warm stone surface and Frank sat beside her.

"Thank you," she murmured. "I'm obliged to you..."

"I'll have a word with him."

"Would you?"

"I'll speak to Edward," Frank assured her. "The master, I mean. Let me talk to him about this, about your... your distress."

"But... no, I shouldn't..." A wave of nausea struck her and she closed her eyes. Perhaps it was the heat causing her headache and this sickness. The overwhelming humidity.

"Only if you wish me to, of course," he said, "but I know how to... how to get around him perhaps. I've known him all my life. Let me talk to him."

"Would you? That would be kind of you and I... well, I've tried but I don't seem to have success at getting him to listen."

She heard the rumble of carriage wheels. Horses' hooves rang out as the two bays and the landau driven by Edward hurtled under the arch and into the yard.

He leaned back and hauled on the reins. "Whoa! Whoa there! Damn you!"

Frank nodded at Peter to go to his master's assistance. The young man ran over and grabbed the reins, while Edward jumped down and tossed his driving whip to him.

"Bloody animals!" He turned to Frank and Rosalind, striding over to them. "What's going on here? Rosalind? What's going on?"

She kept her eyes on the ground while Frank murmured, "Mrs Thornton is unwell, sir. I've sent Miss Harriet into the house to fetch a glass of water to help revive her."

"Faint?" Edward peered into her face. "Not surprised with the damn weather. We'll have a mighty storm later, I'm sure of it. Peter, get those horses washed down. They're caked in dust."

White foam frothed around the mouths of the bays and their heaving flanks dripped sweat.

Frank narrowed his eyes. "Driving them hard, were you?"

Edward laughed. "I wanted to see what they're made of. Have to impress Hugh sometimes. I managed to get the pair to canter up the avenue to Ardlackan House. He was breathless and clinging to the seat by the time we reached the front door. Frightened the life out of him, I did." Edward chortled with amusement and sat down beside Rosalind. "What's the matter, my love?"

She shook her head and closed her eyes.

He moved closer and she could smell alcohol and cigars on his breath. "Come on, you're not as frail as you think."

Rosalind got to her feet and Frank reached out to support her.

Edward pushed him away. "Get your grimy hands off her, man! Here, Ros, take my arm and I'll help you into the house. It's the weather, this cursed heat, that's all and those tight corsets you vain women insist on wearing. Get on with your work, O'Rafferty, I can handle this."

Rosalind cast an apologetic glance at Frank. "Thank you for your help. I'm grateful for your sympathy."

Edward grinned. "Sympathy! What nonsense! I've never received much sympathy from Frank over the years."

His head lad forced a smile. "Not sure you deserve it."

Edward gave him a playful push and staggered slightly before steadying himself and walking towards the door into the garden, one hand gripping Rosalind's arm as he hauled her after him.

He must have been drinking with Hugh again. His cousin's capacity for whiskey was considerably greater than his. The thought of Edward driving the lively pair of horses while three sheets to the wind was terrifying. He could have wrapped the carriage around a tree trunk and killed both himself and his cousin. Hadn't he done enough damage already to Beatrice and her unborn child? Rosalind's eyes flooded with tears again but she hastily wiped them away with the sleeve of her riding habit. No point trying to remonstrate with her husband now in his inebriated state because he wouldn't listen and would only accuse her of making an unnecessary fuss.

"This way, my dearest," he muttered, negotiating the gravel walk beyond the door and almost toppling into the herbaceous border on the right, as a flash of lightning lit the darkening sky and thunder growled closer.

She wrenched her arm away from his grasp. "Thank you. I'm

feeling better now and able to walk on my own." He would only deposit her in the middle of the delphiniums. She walked on along the path ahead of him.

"What were you and Frank doing anyway?" His voice sounded slurred.

"What are you talking about?"

"You looked a close pair there on the mounting block, eh? Far too close for my liking... for a husband's liking."

"For goodness sake, don't talk nonsense. I was feeling a bit faint and he helped me over to sit down, that's all it was."

"A fine sight to see as I drove into the yard! My wife and the coachman almost on top of each other with all the boys watching... and Harriet as well, I suppose?"

"You're being ridiculous, please stop."

He lurched forward and grabbed her shoulder. "Oh, I am, am I? Don't walk away from me like that. I want to talk to you... this has got to end, this hobnobbing with the stable staff and your unseemly friendship with O'Rafferty in particular. Mama is concerned about Harriet mixing with the boys. I told you before to request them to bring the riding horses to the front door. You and Harriet are not to go near the stable yard. Damn it, do you ever see Beatrice loitering in their yard? She has the good sense and breeding to alight from her horse or carriage at the front of the house."

Rosalind stepped sideways and ducked out of his reach as he missed his footing and fell over the stone edging, landing on his back on the lawn. He lay there for several seconds, speechless and winded.

Rosalind looked down at him and held out her hand.

He gripped it, making her wince. "Get me up, for God's sake."

"What will your dear Mama say when she sees you in this drunken state, I wonder?"

"What did you say?"

"Gertrude will not be impressed. She told me Hugh drinks too much."

"Mama won't care. She loves me… she loves me more than you do, that's for certain."

"Don't be silly and please hold your tongue. Troy is coming from the kitchen garden with the wheelbarrow. Here, allow me to help you up."

At the sight of Troy, Edward struggled to his feet and hurried them both into the house through the basement door. More lightning cracked and rain splattered on the steps behind them. In the cool dark interior, he leaned against the wall and reached out to smooth her hair. He slid his hand behind her head and jerked her towards him, kissing her roughly on the mouth.

Rosalind thrust her palms against his chest and pushed him away, turning towards the wooden stairs to the front hall. She hurried up them, blood pulsing through her veins.

Chapter Thirty-Five

The past - 9th July, 1891

"It's been one week." Rosalind stood in front of Edward's desk. "Another week has passed since you promised to talk to Hugh and Beatrice… since I told her I would take the carriage over to bring Ivor home. I don't understand why you have done nothing about this."

He glanced up from the ledger in which he was writing lists of horses' names and entries for upcoming races. His spidery handwriting crawled across the page; the initials of the stable boys who looked after each animal entered in a box on the right-hand side.

Behind him shelves of stud books sat in glass-fronted bookcases and a portrait of Ardlackan Lass hung on the wall, standing alert in the middle of the yard with her flaxen mane and one white sock, the cerise flowering rose and stone mounting block behind her. Edward had never had a portrait painted of his wife or daughter. Even his father, renowned for his lack of interest in family and for his abiding obsession with horses, had commissioned one of himself and another of Gertrude and these were on display in the dining room on either side of the marble mantelpiece.

Edward grimaced and ran a hand through his already tousled

hair. "Must you go on about this incessantly? I told you then and I'll tell you again now that it is good for Beatrice to have Ivor with her. Hugh says she is feeling better… her health is improving and she's showing more interest in life since Ivor went to stay with them. Another few weeks are all it might take for her to be completely well again and then she may consider trying to have another baby. Please don't be so selfish, Rosalind. It's not like you to be so thoughtless. He will be back soon."

Rosalind swung away, stepping over to the window and staring out at the lawn sweeping down to the woods.

"He'll be back soon," Edward repeated.

"You say that every time I mention Ivor. You think I'm selfish and should consider Beatrice's feelings. Well, Beatrice doesn't care about mine so I've spoken to Dr Richards. I went to see him."

He lifted his eyes and fixed them on hers as she turned to face him. "That was foolish and unnecessary. No need to bring him into this. This is a family agreement between Hugh and me and it's got nothing to do with the good doctor."

Rosalind picked at a piece of loose paint on the wooden shutter. She rolled it between her fingers, crumbling it and flicking the flakes out through the open window.

Edward bent over his ledger again and murmured, "Perhaps you should ask Dr Richards for something to calm your nerves. You seem overwrought these days."

"Overwrought? Can you blame me?"

"Mama is concerned about you, you know. She thinks perhaps…"

"Well? Do go on. What does Mama think now?"

He twirled the fountain pen in his fingers, frowning at her sarcasm. "She thinks… she thinks you seem a little hysterical this week. Overwrought, yes, that's a better word. She suggested Dr Richards might give you something to help. One of his potions for ladies with…"

Rosalind regarded him in silence.

He twisted his mouth to one side and shot a quick glance at her before dropping his eyes to the desk. "Fixated, Mama said. She believes you're fixated about the baby and not able to accept that this... um... this arrangement is only for a short time."

Her fingers shook and she clasped them in front of her so that he would not notice. "How dare she! How dare she say that about me! I'm not the one who needs a doctor. It's Beatrice who's not well. Have you told Gertrude about the wager with Hugh and how you lost your son in a gamble on a race?"

No reply.

"Well? Have you? And then Hugh, and possibly Beatrice too, arranged for someone to slip out of the crowd to frighten your mare and she threw you off. Can't you see what's happened here? They cheated. They cheated and now they've taken our son." Her voice rose in anger as she paced across the room and stood looking down at him, laying the palms of her hands on the desk and leaning towards him, willing him to understand.

He ran his finger down the list of horses' names and ignored her.

Rosalind reached forward, snatching the ledger and flinging it across the room. It crashed against the wall beside the window and fell to the ground, pages flapping like a wounded bird. "That's what I think of you and your spinelessness. I will go and get the boy myself. It's the only way, I see that now. I will ask Frank to help me."

Edward stood, stretched towards the wall behind and pulled the bell lever. "You are overwrought. I'm sending for Sadie to take you to your room. I'll ask Patrick to ride for Dr Richards straight away. I'm afraid you are losing your reason, Rosalind. You're creating a huge drama out of this and need something to calm you."

She wanted to open her mouth to scream but managed

to suppress the urge because she realized it would alarm her husband even more.

Was she overreacting? She'd been finding it difficult to sleep during the last week and often spent hours lying awake staring into the darkness, while her husband snored peacefully beside her. She felt limp and exhausted in the morning until she dressed and took her morning walk with Harriet around the garden and down to the beach. Perhaps he and Gertrude were right; perhaps she really was beginning to lose her mind.

Aunt Catherine had avoided talking about Rosalind's mother during the visit to Hampstead but her last letter had included more details. Mama's illness started with terrible headaches and she had to take laudanum and lie down in a dark room. She began to have seizures and these gradually worsened. Papa had been left with no choice when the doctors insisted that she needed to go to a sanatorium where she would receive expert treatment. Her mother must have been seriously ill; she'd needed medical care soon after Rosalind was born. It sounded like Hugh might not have heard the true story. Perhaps he'd picked up gossip and lies.

Beatrice was the one Dr Richards should be worried about; Beatrice with her sudden strange moods and obsessions. The tragedy of losing her baby had made everything so much worse.

The door opened and Sadie appeared. Rosalind glanced at her calm expression and relief swelled inside her. Sadie would understand her frustration.

Edward returned to his desk and sat down. "Ah, Sadie, your mistress is unwell. Take her to her room and make sure she is comfortable. I suggest a few hours in bed. I'll send for Dr Richards."

"Oh, my poor mistress," Sadie murmured, "I will help her, sir, I will. Come with me, ma'am. We'll go upstairs. Is it one of your headaches again?"

Rosalind opened her mouth to deny any illness but Edward

picked up his pen and was writing another name in his ledger. Tears flooded into her eyes and a wave of helplessness swept over her. She moved towards the maid, allowing her to put an arm round her waist and lead her out into the hallway.

At the top of the staircase Rosalind hesitated. She shouldn't go along with this. If she permitted her husband to treat her like an invalid, it would only add more substance to his claims that she was acting out of character.

"Shall I give you some of my drops for headaches?" Sadie asked. "You remember last time, the night of the thunderstorm? You were so upset that night and it worked then, didn't it? It sent you off to sleep."

"Sadie, listen to me please. I don't have a headache. There is nothing wrong with me."

"But the master said…"

"I don't need the doctor. This charade has gone on long enough. All I want is my baby… I want my son to come home."

Sadie gave her a gentle push in the small of her back. "This way. Let's go into your bedroom where you can have a lie down. You'll feel more yourself after a sleep."

Rosalind followed her along the corridor where more family portraits, generations of Thorntons, looked on. She imagined them judging her: the young and foolish wife Edward had brought home from England, who knew nothing about horses or racing and whose mother spent her last days incarcerated in a sanatorium with a distressing illness.

She was shaking all over by the time she reached the bed and her fingers felt ice cold in spite of the warmth of the day. Perhaps she was coming down with a fever. The headaches and chills might be the forerunners of something worse. She allowed Sadie to undress her and help her into her nightgown. She would be patient and wait to see if she felt better after a rest. Only three hours sleep the night before and her head throbbed; her eyes bloodshot when she glanced in the looking glass at a face pale as milk.

She climbed into bed and lay back on the pillows, while Sadie pulled the bedspread up round her shoulders and smiled down at her with such sympathy that tears ran down Rosalind's cheeks and soaked the linen of the uppermost pillowcase.

Sadie reached out and stroked Rosalind's hair away from her forehead. "There, there, don't weep so. You'll be feeling better in no time… and Dr Richards will soon be here. Such a kind man and he'll know how to help you."

Loud sobs forced their way up from Rosalind's chest and she buried her face in the pillow.

Sadie continued stroking her hair and murmuring how she needed to relax and not worry about the baby. He would be home soon, she said, and there was no point making herself anxious, ill and distressed.

Rosalind turned her head to gaze at her. "How do you know that? How do you know he will ever come home? I believe my husband and his cousin have come to an agreement that my baby will never come home… never. I think I've lost him forever. Ivor will never be mine again now Beatrice has employed a nursemaid and is showing him off to local families as if he's her adopted son." More sobs burst from her throat and she took the handkerchief that Sadie offered and wiped her stinging eyes. "Oh, God, what can I do? Dear God, what can I do to stop this madness?"

"Hush, hush. You're not mad. You're just tired and upset."

Rosalind sat up. "I don't mean me. I mean this nonsense… this stupid arrangement or whatever it is between my husband and his cousin."

Sadie remained silent, sitting on the edge of the bed and watching her.

"You must have heard," Rosalind whispered. "You must have

heard what happened. Tell me what you've heard."

"Dr Richards will be here soon, don't worry. Would you like me to fetch you a glass of water? Or perhaps a little wine?"

"Sadie, please listen, please tell me I'm not imagining this. My husband and Mr Hugh had an agreement... a bet on the result of the race... you remember the match? You remember that Major Langstown told me a man barged out of the crowd by the fence and frightened the master's mare? It must have been deliberate. Whoever did that must have been put up to it by Hugh and Beatrice so that they could take my baby, my darling boy."

The maid rested her hand on her mistress's forehead. "You're very cold. Shall I send for a hot drink? Some tea perhaps or wine?"

Rosalind threw off the bed covers. "Stop this! Stop talking and listen to me. Am I the only one around here who believes that something bizarre is going on? I feel you suspect something and I know Frank O'Rafferty definitely does. I want to speak to Frank. Please fetch him for me."

Sadie's blue eyes widened. "Oh, I can't. Not now you're... well, you're in bed and what would the master think? Wait until Dr Richards comes. You're upset, of course you are."

Rosalind tried to get out of the bed but Sadie restrained her; surprisingly strong for her slight build. "No, ma'am, stay here and rest. We'll talk about this later after Dr Richards has been. You'll be able to think clearly then, when the headache has gone."

"I don't have a headache. Why do you think I have a headache?"

"The master... didn't he say you had a headache?"

Rosalind lay back. She couldn't think straight. Edward hadn't mentioned that. He'd thought her overwrought and hysterical.

She knew she needed to remain calm when the doctor came because it would provide an opportunity to reiterate what she'd already told him the day she visited him after seeing Beatrice.

She'd explained that she was worried about her friend and wanted his opinion on Beatrice's ability to look after Ivor. Was she capable of caring for him?

Dr Richards had been his usual tactful self. He was Hugh and Beatrice's physician too, of course, and had been reassuring but cautious. Beatrice had recovered from her melancholia, he'd said, she was restored to health thanks to the wonderful prescription he'd given her. Of course she would be able to look after the baby and she'd been kind to take care of both children while they were away in France. He'd responded as if Rosalind had been making a fuss about nothing. Heat rose to her cheeks when she recalled the kind but rather patronizing glimmer in his pale eyes.

Perhaps this was a conspiracy between all of them? They'd come together to dream up this plan to stop her getting her son back. Her limbs trembled at the thought and she closed her eyes. No, no, she was really beginning to feel overwrought and her imagination was running away with her. She would listen to Sadie and have a rest. She needed to sleep and then she would be able to think clearly. She would know what to do once her mind was calm.

Sadie left the room and returned in fifteen minutes with a small glass of wine. Rosalind sat up and allowed the maid to rearrange the pillows behind her.

Dr Richards arrived soon afterwards with Gertrude, who'd been summoned from the garden. Her mother-in-law ushered the doctor into the bedroom and waved a dismissal at Sadie, who glanced reassuringly at her mistress before leaving the room.

"Mrs Thornton has been poorly since she returned from France," Gertrude said. "Perhaps something she picked up there? Some nasty foreign germs?"

Dr Richards sat on the side of the bed and examined Rosalind's throat, his cool fingers lingering on her glands. "Hmm, I'm not so sure that's what this is. Perhaps a cold coming on?

How do you feel, my dear?"

"I feel perfectly well," Rosalind replied, trying to keep her voice level. "Perhaps I haven't been sleeping but..."

That was the wrong thing to say. The doctor surveyed her from under his bushy eyebrows. "Not sleeping, eh? That's bad, that's most unfortunate. How long has this been going on... this lack of sleep?"

She shouldn't have mentioned her insomnia but too late to withdraw the words now. "Perhaps a week or two. Perhaps since we came back from France."

Gertrude's lips parted in a thin smile. "You see? I told you so, Doctor. I know a foreign illness when I see one. Some disgusting Gallic disease."

The doctor turned to Rosalind's mother-in-law. "Would you mind if I examined her on my own for a few minutes? If you please, Mrs Thornton... I would like to ask her a few more... er... personal questions."

Gertrude inclined her head. "Ah, I see what you mean. A few questions about her state of mind. She's been a bit hysterical..."

"If you please, Mrs Thornton."

Gertrude hesitated before leaving the room, pulling the door closed behind her.

If only Sadie could have stayed to provide moral support.

Dr Richards walked over to his large black bag that he'd left on the floor near the window. "Tell me now that we're alone, what is troubling you? I don't believe for one minute that you've picked up something in France. It's this anxiety about the baby, isn't it?"

Rosalind swallowed to clear her throat. "Yes. No one seems to understand why I'm upset. They've taken my baby boy and nothing I say makes them appreciate how unfair... how odd this is. It's as if they think I am creating a fuss about nothing."

He murmured, bending over his bag and rummaging in its

depths, "Not really so odd, dear lady. Hugh and Beatrice offered to look after the baby for a few weeks while you were away. He'll soon be back with you. I met Hugh this morning in the village and he happened, quite by coincidence, to mention the baby and how much they would miss the little fellow when he leaves them."

Rosalind's heart skipped a beat and began to dance in her chest. "Did he say that? Oh, Dr Richards, oh, thank you, that's wonderful news! They really mean to send Ivor home after all. I thought…"

Dr Richards moved back to the bed, a bottle in his hand. "You thought they meant to keep him, didn't you? But they won't do that. They would never do that. He's your baby, after all, and Edward would never allow them to hold onto him for too long."

"Yes, but he said…"

The doctor sat on the edge of the bed, his right hand gripping the bottle, fingers twisting around the glass and obscuring the label. "Your family is very concerned about you. They're worried you've been under a lot of strain and now, with this insomnia, your nerves are frayed so I've got just the thing to help you. A spoonful twice a day and you'll soon be better. Then we can see about the baby coming home but, at the moment, I fear a little baby would be too much for you to manage. When you've recovered, we can think about it and, in the meantime, he is safe with Hugh and Beatrice. You need have no worries about him whatsoever."

Rosalind sat upright, her throat tightening, and when she opened her mouth no words came. What did he mean? She wasn't ill. She wasn't the one who needed to get better in order to get her baby back. No, Dr Richards had taken her up wrong. Edward must have said something to him about her flash of temper. She should never have snatched the ledger up and hurled it across the study like that. She was usually so placid.

"But I'm perfectly well. I'm…"

"There now, just take this and rest. You're worn out. Here, swallow this spoonful and close your eyes. You'll soon be well again, I promise." He poured liquid onto a spoon and held it out. "Open your mouth, my dear. It will help you relax. One of my best preparations and many of my ladies rely on it."

"What is it?"

"A wonderful tonic for the nerves. In a couple of days, you'll have forgotten all about your worries and you'll be able to cope again. Open your mouth."

Rosalind gripped the bedspread with both hands, pushing her head back against the pillows. When the spoon touched her lips, she slid under the sheet.

"Now, Mrs Thornton, do you want me to have to fetch your husband? He'll be disappointed if you don't try to get well. You do want your baby son back, don't you? I'm afraid I can't advise that unless you make an effort to take your tonic."

Was she in the middle of a terrible nightmare? She wasn't the one who needed medicine for her nerves. It was Beatrice who wasn't well, not her. Or was the doctor warning her; issuing a mild threat? Was he suggesting she wouldn't be able to get Ivor back unless she went along with his treatment?

The tonic was probably only laudanum, or something similar. Perhaps it would be better to swallow the spoonful and be done with it.

She opened her mouth and Dr Richards pushed in the medicine. The liquid ran down her throat and tasted quite pleasant; rather sweet and syruplike. She swallowed and licked her lips.

Dr Richards stood up. "There, that wasn't so bad, was it? I'll leave instructions with your mother-in-law to see that you get this twice a day and I'll come back later this week to check how you're getting on. I'm certain you'll be sleeping better and feeling stronger by then."

He retrieved his bag; gave her a nod before leaving the room.

Rosalind didn't move for several minutes, her mind confused and thoughts jumbled. He sounded so convincing, that elderly doctor, and she almost believed him. He'd said that Hugh mentioned Ivor coming home. Was that true? Perhaps if she complied with the doctor's instructions and took the medicine or tonic or whatever it was, all would be well. If she agreed to let him treat her, perhaps she could convince him and Edward and Gertrude that her mind was perfectly composed. Once the doctor believed her restored to health, then the others would listen to her. This idea calmed her and she yawned, turning on her side and closing her eyes.

Chapter Thirty-Six

The past - 15th July, 1891

Storm clouds buffeted the creaking masts as the ship tossed and pitched amongst rolling waves. A sailor near the prow yelled into the wind, his voice borne away and drowned out by the flapping of sails. He raised his arms above his head, his mouth open and eyes bulging before turning to point into the distance.

Rosalind ran towards him, straining her ears to catch his words and clutching at ropes to maintain her balance as another wave crashed over the deck. Her bare feet slipped on the sopping planks and she landed with a thud of pain, the gale howling in her ears while salt water mixed with blood seeped through her nightdress.

"Ma'am, ma'am... oh, oh, what has happened? Mary, run to fetch Mrs Thornton, hurry, girl. Don't just stand there gawping, get a move on!"

Rosalind lay where she'd fallen, dimly aware of Sadie's voice and a throbbing spasm in her left leg.

"Mrs Thornton, can you hear me?"

Rosalind opened her eyes and the ceiling of the bedroom lurched towards her. She turned her head to one side and groaned.

Footsteps rang out along the corridor and the door burst

open, banging against the wall. Harriet's voice cried, "Mama, I met Mary hurrying to fetch Grandmama. She said you are ill."

The girl kneeled beside Rosalind and pushed her face into hers, her breath warm on Rosalind's frozen cheeks and a smell of something sweet, the scent of hay and horses.

Rosalind attempted to sit up but cried out in pain. "I've hurt myself, darling," she whispered. "But you mustn't worry. Fetch Sadie, there's a good girl."

"But Sadie is here beside me. Can't you see her?"

Sadie's matter-of-fact voice spoke. "She fell out of bed, Miss Harriet. That's all. Nothing to worry about. Now, please give her some air to breathe, step back and allow me to help her up."

Harriet refused to be moved aside and was soon pulling Rosalind's hand while Sadie put her arm around her and asked her to straighten her leg.

"Can't..." Rosalind closed her eyes as nausea flooded her stomach, stealing up her throat. She clamped her mouth shut. It wouldn't do to vomit on the rug.

Sadie and Harriet helped Rosalind into an upright position and straightened out her legs. The pain was ebbing away but a blue-black bruise mushroomed on her left shin. Rosalind reached out to touch it.

What had happened to her? One minute she was dreaming about the storm and the ship. She was on the ship, wasn't she? Something terrible was about to happen, something was coming at them out of the tumbling waves. The man shouting and waving had looked frightened out of his wits. He could see what it was. A reef appearing from the deep, perhaps, a barrier of rocks across the bow that would break the vessel into flitters and toss its timbers to the devouring sea.

Rosalind shuddered.

"Where is Mary?" Sadie asked. "Miss Harriet, would you please go down to the kitchen and ask Mrs O'Brien for a pot of tea… and don't forget sugar. Your mama will need sweet tea to revive her."

"But I don't want to leave her. Can't you go?"

"I'll stay with her, my love. I'll be here in case she feels faint again. Just run down quickly, like a good girl, and you'll soon be back. And if you see that lazy Mary on your way, you tell her to get a move on."

"Go, Harriet," Rosalind murmured. "Go and fetch me tea. That would be so kind of you."

Harriet rose to her feet and ran across the rug to the door. She turned, her hand clutching the knob. "You will be all right, won't you? I couldn't bear it if…"

Sadie smiled at the girl. "Of course she will. All she did was roll out of bed in her sleep. It's just a little weakness, that's all. Your mama has been feeling poorly but we'll soon have her back to full strength again. Dr Richards is dropping in later to check on her. Make haste, Miss Harriet, the tea will help your mother."

Harriet pulled the door closed behind her and Rosalind heard her footsteps running towards the servants' staircase on the left.

"Do you wish to tell me what happened?" Sadie sat on her hunkers beside Rosalind, her arm still draped across her shoulders. "You were shouting about rocks, I think."

Rosalind rested her head on the maid's shoulder. Perhaps it had been Hook Head lighthouse looming out of the waves, with its wicked rocks waiting; waiting to crush the wooden vessel and spit back the wreckage to the deep. "A nightmare, that's all. A ship in a storm. There was something coming at us and I fell on the deck and was covered in blood and…"

Sadie's arm squeezed her reassuringly. "You were having a bad dream… indeed you were, but you're safe now. Dr Richards will be here soon. You've been so ill this week. We've all been worried about you."

Leaning on Sadie, Rosalind rose slowly to her feet. She shivered again and glanced at the window. Outside the sun beamed over the pine trees; the call of a herring gull on the warm air.

She laid her head on the bedspread and groaned. "I don't know what's wrong with me. I felt perfectly well until about five days ago and now I'm so weak and nauseous. I was sick yesterday, don't you remember? It's like I've been poisoned by something I've eaten. Has anyone else in the household been taken ill?"

"No one is ill except you. Will I help you back into bed?"

Rosalind shook her head and pushed her hair out of her face. "No, I wish to sit in that armchair near the window where I can look at the sea. I think I've been too long in bed… growing weak from lying here. Perhaps that's what it is."

"Did you take your tonic this morning?"

Rosalind made her way over to the chair, holding onto Sadie's arm, the muscles in her legs shaking with fatigue. "No, I don't think so."

"I remember now that Mrs Thornton had to go out this morning. It went out of my head when I saw you lying on the floor. It's no wonder poor Mary can't find her and is taking so long. The master had a fall on the gallops and Mrs Thornton was called."

Rosalind's fingers gripped Sadie's arm. "Edward had a fall? Is he injured?"

"No, Mrs O'Brien said he was just winded but his mother went to check on him."

"Then I needn't worry."

Edward moved into the blue guest bedroom when she was taken ill, to give her some peace supposedly. The dreariness of the days now! One day crept into the next, the hours stealing past in a haze when she woke up every now and then to stare at stars or a cloudless sky through the windowpanes; hours interspersed with vivid dreams.

Did she have a fever or some kind of delirium? Perhaps she'd caught some strange foreign disease after all and Gertrude's fears were justified.

Rosalind sat in the armchair facing the window while Sadie draped a blanket over her knees and tucked it behind her.

"Are you comfortable?" she asked. "I'll do your hair now, will I? I'll make you look respectable for Dr Richards."

Outside on the lawn Troy and Patrick spoke in low voices, their heads close together. Patrick held a cigarette in one hand while the older man's wrinkled face wore a grim expression. Whatever Patrick was telling him, Troy didn't believe it.

Rosalind watched as this familiar scene played out between the head gardener and his inexperienced apprentice brought her back to reality; anchored her in the present. It would do her good to sit up and see what was happening in the world outside her bedroom. She'd felt so isolated and alone; so tired of sleeping.

"Sadie, I don't want to see Dr Richards today. Will you tell Mrs Thornton please? Tell her I don't feel up to it."

"But ma'am, that's why you need to see him, because you're still feeling poorly."

"He's not making me better. I feel worse… don't want any more of his tonic. It doesn't agree with me… stomach cramps last night, so bad I thought I was going to be sick again. Ever since I started taking that medicine, I've felt worse, I tell you. I won't have any more of it."

She sounded like a petulant child but she didn't care. She wouldn't allow them to force the medicine down her throat. She would throw the contents of the bottle out of the window. Do that now before Gertrude arrived. She pointed at the bedside table. "Will you fetch the medicine for me, please?"

"Are you going to take it after all? Probably best. Dr Richards knows…"

"Just bring it to me, will you?"

Sadie gave her the bottle and a spoon.

"Thank you. I won't need the spoon." Rosalind removed the cork in the neck of the blue bottle. She sniffed it and read the label again. *Nerve Tonic. For Nervous Headache, Debility and Want of Sleep. Highly recommended by the medical profession.* So much for that! The medical profession didn't have to drink the disgusting potion. She stepped towards the window.

"Careful, you're going to spill it." Sadie reached out.

Rosalind was too quick for her. She tilted the bottle and deposited the remains of the liquid on the rose bed below her window.

"Oh ma'am!"

Rosalind flopped back onto the armchair. "Now we'll see if I feel stronger this afternoon. I think I'd like to get dressed."

"But Mrs Thornton said you should stay in your room for another couple of days."

Rosalind closed her eyes and yawned. No, perhaps she wouldn't get dressed yet. She felt so tired, but she would love to see her baby.

Perhaps Frank would drive her up to the big house.

Edward had told her to stay away until she recovered but surely Beatrice wouldn't mind if she only visited for a few minutes. She needed to see Ivor and check he was happy and well fed. She yearned to see his chubby little face and dimples. He was growing hair now, light brown curly hair like hers.

He would take after her, she was sure of it. He wasn't going to be a Thornton.

"Perhaps this afternoon instead, Sadie. I might feel stronger by then."

A frown still creased the maid's brow. She obviously worried about Rosalind defying her mother-in-law. How Gertrude Thornton struck fear and dread into the hearts of the servants at Ardlackan! Even Beatrice's maids were nervous of the woman. Only Edward was immune to her sharp criticism; oblivious to her displeasure, just as he was oblivious to anything that didn't concern him.

Rosalind sensed she'd also become invisible to him now due to more pressing concerns, such as the new plans for the stable yard and his growing debts. What money he'd won on Ardlackan Lass's win at Fairyhouse would soon be spent. She knew of his increasing financial worries; could tell by the way he'd paced about the room and sat on the armchair that she occupied now, his head in his hands and not paying attention to a word she was saying. He would never change. He never would. Nothing she could say would make any difference. He would continue to squander his way through her money just like he'd spent his way through Gertrude's before his marriage. No wonder Hugh Thornton held him in the palm of his hand. No wonder he was willing to come running when Hugh whistled. Edward was like an obedient spaniel, eager to answer his cousin's command.

Rosalind turned the bottle in her fingers. Earlier in the week, her mother-in-law had locked the bedroom door from the outside. Locked her into her room like a disobedient child in case she took it upon herself to get dressed and go downstairs. Rosalind had given up trying to argue with her. Too exhausting.

She heard Harriet calling from the bottom of the servants' staircase; her loyal kind daughter hurrying back.

How would she cope without Harriet and Sadie? Tears pricked the back of her eyes at the thought of being alone in the house with just Gertrude and Edward.

"Here comes Miss Harriet. I hope Mary will appear close behind her with your tea."

Rosalind beckoned to her. "Come nearer, I want to ask you something. Don't be shocked now…"

Sadie moved closer, her golden curls brushing against her mistress's cheek.

Rosalind handed her the bottle and whispered, "Can you fill

that up with water for me? I don't want anyone to know I've thrown the contents out of the window."

The maid hesitated. "Oh, but Mrs Thornton will…"

"Mrs Thornton won't notice the difference."

The maid looked away and didn't reply.

"Go on. I'll say it was me if I get caught. You won't be blamed… I promise you that."

Sadie walked over to the jug standing on the bedside table. She lifted it, slowly pouring water into the bottle and setting it back where it had been with the spoon beside it.

"I would like you to do something else for me. Would you mind?" Rosalind asked.

"Mind? I'll do whatever you wish."

"I haven't got much time because Harriet is nearly here but would you… would you…"

"What is it you want me to do?"

"Would you take a note to Frank O'Rafferty from me? Don't breathe a word to anyone else though. Would you do that?"

"Oh, well… I don't…"

"Would you? I'll pay you to do it. I'll give you…" Rosalind looked at the dressing table beside them. "I'll give you that brooch of the lily, the one you've always admired. Or the one like a shell?"

Sadie's blush spread from the lace collar of her maid's uniform up her already rosy cheeks. "Oh no, of course you don't need to give me anything. I'd be happy to do it for you. If you think…"

"I think it's my only chance of seeing the baby. How will you get the note to him? No one else should see you." Frank was her only hope. He'd offered to help her, hadn't he? If she ever needed him… She needed him now; needed his help desperately.

Harriet's footsteps sounded in the corridor.

"Frank comes into the kitchen with the stable boys at four o'clock," Sadie said. "I might be able to slip the note to him when he's leaving. I could follow him out into the garden so that Mrs O'Brien won't see me."

"Mama! I'm here."

Rosalind called out as her daughter pushed open the door. "I can see that, my love. Did you find Mary?" She reached out to touch Sadie's hand and added in a low voice, "This afternoon… come back after lunch and I'll give you the note. Not a word to anyone though, you promise?"

Sadie nodded. "I promise."

Chapter Thirty-Seven

The past - 15th July, 1891

Gertrude ushered Dr Richards into the bedroom, holding the door open and beckoning to Harriet with a forefinger. The girl rolled her eyes and shook her head.

"Now, child," Gertrude said. "Don't make me raise my voice. Your manners are appalling and you have no respect for your grandmother."

Harriet sighed and got to her feet, leaning across the bed to kiss her mother. As she walked past, Gertrude prodded her shoulder. "You watch out, young lady. You'll be off to boarding school before long and it won't be a day too soon." She turned to the doctor to apologize.

Harriet stood outside the door, grinning at Rosalind and sticking out her tongue behind her grandmother's back.

Rosalind suppressed a smile and Gertrude swung round to push the door shut in the girl's face.

Dr Richards deposited his black bag on the end of the bed. He reached out and took Rosalind's wrist in his fingers and felt her pulse. "How are you today, my dear? You look a little brighter."

"I'm feeling better, Doctor, thank you." She had to sound convincing. "Your tonic has made a difference. I'm feeling a good deal stronger than yesterday. "

Did he look slightly confused? He glanced at Gertrude and stroked his beard. "Ah, good to hear, very good indeed." His eyes moved in the direction of the bottle and he studied it. "You still have quite a lot of tonic left. Have you been taking it regularly?"

Sadie must have overfilled it. Rosalind hadn't noticed at the time.

"Of course," she said. "I've been taking half a spoonful just as you instructed."

His hand stroked the beard a little faster. "Half a spoonful, eh? I meant you to take one full spoon morning and evening. I wrote it on the label."

"Did you? I never read that, I'm sorry, but half a spoonful has worked wonders. I'd like to get up this afternoon."

"Is that wise?" Gertrude stepped closer and squinted at the bottle, holding it at arm's length. "Dr Richards, I would value your advice. Isn't there a danger of her becoming overtired? Why, only yesterday she was as weak as a kitten."

The doctor's eyes lingered on his patient.

"How is Edward? I heard he had a fall on the gallops." Rosalind decided to change the subject.

Gertrude sniffed. "Nothing serious. No bones broken and only his pride took a tumble. I do wish these stable boys wouldn't make such a fuss. When Peter arrived at the back door, I thought poor Edward had broken his neck at the very least."

She turned to Dr Richards who inclined his head and murmured something about the heavy burden of motherhood, full of care and worry.

Rosalind pushed herself up on the pillows. "I'd like to get dressed and see how I feel when I'm downstairs. I think staying too long in bed is making me weak."

The doctor exchanged another glance with Gertrude. "Hmm, perhaps for an hour or so and only in the drawing room where the fire is alight... and no visitors, mind. We don't want you exhausting yourself, do we?"

She hadn't expected him to give in so easily.

She was wrong. The doctor opened his bag and pulled out another bottle, larger than the first one. "Perhaps I'll change your prescription now that you're feeling better. This one should help restore you to your former self. How are the worries, my dear? No tears today?"

In spite of a surge of irritation at being treated like a child, she forced the brightest smile she could muster. "None at all."

He placed the bottle on the table. "Still, I'd like to err on the side of caution. One dessertspoonful twice daily. A whole spoon, not half. You understand me this time?"

She was aware of Gertrude's sharp eyes watching her.

"I'll see she takes it, Doctor," her mother-in-law murmured.

He inclined his head again, a slight bow towards Rosalind, and closed his bag. Following Gertrude to the door, he turned to take another look back at his patient before he walked out into the corridor.

Rosalind waited until she heard their footsteps reach the main staircase. Then she slowly got to her feet, picked up the new bottle of medicine and stepped to the window. Her legs shook and she reached out to grasp the back of the armchair, waiting a few seconds until the dizziness receded. She wouldn't take more of the doctor's potions. Was there a conspiracy between him and Gertrude? They'd exchanged so many glances.

She slid up the bottom sash of the window and leaned out. The lawn was deserted except for a couple of magpies that hopped and chattered near the summer house. She pulled the cork out of the neck of the bottle and poured the contents out. The poor roses; a double dose of medicine and if they were dead the next day, she would know what caused their demise.

She almost laughed out loud at the thought. Defying Gertrude sent a thrill coursing through her. Perhaps this was how Harriet felt. Rosalind determined to become more strong-minded like her daughter. She'd been too meek and forgiving all her married life while Edward did as he pleased. That would have to change. Aunt Catherine's words of advice to obey her husband on the eve of her wedding had proved a hindrance rather than a help. Rosalind would see what Edward thought of a more determined wife and perhaps he would treat her with more respect.

A knock rapped on the door and Rosalind called out in alarm, "Just a minute, please. I'm in the middle of something personal." Breathless, she hurried to the bedside table and filled the bottle with water, placing it back where Dr Richards had left it.

After a few minutes the knock came again and Sadie's voice asked, "Ma'am? Is it all right for me to come in?"

"Of course, I'm ready to be dressed."

The maid closed the door behind her and approached the bed. "I met Mrs Thornton in the hall. She said you wished to get up for an hour or two."

"Yes, indeed I do. I wish to go over to visit Baby Ivor. I want you to take this to Frank and ask him to bring the carriage round in half an hour. If you put out my walking dress and boots now, I will start dressing while you find him." Rosalind took the sheet of paper from under the pillows and pressed it into Sadie's hands. "It's not a note. I thought you might get caught by Ellen… or my husband or mother-in-law. It's a section of a poem I wrote out a few months ago that I found in a drawer. If anyone asks you, just show them this. Tell them you're giving it to Frank. They'll believe that because half the women in the county seem to be in love with the man."

The maid's lips twitched as she read the first few lines. *She is coming, my own, my sweet…*

A flush bloomed on Rosalind's cheeks. "I know, it sounds silly and romantic but it's not really… Tennyson's poem is… oh never mind that now, Frank will understand it's just a… just give it to him and explain… tell him about the carriage. If you get caught, hand over the poem and no one will be any the wiser."

Sadie pushed it into a pocket in her apron. "Better than them finding me carrying a note with instructions from you."

"Indeed. Don't say anything to the others. Frank is the only one I trust apart from you. He knows that my husband and Hugh had an arrangement… knows what happened in that race."

"But what will they say if they see Frank at the door with the carriage?"

"I'll try to creep out before Gertrude catches me. You can walk on ahead and give me a signal when there is no one about. Perhaps I should meet Frank just outside the gate into the yard. Yes, that's a better idea. Please ask him not to bring Romeo to the front. I'll wait for you here and we'll go down the servants' stairs and out the back door and round to the yard."

"Yes, ma'm." But a glimmer of fear lingered in Sadie's eyes.

Rosalind stepped over to the dressing table and picked up the rolled gold and shell cameo brooch and held it out to the young woman.

"Oh no, no indeed, I can't take it."

Rosalind pushed it into her hands. "Please, you must. I want you to have it. You've been so kind to me all these years… don't know what I would have done without you. Go on, please take it. I know you've admired it."

Still Sadie hesitated.

Rosalind turned away. "It was a present from Gertrude for my twenty-second birthday. I never liked it. You take it."

"Suppose Mrs Thornton sees me with it? She might suspect I stole it."

Sadie had a point and Gertrude's face would freeze when she saw her present on the maid's best Sunday outfit. No, that wouldn't do. It would be foolish to take that risk.

Rosalind reached for the brooch. "I'll keep it for you. One

314

day it will be yours, I promise you. Now go, make haste before Frank leaves the kitchen. I know he'll be there at this time. Go!"

Chapter Thirty-Eight

The past - 15th July, 1891

Edward stormed in with his dark eyes blazing. He strode across the rug and gripped Rosalind's arm.

She gasped and stumbled back, reaching for the armchair to maintain her balance. "Ow, Edward! You're hurting me... please! Please stop... please, I beg of you!"

He pushed his face close to hers; a sharp smell of wine on his breath. "How dare you! You... I can't believe that you... that my wife could be so defiant." He shook his head. "Look at you! Half-dressed to go out. Where are you going, my lovely innocent wife? Oh, you needn't try to explain. I know exactly what you are up to even though that man... even though that snake O'Rafferty swore blind that you'd nothing to do with the fact he was loitering at the yard gate with Romeo in the shafts of the brougham. He's a loyal blackguard... I'll say that for him. Loyal to his mistress and a traitor to his real master, damn him!"

"No, Edward, that's nonsense."

"Do you know what he told me? Eh? Just wait until you hear these impertinent lies. He said he was going to collect his grandmother and take her to the fair in Enniscorthy... over an hour's drive away, if you please."

Rosalind tried to wrench her arm from his grasp.

"Can you believe that tale?" Edward sneered. "Off buying more herbs to put in her potions no doubt, the vile old crone... but I know he was waiting for you. I know when the man is lying. I'm not as stupid as you both seem to think."

She'd never seen him this inebriated so early in the day. She opened her mouth to call for Sadie but thought better of it. Gertrude might only rush to the room and take her son's side.

"Edward, please... let me go. Let me explain."

He gave her a shove that sent her sprawling on the armchair, her hair wild and unpinned, the buttons of her walking dress half-fastened.

He pulled over the stool at the dressing table and sat beside her. "Perhaps you will be kind enough to tell me where you thought you were going. A romantic meeting with O'Rafferty, eh? Where was he taking you? Answer me!"

So that was it. He'd worked himself into a frenzy of jealousy because he imagined them stealing away to indulge in some act of forbidden passion.

The thought almost made her laugh aloud. Poor Edward. He thought he wasn't foolish but... She turned her face away.

He grabbed her hand and pulled her round to look at him. "Where were you going? Do you mean to make me the laughing stock of the county? I won't have men jeering at me and thinking me a fool for tolerating my wife carrying on with the coachman. What do you take me for? I've been far too lenient with you and now I know I should have listened to my mother."

"This is all in your imagination. Frank never would... I wouldn't..."

"I don't believe your excuses, my lovely. My mother always said your beautiful face would attract trouble. You can't keep men away from you, can you?" He dropped her hand and got to his feet. "I'm going out now to deal with O'Rafferty and give him a good hiding. He won't get away with making a fool of me like

317

that in front of all the boys in the yard."

"No, Edward, please… don't blame Frank. I asked him to help me… it's my fault. I asked him to drive me over to see our son. That's all it was. Please listen, please…"

He glared down at her. "A likely story. I've seen the two of you. The other day in the yard… you were there in full sight of all and Harriet watching. What sort of example are you showing the child?"

"I promise you I'm telling the truth. There's nothing going on between Frank and me… nothing. I've never been unfaithful to you… I never have. I was only thinking of the baby, that's all, and I'm sorry now that I've got Frank into trouble. I'm sorry to come between you both because you used to get on so well and he's invaluable to your racing yard. He's the one…"

She'd touched a nerve because Edward kneeled beside her and stared into her eyes. "He's the one who trains the horses, isn't that what you were about to say? He's the one who trains the winners while I'm just the idiot who pays the bills."

No, she was the idiot who paid the bills, not him.

He stood up. "I don't know whether it was O'Rafferty or the baby… perhaps it was both… I don't care. I'm going to make sure that you go nowhere in future without my permission. Mama tells me you haven't been taking the doctor's prescription. Another display of disobedience. Now I know why you're growing more unbalanced as the days pass. You defy us all. You won't listen to reason and you don't recognize how irrational you are. A sure sign of insanity, mark my words."

"I'm not insane… but I might end up raving if I listen to you, your mother and Dr Richards… I know I'm in my right mind. I want my son back, that's all. I don't want to sacrifice him for money and grandeur and the finest racing stables in the land. I don't want to hand him over to your cousin Hugh as his heir. I want Ivor back."

"You're my wife and you'll do as I say. Do you hear me? If I want our son to be brought up where he will have a good home and opportunity... more wealth and prospects than we can ever give him, you will go along with my wishes. I think another week in bed is what you need and I'll make sure you take the doctor's medicine this time." He moved over to the table and snatched up the bottle and spoon, returning to her and holding it out. "Take it. Here, take it now."

Rosalind meekly held out her hand and took the bottle, popped out the cork and placed it on the dressing table. She wondered if it would look more convincing if she showed resistance but decided that she'd annoyed him enough already.

"That's better, you take the spoonful. Here, let me help you pour it out. It will soothe your nerves and might bring you to your senses." He watched her swallow the water. "Good. Now, tell me who delivered your message to O'Rafferty. Who was your little messenger?"

Poor Sadie would be in trouble and be dismissed if he found out. Rosalind kept her gaze on the floor rug at her feet and tried to think while her mind whirled. What could she say? A lie, it would have to be a lie. He was waiting, fingers tapping on his hip with impatience.

"It was me," she said. "I saw Frank out on the lawn and I called him and dropped a note down to him. It was my fault. He never knew that I wasn't meant to be going to visit Beatrice. He hardly even knew I'd been poorly."

Edward snorted and crossed his arms. "As if he doesn't ask me every morning how you are? I don't believe that. However, it's quite possible that you were brazen enough to drop a note out of the window to him. What must he have thought? Is that the way for the mistress to behave? Is that the way for my wife to conduct herself in front of the servants?"

"No, I'm sorry. I was desperate and I thought that you and

Gertrude would try to stop me going."

"You're right about that." His face relaxed; his anger dissipating. "I believe that, at least. Well, as it happens, you won't be going to visit Ivor for quite some time. Mama has dreamed up a plan for both you and Harriet but I'm reluctant to put it into place just yet. I'm not as cruel as you may think. I don't want to send either of you away but I'll make certain that you follow my orders and don't leave your room without my permission."

She took a deep breath. "Send us away? What can you mean?"

He slipped a cigarette from his silver case and struck a match. "She's trying to persuade me to send Harriet to boarding school in Dublin and you to an asylum where you would be looked after. I can sign you in with the help of doctors and there you'll stay until I decide to permit you to leave."

Cold, numbing fear crept up her spine and across her shoulders. Did he have such power? Surely there were laws nowadays against such tyranny? How could Gertrude be so heartless? And poor Harriet packed off to a cold, miserable place in the city where she would know no one and never see her beloved pony for months on end. No, it couldn't happen.

"An asylum," she murmured.

"To a private asylum like your mother. Aha, you didn't think I knew about her, did you? My kind cousin Hugh informed me… thought it best I discovered what your deceitful family declined to tell me. No, my lovely, the place we have in mind for you will be somewhere where you'd be well taken care of. Perhaps Dublin might be best. That way O'Rafferty won't be able to rescue you."

"Oh, please no… no, not that."

"But don't worry… I'll only consider this as a last resort. I'm sure we can come to some arrangement here that will suit us all and keep Mama and Hugh happy too. I have another plan for the time being. You will move up to the servants' floor where Ellen can keep an eye on you. The bedroom at the end of the corridor beside hers is empty and perfectly adequate. But if I hear or see that O'Rafferty…"

She placed her arms around her knees and tilted forward, considering. Perhaps best to keep him calm, to agree to what he suggested. "Yes, I understand… no need to threaten an asylum. I'll do as you say."

Chapter Thirty-Nine

The past - 25th August, 1891

"Mama, I can't live without him." Harriet fixed her puffy, bloodshot eyes on Rosalind. "I can't, I can't. Please will you talk to Papa? Please tell him that I have to keep Bumblebee. I can't bear to give him away." She burst into loud sobs and flung herself face down on the bedcover.

"My poor darling." Rosalind put down her book of Alfred Tennyson's *Lyrical Poems* and stroked her daughter's hair. "I know how much you love that pony…"

"He's my best friend." Harriet raised her head, tears streaming down her cheeks. "Papa just took… just took him away and never even told me. I went to his stall and he was… was gone."

Heartless and unnecessary. Why must Edward behave like this? He knew how Harriet doted on the little pony so how could he do this to her with no warning? Had it come to this now? Had she no longer any influence over her children's future?

"Would you like to ask Sadie to bring us up tea and some of Mrs O'Brien's coffee cake? I hear she made several this morning and you love coffee cake."

"No, thank you, I'm not hungry."

"Not even one tiny little slice?"

Harriet sniffed. "I'm never going to eat again. I won't eat anything until they bring Bumblebee back."

"I'm sure they'll allow you to go and see him. Irene will look after him. She's only six but she loves animals and she knows he'll always be yours." Rosalind pressed her finger tips together in an effort to quell the anger that coursed through her. Was this Gertrude's idea? If so, how dare she!

Harriet sniffed again and rubbed at her wet eyes with the back of her hand. "I hate Papa! I don't want to live here anymore. I want to run away. I won't go to boarding school after the summer, I won't."

So that had been decided too. Again, Rosalind hadn't been consulted, hadn't been asked for her opinion and this was how it was going to be from now on with Edward and his mother making all the decisions for the family. She heard nothing now, confined to the top storey bedroom for one month since the last visit of Dr Richards. All pretence of illness had been abandoned; Edward locked the door behind him after his visits and instructed Sadie to ask Gertrude for the key when she was required to tend to Rosalind. Edward informed the servants that anyone caught speaking about the mistress outside the family home would be dismissed.

Sadie said they were all concerned, some downright disbelieving, especially Mrs O'Brien, but they valued their positions and kept their mouths shut.

Edward had brought a document into the room the previous week and asked her to sign it. A legal consent agreeing to the adoption of the boy by Hugh and Beatrice. Ellen accompanied him to act as a witness to the signature. Rosalind snatched the papers and tore them into pieces before throwing them on the floor. She would never sign away her baby.

Ellen watched aghast, probably convinced that the mistress was not in her right mind but Rosalind no longer cared.

She knew the building of the new stable yard was planned for September. Her husband produced yet another document for her to sign, a letter to her solicitor requesting more funds to be transferred to her husband's bank account. She'd scrawled her signature without objection. The money didn't matter anymore.

"I want to run away," Harriet repeated, holding onto the skirt of her mother's pale blue linen dress. She gave it a tug. "Don't you want to run away too? Don't you hate being locked in here and not allowed out? Why? Why do you have to stay here all day and all night?"

Rosalind walked to the window. She could never have imagined that Edward and Gertrude would behave in such a ruthless manner. They would find a quiet institution for Rosalind where no one would know who she was, just like Edward hinted. He would accompany her, playing the role of worried spouse; deliver her into the care of more doctors. Did he really have the power to do that? Perhaps he'd force her to sign herself in or get Dr Richards to sedate her. Edward might never return, leave her there for the rest of her life. She'd read about that happening to helpless women.

"Mama, do you want to run away with me?"

She looked at Harriet. Often during long and tedious days spent on her own, Rosalind dreamed of escape. Yes, she would love to run away but she wouldn't leave without her baby son.

"We could leave Ardlackan, couldn't we? But where would we go?" Harriet twisted one of the metal buttons on Rosalind's dress.

Rosalind gently removed her fingers from the button. "Careful, darling, you'll pull it off. I don't think we should risk running away."

"We could ask someone to help us. What about Aunt Catherine?"

Rosalind had already tried writing to her aunt but hadn't

received a reply. She suspected that Gertrude opened her letter and threw it in the fire. What would her aunt think if they appeared on her doorstep, her aunt who'd been so insistent that Rosalind should be a dutiful wife?

"We could steal the key from Grandmama," Harriet murmured, still fiddling with the button. "I know where she keeps it. It's in a little rosewood box on the mantelpiece in her bedroom."

"How do you know that?"

Harriet's broad grin lit up her features. "I spy on her. I waited until she went out to the garden and then I searched her room."

Rosalind had given up reprimanding her daughter for her unorthodox ways because Harriet's courage was an inspiration now.

"Frank might help us." Harriet breathed on the windowpane and drew a large H. "I could ask him."

"No!"

"Why not? He likes us. He likes you, I know he does. Yesterday I met him in the garden near the kitchen door and he asked most particularly after you and hoped you were feeling better."

"Did he?"

The girl laughed. "Of course he did. Frank said he misses us. He said it's a long time since he's seen you and I think he's worried about you because his eyebrows joined together and all those wrinkles came on his brow and…"

"Don't talk nonsense, child." Dear Frank. She missed him too. She missed their conversations and his kindness.

Harriet swung away from the window, turning in a circle with her arms outstretched. "I could leap out the window and fly away if only there weren't bars. Do you know where I hid my stories?"

Rosalind pointed to the loose floorboard under the wardrobe near the left window. "Under that board? I've seen you put things there. You're like a little jackdaw, my love, or a squirrel. You've always loved hiding secret messages and riddles. What are you writing about?"

"Oh, this and that… lots of things. I write how horrid Papa is and how I hate Grandmama. I'm going to write about how they stole Ivor and how they've taken away Bumblebee." Her eyes filled with tears again. "I hate living here."

"What happens if they find your writing? They will be angry with you."

Harriet reached out and took her mother's hand. "They won't find it. No one knows about that loose floorboard apart from you and me. Frank thinks it's strange you never see him now. He asked me if you were still poorly."

"What did you tell him?"

"I said you weren't as ill as Papa and Grandmama would like him to think."

"Harriet, you didn't! Why would you risk saying that?"

She smiled and tapped her right ear. "Frank knows I listen at doors. He thinks I'm clever." Harriet put a fingernail in her mouth and nibbled at it. "He has a bruise on his face. I thought he might have fallen off a horse but Peter told me that Papa hit him."

"Surely not."

The girl danced away across the rug. "Oh yes, Papa went into the stable yard last week and hit Frank. Peter told me all about it. Papa was very angry and walked up to him and punched him in the eye."

Rosalind clutched the top bar on the window. "Poor Frank."

"Peter said Papa hit Frank several times before. They had a fight, he said, and none of them knew why Papa hit him. Papa just stormed off without saying a word. The boys think it might be because of something Frank said about Mick Maguire."

"What would Frank have said?"

Harriet spun in a circle. "Peter thinks Frank didn't like the way Cousin Hugh insisted on making a bad jockey ride Ardlackan Lass. Peter said it was to confuse the… the man who gives the horses their weights for races."

"The handicapper?"

"Yes, him. Peter said Frank believes Maguire and the men he works for are dangerous."

Footsteps echoed on the wooden floor of the corridor. Sadie coming to unlock the door perhaps and check if Rosalind required tea. Hopefully it wasn't Gertrude. She held her breath as the door swung open.

"Would you like tea and cake?" It was Sadie.

Rosalind turned from the window, smiling. "Thank you, that would be lovely."

"Miss Harriet, your grandmother is looking for you," Sadie told the girl who made a face and cast her gaze to the floor. "Perhaps you could ask Mary to bring tea, please."

"I don't want to go. I want the cake too."

"I thought you said you weren't hungry and you'd never eat again," Rosalind teased. "You had better go or Grandmama will come up here to search for you and I might not be allowed to have a visitor for days. You've been prevented before when you misbehaved."

Harriet skipped towards the door, stopping to whisper in the maid's ear as she passed, "We're going to run away. Hush, don't tell anyone." She giggled and ran from the room.

"Ma'am?"

Rosalind waved a hand. "Oh, ignore her… just a girlish fancy, that's all. I couldn't go because I would have to leave my baby behind."

Sadie stroked a crease out of her apron. "Where would you go?"

"I don't know. Have you heard anything about plans to send Harriet and me away from here?"

The maid hesitated.

"I know you hear a lot more than you say. I've known for years that everyone in the kitchen hears everything that goes on in this house. Harriet says she is to go to boarding school."

"Didn't they tell you?" Sadie's voice rose and her eyes rounded.

"Oh, they don't tell me much these days. One day soon they'll send me away. My husband will place me in a lunatic asylum so I'll no longer be a nuisance to them here. I'm sure half the county has heard the story by now of poor insane Rosalind going the same way as her mother. I'm the woman people will whisper about in years to come."

"We are at the mercy of these men, all the same. They have such power over us." An unusual bitterness in Sadie's soft voice. "Shouldn't you go back to bed before Mary brings tea? If Mrs Thornton comes looking for Harriet, it might be better she finds you in bed. She's kinder to you when she thinks you're unhappy."

"Yes, you're right. If she thinks I've given up and am too weak and incapable of planning an escape, she won't watch me so carefully."

Sadie followed her to the bed and helped her out of her dress. "We'll put your nightgown back on. Would you really consider getting away from here?"

Rosalind held up her arms as Sadie untied the bustle pad and lifted her petticoat over her head. She stood in the middle of the room in her chemise, her eyes still on the summer sky outside. She would love to escape but it was impossible. No point dreaming about it.

"I could help you." Sadie laid the petticoat on the bed and picked up the white cotton nightgown with the ruffle at the neck and cuffs. It was old, one of several given to her by Aunt Catherine for Rosalind's honeymoon in Switzerland, soft cotton lawn and a yoked bodice with lace.

"How could you help me?" Rosalind pulled the nightgown

328

over her head and lifted the bed sheet to slip under it.

Sadie came closer and reached out to touch her mistress's arm, glancing towards the door before whispering, "I could help you and Miss Harriet get away from here, if you wish. I know what they're planning. I overheard the old lady talking to the master two hours ago. I was in the hall and they were in the dining-room…"

Rosalind sank back on the pillows and closed her eyes. So, it was true and not just a threat. Edward really intended to get rid of her.

"I'm sorry if I'm speaking out of turn but I feel you should know." Sadie raised her voice. "It's not right. I can't stand back and let this happen without offering to help you. It's that Beatrice Thornton who should be sent away. She's the lunatic, may God forgive me for saying so, but it's the truth. There are some that say…"

"Say what? What do some say?" Rosalind sat upright.

"They say she's obsessed about poor little Ivor. They say she goes to the nursery at night and wakes him up deliberately to check he still breathes. She can't bear to let him out of her sight and the nursemaid has left already… didn't last long."

"Magdalene, was that her name? How do you know this?"

Sadie picked at the bedcover with her fingernail, finding a loose thread and twisting it. "There's a kitchen maid there called Ruby and she's a niece of Mrs O'Brien. She's only thirteen but she's been working in the house six months or more. She says quite a few of the servants have left. Their mistress drives them away with her strange moods and temper tantrums. The nursemaid stayed less than a month and now the mistress looks after Ivor herself."

Rosalind put her hands to her face. Beatrice would have no idea how to look after the baby.

"Ruby says he cries a lot. It's his teeth, I suppose, and the mistress goes quite distracted with agitation. Ruby sees her giving poor Ivor medicine to sooth him. He sleeps for hours and hours, he's that drugged. It can't be good for the boy."

"Oh Sadie, don't tell me anymore, please don't. I can't bear the thought of that woman with my baby. Oh please... you said you'd help me... help Harriet and me get away. But I can't leave without Ivor."

"You must take him too."

Rosalind reached out and took Sadie's hand and squeezed it. "But how? Please help me before I'm taken away and locked up in some terrible place." Her voice broke. "Oh, oh... poor baby... poor little Ivor."

"Have courage. We'll think of something."

"We'll have to be careful because I couldn't bear the thought of them finding out and punishing you... sending you away from me. I couldn't bear that. You must come with me... promise me. I can't do this on my own. Come away with us." She gripped the maid's hand so hard that Sadie winced.

"I promise. Together we'll think of a way to get everyone to safety." Sadie lifted her other hand and touched Rosalind's hair. "I don't want to stay here, that's the truth. I couldn't stay without you. I'll be happy to leave."

"Is she trustworthy, this girl Ruby?"

"I think so. She's a good girl and sensible for her age. Let me talk to her. I will visit her at home in the village and say I have a message from Mrs O'Brien. I'll try to get her on her own and find out what I can about the baby. She told me all this when I met her on the road to the village last week. When I was in the big house while you and the master were in France, Ruby attached herself to me because she was lonely and frightened. She's afraid of her mistress and the way she suddenly flies at the servants in a fury."

A knock on the door made Rosalind drop Sadie's hand. "That will be Harriet back or perhaps Mary with the tea. Not a word to anyone for the moment. You talk to Ruby O'Brien and see what she says."

Chapter Forty

Daphne waved a hand towards the battered green trunk. "That's it there. If you could help me lift it down to the car... thank you, Ben. I'm finally going to send poor Charles's old clothes off to the charity shop."

I gave her an understanding nod. "I suppose it's time and someone else will put them to good use."

Ben pushed aside a cardboard box filled with what looked like Christmas decorations; a mixture of bright lights on wires and sparkling tinsel.

"I found out about Aunt Catherine in the house in Hampstead," I said, looking at the barred window where Archie sat staring forlornly at me. "Just had a letter this morning from the man who owns the house in Church Row." Poor dog. I'd promised him a walk in the morning. He never could understand why humans talked so much instead of hurrying out of doors and down to the beach.

Daphne picked up a trilby hat. "Do you remember Charles wearing this to the races? He called it his lucky brown hat. He wore it the day he won the Irish Grand National for the second time."

"Yes, I remember it well."

Daphne looked down at her hands. "What did he say?"

"Charles?"

"No, dear. The gentleman in Hampstead."

I smiled. Daphne flitted from one subject to another like a butterfly in her herbaceous border and it was sometimes hard to keep up with her. "He's a retired accountant and he wrote that he inherited the house from his mother about thirty years ago. His grandparents bought it in 1902 from a Catherine Farrow so that sounds like Rosalind's aunt. We didn't know Rosalind's maiden name, did we? So she was Rosalind Farrow before she married Edward... though her name would be in the church records here, of course."

Ben bent to lift a box from the top of the trunk. "So where did she go after selling the house?"

"The accountant has a file with the original deeds and old letters from lawyers about the house. Catherine Farrow was a pillar of Hampstead parish, apparently. She worshipped in St John-at-Hampstead at the end of Church Row. It sounds a nice road. Two terraces of houses dating back to the 1720s with a line of trees down the middle. But she's not buried in the graveyard there. She left the area after selling the house."

"1902, you say?" Ben asked. "Did she go somewhere with Harriet and Ivor, do you think?"

I shrugged. "Maybe. I'll have to keep searching now that I know her full name."

Footsteps echoed in the corridor. Daphne dropped the trilby and I stepped over to the door and peered into the shadows on the right.

"You gave me a fright." Dominic stood in front of me, his voice rising. "Fiona, I can't cope with this place for much longer. The internet signal is terrible... useless. How can I get anything done? And as for the noise in my room..."

I held up my hands to warn him that Daphne was on the other

side of the door. Ben appeared and I introduced him to my husband; ex-husband I repeated with emphasis. The two men shook hands.

"You've still got a noise in your room?" I asked. "What sort of noise?"

Dominic ran a hand through his floppy brown hair. "Mostly at night. Scratching and scraping and creaking of floor boards. There's something up here."

"Something?"

"And noises in the chimney. Chirping noises. I swear the room is alive with creatures."

"Baby birds," Ben replied with a grin. "I've got a zoo in the apartment in the yard. Birds, bats, mice... you name it."

"Huh... bigger than mice." Dominic ignored him and glared at me, as if it was my fault. "Something banging around at night. I can't get any sleep, I tell you. The sooner you organize for us to go back to Dublin to your father's house the better. I can't do anything here without internet. How do you stick it? What a backwater!"

I rolled my eyes. "Dominic, you can't return to that house. You're going to have to find somewhere else to live."

"It's not fair," he moaned. "You can't sell your father's house now. I've nowhere to go, as well you know. You'll have to wait."

Ben shot me an amused look and I thought again how mature and placid he seemed compared to my husband. Aged twenty-one, Ben was more grown-up and independent than Dominic would ever be.

"Show us your room," I suggested for the sake of peace. "Show us where the scratching is coming from."

Dominic led the way to the end of the corridor as Archie danced around our ankles. At last he was going somewhere.

Dominic swung open the door and waved us in. "It's a mess."

His clothes were strewn on the floor, shoes abandoned

and socks in a heap. A damp towel hung on the top bar on the window. The duvet dangled off the end of the bed and one of the pillows lay at my feet.

I bent to pick it up. "What do you do up here at night? It looks like you've been burgled."

"I can't sleep, I told you, it's too hot and the noises keep waking me up. The worst noise is from under the cupboard by the window. A sort of rustling."

Archie ran to where Dominic pointed, sniffing the floor and his tail wagging faster.

"Must be mice," Ben said. "What else could it be?"

Archie scratched under the wardrobe with his front paws, whining with excitement.

"There, that's what your damn dog does most nights. He comes up here when I've eventually got to sleep and wakes me up again. Every time it's the same spot. There must be a creature under the floor. A hedgehog or something. Don't hedgehogs drive dogs crazy?"

I laughed. "No way we'd find a hedgehog up here. How would it get here?"

"A rat then," Dominic said, scowling at me. "One of you take a look."

"I will." Ben stepped forward. "I'm used to the wildlife inhabiting these old houses. It'll be mice, I'm sure, especially if the dog is interested in it after dark."

He bent down beside Archie, stroked his head and pulled at the floorboard. It took him a few minutes to ease one end out and lift it up. He gently manipulated the other end until it came away and he placed the board on the floor, leaning forward to peer into the hole. I stepped closer as Dominic hesitated by the door, getting ready to run if a rat jumped out at us.

"I think there's something down here but it's difficult to see." Ben took his mobile out of a pocket and switched on the flashlight, shining it into the open cavity.

"A dead mouse?" I asked.

"No, a package of some sort. There are pieces of paper here that have been chewed by mice. Maybe a mouse's nest, by the look of it. Perhaps that was the rustling you heard."

"A mouse's nest," Dominic repeated with disgust.

"It's an oilcloth. An oilcloth with something wrapped up in it." Ben lifted a dark green material out of the hole. "What's this, I wonder?"

I kneeled beside him, a tingle pulsing through me. "Open it up. Let's see what's inside."

"I'm going out," Dominic muttered behind us. "I've got better things to do than root under dirty floorboards and touch things filthy mice have been chewing. If you need me, I'll be down in the village café where there's a Wi-Fi signal."

We ignored him as he walked away. Ben, Archie and I sat looking at the grimy package.

"Open it," I said again.

Ben placed the bundle on the floor and untied the faded red ribbon that held it together. He unfolded the cloth and spread it out. Sheets of paper covered with handwriting lay in the middle, some nibbled at the edges and yellow with age.

I picked up a page and exclaimed, "Hey, check out the writing!"

Ben held up another sheet. "Yeah, looks like Harriet's. There's a lot more here."

I read aloud, my voice slightly breathless:

"Mama has been locked in this room for more than a month. I hate Papa. He has given away my pony and is going to send me to boarding school. Mama hates him too and we are going to run away. Frank is going to help us escape and then we will be free."

336

Ben's dark eyes sparkled. "It's definitely Harriet. It's her writing, isn't it? Oh my God!"

"Read yours out… read it out please. To think these pages have been here all this time, right under our noses, lying hidden under the floorboards for generations…"

Ben turned back to the first page in his hand. "This is what she says:

> *"I hate Cousin Beatrice and Cousin Hugh. They have stolen my baby brother Ivor and they won't let him come home. Sadie says Ruby will help us get him back. Ruby is Mrs O'Brien's niece and she has hair the same shade of auburn as mine. I like Ruby. Mama is very unhappy and cries a lot because Papa says he is going to send her to an asylum where the lunatics go but I know that Frank won't let that happen. Frank has a friend with a boat. I know that because I heard Mama and Sadie discussing how we are going to escape. I was listening outside the door. I hear a lot more when no one knows I am there."*

Ben and I stared at each other and I guessed immediately what he was thinking. Like me, he could imagine those years, one hundred and thirty years, peeling back and Harriet Thornton, the indignant but intelligent child with decided opinions for one so young, standing in front of us while the sunlight flickered and dust motes danced round the bars of the windows.

Chapter Forty-One

A mist swirled in from the sea, creeping over the lawn and herbaceous borders, curling damp fingers round the corners of the house. The shrubbery lay shrouded, only the tops of pines and evergreen oaks in the wood rearing above the grey blanket of fog.

A blessing, this fog. Visibility would be difficult and it might muffle the horse's hoof beats and rattling of carriage wheels.

Rosalind moved away from the window and checked her pocket watch again. Three hours still before Sadie's soft knock on the bedroom door. Three hours before Harriet would be silently awoken from her slumber.

Rosalind's pulse raced. She put a hand to her chest and sank onto the bed. She had to take this brave step into an unknown future for her sake and for the sake of her children. God grant her the confidence to leave Ardlackan far behind.

The mist would help.

She welcomed its cold breath on the glass and mouthed a silent prayer that all would go well; that they would not be discovered. If they were found out... but she couldn't contemplate that. Rosalind pressed her fingers together and closed her eyes. She would focus on remaining purposeful, on following their escape route step by step and keeping her fear reined in.

It had taken nine days to perfect their getaway plan. Sadie had carried messages to and from Frank disguised as poetry, while Harriet scribbled her account, lying on the bare wooden floorboards with her tongue peeping out of the side of her mouth. She concealed the sheets of paper in her hiding place before Gertrude arrived to evict her and lock Rosalind in, bearing away the key with the smugness of a jailer.

Frank had grown inventive, changing Tennyson's words to suit his purpose. It was well that he used poetry because Sadie had been spied on and caught by Ellen the day before as she slipped in the kitchen door, Gertrude's maid demanding to see what Frank had handed her. Ellen glanced suspiciously at the sheet of verse before she scoffed and tossed it back. Sadie assured her it was written by Lord Tennyson and Ellen said she would do well to ignore the coachman's sweet talk because that man said more than his prayers and poetry was often used to coax pretty girls to sin.

Rosalind read the words again, with their hidden message, and silently thanked Frank for his ingenuity.

Come into the garden, Maud,
For the black bat, night, has flown,
Come into the garden, Maud,
I am here at the gate alone;
And the woodbine spices are wafted abroad,
And the musk of the rose is blown.

Come into the woodland, Maud,
For my heart yearns for thee;
Come into the woodland, Maud,
As I stand in the clearing at three.

Sadie had also met Ruby in the village the previous week and had given her instructions. She took Rosalind's money to the village market and purchased what they required.

Harriet too had begged to play a role, one that suited her years of spying on family members. Earlier that evening, an hour before Gertrude retired to bed and extinguished her lamp; the girl slipped into her grandmother's room and removed the key to the locked bedroom from the rosewood box on the mantelpiece.

Rosalind bent to look under the bed at the tapestry bag packed by her maid. Only one change of clothes. Beside the bag lay the heavy wool cloak bought by Sadie at the market. Her own was almost identical, the maid explained, and Rosalind wouldn't look out of place when they were among poorer folk. Her fine coat with the fur cuffs and collar would remain behind in the wardrobe, hanging with her useless silk and linen dresses. She would have no further need for them where she was going.

Rosalind shook out the dark blue cloak and pulled it around her shoulders, lifting the hood over her hair and regarding herself in the mirror. Her pale face stared back, her eyes glittering in the half-light. A dark, shadowy figure that would disappear into the fog outside. She could be anyone in that cloak.

She looked down at her hands and, on impulse, pulled off her wedding and engagement rings. They should stay behind too; she would leave them on the dressing table as a statement for Edward. She'd considered writing him a letter to say why she was leaving; the hurt caused by his uncaring treatment of his wife and children; the cruelty of his mother's obsessive ambition but no, she would say nothing. She would steal away like a thief in the night and give him no clue as to where she'd gone. He would suspect the local train and the steamship from Dublin, no doubt. Hopefully he would check there first.

Rosalind shivered and pulled the cloak closer around her. If she was honest with herself, she was beginning to feel a frisson of excitement. She would soon be free; free to live another very different life.

She slipped off the cloak and rolled it into a bundle before pushing it back under the bed. She lifted the bed covers, sliding under them and lying with her head on the pillow, her gaze fixed on the ornate plasterwork above the window. Impossible to sleep but she would close her eyes for the last remaining hours in Ardlackan Lodge and try to rest for she would need every ounce of strength for the journey ahead.

After what seemed only a few minutes, Rosalind woke with a start. She gasped as a figure bent over her.

"Ma'am? Don't be afraid, it's me," Sadie murmured. "Are you dressed?"

Rosalind attempted to keep her voice as steady and confident as her maid's. "Yes, yes I am. I got into bed in my clothes. And Harriet? Is she ready?"

"Yes, she's in the corridor outside. I asked her to take her boots off because I was afraid someone might hear her. Ellen has sharp ears and doesn't sleep well. I'll carry your bag. Here, let me help you put on the cloak."

"I'll carry my own belongings from now on, Sadie. You have enough already with your own and Harriet's. And the clothes for the baby? Did you pack those?"

"Of course," Sadie whispered and put a finger to her lips. "Now we must be silent. Come along, it's time to leave. Isn't the fog a mercy? I will lead the way down the corridor and servants' stairs to the back door."

Rosalind wrapped the warm comforting cloak around her and bent to pick up her boots and tapestry bag.

The mist still covered the garden; the moon obscured. She cast a final glance about the room, her eyes lingering on the rings on the dressing table for a few seconds. She would not be sentimental. She would not cry. No, she would go boldly into the darkness outside with Sadie and her daughter.

Even so, her heart pounded when she saw Harriet's expression; her white face where fear and excitement mingled. Harriet opened her mouth as if to speak and Rosalind tipped her head towards Sadie's retreating back as a signal to stay silent and follow her. Harriet smiled and turned away. If they could get out of the house without being caught; if they could reach the trees on the far side of the lawn under the concealing cover of this mist, they would have a good chance. Would Frank be waiting with Romeo and the carriage? Of course he would. He would never let them down.

Sadie reached the door to the servants' stairs and slowly turned the knob. A sharp click rang out and Rosalind held her breath. A moan and a sigh floated from behind a bedroom door and she froze. Mary's room. They waited for a few seconds but silence fell again. Sadie pulled the door towards them and moved onto the top step.

Their stocking feet made no sound on the wooden stairs as they clung to the handrail and felt for the next step in the darkness. One mistake, the merest sound and they might be discovered and their flight prevented.

They reached the corridor below and crept along the flagstones, past the kitchen, past the entrance to the boot room and down to the heavy oak door at the end.

A six-inch key hung on the right on a nail in the wall. Sadie reached for it and pushed it into the lock. An echoing click made them all freeze, holding their breath in the cold air of the corridor.

Was that fog creeping under the door? The chill numbed Rosalind's fingers and she clasped her cloak with one hand while the other gripped the handle of her bag. The kitchen clock struck the hour, resounding chimes that made them all flinch. Three o'clock in the morning and no one awake out there in the gloom. Except for Frank, of course, and his accomplice down by the sea.

A blast of damp air hit them as they stepped out onto the gravel path running along the garden wall.

Sadie eased the door shut and whispered, "We'll put on our boots now and move onto the lawn. The gravel makes too much noise underfoot." She didn't bother to lock the door after lacing up her boots. She stepped across the stones and onto the grass.

Two hundred yards to reach the trees bordering the wood. Sadie had paced it out during the week to assist them in the dark. Rosalind looked up at the house. No lamps glowed behind the shutters. No voice of alarm cried out in the darkness. She gripped Harriet's arm with her right hand and held it. Together they crept across the sopping grass.

They'd almost reached the sanctuary of the laurels at the edge of the trees when a rattling sound caused them to stiffen.

Rosalind tightened her grip on her daughter's arm.

The sash of a window halfway along the top storey rose up.

So nearly away and now their flight had been discovered. A hand came out and a tiny red light glowed. Who was this and would he, or she, spot the figures below?

Sadie laid a finger on Harriet's lips.

Rosalind's heart flipped several times and thumped painfully against her ribcage. Panic swelled in her throat as if trying to claw its way out. She swallowed and closed her eyes. This was no time to be weak and foolish; a few more steps and they would reach the shelter of the wood.

Harriet hid her face in her hands, as if hoping that would obscure her.

After a few minutes, the red glow died and a man coughed before closing the window.

"Who was that?" Harriet whispered.

"That's Patrick and his cigarette." Sadie's voice was barely audible as she stepped round the laurels. "He gave me a fright though for I feared it was Ellen about to call out to us. Thank the

Lord it wasn't her. This way now, follow me. We have to pick our way through the trees and there'll be briars and rabbit holes. Take care where you place your feet."

Moisture dripped from Rosalind's curls and ran down her face. Silence hung in the air, no sound of the sea below on the beach, no murmur as the tide crept across the sand.

"Ma'am?" Sadie's voice whispered near her ear.

"Call me Ros, please. I'm no longer your mistress after tonight."

"Oh, indeed I cannot. It doesn't sound right."

"As you wish," Rosalind said, "but you'll have to get used to it eventually. Lead on, brave Sadie, lead on and we will follow."

"I wish I felt brave. My poor heart is pounding and my knees are weak."

"All our hearts are aquiver. Except perhaps Harriet's."

"Mama, I thought I was going to be sick with fright but I feel calmer now. I was so afraid that Papa might hear us. What do you think he'll say when he finds us gone? And Grandmama, she will be so angry. It makes me laugh to think of her face in the morning."

"Don't," Sadie warned. "Please don't laugh just yet. Let us get far away before you dare to do that."

In the gloom, the corners of Harriet's mouth curled into a smile. "I'll laugh in silence then. I'm laughing inside." The amusement slid from her face and she clutched her mother's arm. "Oh, I packed my book of riddles but I've forgotten my writing... my story about our escape. I'll have to go back."

"No, dearest, you can't. We can't risk that now. No one will find your hiding place and, even if they do, it will be too late. We'll be long gone."

They made their way through the undergrowth, pushing bracken out of the way; the hems of their skirts heavy with dew while briars snatched at the fabric. Harriet stopped twice to untangle wicked thorns from the hem of her cloak. Sadie stepped into a rabbit hole and twisted her ankle; lying in the pine needles, breathing heavily.

"Are you in pain? Will you be able to keep going?" Rosalind asked. "Here, lean on me."

Sadie gathered her strength and climbed to her feet, limping on towards the avenue where the trees spread further apart.

Rosalind's eyes had grown accustomed to the dark and she glimpsed a blacker outline ahead; a soft snort floating towards them. It was Romeo, blowing down his long nose, and Frank, dear kind Frank, standing at the horse's head with his collar raised against the damp.

Chapter Forty-Two

They approached the carriage, an older one Rosalind didn't recognize that looked like an outside car used by the local country people. Frank held an unlit lantern in his hand. The fog had lifted in patches of the wood.

"I'm relieved to see you ladies, I can tell you," Frank said, stepping forward to take their bags. "I feared you might not get away without the alarm being raised. Now look over here, Mrs Thornton, see what I have for you." He beckoned her to the sidecar and held out his hand to help her onto the step. "See him asleep in the basket... sound asleep and has been since we left Ardlackan House."

Rosalind let out a cry of joy and reached out to touch the baby but Frank snatched up her hands and secured them in his. "No, please... don't wake him. If he takes fright and starts to cry.... He's been so good, the tiny lamb. Don't disturb him yet."

Ivor stirred a little and Rosalind moved away. So tempting to pick him up and hug him to her but Frank was right. The baby might howl, attracting attention in these silent woods. She couldn't risk someone hearing him. Poachers out snaring rabbits, perhaps, or anyone who might be curious enough to come close. There could be people among these trees at night; people with no wish to be seen, using the cover of darkness to go their dubious ways.

"Oh, thank you, Frank, I can't thank you enough."

"Can I see him?" Harriet pulled herself up on the carriage step and almost pushed her mother off in her haste. "Oh look, he's so peaceful. He's grown a lot in the last month."

Sadie stood in silence on the pine needles, smiling.

"It was easy in the end," Frank murmured. "Ruby O'Brien is a sensible girl and didn't panic. At the time arranged with Sadie, she brought him down to the library window and passed him out to me. That room looks out on the avenue side of the house... on the shrubbery so all I had to do was slip back into the laurels with the little man and we were invisible."

Rosalind thanked him again and silently praised Ruby who'd managed to gain Beatrice's trust since the nursemaid Magdalene's departure and had been allowed to assist with the baby. It was easy for her to sneak him away when the family was asleep as Ivor had grown accustomed to her presence. Beatrice and Hugh would get a shock in the morning when they found him gone.

Frank's teeth gleamed white in the moonlight and his eyes creased into a smile. "And young Ruby played her part well, to be sure. As luck would have it, the mistress had one of her bad headaches and our brave Ruby offered her my grandmother's sleeping draught... better than a double dose of Godfrey's Cordial any day and enough to knock out a bull. Her ladyship will be comatose for hours but we better not delay here talking. We'd best make haste before the dawn arrives. Allow me, Mrs Thornton; allow me to help you onto the sidecar."

He handed all three of them up to their seats and they sat facing outwards. Frank climbed up to the driver's seat, picking up the reins and clicking at Romeo to step forward. He kept the horse at a walk along the edge of the avenue where fallen leaves and pine needles dulled the beat of his hooves.

Harriet peered into the darkness around the tree trunks. "Do you think there's anyone out here tonight? Patrick told me about the headless horseman in these woods. He appears when the moon is full."

Rosalind raised her eyes to the treetops. No full moon tonight, just a crescent hanging in the sky. A light wind had risen, carrying away the sea mist and whispering through the pines.

Frank spoke softly. "That's what people say. The horseman rides a grey steed and gallops through the trees. Let's hope we don't meet him tonight."

Harriet shivered and pulled her cloak tighter around her but her eyes gleamed. "I wouldn't be afraid, not with you here. I don't think the horseman could harm us."

"We have more to fear from the living." Frank turned his head to grin at her. "They're much more dangerous."

The carriage rumbled on, Romeo moving forward with his usual lack of enthusiasm and Frank shaking the reins on his back and murmuring encouragement.

Rosalind put her arm across Harriet's shoulders, her eyes on Ivor asleep in his basket with his tiny hands curled into fists. Ruby had dressed him snugly for the night air, a bundle of wool and white lace on cotton lawn with only his face peeping out of the folds of the blue check blanket covering him.

She imagined Beatrice's reaction the next morning. If Grandmother O'Rafferty's sleeping draught worked, Beatrice might remain in bed longer than usual. Though perhaps she would wake up when Ruby pretended to tend to the baby at her usual time and raised the alarm about him missing.

How panic-stricken Beatrice would be when she discovered! She would scream for a search party and berate the servants for their carelessness. The corridors of Ardlackan House would reverberate with her fury.

"Frank, what will happen to Ruby?" Rosalind asked. "I hope

she won't be punished if they discover her role in our escape."

"If she's dismissed, she's been paid well for her assistance, never fear. I slipped her an envelope of money."

"Oh, that's kind of you. I never thought… you must allow me to recompense you."

He shook his head and explained that it was a gift, a parting gift to a family he would sorely miss. Ruby had been sworn to secrecy but should Beatrice's rage cause the girl to break down and confess what she'd done, there would be others who would help her. If Ruby was dismissed without a reference, her aunt Betty O'Brien would ensure that she found other employment. Frank said he would keep an eye on the girl to make certain she was looked after and no doubt Ruby would be glad to leave the employment of Beatrice Thornton.

They were nearing the front gates beside the lodge and Frank directed Romeo onto a track to the left, away from the gravel sweep at the entrance.

"Another way out?" Rosalind asked.

"Yes. The old woman in the lodge is a poor sleeper at the best of times and I won't risk opening the gates. She'd come running out like a ferret demanding to know what we're up to. This way is longer but there's a lane leading to the road beyond and I can move the fence aside to get the sidecar through. I walked that way yesterday and loosened the palings so they should pose no problem to us."

The track was rough and the swaying carriage nudged its occupants against each other. In the basket, Baby Ivor moved and yawned but slept on.

They continued for another quarter of an hour in silence until Rosalind felt Sadie stiffen. She followed her gaze and her heart missed a beat.

A man stood ahead about two hundred yards away where the trees cleared in a circle and a shaft of moonlight filtered down.

Rosalind saw only his silhouette in a long coat and cap but he appeared to be facing the other way.

She tapped Frank on the shoulder. "See ahead of us," she whispered and pointed.

Frank glanced up the track. "A poacher, by the look of him. We'll stay here and remain silent. Perhaps he'll move off in another direction and not see us."

Rosalind motioned to Harriet and laid her finger on her lips. Ivor moved in the basket and opened his eyes. Seconds passed as he glanced up at the faces above him. He opened his mouth. On impulse Rosalind pushed the tip of her forefinger between his lips and Ivor began to suck, closing his eyes and drifting back to sleep.

The dark figure ahead on the track stepped away, slipping into the trees on his right. Rosalind exhaled with relief and Frank waited another five minutes before moving forward.

A twig snapped in the undergrowth. Frank held up his hand, a silent command for them to stay quiet, nodding towards the trees on the right of the carriage.

Rosalind strained her eyes and saw a large hairy dog regarding them, alert but immobile, sniffing the air. More seconds passed before the hound turned and loped away.

"Mick Maguire's lurcher," Frank said. "The poacher's dog. Lucky that he's a silent creature and saw no harm in us."

"That was frightening," Harriet muttered. "I thought he was going to bark and bring the man."

"And what would Maguire think of us?" Sadie shifted on her seat and yawned. "In the dark, he'd likely judge us to be a local family on our way home. We don't look like we've come from Ardlackan Lodge, especially you, Miss Harriet, with your hair all over your face and your cheeks streaked with dust."

The young girl smiled. "And you don't look like Sadie the lady's maid. Your face looks dirty too. Even Mama looks like a poor woman in her cloak."

"Still, I'm relieved he didn't think to look this way." Frank flicked the reins and Romeo snatched a final mouthful of grass before lumbering on. "He might have recognized me even with my cap pulled down over my eyes. He knows me well but I could always claim I'm giving some of my relations a lift home after a family funeral. There are enough of us for people to lose count." He laughed softly and Rosalind felt another surge of gratitude towards him.

She would miss Frank; would most likely never see him again if their plan succeeded. She'd tried not to think about that, keeping her mind on the planning of their flight. She pressed her fingertips together but tears pricked at the back of her eyes. She couldn't help glancing up at the man in front of her with his dark curls. He had his back to her and was guiding Romeo along the lane, giving him an occasional reprimand, a soft admonishment, for trying to lower his head and grab at more vegetation.

They drove on for another half an hour until a glimmer of light flickered further along the lane, a long way in the distance. The dawn coming? The sun rising? Surely not this early. Rosalind twisted to peer round Frank's side.

The light vanished. Perhaps it was just her imagination. She breathed out and gave Harriet's hand a reassuring squeeze. Her nerves felt on edge, every sinew in her body strung taunt like a violin.

Frank pulled the reins. "Whoa, Romeo, whoa there, old boy. Now what have we here?" He spoke under his breath but Rosalind's stomach lurched at his words. "Another man out in the dark woods tonight. Or is it the same one? No, it's a different man... a rider this time."

Ahead of them a second light flared and died away. A red glow appeared. A man striking a match to light a cigarette, like Patrick at the window. The mist swirled about them again and, in the gloom, she could just make out he was sitting astride a grey horse.

"How far to the road?" Sadie whispered.

"Just beyond the horseman. We're nearly there. Hush now, don't breathe a word and we might be lucky for a second time. We'll linger here a moment or two."

Harriet clutched at her mother's cloak. "It's the grey horse, look. It's the phantom of the woods."

Frank shook his head. "Not him, my love. This phantom looks too real for my liking."

The red glow moved to the left and back to the right, the smoker riding back and forth. The light seemed to be getting closer and Rosalind's mouth went dry. She swallowed and licked her lips, pulling the hood of the cloak over her face.

"That's definitely no phantom, child," Frank murmured. "Better for us if it were."

Romeo raised his head and pricked his big ears, suddenly alert. He let out a whinny that echoed through the woodland, followed by another louder one as he pulled forward. A third whinny answered, more shrill than the cob's.

The grey horse advanced towards them. Sadie raised her head and peered into the darkness.

Frank muttered, "Whoa there, you old fool, stand still! You'll draw attention to us."

Too late.

Shrill whinnies from the second horse rang out again and hoofbeats on the stones, louder as they approached.

"Who's there?" A familiar voice called. "Show yourselves! Where are your carriage lamps? Show yourselves, I say!"

Edward! Edward riding Sally, his grey mare.

Dear God, what could they do? Jump off the carriage and run into the trees? Hide in the darkness while he demanded to know what Frank was up to in the woods at this hour.

Rosalind clutched Sadie's arm. "It's my husband. We have to get down now."

Frank swung round on his seat, his voice urgent. "I'll pull the carriage across the lane to conceal you as you climb down. He may not have noticed how many are here. Away with you all into the trees and hide while I try to fob him off with some yarn about my relations. Go, go quickly!"

Rosalind helped Sadie down; Harriet's breath warm on her mother's neck. Sadie turned to assist Rosalind while the girl leaped off the seat, landing on the pine needles and running towards the cover of the trees.

"Who's there? Stop, I say!" Edward kicked the mare into a canter.

Rosalind whispered to Sadie, "What about Ivor? We can't leave him behind. Frank, pass me the basket. Hurry!"

He lowered the precious bundle and together the two women carried the basket across the lane into the darkness of the trees. They placed it on the ground behind a clump of dogwood and kneeled beside it. Harriet was lying behind a tree trunk on their left.

"Come forward!" Edward shouted. "Show yourself this instant!"

Frank ensured they were out of sight before he urged Romeo into a walk. "It's only me, sir," he called out. "I'm on my own."

Chapter Forty-Three

The grey mare snorted and shied at the side car as Edward pulled on the reins. She stood with her nose pressed against Romeo's, blowing into his nostrils before squealing and kicking out with a foreleg.

Edward shouted a curse at her and Rosalind held her breath as her husband demanded to know what Frank was doing out in the middle of the night.

The coachman murmured a few words and she strained her ears to catch them. Family funeral, dropping his cousins home, poor uncle somebody had died suddenly...

"Yes, yes," Edward snapped. "Enough of that. What are you doing here in this area of the wood? That's what I want to know. Why didn't you continue up the avenue when you came to the front gates?" He turned to look behind him and then to the side, staring into the darkness of the pines.

Rosalind crouched lower to the ground and prayed that he wouldn't notice Harriet, who wasn't completely concealed behind the tree trunk.

The mare stamped her hoof and squealed again when Romeo had the audacity to nip at her.

"Damn you, Sally, be quiet and stand still!" Edward moved

her a little further away from the cob. "Well, O'Rafferty? I'm waiting for you to answer my question. What the hell are you doing here instead of heading back to the stable yard? I'm not sure I believe your story about your dead uncle whatever his name is. I know you're a born liar."

Sadie's face was pale in the dim light. If only Edward would go on home and leave Frank alone. What was her husband doing in the middle of the wood and why was he riding through the trees on this quiet path at four o'clock in the morning? Had he been out carousing with his racing friends? His words sounded slurred so perhaps he'd been drinking until now and had mistakenly taken the wrong path off the road in the woods. Unlikely though, because both Edward and Frank knew the woodland well.

Had Edward encountered Maguire? Was there business between them that couldn't be conducted during the daylight hours? Rosalind had heard that Maguire worked for some of the wealthier bookmakers and Martin Chance sprang into her mind. Surely her husband hadn't been foolish enough to owe him money? Harriet assured her the stable boys claimed Chance was a man without mercy.

Ivor stirred in his sleep and snuffled.

"What's that?" Edward asked Frank.

"I hear nothing."

"That noise, damn you!"

Ivor obligingly gave a little yawn and opened his eyes. Rosalind's heart fluttered in her chest.

Frank again murmured that he'd heard nothing. "A fox, perhaps, or an owl."

"A fox? You hardly think a fox would snuffle like that, for God's sake, man. Don't talk nonsense. It didn't sound like an owl. Be quiet for a moment and listen."

Rosalind willed Ivor to remain silent. He looked up at her from the depths of the basket and held out his little hand. She shook her head, hoping he would know what it meant. Ivor's mouth curved and he gurgled.

"That bloody noise!" Edward shouted. "It sounds like a child… a baby. Have you got a baby on that sidecar?"

"No sir, no baby at all, just myself and Romeo. There was a small child here earlier though before I dropped her off with the mother and father in the village and…"

"Stop blathering and listen. I think it came from over here." Edward kicked the mare forward. He examined the pine trees.

"I should be getting home." Frank picked up the reins. "This poor cob needs to get back to his stable."

Edward ignored him, looking straight at the dogwood bush, his head to one side as if straining to hear.

"Will you accompany me, sir?" Frank sounded a little desperate.

Rosalind's throat tightened. Please God, no. He couldn't find them now, just when they had so nearly got away.

Ivor, disappointed he no longer had his mother's full attention, gurgled again and gave a small cry. Rosalind held out her hand but the baby uttered a loud wail.

"It is a baby!" Edward swung round and glared at Frank. "You knew all along, didn't you? Get down this instant and fetch it. What's it doing in the wood and who does it belong to?"

His own son. He didn't even recognize the cry of his own son. Rosalind looked at Sadie and saw fear etched on her face.

"I'm talking to you, O'Rafferty," Edward said. "All right, I'll get off the mare and find the baby myself if you won't oblige. Come down from that seat and hold her for me."

Frank threw a glance towards the trees, as if to apologize for his failure, and lifted his boot to step down.

Harriet sprang to her feet, snatching up a long branch lying in the dead leaves and ran screaming at her father on his horse.

Her shrieks pierced the darkness.

The mare snorted and leaped sideways, spinning in a half circle and rearing. Edward lurched forward, grabbing at her mane to keep his balance.

"No, Harriet, no!" Rosalind cried. "Oh no… no!"

Harriet smacked the branch on the track and roared, "You won't take him back, you won't! Ivor has to stay with Mama. I hate you! I hate you!" She burst into sobs and flung the branch at her father.

Sally reared again in terror, frantically shaking her head. She spun around and bucked, sending her rider hurtling to the ground. He hit the stones head first and lay still, his legs and arms splayed. The mare snorted and galloped off in the direction of the avenue.

Frank ran to him and held his fingers to Edward's neck, feeling for a pulse.

Harriet's shoulders heaved and tears rolled down her face. Sadie hurried to her and put her arms round her.

Rosalind picked up the now screaming baby and tried to comfort him.

"I've killed Papa, I've killed Papa!" the girl shrieked.

Frank stood up, shaking his head, as if in disbelief. "No, you haven't killed your papa. He's still breathing, thank the Lord."

Rosalind emerged from the trees, cradling Ivor and rocking him. His wails subsided as she hugged him to her. "Oh Frank, what will we do? What will we do now?" She stood looking down at Edward's prostrate body, his nose pressed against the stones and a trickle of blood from above one ear. "We can't go on now. We can't just leave him lying here for dead."

Harriet screamed again. "Dead? Is he… is he really dead?"

Frank turned to her. "Not dead, child. Just unconscious. He's had worse falls from his horse and survived to face another day. This is no different. He's only concussed and will come around after a while."

"Frank?" Rosalind looked into his eyes.

"We should go on," Frank replied, holding her gaze. "We set out to get you and the children to safety and that's what we should do."

"But Edward… will he…? What will happen to him?"

Frank held out his hand to assist Harriet up onto the seat. "Edward will recover consciousness and I'll return to make sure he gets to bed. I'll take him home. Do as I say now and we'll finish what we set out to do this night. Sadie, fetch the baby's basket from the trees while I help the mistress up." His hand gripped Rosalind's, a firm squeeze of encouragement and she saw the determination in his eyes. He was right, of course he was right. For all their sakes they had to continue. They had to get away now because they might never have another chance.

Still she hesitated.

"Your husband will have recovered in a day or two," Frank's voice sounded urgent. "A sore head tomorrow, perhaps, but he'd have had that anyway judging by the amount of whiskey he's obviously consumed tonight. I have to tell you that this is the first time I've ever been thankful that your husband's balance on a horse leaves a lot to be desired. Now, climb up please and we'll be on our way." He got back onto the driver's seat.

Sadie returned from the trees holding the baby's basket and brushing leaves off her skirt. Her hair had come unpinned and hung down over her shoulder on one side, long blonde tresses gleaming in the moonlight.

The air felt warmer, the scent from the pine trees sharp and fresh. A faint glimmer of light shone in the east. Dawn coming. They would have to move fast if they were to get away unseen.

With everyone back on their seats and Harriet rubbing her swollen eyes, they made their way on along the track to the fence bordering the woodland. Frank climbed down and lifted the planks out of the way, leading the cob through the gap.

"I thought I'd killed him," Harriet said. "I was so angry but what if I've killed him…"

Rosalind hugged her close. "Hush, my love. I was afraid you'd be trampled under the horse's hooves. If anything had happened to you, I don't know what I'd have done. As for Papa, Frank says he'll recover consciousness soon."

But how would Frank explain what had happened? What would he tell Edward about Harriet and the baby? Edward would know now that the coachman had played a part in their flight.

"Will he remember this… that we were here?" she asked him.

Frank was silent for a few seconds before he murmured, "I'll think of something, don't worry. If we're fortunate, he might not remember. It depends how much he had to drink. If he does recall the incident tonight, I'll tell him the truth. What can he do? I've committed no crime, after all."

"But… your position here… at Ardlackan with the horses, I mean. Edward will dismiss you."

Frank didn't turn to look at her. "Ah well, if that comes about, I will have to seek employment elsewhere. Someone will take me in, don't you worry. I'll be grand."

"I'm worried he might attack you, though. He hit you before, I know he struck you. A jealous streak at the best of times but if he thinks you helped us to get away from him… I don't know what he'll do."

"I'll take a chance," Frank replied. "I'm not afraid of Edward Thornton."

They continued down the hill towards the sea and turned left before the village, along an overgrown lane with grass sprouting between the cart tracks. Rosalind had never been this way before. The carriage jolted and rocked over loose stones and she clutched the wooden seat to keep her balance.

A smell of salt and seaweed rose on the air as light spread across the sky, a faint pink glow.

Romeo plodded on and Frank remained silent. Rosalind

decided he was wondering what would happen later when he returned to find Edward. Thank God Edward hadn't been seriously hurt. Much as she longed to get away from him, she could never have left him lying severely injured in a pool of blood. He only had that slight trickle from above his ear so he wouldn't bleed to death. The last thing she should do now was feel sorry for the man who would have seen her banished to an asylum.

If only Edward had been stronger, if only he could have stood up to his mother and his cousin Hugh. And yet fate had played its part too. If Edward had never had the accident with the landau and the two bay horses; if Frank had been driving that day, Beatrice's baby would have survived. Edward wouldn't have felt obliged to make amends for the tragedy.

The sound of waves floated on the breeze, a sucking and slapping against rocks; the wind gathering strength.

The sidecar turned a corner and Rosalind glimpsed a steep drop leading down to a jetty of grey stone, stretching out into the dark water. A fishing boat rose and fell on the swell, a long wooden vessel with masts both fore and aft, sails lying ready to be hoisted.

Harriet sat up. "Oh, is that the boat? Will we really be able to go all the way to Wales in that?"

"Of course." Frank positioned the carriage close to the pier. "My friend's first cousin is an experienced man when it comes to ferrying passengers across the Irish sea. He's done it many times before."

He grinned at Rosalind. What sort of passengers was he talking about? She guessed they were avoiding the usual means of transport for reasons of their own. Men who preferred not to travel on trains and steamships because they might be picked up by the Royal Irish Constabulary. Smugglers or republicans.

The ladies stepped down from the sidecar and Frank

handed their bags to a young man with a broad local accent who respectfully removed his cap. His father came ashore and shook the coachman's hand.

"This is the cargo my friend was telling you about." Frank nodded in Rosalind's direction. "A fair cargo indeed."

The older man screwed up his eyes and peered at them. He was wearing a faded coat with a red kerchief round his neck. His gaze lingered on Sadie. "Very fair indeed. Does my cargo comprehend this is no luxurious crossing? And, Frankie boy, you've enlightened them as to the lack of comfort on my vessel?"

"Aye, I have." Frank turned to face Rosalind. "We'll say farewell, then. May God watch over you and keep you safe. At least you have a reasonably calm morning for the sea voyage."

This was it. This was where they parted after all these years. Ten years of companionship and laughter; the moment had arrived to bid farewell to the one man she trusted in the world; the man who'd never let her down.

Harriet stroked Romeo's long nose, murmuring goodbye to him as tears ran down her cheeks. Sadie took out a handkerchief and passed it to her.

"What's the matter, little one?" Frank put his arm round the girl and kissed the top of her head. "You'll be grand, my sweetheart. You're on your way to a new life… just think how exciting that is. You promise me something…" He took her face in his hands. "You look after your mama for me, please. She's a very special lady, your mother."

Harriet sniffled. "I will but… I don't want… I don't want to leave you, Frank. Can't you come with us?"

His eyes softened. "No, I'm afraid I can't. I've got to go back and get your foolish father home and into bed. I can't go gallivanting off across the ocean with you ladies." He flicked his gaze to Rosalind's face. "Much as I would love to… much as I would love to." He gave Harriet another hug and pushed her away. "Go now, climb on board and don't be sad. We might meet again someday, you never know."

It was Sadie's turn next and she primly held out her hand. He bent over it and kissed it, laughing when she pulled it away.

A blush sprang to her cheeks. "You always were a charmer," she said.

"And you always were charming." He helped her to step over the side of the boat. "Goodbye, Sadie. I wish you health and happiness."

Tears stung at the back of Rosalind's eyes and she turned her head away in embarrassment. She reached out to rub Romeo's forehead. "Farewell, old friend. You're a good horse and I'll miss you."

Frank walked over to her and put his hands on her shoulders, gently turning her to face him and lifting her chin to look into her eyes.

"Now, now," he murmured. "Let's have no crying over the cob. Romeo will be well looked after, I promise you that, and I'll make sure he always has a good home." He lifted a hand and touched her cheek. "Goodbye, Mrs Thornton... Rosalind, lovely Rosalind. May you arrive safely at your destination."

Her tears overflowed and she blurted out, "I won't forget you. I won't forget what you've done for us... all the help you've given me over the years. I don't... I don't know how I would have coped without you."

He shook his head. "Ah, you'd have managed well enough. You're stronger than you think. Don't forget that. You're stronger than you think. There are few women I know with your courage... few who would have even tried to stand up to a husband. I hope you make a new and happier life for yourself and I'm only sorry that you will remember us... that you'll remember Ireland as a place of torment."

"Not torment, no, not that. I had happiness here until

Edward… until his gambling and his drinking… and his family's ambition got the better of him. You will look after him, won't you? Don't leave him lying there too long."

"Of course. He'll be safe with me."

"Frank?"

"Yes?"

She glanced at the boat to check Harriet and Sadie had their backs turned, both looking at Ivor in his basket, the little centre of attention. She leaned forward and kissed him on the cheek. His skin felt cool in the warming air. "Thank you. Thank you for everything."

For several seconds they stood looking into each other's eyes. Her tears had dried and she held out a trembling hand. He took it and lifted it to his lips, kissing it twice.

"Don't say anymore," she said. "Please. Just let me go now. Goodbye Frank. Goodbye and God bless you."

She hurried to the side of the boat but he followed to take her arm and help her on board. She felt the swell of the sea shifting beneath her feet and turned to look up at him.

"I won't forget you," he murmured. "I will never forget you."

"God bless you," she said again, as she rubbed her sleeve over her eyes.

She saw Frank walk back to the sidecar, hiding his face against Romeo's stout neck for a few moments before giving the horse a pat. He climbed onto the driver's seat and held up a hand to wave.

Rosalind took her place at the bow of the boat and slid her arm round her daughter's waist, while the men cast off the ropes. As the dawn light flickered, she watched the carriage moving up the hill taking Frank away from her into the shadow of the trees.

Chapter Forty-Four

Patches of light dappled the path in front of the cob as the day dawned. Frank jumped down to lift back the palings across the gap and somewhere to his right a jay screeched; a flash of blue and white wings among the pines.

Romeo trotted on, cheered by the thought of heading for his stable and probably anticipating a manger of oats awaiting him.

Would Edward have regained consciousness by now? Would he remember what had occurred before his tumble from the grey mare? Would he recall the crying baby and Harriet storming towards him?

Frank hoped that Rosalind, Sadie and the children would be out at sea by now, the breeze strong enough to carry the fishing boat far away from the shore before prying eyes of early risers wondered what cargo was on board.

He couldn't dwell on the thought of Rosalind sailing away from him and the ache in his gut. Her departure was painful but for the best. She and her children had managed to get away and his feelings weren't important. He would miss her though; miss her more than he'd ever imagined.

He was nearing the place where they'd left Edward.

Hopefully his master would wake up with a thundering

headache from all the alcohol, with no memory of what had happened. Frank would help him into the carriage and take him home and no one would be any the wiser.

Frank kept his gaze on the lane below the rattling wheels of the carriage. Was it near here? No sign of a body lying on the stones. Or perhaps over there one hundred yards ahead. No, not there. After another ten minutes his eyes rested on a long branch thrown beside the lane, abandoned on the verge of pine needles.

"Whoa, whoa there, stand." He called out to the cob and Romeo came to a halt. That branch? It looked like the one Harriet waved as she ran screeching from the trees towards her father. But surely not, for there was no sign of the fallen man. Where had Edward gone? Frank glanced up the lane and turned his head to look behind him. The trees seemed to draw in on him, the wind whispering among the branches. He climbed down from the seat and bent to feel among the stones with his fingers. He raised the tips to his nostrils. Blood, a few spots of dark red on the ground. Was it Edward's? It must be. This had to be the place.

Frank got to his feet and stared into the trees. Had his master awoken and stumbled into the depths of the pine, oaks and brambles, only half-conscious and with no idea where he was going? If so, how would he find him?

A dilemma, to be sure. What should he do now? He would have to return home and see if Edward had made it back. There was Sally the mare to consider. Where had she ended up after her frantic gallop along the laneway? A riderless horse would usually go back to the stables to be with her companions.

He had a choice: either keep searching for Edward or return to the stable yard. If he was discovered out in the early morning, people would question him, wondering why he hadn't returned home and, when Rosalind and the children were confirmed missing, suspicion would undoubtedly fall upon him. No, it would be prudent to head back, put the cob in his stable and feign innocence. For all he knew, his master might be waiting for him in the yard.

Frank got back onto the seat, clicked at Romeo and on they went, wheels rumbling over the rough way, the early morning growing brighter as birds twittered a cheerful chorus to celebrate the arrival of a new day.

He would hurry back to Ardlackan Lodge and pray that Edward Thornton returned alive but without any memory of the night's events.

As the sidecar rattled into the yard, one of the sheepdogs ran towards it, barking but with a wagging tail when she recognised Frank. He stepped down and stroked her soft coat with a distracted hand, glancing around him. All was quiet. Another hour and the stable boys would be up, Peter and Joseph emerging as usual from the loft bedroom they shared, yawning and rubbing their eyes.

Frank unhitched the horse from the shafts and led him to the stable. He stripped him of the harness and tossed him an armful of hay, checking the level of water in his bucket. What should he do now? The house lay in darkness above the yard wall, no light flickering in the servants' quarters. He wondered if he should wake the household and tell them that the master had met with an accident in the woods, but then they would know he'd been a witness and would connect him with Rosalind's flight. It would cause suspicion; make the family realize she hadn't gone to Dublin on the train to catch the steamship. More sensible to go to his bed and wait for an hour until the boys got up. He should treat it like any other day. That was the best plan.

Frank walked towards his room over the coach house but the clatter of hooves made him swing round. The grey mare cantered under the archway and slid to a halt, her coat steaming and stained dark with sweat.

Chapter Forty-Five

The present - 22nd July, 2019

"What would it have looked like around the beginning of the twentieth century?" Jessica sipped her coffee, holding the large cup between her hands. She turned her head to look back at the grey three-storey Dublin house with its bay windows. "It could have been built as a private asylum. What do you think?"

"I think it was more likely to have been someone's home and they opened it up for private patients," I replied. "That happened in those days. Now it's a guest house, restaurant and café and no one sitting here wonders about the women who strolled round this garden. Do you think Rosalind sat here wondering when Gertrude would collect her and take her home to Ardlackan?"

Bees buzzed in the purple buddleia beside our glass-topped table.

I wondered if the letter from the authorities had arrived for Jessica's father in the afternoon post. Information about residents in hospitals and asylums was confidential and restricted to close family members.

"Nowadays she could probably have lived at home with her family as the medication would be so much better." Jessica twirled the coffee cup on its saucer. "She might have been sitting here where we are on a seat like this." She shivered. "Daphne would have something to say about that."

"Daphne would be able to see her on the seat beside us."

Amusement in Jessica's eyes. "You're joking, I know. You don't share her connection with those who have passed on before us."

"Do you?"

She shrugged. "I sometimes feel if a house has a good or bad atmosphere... that sort of thing."

A young woman emerged from the café and walked across the lawn to lift our empty cups onto a tray.

"Another coffee?" Jessica asked me.

"Okay, why not? We're not in a hurry."

She ordered two more cappuccinos and a slice of carrot cake to share. She leaned back in her chair, twisting her hair in her fingers. "Tell me all about Dominic. How's he getting on?"

"He's not happy that we put him in a bedroom on the top floor." I grinned at her. "Vindictive of me, I admit."

She put the end of her hair in her mouth and chewed; a habit from childhood. "Perhaps he feels a strange atmosphere up there too. Remember that night..."

"Yes." I changed the subject. "Tiffany's gone on holiday to Morocco for two weeks with her mother and has locked Dominic out of the apartment. He spends a lot of time on his laptop in the village café where the internet signal is good. I don't think she's been in touch with him."

Jessica raised her eyebrows.

I shook my head. "I try to stay out of his way. I think I'm learning sense at last."

"You can't go on mothering him for the rest of your life. You can't afford it."

"You're right. I need to save money to find somewhere to live. Dominic, of course, still thinks he's entitled to half of the proceeds from my father's house when it eventually sells. He's muttering about his rights." I watched a dark brown butterfly, a Red Admiral, dancing a jig over a blue globe thistle. The scent of lavender rose from a clump at the edge of the terrace. Daphne would feel at home in this garden, the herbaceous border stretching along the wall and the formal circular pond with water lilies; goldfish hiding beneath the thick green pads.

Jessica tossed her hair and welcomed the arrival of our coffee and cake by reaching out to help the waitress unload the tray. "I still can't believe what you found under the floorboards... what Archie found. Forcing Rosalind to give up her baby son... no wonder she couldn't cope."

"So cruel. Heartless... the male heir mattered so much in those days. Carrying on the family name. A load of nonsense when you think about it. Daphne admits to knowing more about the family than she first told me. She knew Hugh was a difficult and arrogant man but even she was surprised he would take a child without the mother's consent."

"Perhaps his wife was desperate after losing her own son. What happened to her?"

I reached for the carrot cake. "Can I have some before you eat it all? Thanks. I don't know why she lost the son... miscarriages happen even now."

Jessica frowned. "Ruthless though, wasn't it, to take Rosalind's. Particularly ruthless of Edward to agree to hand the baby over without telling his wife. You're indebted to Harriet's indignation and love of writing for the truth. If only we knew what happened later that night when they planned to escape. Do you think they were caught? Did Frank turn on Edward in the woods and lose his temper?"

I nibbled the cake. "I don't want to believe it was Frank but if he was in love with Rosalind... if Edward turned nasty... I don't want to admit that Tiffany Ryan might be right."

"At least he wasn't a family member though. He wasn't a

Thornton. Daphne would prefer him to be the killer."

"Would you like to hear my list of suspects for Edward's murder?" I asked. "It's quite long."

"Yeah, sure. I might be able to help you."

"With your banker's analytical brain, you mean?"

She cut the slice of carrot cake in two. "Yes, I'm good at processing information. A walking computer, my dad calls me." She grinned and glanced at her phone. "He said he'd ring when the post arrives."

I pulled my notebook out of the depths of my handbag. "I need a walking computer right now. Okay, let's see… might as well start at the beginning. First, we have Rosalind, the wife of Edward who was the one Tiffany suspected because she'd been told by an Ardlackan local that she was a crazy lunatic. Unfortunately, the journalist might be correct."

"Poor Rosalind, I know you feel an affinity with her. You have something in common… both married to gamblers. Go on."

"Then there's Frank O'Rafferty, the coachman and head lad in the racing stables, who worked for Edward. A crime of passion, Tiffany thinks, a juicy love triangle that will appeal to viewers who like sensational murder stories."

"I can see the appeal of that. A Victorian scandal hushed up by my family."

"But Kitty O'Rafferty thinks Frank would have known his place in those days and would never have succumbed to an affair with the mistress. Besides, he went on working for Gertrude and Hugh Thornton afterwards before he sailed to America. Hardly the sort of thing a murderer would do, is it?"

"Not unless he had nerves of steel. He'd have vanished earlier after the event, I think."

I ran a forefinger down my handwritten notes. "Okay, there's a man called Mick Maguire who was mentioned as a nuisance… an unpleasant shady character in Rosalind's Aunt Catherine's letter. He also makes an appearance in Harriet's book of riddles. A tout and connected in some way with a race that was held in early April 1891. A tout who used to spy on racing stables and sell information to bookmakers or to gamblers. Harriet wrote that it was a match between her father and his cousin Hugh."

"A gamble on a race. That might be significant if Harriet thought it was important enough to write a riddle about it."

"Her riddle implied it was dangerous." I watched a bumblebee land on the lavender, a striped furry body hovering from flower to flower. "Ben told me about match races and they're not held very often nowadays. They would have been private gambles between the owners or riders of the horses involved, usually two horses. Was there a falling out over the result of the race? Harriet's book has a drawing of her father falling off and Maguire is pictured beside the carriage."

"Who knows? If Maguire was a rough sort of fellow, would he have been working for someone else? The thug who collected the money for a boss? It's a possibility."

"I like your analytical thinking so far, my friend. A big boss in the background. Someone who wanted Edward out of the way. But why?"

Jessica waved her hand. "Write that down before we forget. Gambling was the ruination of many racing families. I remember Uncle Charles telling us when we were staying at Ardlackan, saying it was why he wouldn't have anything to do with owners who were known to be serious punters. Too much pressure for him, I suppose, and then they'd blow all their money and not pay the training bills."

I made a few notes in the margin. Jessica might be onto something there. Edward might have owed money to the boss Maguire worked for, or to Maguire himself.

Jessica slurped her coffee. "I'm enjoying this. Now, who's next or is that all the suspects? What about Beatrice?"

"Why would she kill Edward? And it was a violent death, a blow to the side of his head. It doesn't sound the sort of murder a lady would commit. She'd have resorted to poison or smothered him when he was asleep in bed."

"Unless she paid a man to do it."

I closed my eyes, attempting to imagine the scene, the lady from the big house paying a hit man. No, too unlikely.

"Anyone else?" Jessica asked.

"There's Harriet, who was only eight. A most unlikely suspect and yet Ben told me that his grandmother said Harriet worried she'd killed her father."

"You realize Ben is now a relation of mine, don't you? Some sort of distant cousin."

She was correct. Her brown eyes and hair resembled her father's and he was a handsome man like his older brother when he was young. They all shared the dark Thornton looks.

"There's someone else we should consider who you haven't mentioned." Jessica drained her coffee cup.

"Who's that?"

"Hugh. Cousin Hugh Thornton, Beatrice's husband who took over Ardlackan Lodge and lived there until he died."

"Hugh? But what would his motive have been?"

"The match with his cousin? A gamble? Maybe Edward owed him money and didn't pay up. Or maybe he was furious if he discovered Rosalind that night trying to escape with the baby."

"Such a pity John Thornton's daughter died young. She might have known something about Hugh. Daphne doesn't know where she went but she left Ireland in her twenties."

Jessica peered at her mobile. "It's nearly four o'clock. I have to go home and help Mum with a dinner party... a family gathering tonight. Would you like to come?"

"Thanks but no, I'd better drive back to Wexford and help Daphne with Dominic. I don't want her to have to cope with him on her own for too long because she's been kind to give him a bed. You know what he's like… he'll be waiting for his dinner and wondering when she's coming in from the garden. I'll pick up something to eat on my way back there." I added, "There's Rosalind's Aunt Catherine in London too."

"She'd hardly have killed Edward."

"No, I don't mean that. Surely she would have known what happened to Rosalind. Harriet spent her mature years in London according to Ben so Aunt Catherine would have kept in touch. She moved away from London so I'll have to research the death records in England. She could have kept an eye on Harriet and Ivor, unfortunate children with no father and their mother living in an asylum in Dublin."

Jessica stood as her mobile rang. "Hello, oh Dad… yes, yes I'm here with Fiona. What's that you said?" Her hand reached for her hair, twirling it in her fingers. "Wow, that's a surprise! Are you sure? Huh, well we were wrong about that. Thanks Dad, see you soon."

"What?" I asked. "We were wrong about what?"

Her dark eyes glowed. "Rosalind. It wasn't her. Beatrice came here, not Rosalind."

Chapter Forty-Six

I found Daphne in the middle of the rose border, dead-heading faded blooms with the enthusiasm of an axeman. She glanced up as I approached across the lawn, while Archie ran in circles with a tennis ball clamped in his mouth.

"There you are, Fiona. I'm just tidying up here before dinner. It's supposed to rain tomorrow so I mightn't get another chance for a few days. This 'New Dawn' needs a bit of a trim." She chopped with her secateurs and tossed another brown flower into her basket. "How did you get on?"

Archie dropped the ball at my feet and I kicked it as far away as I could. The little dog scampered after it. "She wasn't Rosalind."

Daphne's pink floppy hat stopped moving among the rose bushes. "Not Rosalind?"

"No, the woman in the asylum was Beatrice, Hugh's wife."

She blinked behind her round glasses. "Beatrice, my goodness. I had such a strong feeling that… not Rosalind… and I've thought all these years that…"

"Beatrice was there from early 1902 until she died in 1905. Her medical notes state she was a pyromaniac and that's why she burnt down the house."

Another rose head landed in the basket.

Daphne said nothing so I continued. "She set fire to several things apparently. First it was the bedroom curtains, then a pile of books in the middle of the kitchen garden, then the potting shed... before she turned on the house. Poor woman must have been very ill and distressed. She lost a child... a baby, you see."

Daphne glanced up at the top of the house.

I raised my eyes but saw nothing but the window panes glinting in the sun and house martins circling over the slates.

"Daphne?"

She chopped off another flower. "Beatrice Thornton was a pyromaniac? How fortunate she didn't come to live here with her husband or there might not have been a house for John to inherit. I suppose that awful woman, the journalist, what's her name... she'll make a big song and dance about this. Honestly, it just gets worse."

"I'm sorry." Archie was back, panting and rolling on the grass at my feet with his pink tongue hanging out. "But isn't it better that the woman who lived here wasn't sent to an asylum? Even if it was a well-run private asylum? I'm relieved Rosalind didn't end up there." I bent to tickle the dog's stomach. "I hope Dominic hasn't been driving you crazy all afternoon. Did he go off to the village?"

"He's gone."

"I expect he'll be back soon for dinner. I bought a takeaway for us tonight... duck in plum sauce with rice."

Daphne looked away, the pink cotton ribbons on her hat swinging. "That's kind of you, dear. Dominic has gone... gone away. Back to Dublin, he said. He took his suitcase so I think he meant it."

"To Dublin? Where's he going to stay?"

"Are you upset? I'm sorry, perhaps I should have been less blunt but you're better off without that man. He needs to learn to fend for himself. He mentioned a friend with an apartment."

A relief he was gone. But he could have told me he was leaving. Perhaps he'd left a note like the last dramatic departure. *Dear Fiona, I'm sorry but I can't cope without internet.*

"I expect he'll turn up again soon now that my father's house has been sold. I heard from the estate agent today on the way back from Dublin."

"That is good news, very good news. Now don't you go giving that Dominic any more money. You've done enough for him."

I agreed. "Perhaps it was for the best he came to stay here because now I know for sure that I don't want him back. My marriage is over. Finally over."

"All things happen for a reason," she said, "which reminds me, I had a phone call from Kitty O'Rafferty... the woman you went to see... who bought the painting from me last year. She sounded quite breathless on the phone. She was looking for you and almost overcome with excitement. She's driving here now and should arrive any minute."

I looked up from stroking Archie. "Really? Did she say why she's coming?"

Daphne waved her gardening glove. "A letter she's found or something. She'll explain when she gets here."

"Sounds interesting. You realize that I'm homeless now?"

Her wrinkled face lit up. "And I have a big empty house to share with only the shadows of the past. Stay with me a while, my dear, until you get settled... until you find your way somewhere else."

"Thank you, thank you so much. I might have to take you up on that. You've been so kind... I don't know what..."

"Nonsense." She cut me short with another chop of her secateurs and tossed the clipping away. "You'll be doing me a good turn. Let's go and eat the duck you bought while we wait for Kitty to arrive. I hope she hasn't found something else scandalous about poor Charles's family."

When Kitty arrived, she reminded me again of a young girl, a teenager with a daring secret to divulge. Her long cotton dress was a shade of cornflower with a wide leather belt and dark brown sandals. Her nails, no longer turquoise, were painted the same blue as her outfit.

"How are you, Daphne?" she asked.

"Very well, thank you. I'm getting used to having company around me now. I've got Fiona and Ben. It will be hard to let them go."

Kitty let out a high, rather shrill titter. "You're lucky. I have to make do with my two boys, my little dachshunds. Such bold little rascals."

The two women exchanged pleasantries while I made coffee and placed the mug beside Kitty as she opened the shoebox and took out a letter.

"This," she glanced at me. "This is the one I found. An unopened letter. How could it never have been read you ask? All those years since 1964 and nobody ever saw the contents. You see it has an Australian stamp? And the date is the sixteenth of October."

"I presume you opened it," I replied.

"Addressed to Vera, Johanna O'Rafferty's niece. Vera had died, poor woman, by the time the letter arrived." Kitty was enjoying her moments of suspense.

"How do you know she'd died?"

"I checked her name on the births, deaths and marriages website. They have all the records since 1864… there she was… died on the twenty-third of October from a heart attack. I suppose somehow the letter was forgotten and whoever cleared out her house must have bundled it away with other correspondence going back to the 1950s. It wasn't the only unopened letter in this box. There were other bills and a few cards." She gazed at me with triumph in her eyes.

Daphne picked up a morsel of duck from her plate and fed it to her cat. "What does it say?"

Kitty held up the envelope. "It tells us the account of an eye witness in the woods on the night of the murder."

Something fluttered in my stomach. "Who wrote the letter?"

"A relation... a relation of Frank O'Rafferty who went to live in Australia with his wife."

Daphne clutched the table with one hand. She closed her eyes and gestured towards me. "Give it to Fiona. Let her read it first."

Chapter Forty-Seven

I reached out and took the envelope with the Perth postmark. Pale blue paper with several sheets of neat writing in black ink; the handwriting of an organized person. Not scrawled in a hurry, but as if the man had stopped to consider before proceeding with his account. I read aloud:

> *"16th October, 1964*
>
> *Dear Aunt Vera,*
>
> *Please forgive me for taking so long to reply to your last letter. I'm delighted to hear that all the family is well and the twins are up to mischief as usual. Poor Mammy must have been terrified when they let loose the mice in her kitchen. She's in dread of them running around her feet. I can imagine her screaming and leaping on the chair and the boys laughing their heads off at the sight of their grandmother in hysterics.*
>
> *One of the reasons it's taken me so long to write is because I'm sorry to say that I have some bad news. There's no easy way to phrase this so I'll just come straight out with it and tell you Agnes and I have separated. Agnes decided last month that she'd rather be with another man who lives on the far side of Perth. I suppose it was on the cards but men like me can be blind and too busy*

working to notice the signs until it's too late.

Now that she's gone, I feel I can tell you something she told me that happened to her back in Wexford. Do you remember you said when Agnes and I got engaged that you never trusted anyone in the Maguire family? It's a strange story so maybe best to keep quiet about it but I feel I have to get it off my chest. It won't make any difference now to the Thornton family, I suppose, because both Hugh and John are dead but perhaps Charles wouldn't like it talked about."

Daphne's eyes were fixed on the dresser. As if she wasn't listening. But I knew she was; she was taking in every word and dreading what might come next. I continued to read in as calm a tone as possible although I noticed my hand holding the letter was shaking. What if it was Rosalind? What if it was Harriet? Kitty watched me with her eyes alive, as if deriving pleasure from every syllable. Whoever the killer was, it obviously wasn't Frank O'Rafferty. I continued:

"Do you remember Agnes's grandfather Mick Maguire? He was well known in racing circles back at the turn of the century. Agnes was only twenty when Mick was dying and she lived in the cottage with him those last few months, cooking his meals and tending to his needs. It can't have been fun for a young woman but she went on to train as a nurse so maybe she had a vocation. She always longed to be a nurse and that's why we ended up here in Australia.

Old Mick's mind started to wander before the end. He was ninety in 1945, a great age, and he used to come out with outlandish stories and Agnes never knew whether they were true. One day he told her he knew who killed Edward Thornton. That was the mystery that baffled all the locals including your parents. Do you remember how the Thornton family hushed it up and the final inquest concluded with an open verdict? Some thought it an accident, just a fall from his horse. The locals suspected your uncle, Frank O'Rafferty, because he was in love with Edward's wife? That was the gossip they liked to spread back home in Wexford and I remember the boys in school teasing me about it and telling me I was related to a murderer. I hated that, I can tell you!

Agnes made me swear not to tell anyone just in case her granddad was telling the truth – he wasn't a truthful sort of man, if you ask me, but I agreed to say nothing. It happened about a week before the old man died and he'd been sleeping badly and keeping poor Agnes up half the night. Maybe I shouldn't call her poor Agnes now after what she's done to me but I felt sorry for her at the time. Her granddad always had a devious way about him and I never trusted him.

Anyway, Mick was jabbering away about nothing in particular one night and Agnes was hoping he'd drop off to sleep, when suddenly he sat bolt upright in the bed and claimed he knew who killed Edward Thornton. He winked at Agnes and repeated it again. Then he told her he'd been well paid to conceal the truth for forty-four years. Well paid, he added, by the man who committed the crime."

Daphne cleared her throat and picked at the bones on her plate.

"Would you prefer me not to read it out loud?" I asked.

She shook her head and her mouth twitched. "No, go on. You might as well keep going."

I turned back to the letter.

"Agnes was all ears because she said he was suddenly lucid and could remember the date. That sometimes happened in his last few weeks and then he'd lapse back into senility. She said he was grinning at her and she was frightened because she didn't know

what he was going to come out with, afraid he might have seen Frank O'Rafferty in the woods that night because she was engaged to marry me by then. She was terrified her granddad would say it was Frank and that all the old local tales were true. Then I'd be related to a murderer and her family would never let her marry me. They didn't like me anyway because I was an O'Rafferty but a killer in the family would have definitely brought out the worst objections from Agnes's parents.

So, there's Agnes in the middle of the night and old Mick grinning like a Cheshire cat and winking at her. She begged him to tell her and promised she'd never breathe a word to anyone and Mick admitted he was in Ardlackan woods the night of the murder. He was poaching and had his old lurcher dog with him. He hid behind the trees and saw what went on and didn't interfere because he was a coward at heart in spite of all his tales of bravery.

What Mick said next nearly made the hair stand up on Agnes's head. Hugh Thornton and his cousin Edward were having a mighty argument. Mick said Edward's voice sounded slurred, he had blood on his face and was unsteady on his feet. He believed the man was drunk to be honest but thought afterwards it might have been something else after the inquest.

Hugh was in a rage in that wood and was shouting at his cousin because he said he'd been responsible for the premature birth and death of Hugh's own son. Edward had been driving the carriage when Beatrice fell into the river and that's why she lost the baby. Now he'd destroyed his friendship with a big bookmaker with his loose tongue. I know Edward had a reputation for gambling. The final straw, Hugh roared at him, was letting his wife get away with the children and all the money. All the money they needed for the new training stables. It was to be the biggest and best professional training yard in the country. All their plans went awry that night for, with Edward's wife gone, there wasn't enough money to fund the venture.

Old Mick was tired now from all this excitement and slid down the pillows. Agnes had to fetch him a drop of whiskey to get him talking again to finish his story. He told her he saw Hugh Thornton grab his cousin by the throat and shake him like a terrier with a rat. He told him he'd better tell him who helped his wife to get away and he'd go after her and report them to the constabulary.

Edward wriggled and wailed like a baby. Hugh nearly choked him and Edward lay gasping on the ground but was crying now because he didn't want to lose Rosalind. He said he was sorry for the way he'd treated her and he blamed Hugh for that. Hugh had put him up to this and driven his wife away. He wouldn't tell Hugh who had helped her escape so his cousin picked him up and shook him again, demanding to know. Edward eventually claimed he didn't recognize the driver of the carriage and his wife must have hired one from the town.

With that, Hugh lost patience and picked up a big stone and struck Edward on the back of the head with it. He fell to the ground and Hugh rolled him into a ditch.

He got back on his horse, which was tied to a tree trunk, and rode on home with blood on his shirt and hands. Old Mick said he felt faint with shock after Hugh was gone and had to get out his own whiskey bottle which he carried in his coat to revive himself."

"Oh," Daphne cried, "it could be all lies. How can we believe this? Hugh Thornton! How could it be Hugh?"

"And Frank stayed to work for the man." Kitty shuddered dramatically. "Not knowing that he was employed by a killer."

"Shall I continue?" I glanced at the letter. Bad news for Daphne, poor Daphne, because these words implicated the man who'd lived in her house; inherited it when Gertrude died.

"Go on," Kitty urged. "You need to know the truth."

I took a sip of coffee, rather cold by now, and read on:

"That was bad enough and Mick should have gone to the constabulary next day when the news broke that Edward Thornton was found dead in the woods. But of course he didn't. He grinned at Agnes and told her he had a better idea. Mick went to Hugh Thornton and told him what he'd seen and that he would keep quiet about it for a large sum of money. Agnes said Mick was always an opportunist. How much was Hugh's neck worth? A lot, Mick said, but he wouldn't tell his granddaughter the sum, just that Hugh thought it over and decided to pay up.

Maybe you'll think this was all a lie coming from a man like Mick Maguire? Especially one as senile as he was at the time and almost on his deathbed. I thought he was making it up but Agnes swears he was lucid when he was telling her this and kept repeating that he saw Hugh Thornton hit his cousin on the head with a stone and toss him into the ditch.

So what do you think of that story? Agnes wasn't positive it was true and her granddad was buried the following week but she decided to keep it to herself and never tell her family. She also didn't like the thought of my family finding out that old Mick was a blackmailer. He should have gone to the constabulary about the murder and not made money out of it, but that was Mick all over. He was always devious.

I have to go to sleep because I have an early start tomorrow but I just wanted to tell you this. It's nearly twenty years ago now since Agnes found out and she won't thank me for passing it on but I don't feel guilty after what she's done to me. I thought you'd want to hear that Frank was an innocent man.

All the best to you and the family and tell those twins that their uncle in Australia is laughing his head off too at their antics. With love from your nephew,
Kieran"

Kitty sat nodding and smiling. "You see. Frank was an innocent man. That's what Kieran O'Rafferty says. I knew the journalist was wrong, I knew it."

A bombshell for Daphne and the Thornton family though. An unwelcome turn of events. I'd have to pass this news on to Tiffany; but not straight away for I would need to think long and hard about the consequences.

Chapter Forty-Eight

The present - 27th July, 2019

"**D**amn that Sebastian Rotherill! All these months gone to waste." Tiffany tapped her forefinger on the table top. "All my work flushed down the drain… total waste of time." She picked up her glass of lager and swallowed. "It's frustrating, to say the least."

I bit into a crab sandwich and attempted an expression of sympathy. I'd been summoned an hour before when the journalist was driving towards Ardlackan. A short abrupt text message:

Buy you lunch. Meet in O'Mahony's pub 12:30.

How could I turn down an order like that? I longed to see how she reacted to the email I'd sent her attaching a scan of Kieran O'Rafferty's letter about Mick Maguire and exposing Hugh as the killer. Badly, as it turned out. Very badly. She greeted me with a glower and a heavy sigh. I felt obliged to head to the bar counter and bring her back another lager.

Her sharp brown eyes sought mine. "Do you think it's fair? I mean, honestly, all my effort and now I'm only getting paid for a fraction of it. Sebastian says the man who gave him the information in the first place, Grace's grandson, is no longer interested. I know why this has happened. It's all to do with pride... pride and money."

"Why pride?"

"The grandson of Grace Thornton... don't you get it? He doesn't want his ancestor, Grace's father Hugh, exposed as a murderer."

"I see." I was enjoying the irony. Daphne would be amused to hear this.

"And Sebastian Rotherill claims his business partner has just gone bankrupt. Huh, so now there's no money to fund the TV murder series and it has to be dropped. I don't know if I believe that excuse."

I took another bite of crab to smother a smile. "Shame," I murmured, "but Daphne will be delighted. You could have given Ben an acting role."

Her thin eyebrows rose. "What? What are you talking about?"

"Ben is the image of Hugh Thornton when he was young. I've seen a photograph. He could have played the leading role in this drama."

"Well, too damn late now, isn't it? Sebastian has dropped the idea and sent on a payment for about a third of what I've done."

"I think I'd better pay for lunch. I owe you anyway."

"Why?"

"That day in Dublin you bought me lunch, remember? The day you so helpfully put me in touch with Kitty O'Rafferty. You're the one I have to thank, to be honest, as Kitty eventually solved this. If you hadn't sent me... It was really because of Dominic, I think... you were angry when you realized he hadn't told you he was married to me and you kindly decided to help. I'll have to thank Dominic when I next see him."

"Oh, isn't he still here?"

"Nope, he cleared off about five days ago. Couldn't cope with the bad Wi-Fi signal. Haven't you seen him?"

"Nah, don't want to. He tried calling me a few times but I didn't answer… been there, done that and I'm moving on now."

I finished my sandwich and reached for the menu. A shaft of sunlight fell across our table in the window. Outside a gaggle of giggling teenagers strolled past and Tiffany shot them a scornful glance. She'd had her hair re-highlighted and the blonde streaks gleamed in the sunshine. She opened her handbag and pulled out her lipstick.

I decided to be magnanimous. "Would you like a chocolate sundae to cheer you up? Ben says they make good ones here."

She reached for an empty plastic water bottle on her right and crushed it. "Just order me whatever you're having…please." The *please* was added as an afterthought but better than nothing.

I gave our order to the young barman. "A pity really, it would have made an exciting story for TV. A man steals his cousin's baby, leaves him for dead in the woods and his wife loses her mind, burning down their house. No wonder Daphne heard Hugh was reclusive and difficult in his old age. He must have lived under the fear of Maguire telling the truth for the rest of his life."

"Why do you think Frank O'Rafferty stayed at Ardlackan Lodge for ten years before he left for America? Why stay with someone like Hugh?"

"It was a job and he was fond of the horses… an excellent trainer and jockey by all accounts. Maybe he was happy there."

She frowned. "You know what I think?"

"What?"

"I think he probably suspected Hugh and wanted to find out if it was him. The constabulary must have wanted to pursue Rosalind, even though the family hushed the whole thing up, and I'm sure Hugh would have liked to pin the crime on her, get her hanged or locked up so that he would be off the hook. I bet Frank wanted to prove she was innocent… if he was in love with her, that is. And he helped her escape, didn't he? You told me Harriet's sheets of journal prove that. Frank was going to help her, the children and the maid to get away."

"Yes, he must have helped them. They couldn't have done it on their own."

Tiffany glanced at her mobile. "Well, I don't like to think of Hugh Thornton getting away with it... the murder."

"He never faced justice but perhaps he suffered all the same. He lived a lonely secluded life in his old age. It must have haunted him, surely it did? And his wife... perhaps she found out what he did and it tipped her over the edge." I thanked the waiter for the chocolate sundaes and pushed one towards Tiffany. "Maybe you're right. Maybe Frank suspected Hugh. I'm glad Edward didn't give Frank away at the end... felt some loyalty towards him. Edward was a weak man but perhaps he wasn't as bad as we think."

She snorted. "Huh, you're a soft one, aren't you? You'd never make a journalist."

I waved a hand dismissively. "I don't want to be a journalist but I'm considering family history research. I enjoy it and people love tracing their roots these days. I tracked down the aunt, by the way, Rosalind's Aunt Catherine. I found her death certificate and she never married. Moved to Ulverston in Cumbria... used to be in Lancashire in those days, I think."

Tiffany jabbed at the dessert with her spoon. "And no sign of Rosalind? I bet the aunt moved over there to be near her. Rosalind probably settled down under another name or married again. Why else would Catherine leave London?"

"I couldn't find a marriage or death certificate for Rosalind Thornton so I guess she changed her name. It was easier for people to disappear in those days with no computer records."

"Yeah, common enough," Tiffany agreed. "It was why bigamy was rife in that era."

I hoped that Rosalind and her children had found a happier life in Cumbria near their aunt. I was certain that was where they'd gone.

The door of the pub swung open and Daphne and Ben entered with Archie on a lead, his little tail wagging. I waved at them and called out, "Over here! Have a coffee with us. Tiffany and I haven't finished our lunch."

"Archie had a lovely time on the pier," Ben said, pulling a stool out for Daphne and sitting beside her. "He chased every seagull off the wall and barked at all the fishermen in the trawlers."

I gave the dog a pat. "Good man, Archie, you keep those birds under control." I smiled at Daphne. "Tiffany has just told me the good news. Sebastian Rotherill has abandoned the television murder series."

"I've got to go." Tiffany stood up. "Thanks for lunch, Fiona. I can't finish the dessert… not as hungry as I thought." She held out her hand and gripped mine. "I'll see you around. Maybe we could work together on something in the future."

Ben cast me an amused look while I returned Tiffany's offer of friendship with as much feigned sincerity as I could muster. She nodded curtly at the others and left.

"Daphne and I have been discussing our plans for Ardlackan," Ben said. "We're going to do up the yard and rent it out to tourists… so near the sea, it might be popular and bring in some cash."

I raised my arm and beckoned to the young man behind the bar. "Let's have a drink, we've plenty to celebrate. Rosalind's new life, Harriet not a killer, Tiffany vanquished and Daphne finds peace once again. A good week, I'd say."

Ben threw back his head and laughed.

Daphne stretched out her hand and grasped mine. "And I have two wonderful lodgers and my lovely niece Jessie arriving tomorrow for her holiday. A good week indeed."

Chapter Forty-Nine

The past - 7th June, 1902

Rosalind lifted the latch of the front door, pausing for a few seconds to admire the climbing rose entwined in the trellis on the wall of the cottage. Its sweet scent clung to the summer air, mingling with that of a honeysuckle trailing over the window. She looked out across the sands towards the west. The tide was turning and would soon sweep in across Morecambe Bay.

A tough landscape greeted them when she and the children first arrived from Wales eleven years before. Swathes of green farmland interspersed with the great industrial cities of Liverpool and Manchester in the south where cotton mills and iron works lured families to seek work. There were too many Irish in Liverpool, too many friendly families who might send word home about the young woman so she moved further north along the coast to Morecambe and finally settled in the seaside village of Baycliff.

She'd put down roots, like the border of flowers on the left of the door, the hollyhocks and poppies, and somehow she'd flourished.

Rosalind hummed as she walked into the kitchen where Harriet sat at the scrubbed pine table reading a newspaper.

Her daughter glanced up. "Good evening, Ma. How did your day go?"

A saucepan bubbled on the top of the stove; a smell of rabbit stew and onions.

Rosalind took off her hat and hung it on a peg on the wall beside the old dresser. "Very well. The Board of Governors approved the plans for an extension to the schoolroom for the girls and assured me the Inspector thought our pupils displayed remarkable promise."

"I'm glad to hear it. Rabbit tonight, Ma. I walked to the market and bought two fat ones." Harriet looked well these days, her copper hair pinned up on her head and her skin glowing from the sea air.

Mrs Beeton's bible of cookery lay open beside the newspaper, its well-thumbed pages splattered with brown gravy marks and dusted with flour. Harriet and Rosalind had taken to Mrs Beeton.

"And Ivor?" Harriet asked. "Is he with his friend for the night?"

"He'll be back in time for school tomorrow morning. They're going fishing tonight so you can imagine the excitement. Ivor loves the outdoor life, doesn't he?"

She picked up a letter and turned it over in her hands. Addressed to Mrs Alfred Smith. Emily Smith, the village schoolmistress. Nearly six months now since her wedding day and her heart still lifted when she saw her name written on the stiff white paper her Aunt Catherine preferred. The Smith family kept to themselves and nobody suspected a thing.

Rosalind tossed the envelope aside and twirled the gold band on her finger. Not as heavy and expensive as the one Edward gave her all those years ago but a hundred times more precious to her. Why should she care about money and social status when she had the kindest husband in the country? And Harriet adored him. He and her daughter strolled for hours along the local country lanes while Rosalind corrected school tests and essays. They often came home with wild flowers to decorate the house.

In May they'd made a bouquet for her from branches of flowering hawthorn and frothing cow parsley. Her husband had taught Ivor to fish and they sometimes borrowed a little wooden boat.

"Aunt Catherine will be visiting this weekend," she said. "Perhaps you might bake something nice." They could afford a small leg of lamb for Sunday luncheon and she still had an abundance of vegetables in the garden, which her husband helped her weed on warm evenings after work. "I'm sure you'll cook a nice roast for her." Rosalind lifted the lid of the saucepan and peeped in. "It does smell good. I'm going to invite Sadie and her husband too. Aunt Catherine loves their golden-haired daughters." So nice that Sadie had married a local miller's son.

"A Bakewell tart? Would you like that?"

"Thank you. I'm fortunate to have such a wonderful cook in the house. What will I do when you leave home?"

Harriet yawned and pushed the newspaper away. "Not likely to happen yet. I know I'm nineteen years old but I want to look for a work near here. I'd like to save money to go to London. I'd love to be a journalist, as you know. I've been reading about Emmeline Pankhurst... you've heard of the lady who believes women should be allowed to vote."

"Isn't she quite militant in her views?"

"I think I would like to support those who speak up for a woman's right to vote. Surely we deserve to be able to vote, Ma? I've known men more stupid than me."

"You're not stupid, my love. You're an intelligent young woman."

"Well, I'm going to find out about it and see if there's a local group for women's suffrage in Liverpool. I'm..." Harriet left off talking and ran to the window.

"What is it? Who's there?"

A clatter of iron-shod hooves on the road and the creak of the wooden gate at the end of the garden. A familiar whistle of a tune they both knew.

Harriet beckoned. "See there. A magnificent grey horse! Look at his dapples and the gleam on his coat. Oh, what a beauty! I'm going out to have a look at him. Come on, let's go and admire him."

The rider stood beside the gate, holding the reins of the horse in one hand as they hurried out into the garden. Her husband home early from work and without his bicycle.

"What do you think, ladies? Isn't he a fine fellow? Five years old and as quiet as a lamb. Step back, Harriet, don't throw your arms around him like that until he gets to know you. Why, you can't get up on him now. Wait, wait..." He turned to Rosalind, his blue eyes sparkling with amusement. "What do you think of my new mode of transport, eh? I never could take to that old boneshaker of a bicycle."

He reached out for Rosalind and caught her in his arms, planting a kiss on the end of her nose.

She kissed him back and put up a hand to stroke his cheek. "A beautiful horse, to be sure. Is it a thoroughbred?"

"Of course he's a thoroughbred. My employer has given me permission to find him two geldings to buy this summer. Two steeplechasers. The farmer is coming round to my way of thinking. He'll soon have lost interest in his plough horses and machinery and be taking to the racecourse."

Rosalind smiled. "You'll introduce the poor man to the road to ruin. Are you sure that's what he wants, Frank? To spend his money on horses when he could be content with his corn and his cows and his flocks of sheep?"

"Of course that's what he wants. He thinks it's a grand idea. I'm planning to build a stable or two at the back of our cottage as well."

Harriet had clambered onto the gelding's back, pushing her feet into the stirrups. "Frank, please help me with the leathers. I can ride astride as well as any man. Look, my legs are nearly as long as yours now."

"You're a fine tall girl."

"Let go of the reins, let go! I want to ride him to the end of the road. You said he is quiet. Let go!"

Frank raised his eyebrows and tilted his head towards Rosalind. "What say you, Mother? Are you willing to risk your only daughter's neck on an unknown piece of horseflesh?"

She laughed. "I'll trust you to be the judge of that."

He adjusted the length of the leathers for Harriet and released the reins. She pulled the horse round and headed off at a trot towards the bend in the lane, her chestnut curls bouncing as she disappeared out of view to the rhythm of hoofbeats on the rough stones.

"I hope she doesn't fall off," Rosalind said.

"She knows what's she's doing… and she's missed having a horse all these years. The occasional ride on a Shire just isn't the same. Remember how she used to fly down the beach at Ardlackan with the wind in her hair and the little legs of that pony galloping beneath her? Those were the days." He put an arm round her shoulder and pulled her against him. "It's good to see her happy. She worries about it still, you know she does. She'll never forget it was her actions that caused Edward to fall from his horse. If only we knew who…"

"Hush," Rosalind said. "We won't talk about that."

They stood looking out over the green farmland that stretched down to the village. A flock of seagulls flew overhead and wheeled back towards the sea. Frank couldn't have lived far from the ocean, she knew that. Salt water ran in his veins.

He'd helped them find the two-storey limestone cottage with

its magnificent view. At first, he'd only come for a few days at a time and kept returning to Ireland as he still worked as coachman at Ardlackan Lodge and trained a few horses owned by Hugh. He had to save up money and it was vital no one suspected where Rosalind and the children had gone, so he couldn't leave Wexford too soon.

What would she have done without Frank in those days? He'd arranged the boat crossing to Wales and followed them to Liverpool after a few months where Rosalind rented a small terraced house and sought work in a local school.

"You miss Ardlackan." She caught his other hand in hers.

"Sometimes… but now we're here on the coast it reminds me of home. It's not the same but I'm getting used to it and at least my mother knows where I am. She's amused by the letters containing an alternative version of events from her cousin's son Alfie in England, while poor Frank had to emigrate to Virginia. She said Hugh Thornton sometimes asks about me when she meets him in the village."

Hearing Hugh's name always made Rosalind's pulse race. Not as fast as in the early days but still that quickening; that cold nauseous dread in the pit of her stomach.

"She says Hugh isn't the handsome man he used to be," Frank continued. "It appears his gambling and drinking have got the better of him this last year, his racehorses aren't running so well, he's sacked his new trainer and his wife has lost all interest in the outside world since she…"

"Poor Beatrice. I know she was ill but I still can't comprehend how she could set fire to the house. And what did your mother say about me in her letter?"

He tightened his grip on her shoulders. "She said she will never forgive the English hussy who stole away her son. That's what she said." He laughed. "No, don't look at me like that. Don't give me such a fierce stare, my darling. Of course I'm joking.

She's looking forward to visiting soon. When I've earned enough for her passage on the steamship to Liverpool, she can come here to stay with us for a few weeks. We can rely on Mother not to reveal our whereabouts."

Beatrice had once told her that Hugh had spies everywhere; that he discovered people's secrets. If anyone could find out her hiding place and her new false name, it would be him. Please God he never would. That was why Frank had to change his name too. He was only ever Frank to them but in public she was careful to call him Alfie. It came with a price, this life of freedom, and for years to come she would be looking over her shoulder but at least she'd have Frank by her side.

Inventing their new names had amused them. Alfie and Emily and their children Maud and Lionel. Tennyson had married late in life too when he was finally allowed to wed his Emily. Rosalind had disguised both her name and her handwriting when she first wrote to thank Frank and sent him her address.

"Do you miss your wealth?" he asked suddenly. "I've never been rich so I wouldn't know if it's a hardship to give it up."

"No, you know I don't. Aunt Catherine manages to send me a little and I have my employment. I can't trust the lawyers not to give me away."

Gradually over the years Frank had eased out of his old life in Wexford and waited for the opportunity to leave Ireland forever. He informed Hugh and Gertrude he was going to America. Dearest Frank. He'd sacrificed his homeland and his family for her.

She watched the gulls flying back along the coast, drawn by the sea and the fish. A breeze blew a strand of hair over her eyes and Frank bent to push it away.

"You don't regret this, do you?" She gazed up at him.

The evening light played on his face, sun-tanned from working outdoors. "Why would I regret it, my love? Aren't you and Harriet and Ivor the best that's ever happened to me? I'd never have been able to marry you if it hadn't been for Edward and his heartless schemes. Think about that. If he'd behaved like a responsible husband and not squandered your wealth on gambling. . . if he hadn't got mixed up with the likes of Maguire and that bookmaker Chance, I wouldn't be standing here with you now. I'd still be taking orders in the stable yard of Ardlackan and hoping you would send word for me to saddle up Romeo. I'm a lucky man." He took her face in his hands. "I mean it… every word. I'll never regret leaving Wexford for you."

Hoofbeats rang out and the grey horse appeared, Harriet with her feet dangling and the reins hanging loose on his neck.

"Would you look at her ladyship!" Frank pointed in her daughter's direction. "So casual on a horse she's only just encountered. She's a fine rider… a confident young woman. I must tell her about the new steeplechases for ladies. They're popular in Poland, I believe. I can see your Harriet galloping down to the start on my new employer's thoroughbred. I should have a word in his ear about her."

Rosalind laughed, lifting her hand to his chest to give him a gentle push. "Don't you dare, Frank O'Rafferty, don't you dare!"

To the reader

Thank you for reading *The Family Shadow*. I hope you enjoyed it and, if you did, perhaps you would be kind enough to leave a review. This makes a big difference to authors these days and it can be as short as you like. Your help is much appreciated.

If you're interested in receiving my newsletter by email with information about my other novels, special offers, background research, gardening tips, folklore and historical photographs, please visit www.suzannewinterly.com and complete the form. All are welcome!

You can also find me on the following social media platforms:

Facebook
www.facebook.com/suzannewinterly

Instagram
www.instagram.com/suzannewinterly

Pinterest
www.pinterest.ie/suzannewinterly

List of Characters

The present

Fiona Foley - History teacher. Married to Dominic
Jessica Thornton - Daphne's niece
Daphne Thornton - Jessica's aunt
Ben Davidson - Employed by Daphne
Dominic Foley - Married to Fiona
Tiffany Ryan - Journalist
Kitty O'Rafferty - Descendant of Frank O'Rafferty

The past - 1890/91

Ardlackan Lodge
Rosalind Thornton - Edward's wife
Edward Thornton - Rosalind's husband
Harriet Thornton - Daughter of Edward and Rosalind
Ivor Thornton - Son of Edward and Rosalind
Gertrude Thornton - Edward's mother
Frank O'Rafferty - Head lad and coachman
Sadie - Rosalind's maid
Ellen Mangan - Gertrude's maid
Mrs O'Brien - Cook
Joseph and Peter - Stable boys
Cornelius Troy - Head gardener
Patrick - Assistant gardener
Mary O'Brien - Kitchenmaid and niece of Mrs O'Brien

Ardlackan House
Hugh Thornton - Edward's cousin
Beatrice Thornton - Hugh's wife
Grace, Irene and Nora - Daughters of Hugh and Beatrice
Gilton - Butler
Lydia Temple Governess
Magdalene - Nursemaid from Germany
Ruby O'Brien - Maid and niece of Mrs O'Brien

Others
Martin Chance – Bookmaker
Major Langstown – Land owner
Mick Maguire - Tout

Author's Note

The good thing about the last decade of the nineteenth century is that there is still a lot of original material available. The National Library in Dublin was a treasure trove and I spent happy hours there searching through the equestrian and local newspapers. Books published in the late Victorian era brought the period alive for me and I enjoyed being able to pick up exactly the same volume that my characters might have leafed through. I used to work in the horse racing industry here in Ireland and even wrote a number of articles for newspapers and magazines.

Horse trainers in Ireland in the nineteenth century took their best horses to race in England and France. It was fascinating to discover that the Grand National at Aintree was won by Irish-trained horses in ten of the eleven years from 1889 to 1899, an incredible feat when you think that the horses had to be ridden or led to the nearest railway station, then put on a train to Dublin, followed by a steamship to Liverpool.

There are some dramatic differences between the 1890s and the twenty-first century. I read amusing anecdotes including tales of match races between owners where two horses were ridden across country. Tenants and employees resorted to unscrupulous methods to try to ensure that their landlord or master won and, in one match race, a supporter decided to pull a donkey and cart across a fence to obstruct a rival. This attempt at sabotage failed when the horse jumped the fence, donkey and cart in one brave leap!

I can imagine that my character Frank O'Rafferty would have read the latest books about training racehorses. One published by a vet in the 1880s, that I bought second hand, provided me with instructions about building stables, the best feed, the ideal weight of horses and how to manage the stable boys (now called lads).

It also included the author's recommended system to prevent staff passing on information about horses and their form to touts. This involved replacing the horse's name with a number on the stable door, so that only the trainer and the head lad knew which horse was which. I wonder if this actually worked.

Another nuisance mentioned in the late nineteenth century was the number of ballad singers at race meetings. They pestered ladies sitting in their carriages and refused to stop singing until they were paid to go away. The National Library has some wonderful old photographs of Punchestown racecourse in the 1860s where families in carriages mingle amongst three card tricksters and women with roulette wheels.

The poetry of the eminent Victorian poet Alfred, Lord Tennyson is now in the public domain. I was able to find an 1885 collection of his *Lyrical Poems* with a lovely dark green cover and gilt lettering. I imagined Rosalind picking it up to read *Maud* or *The Lady of Shalott* in her new summer house. Tennyson was the longest serving Poet Laureate and so popular in his lifetime it's said that he had to move between two homes to avoid being overwhelmed by admiring visitors. The publication of *Maud*, however, produced a public outcry as readers thought the poem too dark and morbid. His reputation survived the critics and Maud remained one of the poems Tennyson liked best.

Mrs Isabella Beeton and her tomes on household management and cooking are famous and my son gave me one of her books for Christmas, again published in the 1880s. I remember my grandmother using her updated cookery books. Mrs Beeton's advice was aimed at the wives of Victorian business men and industrialists; that new breed of women with money but little experience of how to hire and manage servants. I discovered that the cookery writer also had a connection with horse racing. Isabella and her siblings lived in the new grandstand at Epsom racecourse after her widowed mother married the Clerk of the Course, Henry Dorling. Isabella went on to marry the publisher Samuel Beeton, who encouraged her books. I always used to imagine Mrs Beeton as a grand old Victorian lady but she tragically died at the early age of twenty-nine.

I'd like to thank everyone who helped me with The Family Shadow, especially Hilary Johnson for her invaluable editorial advice. My thanks go to Stuart Bache and his team at Books Covered. It's always a pleasure to see his cover ideas take shape. I am grateful to others who helped me along the way: Jill, Rosemary, Tara, Nicola, Maggie, Alan, Cherry and, of course, my husband William for encouraging me to keep going on days when things didn't go according to plan.

Suzanne Winterly - 2021

About the author

Suzanne Winterly was born in County Tipperary, Ireland. She has an English degree from Trinity College, Dublin and has written articles for specialist newspapers and magazines about horticulture and horse racing.

She has two sons and lives in the country with her husband and a variety of four-legged friends.

Website
www.suzannewinterly.com

Facebook
www.facebook.com/suzannewinterly

Instagram
www.instagram.com/suzannewinterly

Pinterest
www.pinterest.ie/suzannewinterly